# BALTIMORE

## *The Apostle*
## *and the Witch of Harju*

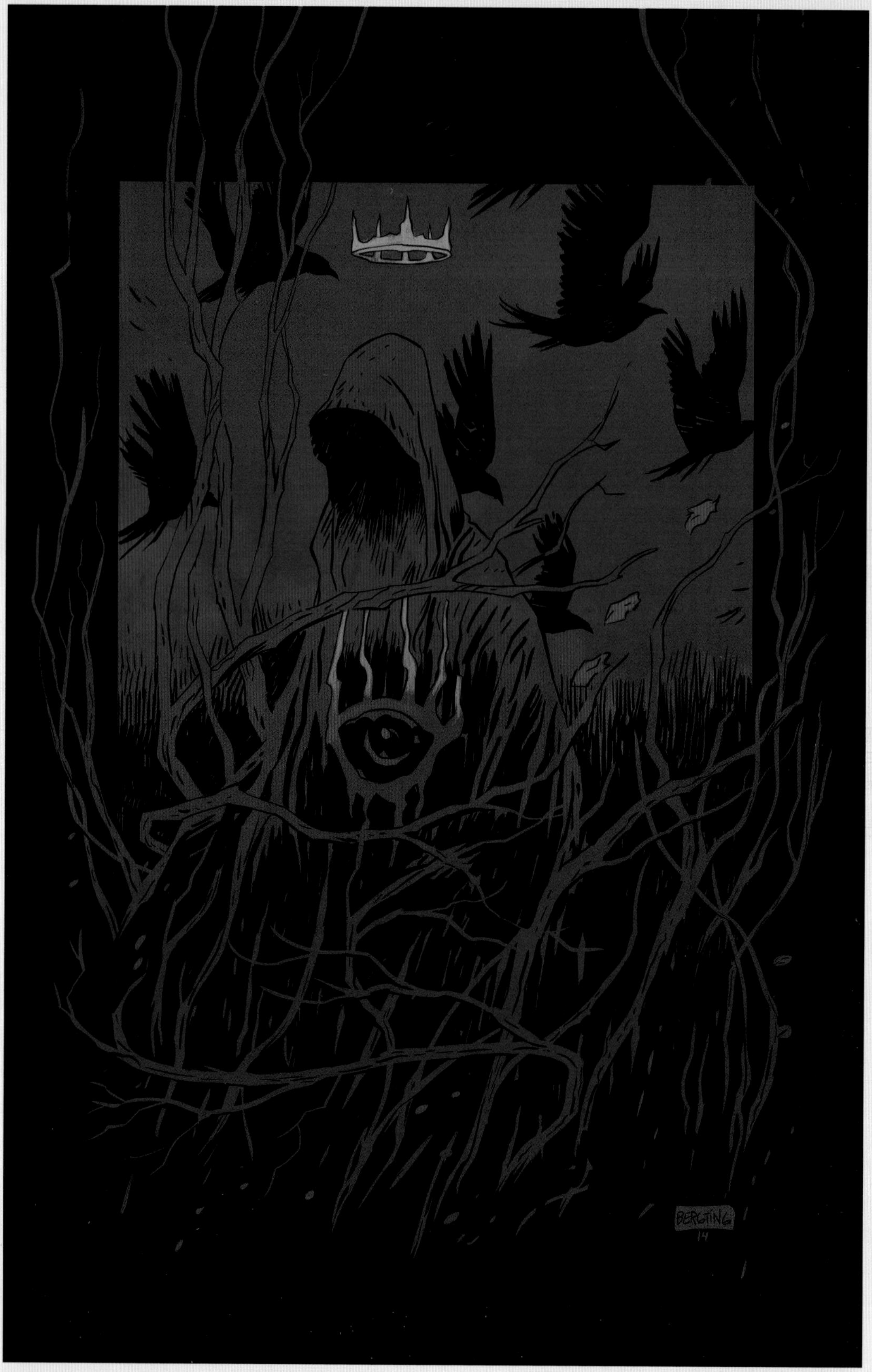
BERGTING
14

# BALTIMORE™
## THE APOSTLE AND THE WITCH OF HARJU

### VOLUME FIVE

*Story by*
**MIKE MIGNOLA**
**CHRISTOPHER GOLDEN**

The Witch of Harju *Art by*
**PETER BERGTING**

The Wolf and the Apostle *Art by*
**BEN STENBECK**

*Colors by*
**DAVE STEWART**

*Letters by*
**CLEM ROBINS**

*Cover Art by*
**MIKE MIGNOLA** with **DAVE STEWART**

*Chapter Break Art by*
**BEN STENBECK**

*Editor* **SCOTT ALLIE**

*Associate Editor* **DANIEL CHABON**

*Assistant Editor* **SHANTEL LAROCQUE**

*Collection Designer* **AMY ARENDTS**

*Publisher* **MIKE RICHARDSON**

**DARK HORSE BOOKS**

Neil Hankerson *Executive Vice President* • Tom Weddle *Chief Financial Officer* • Randy Stradley *Vice President of Publishing* • Michael Martens *Vice President of Book Trade Sales* • Scott Allie *Editor in Chief* • Matt Parkinson *Vice President of Marketing* • David Scroggy *Vice President of Product Development* • Dale LaFountain *Vice President of Information Technology* • Darlene Vogel *Senior Director of Print, Design, and Production* • Ken Lizzi *General Counsel* • Davey Estrada *Editorial Director* • Chris Warner *Senior Books Editor* • Diana Schutz *Executive Editor* • Cary Grazzini *Director of Print and Development* • Lia Ribacchi *Art Director* • Cara Niece *Director of Scheduling* • Mark Bernardi *Director of Digital Publishing*

*DarkHorse.com*

*Published by Dark Horse Books*
*A division of Dark Horse Comics, Inc.*
*10956 SE Main Street*
*Milwaukie, OR 97222*

*First edition: March 2015*
*ISBN 978-1-61655-618-1*

*1 3 5 7 9 10 8 6 4 2*

*Printed in China*

This volume collects *Baltimore: The Witch of Harju* #1–#3 and
*Baltimore: The Wolf and the Apostle* #1–#2, published by Dark Horse Comics.

# THE WITCH OF HARJU
*Chapter One*

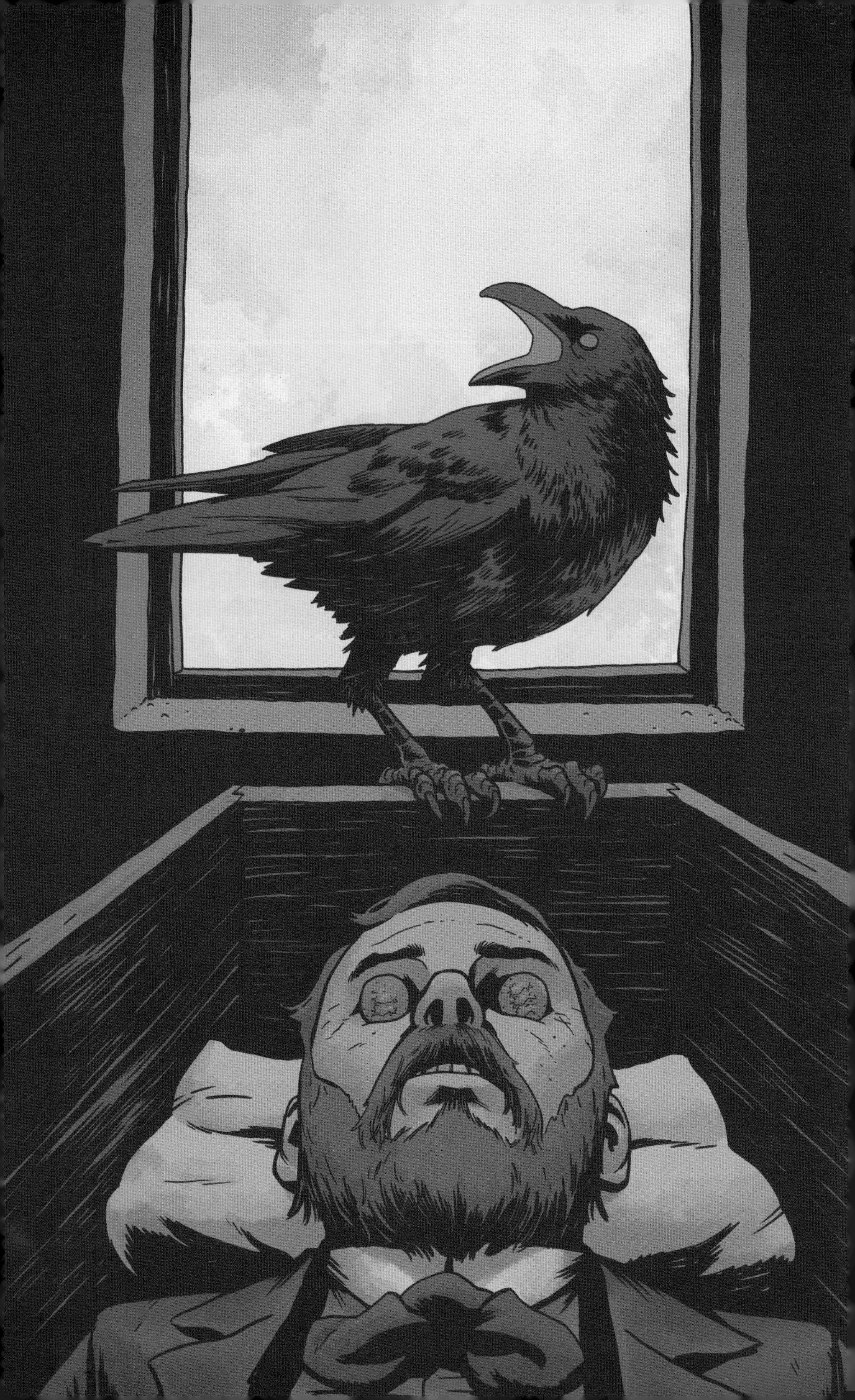

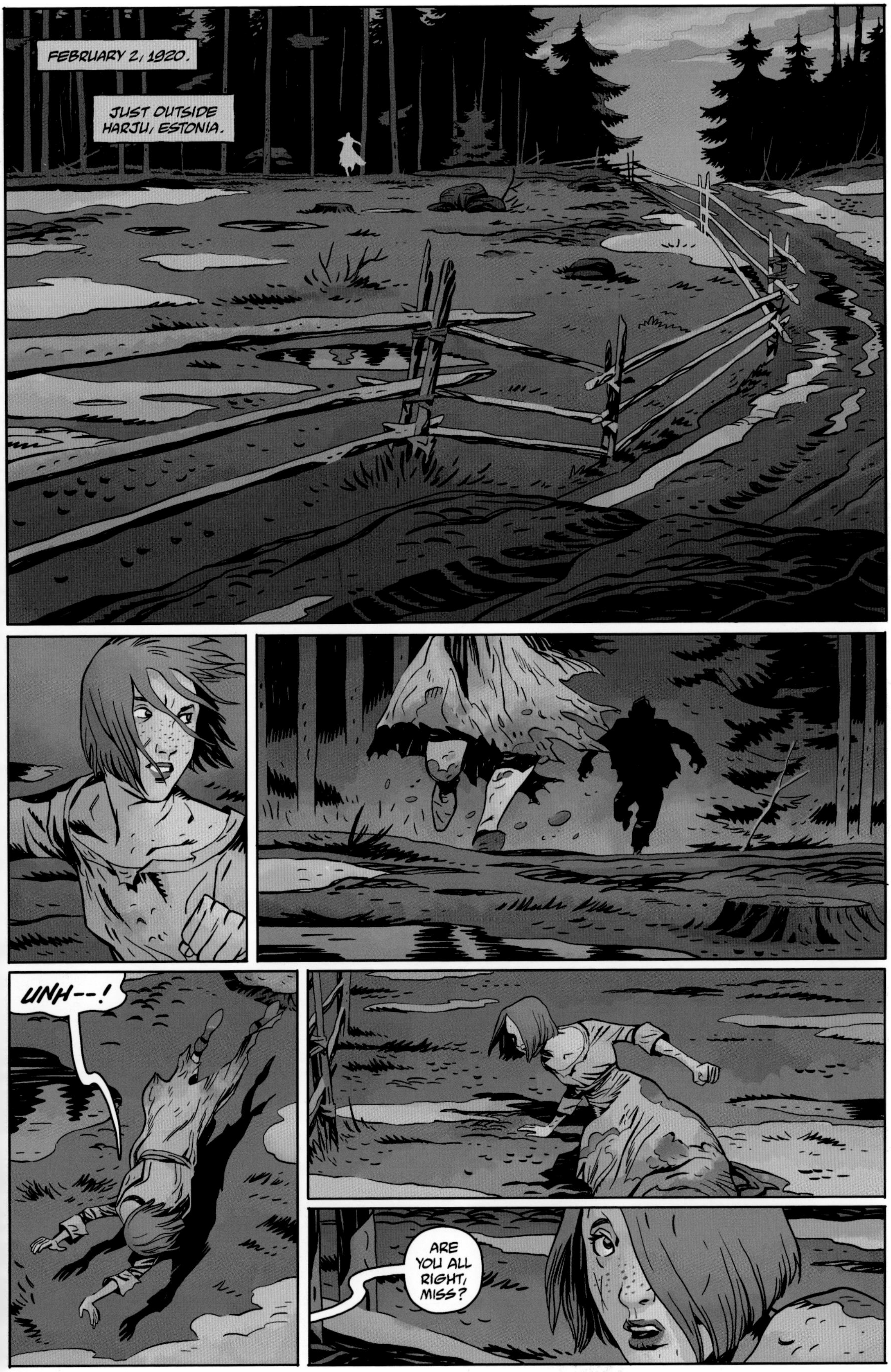
FEBRUARY 2, 1920.
JUST OUTSIDE HARJU, ESTONIA.
UNH--!
ARE YOU ALL RIGHT, MISS?

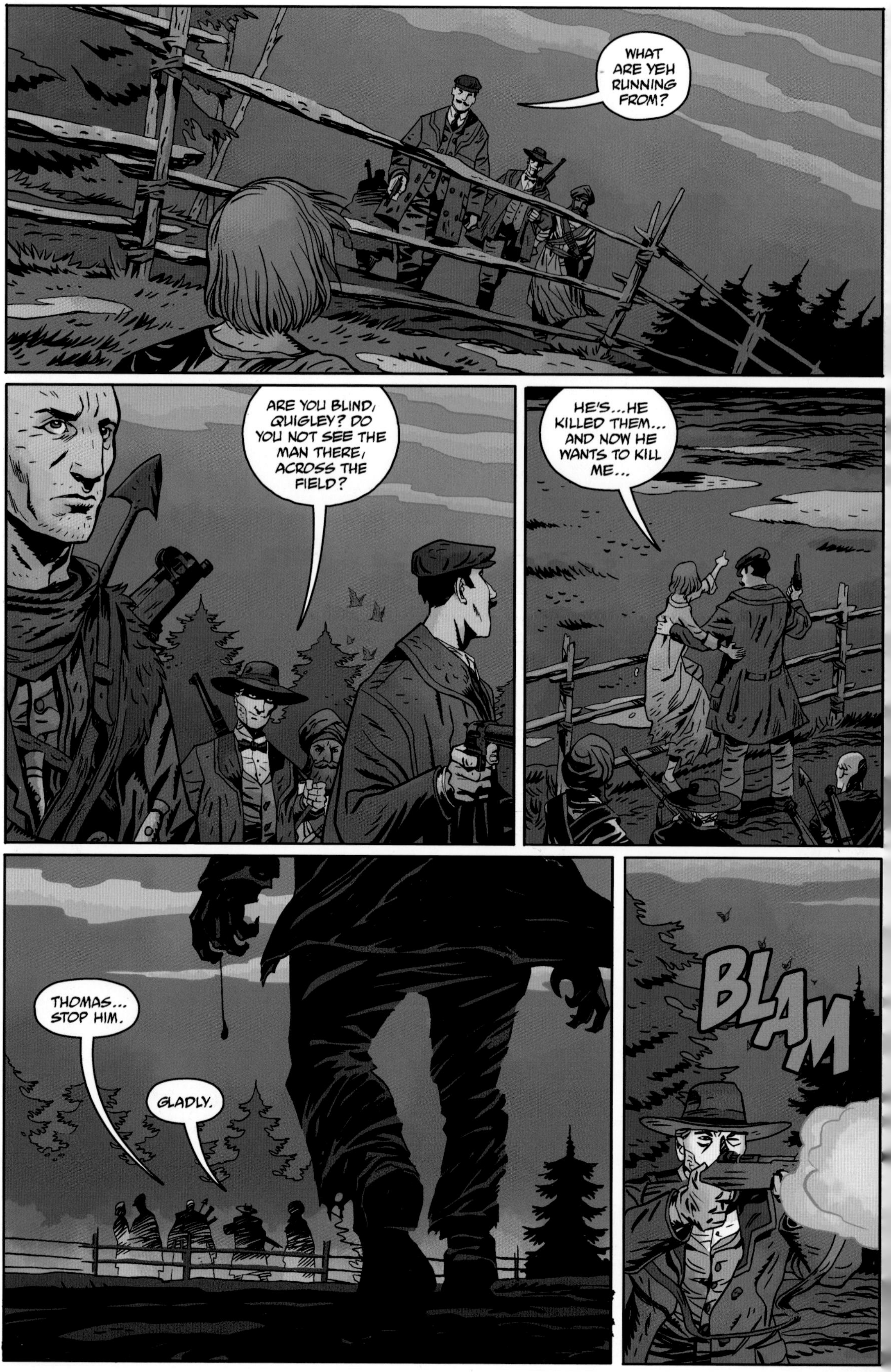
WHAT ARE YEH RUNNING FROM?
ARE YOU BLIND, QUIGLEY? DO YOU NOT SEE THE MAN THERE, ACROSS THE FIELD?
HE'S...HE KILLED THEM... AND NOW HE WANTS TO KILL ME...
THOMAS... STOP HIM.
GLADLY.
BLAM

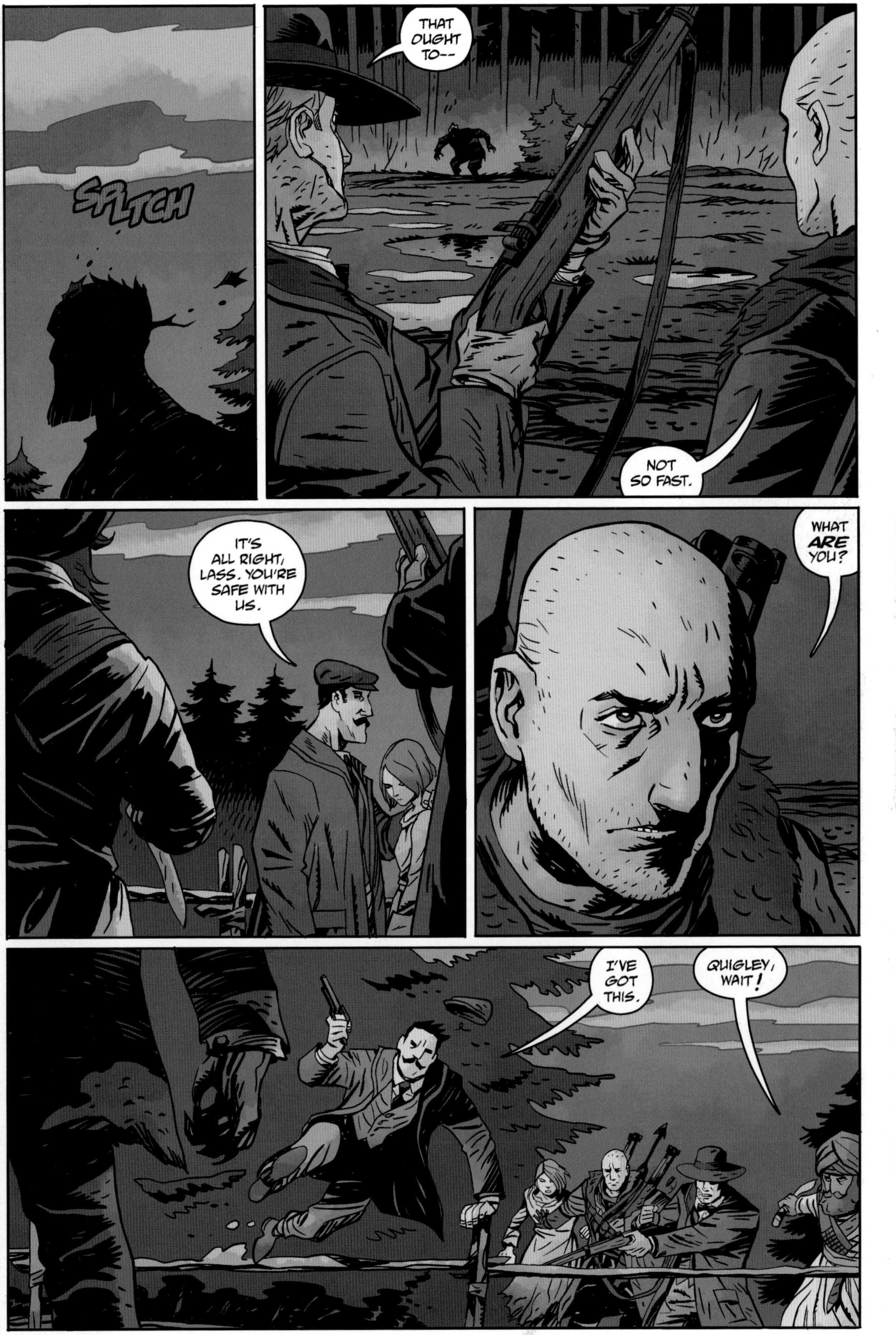
SPLTCH
THAT OUGHT TO--
NOT SO FAST.
IT'S ALL RIGHT, LASS. YOU'RE SAFE WITH US.
WHAT ARE YOU?
I'VE GOT THIS.
QUIGLEY, WAIT!

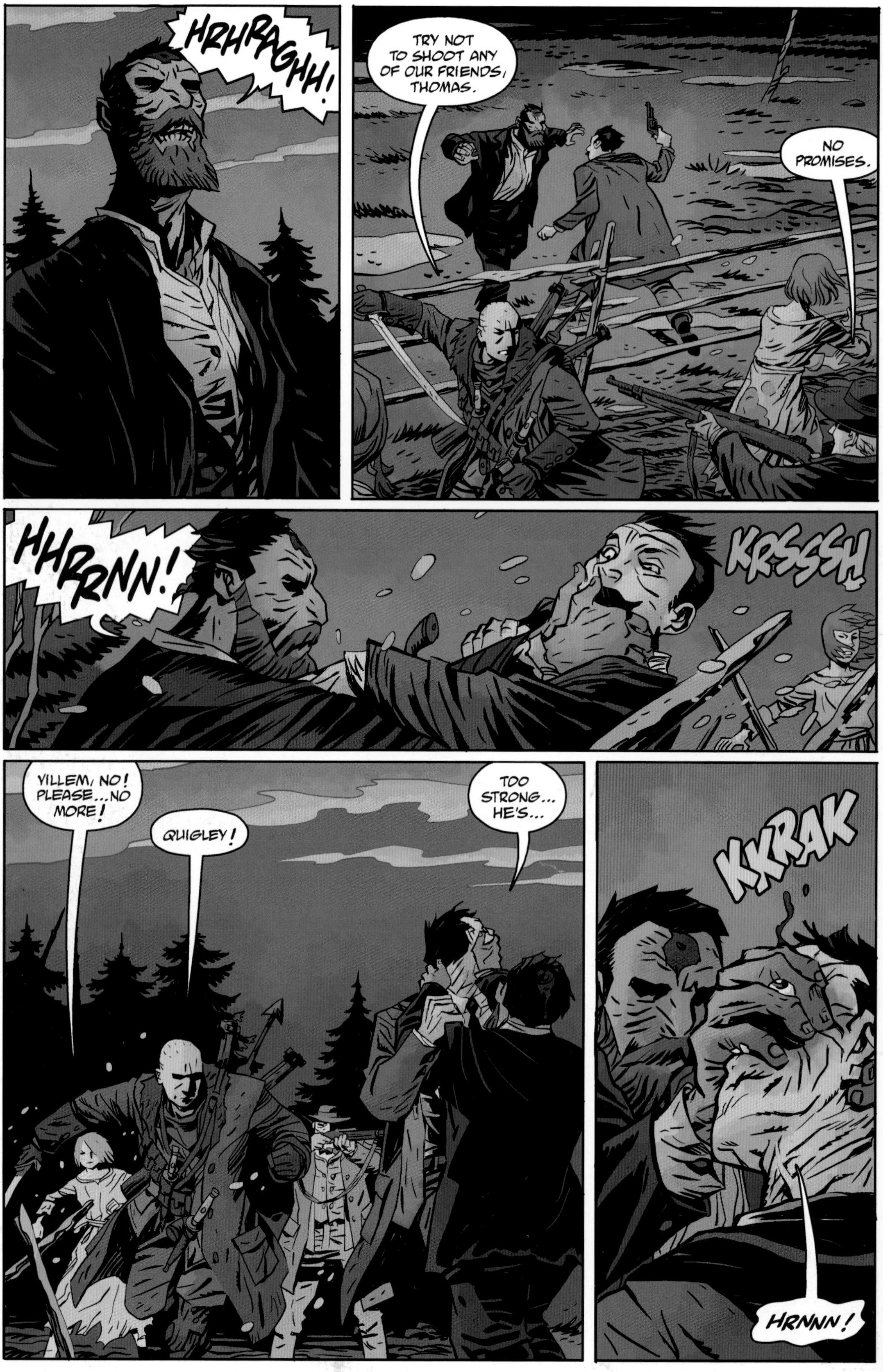
HRHRAGHH!
TRY NOT TO SHOOT ANY OF OUR FRIENDS, THOMAS.
NO PROMISES.
HHRRNN!
KRSSSH
VILLEM, NO! PLEASE...NO MORE!
QUIGLEY!
TOO STRONG... HE'S...
KKRAK
HRNNN!

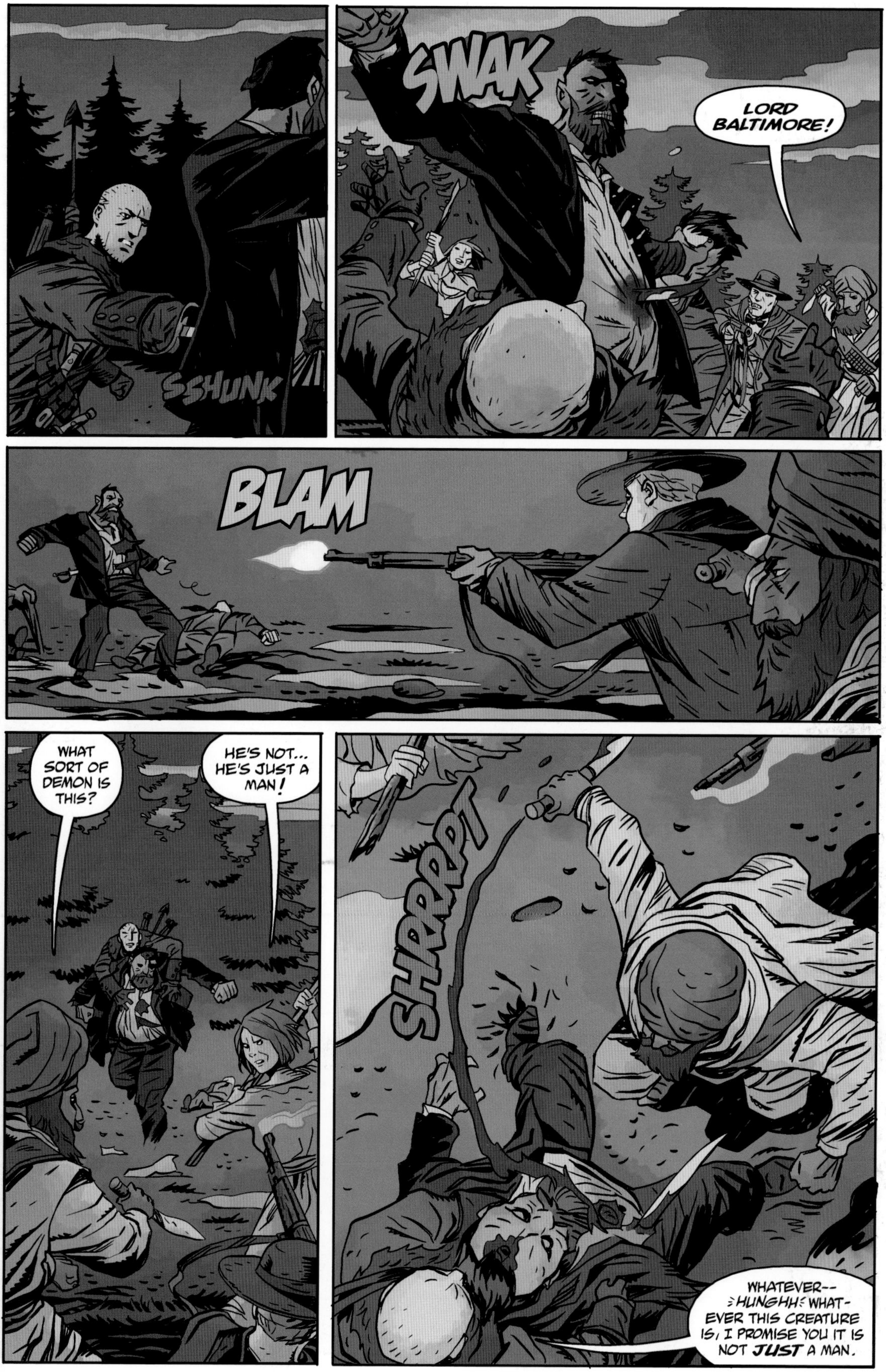
SSHUNK
SWAK
LORD BALTIMORE!
BLAM
WHAT SORT OF DEMON IS THIS?
HE'S NOT... HE'S JUST A MAN!
SHRRRPT
WHATEVER-- HUNGHH WHAT-EVER THIS CREATURE IS, I PROMISE YOU IT IS NOT JUST A MAN.

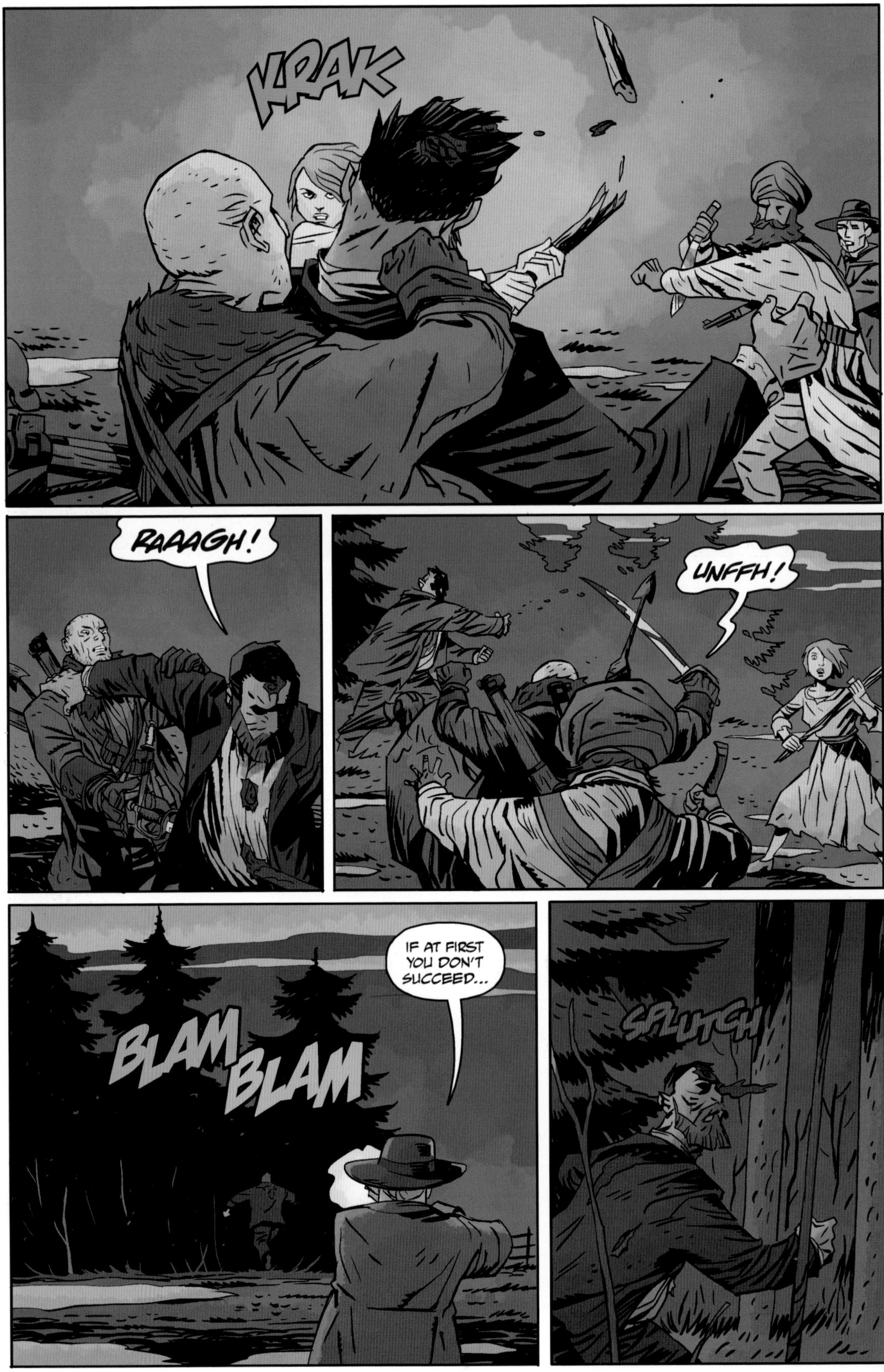
KRAK
RAAAGH!
UNFFH!
BLAM BLAM
IF AT FIRST YOU DON'T SUCCEED...
SPLUTCH

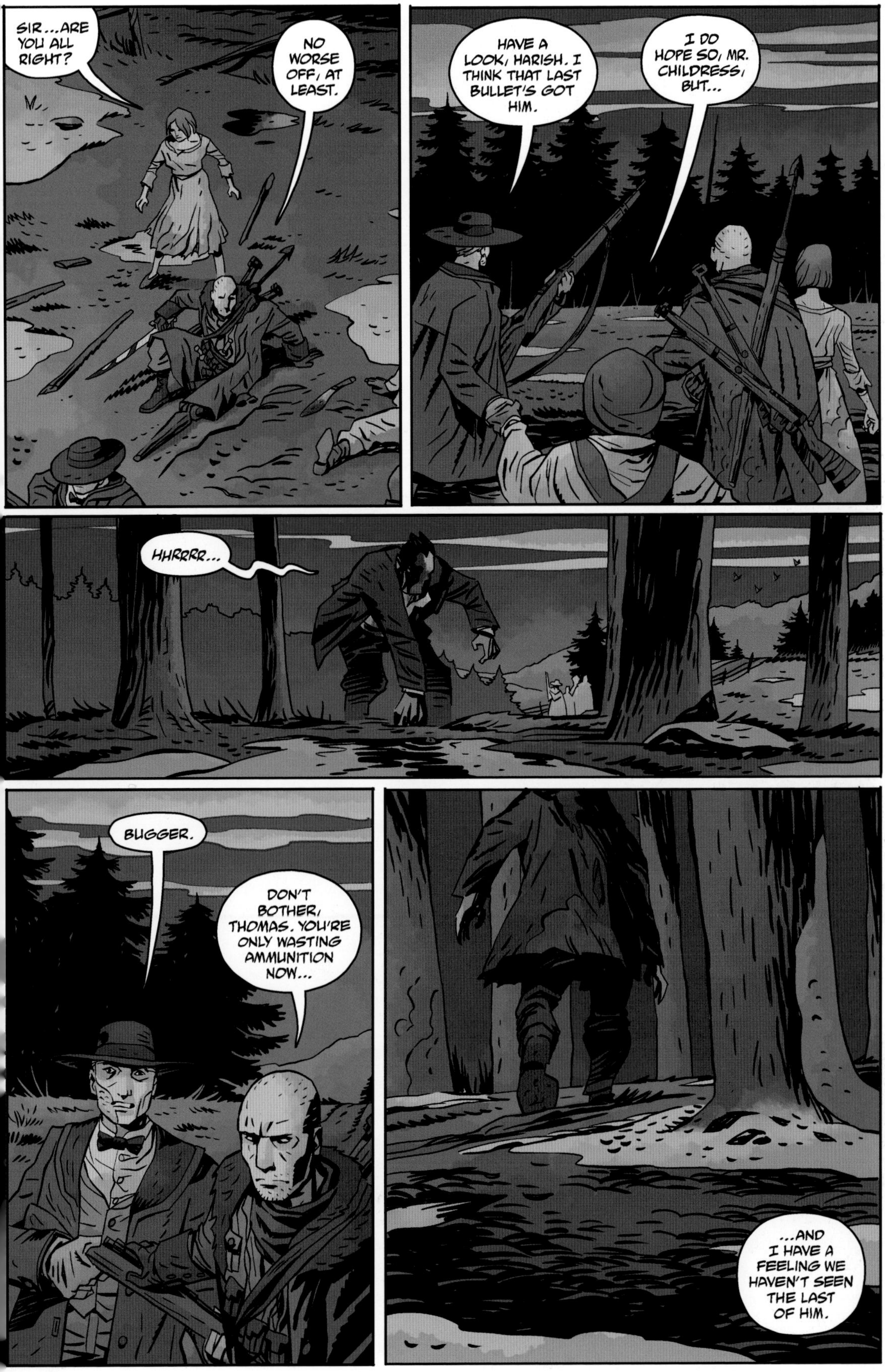
SIR...ARE YOU ALL RIGHT?
NO WORSE OFF, AT LEAST.
HAVE A LOOK, HARISH. I THINK THAT LAST BULLET'S GOT HIM.
I DO HOPE SO, MR. CHILDRESS, BUT...
HHRRRR...
BUGGER.
DON'T BOTHER, THOMAS. YOU'RE ONLY WASTING AMMUNITION NOW...
...AND I HAVE A FEELING WE HAVEN'T SEEN THE LAST OF HIM.

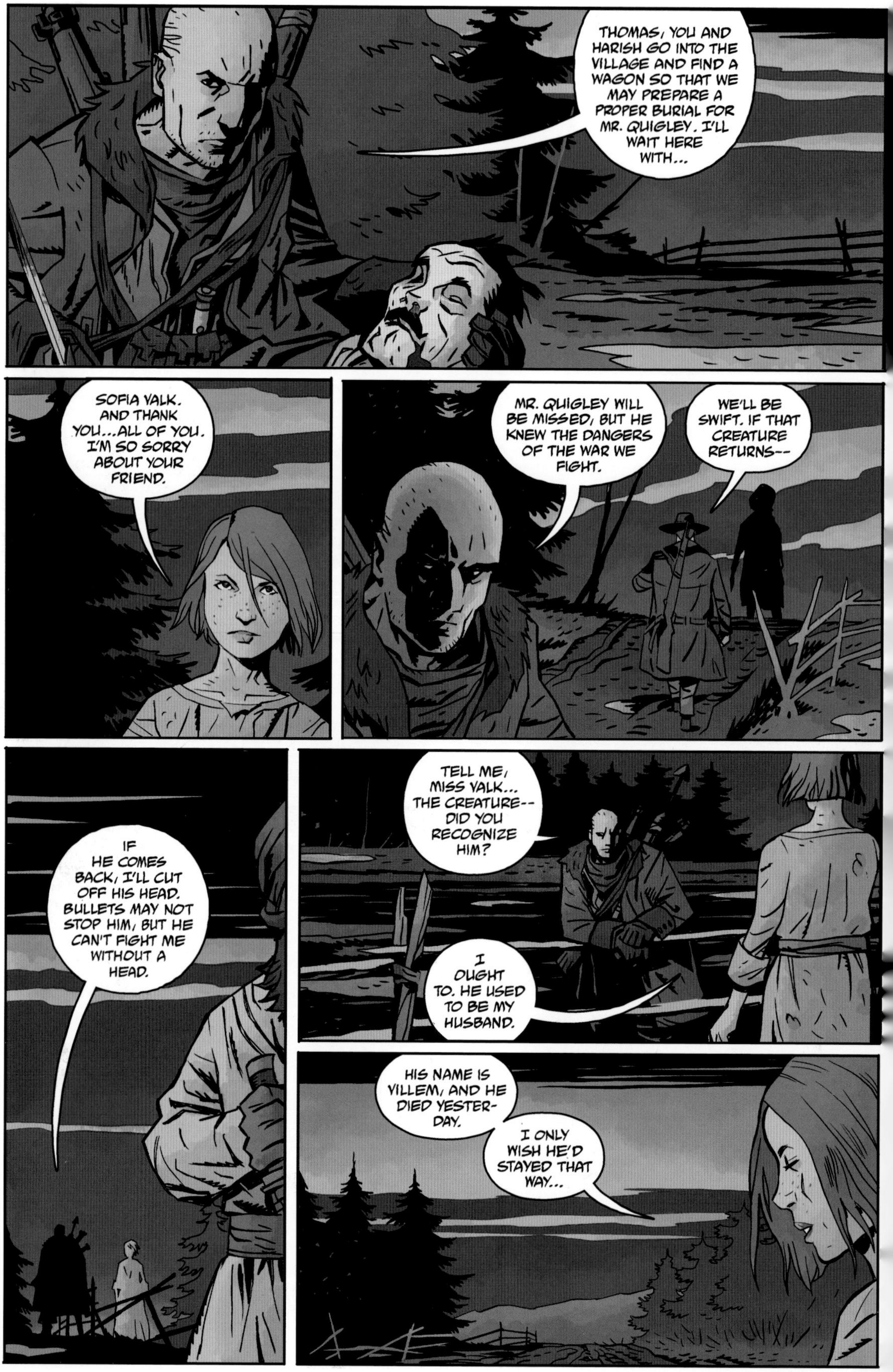
THOMAS, YOU AND HARISH GO INTO THE VILLAGE AND FIND A WAGON SO THAT WE MAY PREPARE A PROPER BURIAL FOR MR. QUIGLEY. I'LL WAIT HERE WITH...
SOFIA VALK. AND THANK YOU...ALL OF YOU. I'M SO SORRY ABOUT YOUR FRIEND.
MR. QUIGLEY WILL BE MISSED, BUT HE KNEW THE DANGERS OF THE WAR WE FIGHT.
WE'LL BE SWIFT. IF THAT CREATURE RETURNS--
IF HE COMES BACK, I'LL CUT OFF HIS HEAD. BULLETS MAY NOT STOP HIM, BUT HE CAN'T FIGHT ME WITHOUT A HEAD.
TELL ME, MISS VALK... THE CREATURE-- DID YOU RECOGNIZE HIM?
I OUGHT TO. HE USED TO BE MY HUSBAND.
HIS NAME IS VILLEM, AND HE DIED YESTER-DAY.
I ONLY WISH HE'D STAYED THAT WAY...

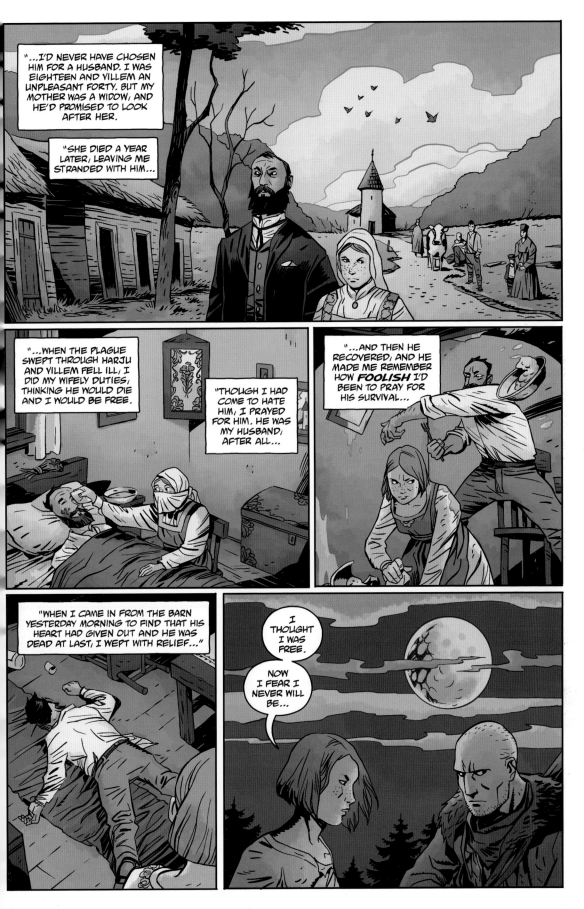

"...I'D NEVER HAVE CHOSEN HIM FOR A HUSBAND. I WAS EIGHTEEN AND VILLEM AN UNPLEASANT FORTY. BUT MY MOTHER WAS A WIDOW, AND HE'D PROMISED TO LOOK AFTER HER.

"SHE DIED A YEAR LATER, LEAVING ME STRANDED WITH HIM...

"...WHEN THE PLAGUE SWEPT THROUGH HARJU AND VILLEM FELL ILL, I DID MY WIFELY DUTIES, THINKING HE WOULD DIE AND I WOULD BE FREE.

"THOUGH I HAD COME TO HATE HIM, I PRAYED FOR HIM. HE WAS MY HUSBAND, AFTER ALL...

"...AND THEN HE RECOVERED, AND HE MADE ME REMEMBER HOW *FOOLISH* I'D BEEN TO PRAY FOR HIS SURVIVAL...

"WHEN I CAME IN FROM THE BARN YESTERDAY MORNING TO FIND THAT HIS HEART HAD GIVEN OUT AND HE WAS DEAD AT LAST, I WEPT WITH RELIEF..."

I THOUGHT I WAS FREE.

NOW I FEAR I NEVER WILL BE...

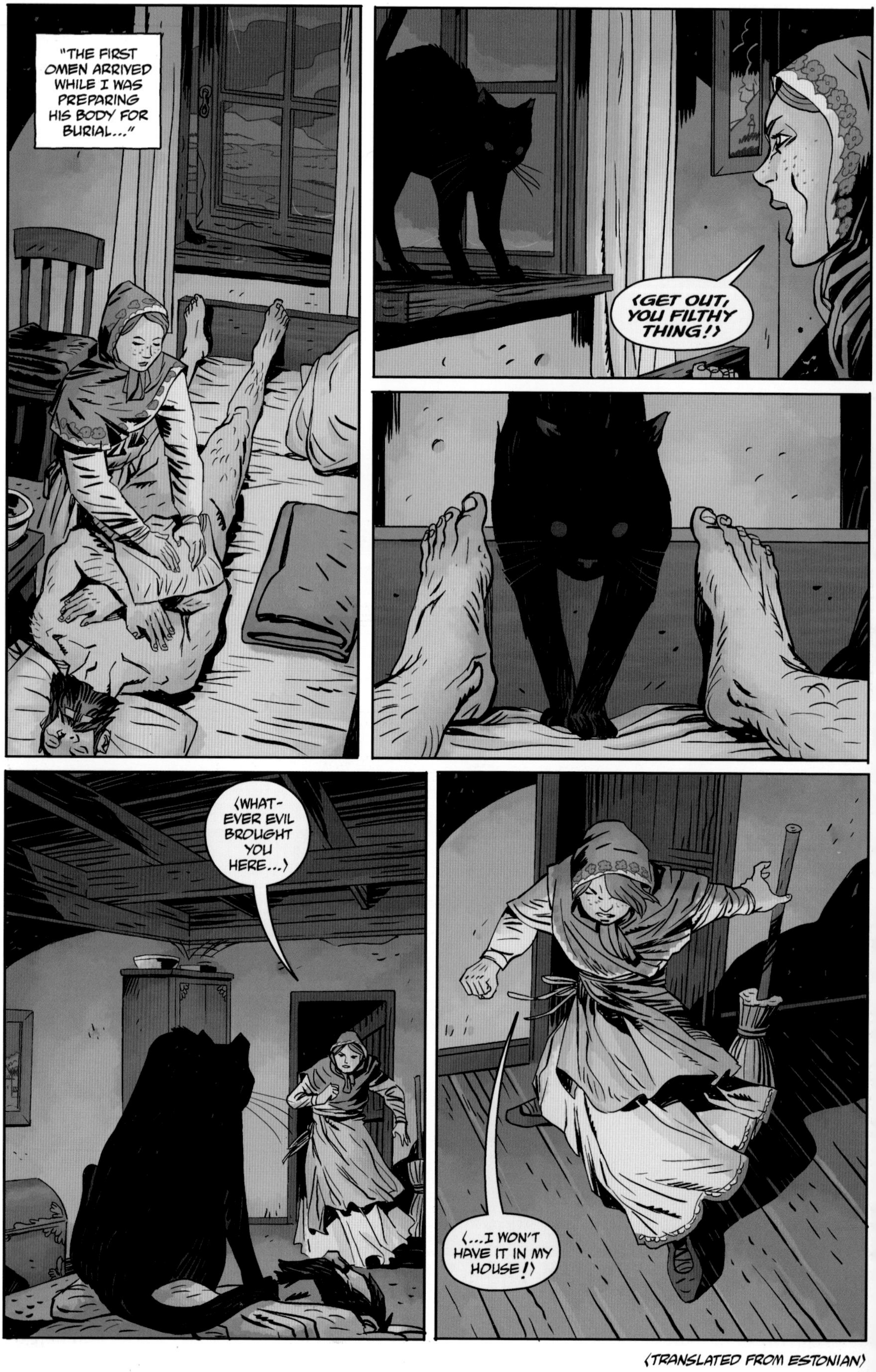
"THE FIRST OMEN ARRIVED WHILE I WAS PREPARING HIS BODY FOR BURIAL..."
‹GET OUT, YOU FILTHY THING!›
‹WHAT-EVER EVIL BROUGHT YOU HERE...›
‹...I WON'T HAVE IT IN MY HOUSE!›

‹TRANSLATED FROM ESTONIAN›

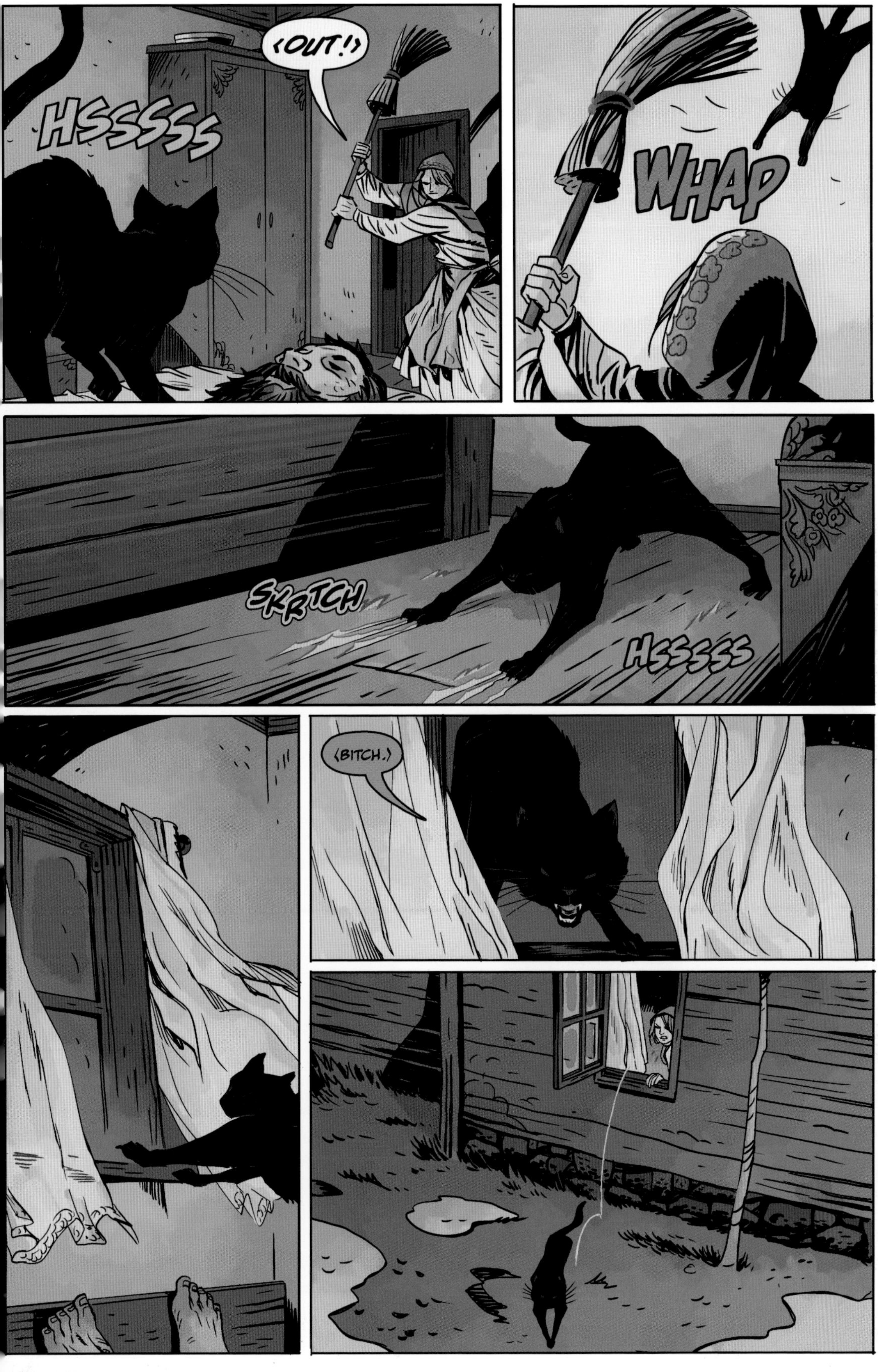

HSSSSSS
‹OUT!›
WHAP
SKRTCH
HSSSSS
‹BITCH.›

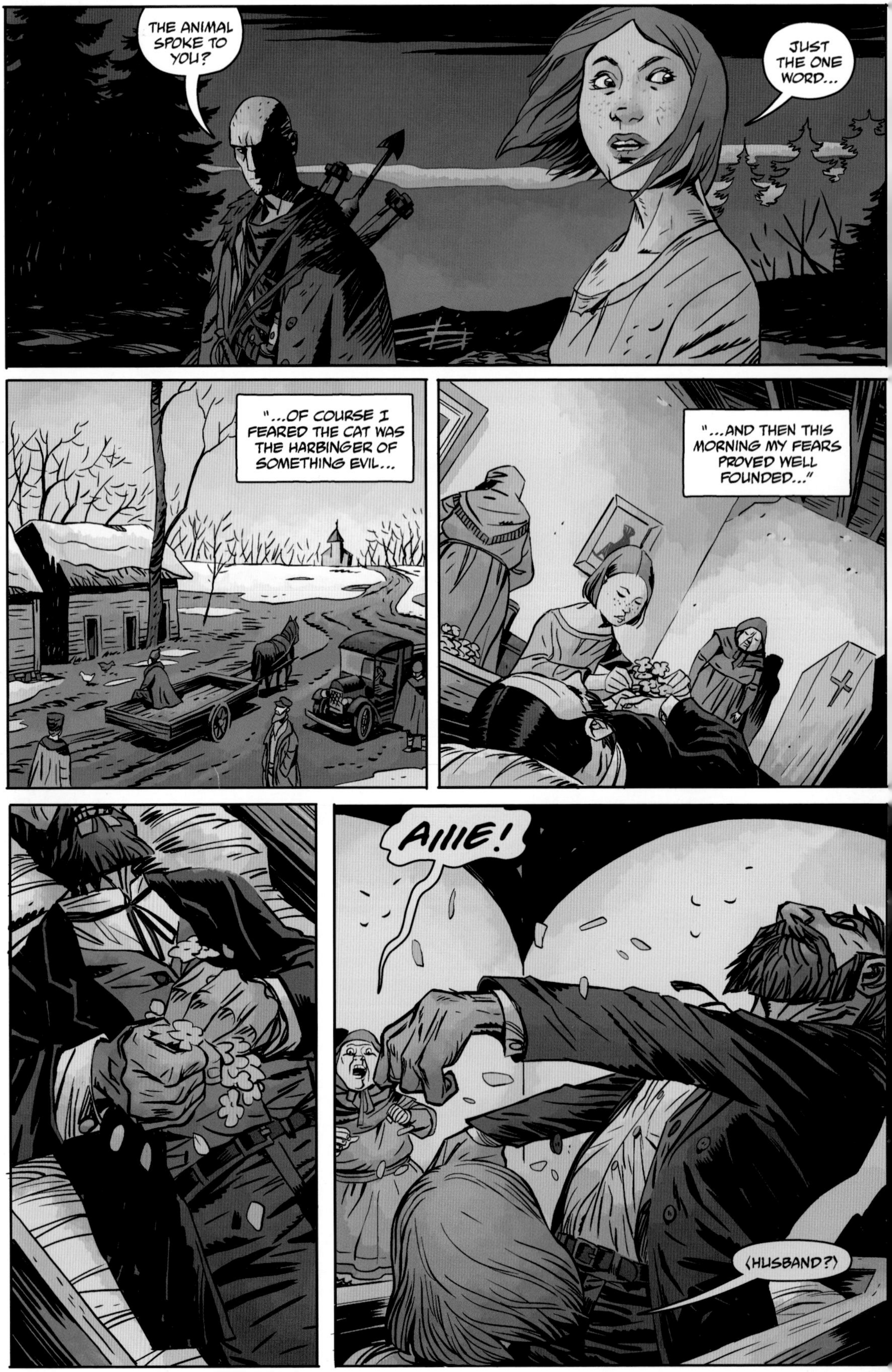
THE ANIMAL SPOKE TO YOU?
JUST THE ONE WORD...
"...OF COURSE I FEARED THE CAT WAS THE HARBINGER OF SOMETHING EVIL...
"...AND THEN THIS MORNING MY FEARS PROVED WELL FOUNDED..."
AIIIE!
‹HUSBAND?›

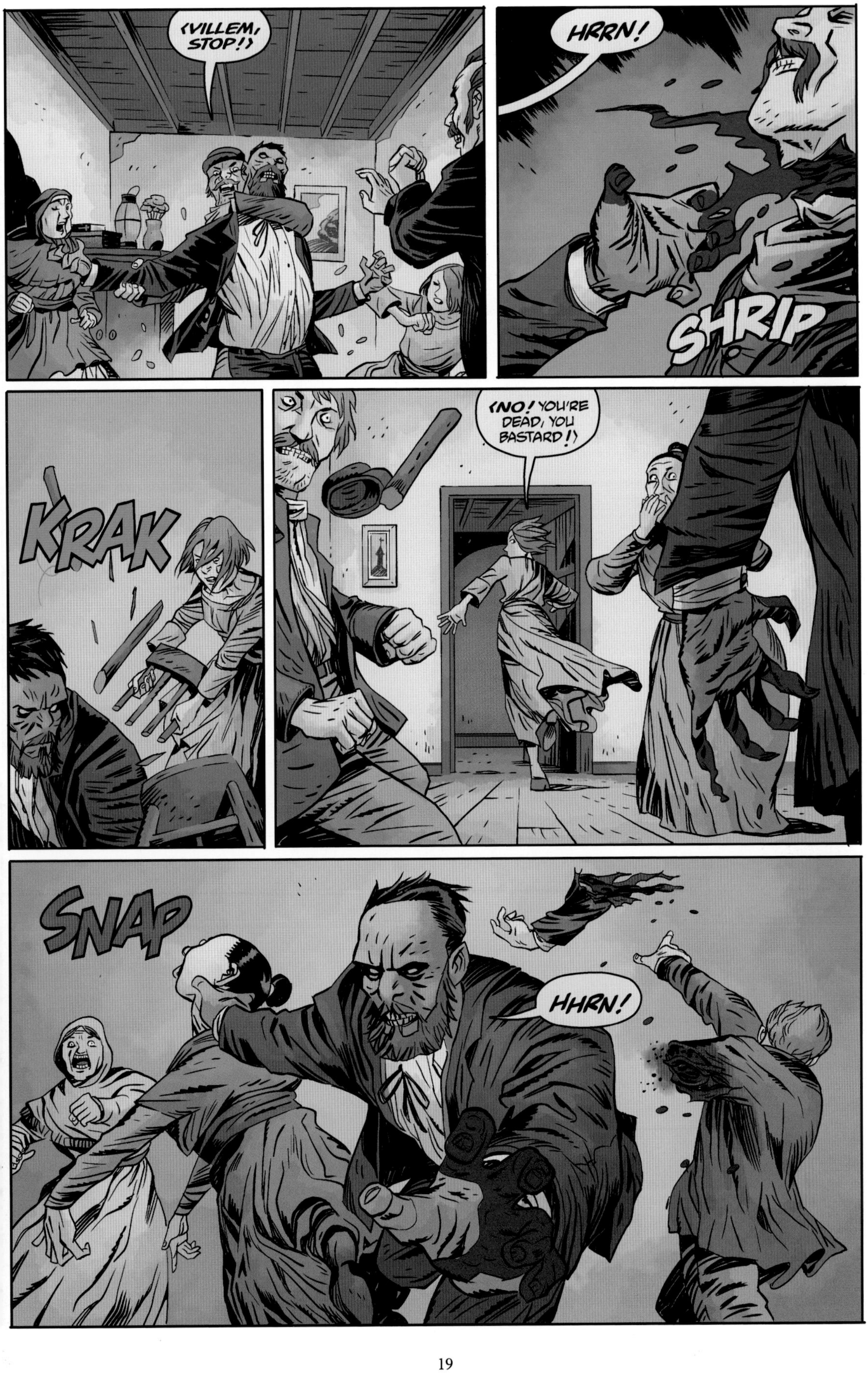
‹VILLEM, STOP!›
HRRN!
SHRIP
KRAK
‹NO! YOU'RE DEAD, YOU BASTARD!›
SNAP
HHRN!

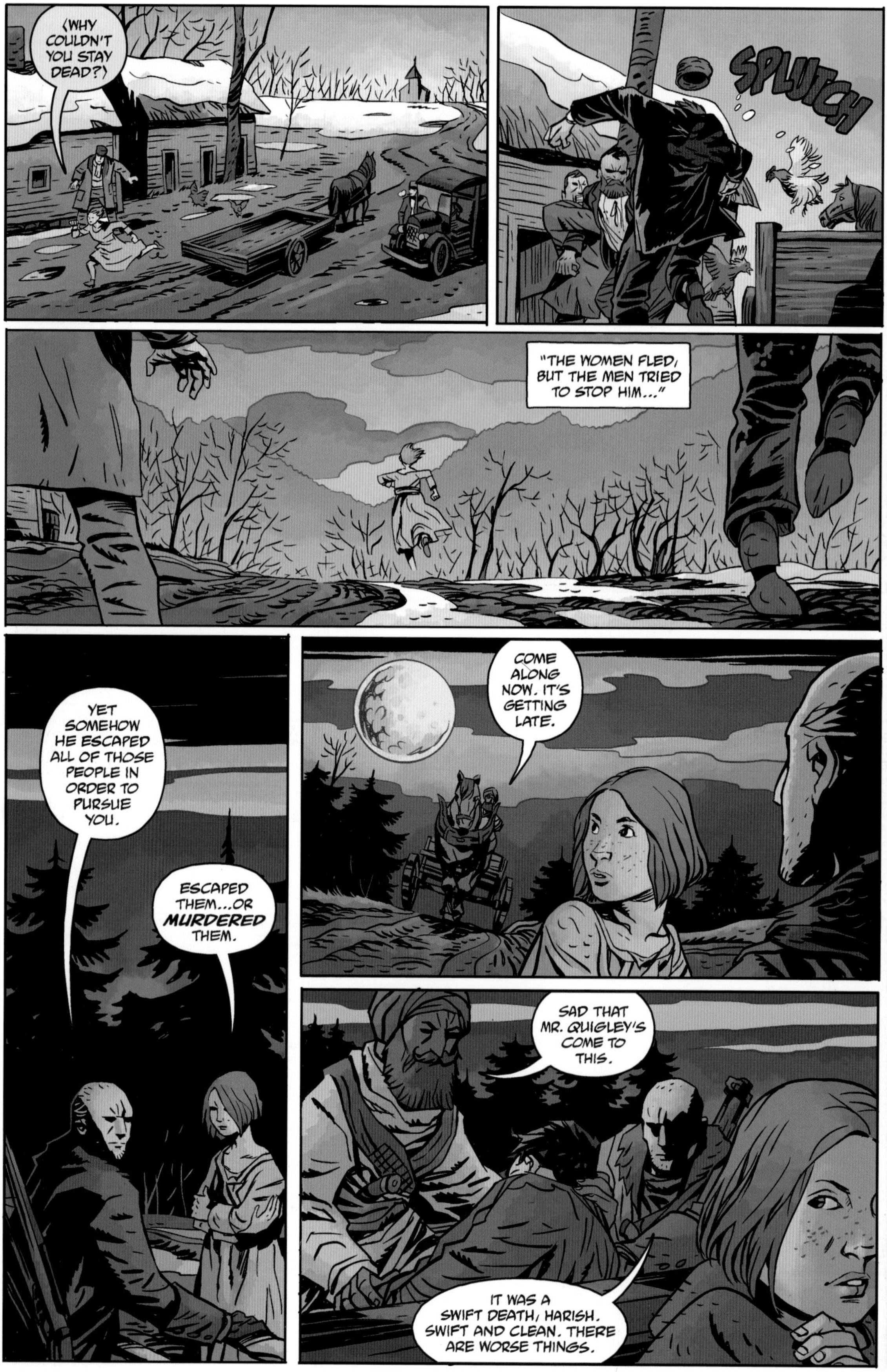

‹WHY COULDN'T YOU STAY DEAD?›
SPLUTCH
"THE WOMEN FLED, BUT THE MEN TRIED TO STOP HIM..."
YET SOMEHOW HE ESCAPED ALL OF THOSE PEOPLE IN ORDER TO PURSUE YOU.
ESCAPED THEM...OR MURDERED THEM.
COME ALONG NOW. IT'S GETTING LATE.
SAD THAT MR. QUIGLEY'S COME TO THIS.
IT WAS A SWIFT DEATH, HARISH. SWIFT AND CLEAN. THERE ARE WORSE THINGS.

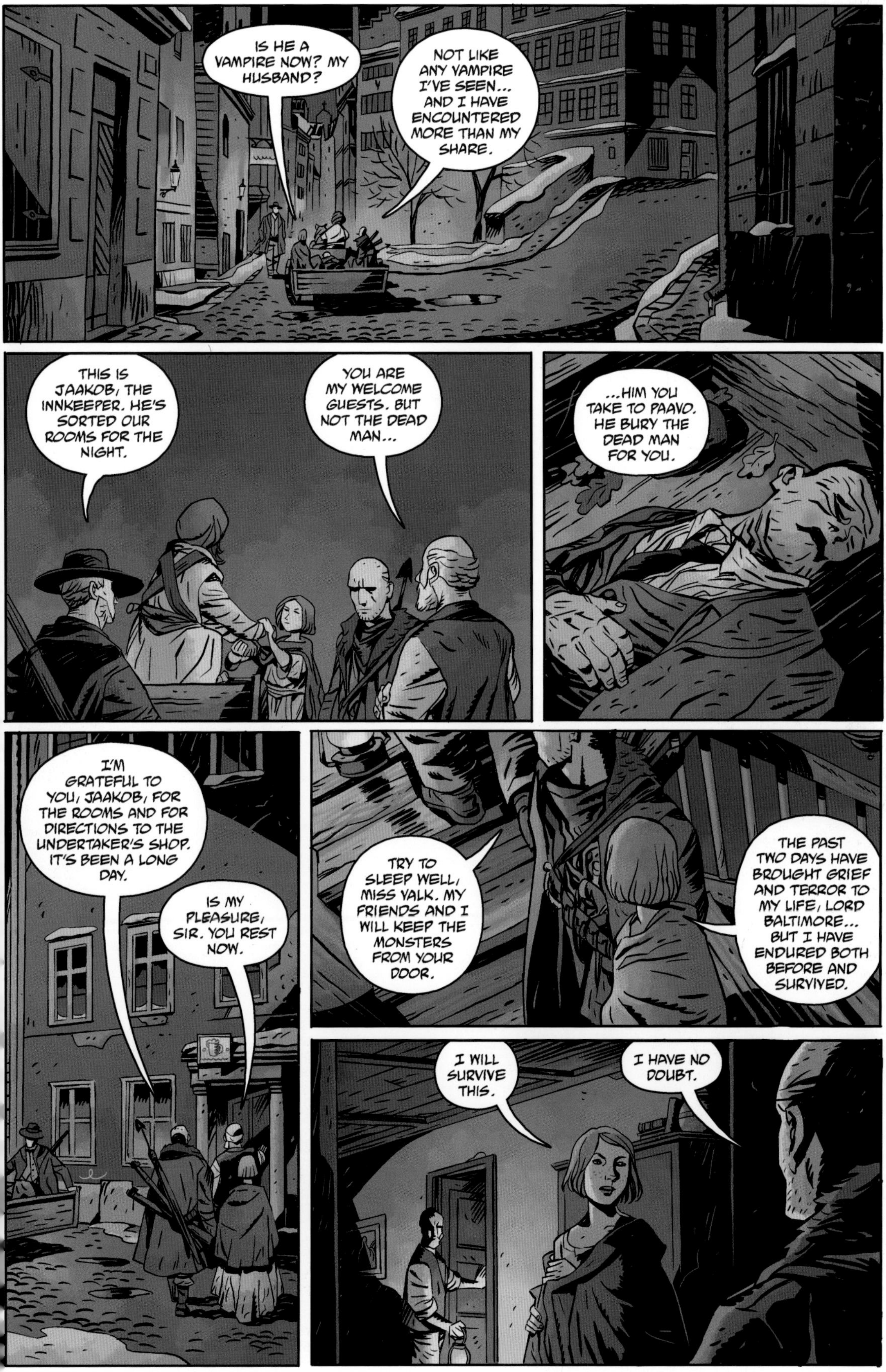
IS HE A VAMPIRE NOW? MY HUSBAND?
NOT LIKE ANY VAMPIRE I'VE SEEN... AND I HAVE ENCOUNTERED MORE THAN MY SHARE.
THIS IS JAAKOB, THE INNKEEPER. HE'S SORTED OUR ROOMS FOR THE NIGHT.
YOU ARE MY WELCOME GUESTS. BUT NOT THE DEAD MAN...
...HIM YOU TAKE TO PAAVO. HE BURY THE DEAD MAN FOR YOU.
I'M GRATEFUL TO YOU, JAAKOB, FOR THE ROOMS AND FOR DIRECTIONS TO THE UNDERTAKER'S SHOP. IT'S BEEN A LONG DAY.
IS MY PLEASURE, SIR. YOU REST NOW.
TRY TO SLEEP WELL, MISS VALK. MY FRIENDS AND I WILL KEEP THE MONSTERS FROM YOUR DOOR.
THE PAST TWO DAYS HAVE BROUGHT GRIEF AND TERROR TO MY LIFE, LORD BALTIMORE... BUT I HAVE ENDURED BOTH BEFORE AND SURVIVED.
I WILL SURVIVE THIS.
I HAVE NO DOUBT.

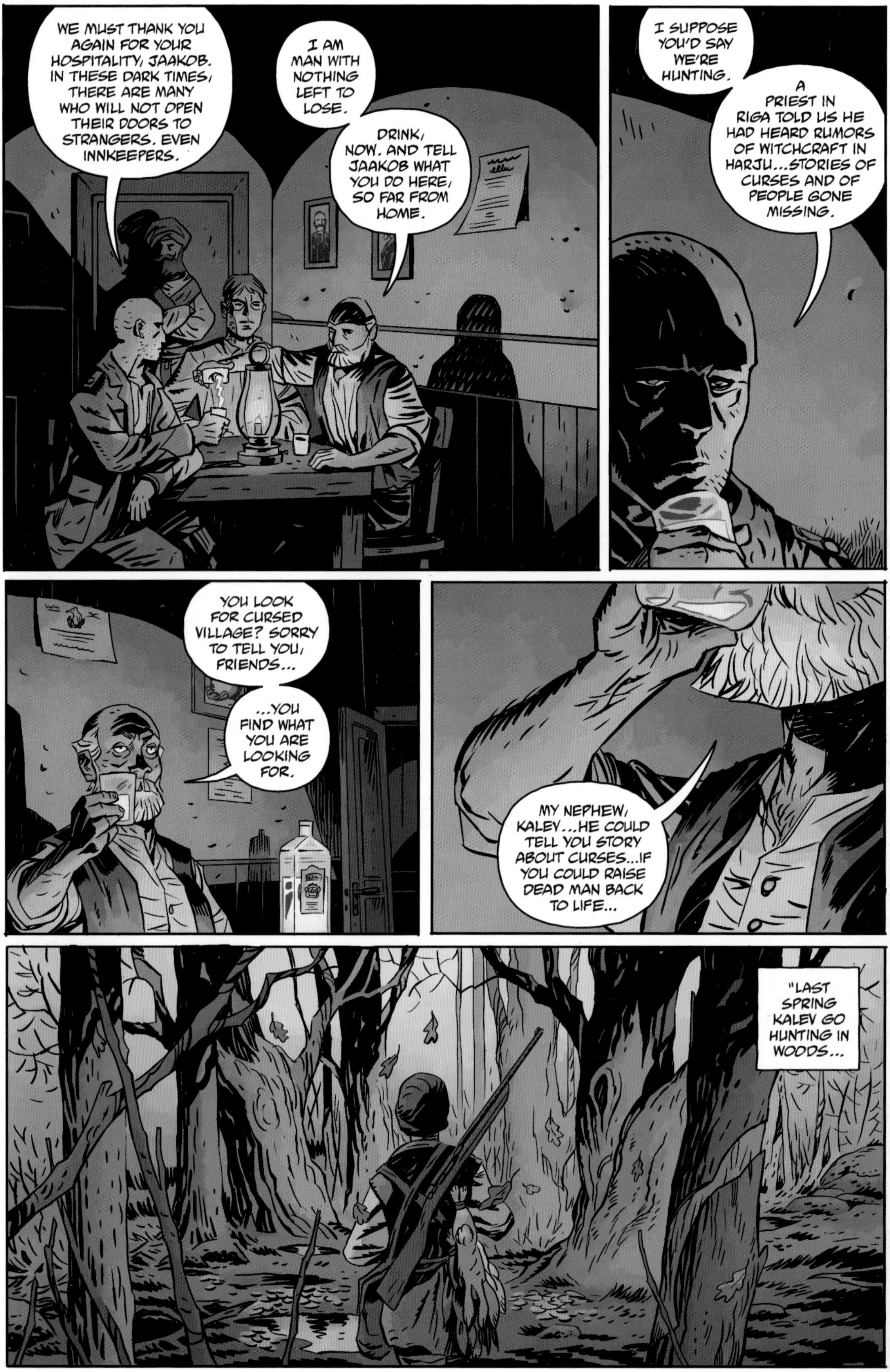
WE MUST THANK YOU AGAIN FOR YOUR HOSPITALITY, JAAKOB. IN THESE DARK TIMES, THERE ARE MANY WHO WILL NOT OPEN THEIR DOORS TO STRANGERS. EVEN INNKEEPERS.
I AM MAN WITH NOTHING LEFT TO LOSE.
DRINK, NOW. AND TELL JAAKOB WHAT YOU DO HERE, SO FAR FROM HOME.
I SUPPOSE YOU'D SAY WE'RE HUNTING.
A PRIEST IN RIGA TOLD US HE HAD HEARD RUMORS OF WITCHCRAFT IN HARJU...STORIES OF CURSES AND OF PEOPLE GONE MISSING.
YOU LOOK FOR CURSED VILLAGE? SORRY TO TELL YOU, FRIENDS...
...YOU FIND WHAT YOU ARE LOOKING FOR.
MY NEPHEW, KALEV...HE COULD TELL YOU STORY ABOUT CURSES...IF YOU COULD RAISE DEAD MAN BACK TO LIFE...
"LAST SPRING KALEV GO HUNTING IN WOODS...

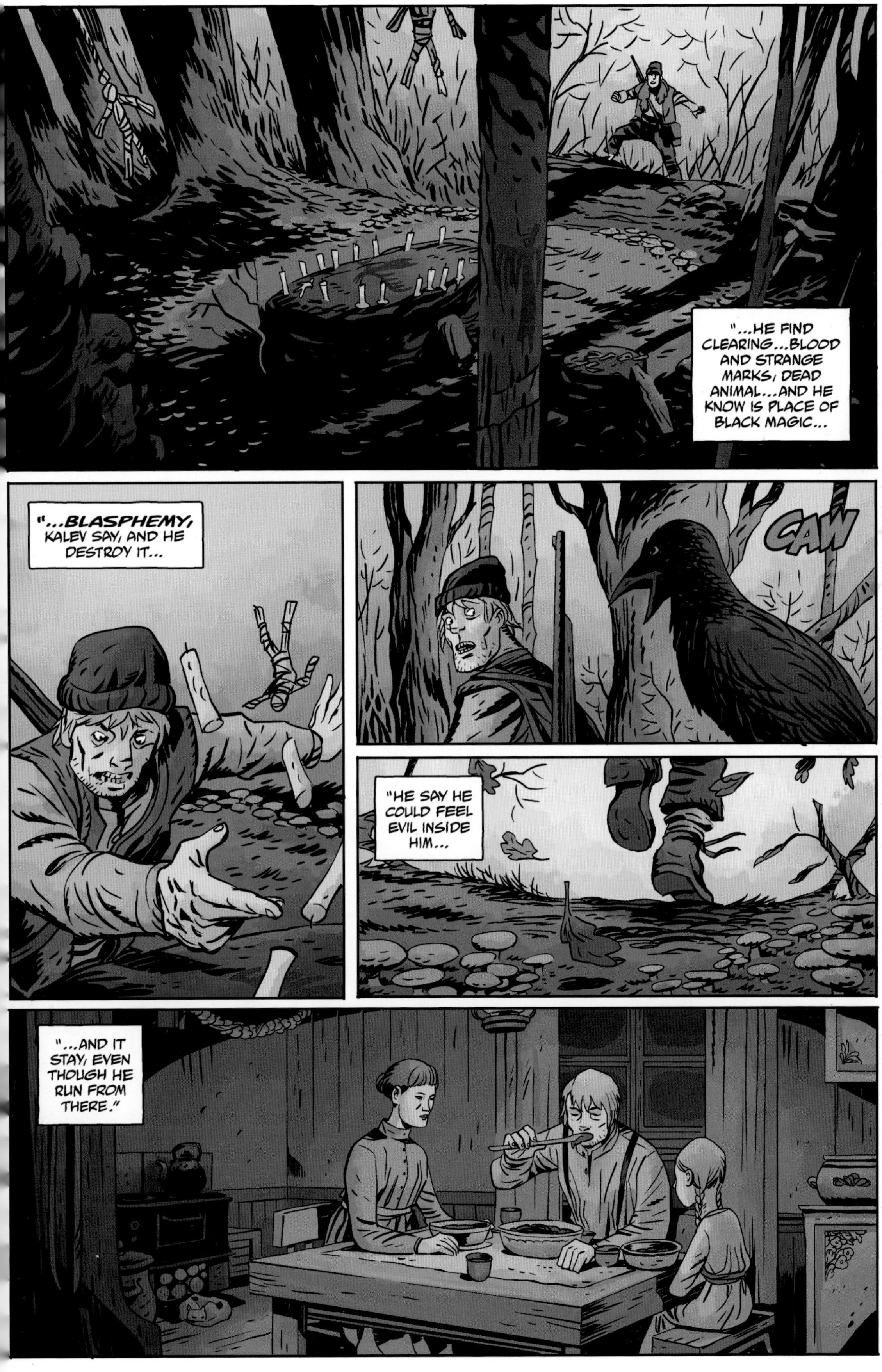
"...HE FIND CLEARING...BLOOD AND STRANGE MARKS, DEAD ANIMAL...AND HE KNOW IS PLACE OF BLACK MAGIC...
"...BLASPHEMY, KALEV SAY, AND HE DESTROY IT...
CAW
"HE SAY HE COULD FEEL EVIL INSIDE HIM...
"...AND IT STAY, EVEN THOUGH HE RUN FROM THERE."

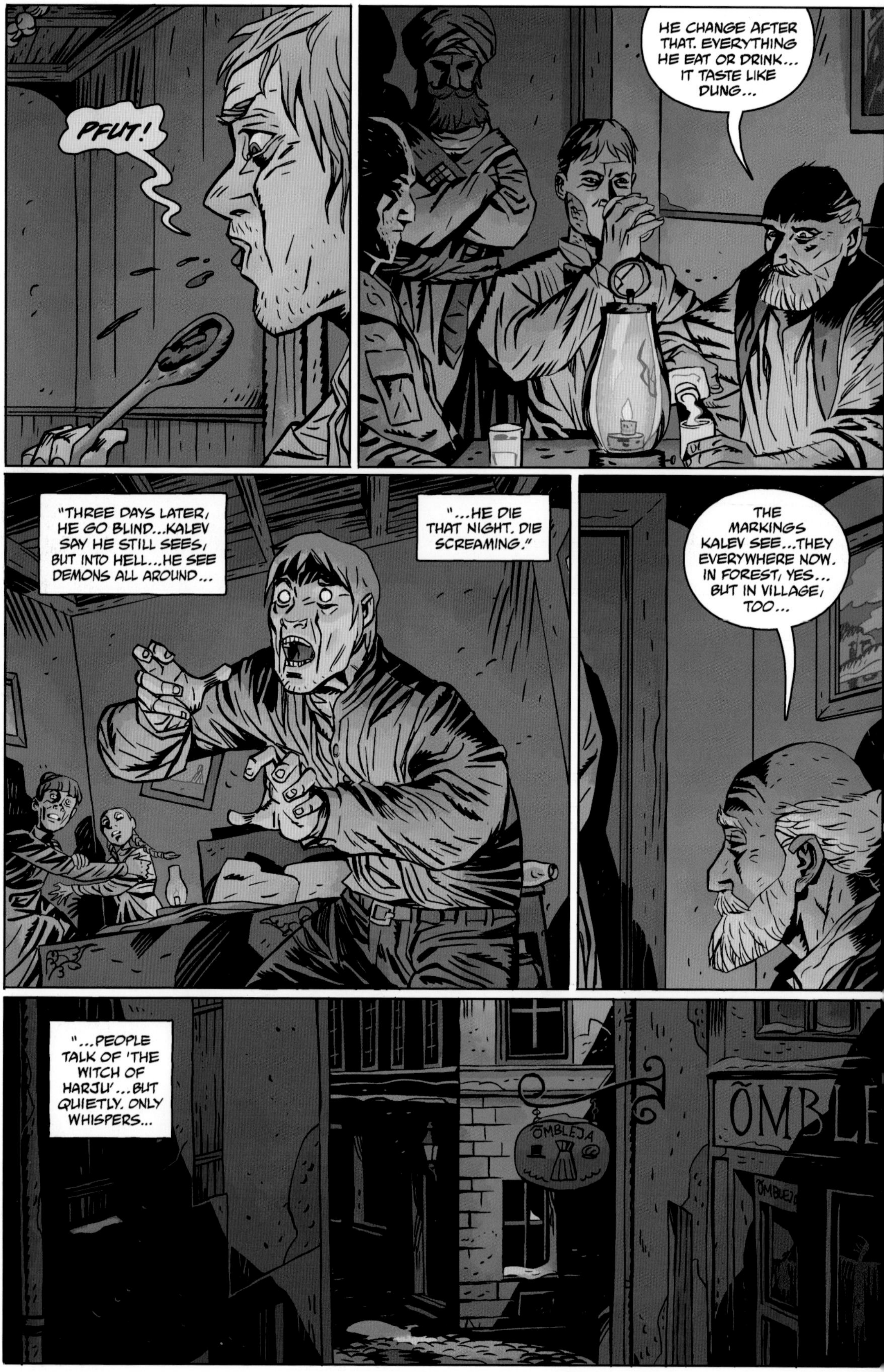
PFUT!
HE CHANGE AFTER THAT. EVERYTHING HE EAT OR DRINK... IT TASTE LIKE DUNG...
"THREE DAYS LATER, HE GO BLIND...KALEV SAY HE STILL SEES, BUT INTO HELL...HE SEE DEMONS ALL AROUND...
"...HE DIE THAT NIGHT. DIE SCREAMING."
THE MARKINGS KALEV SEE...THEY EVERYWHERE NOW. IN FOREST, YES... BUT IN VILLAGE, TOO...
"...PEOPLE TALK OF 'THE WITCH OF HARJU'...BUT QUIETLY. ONLY WHISPERS...
ÕMBLEJA
ÕMBLE
ÕMBLEJA

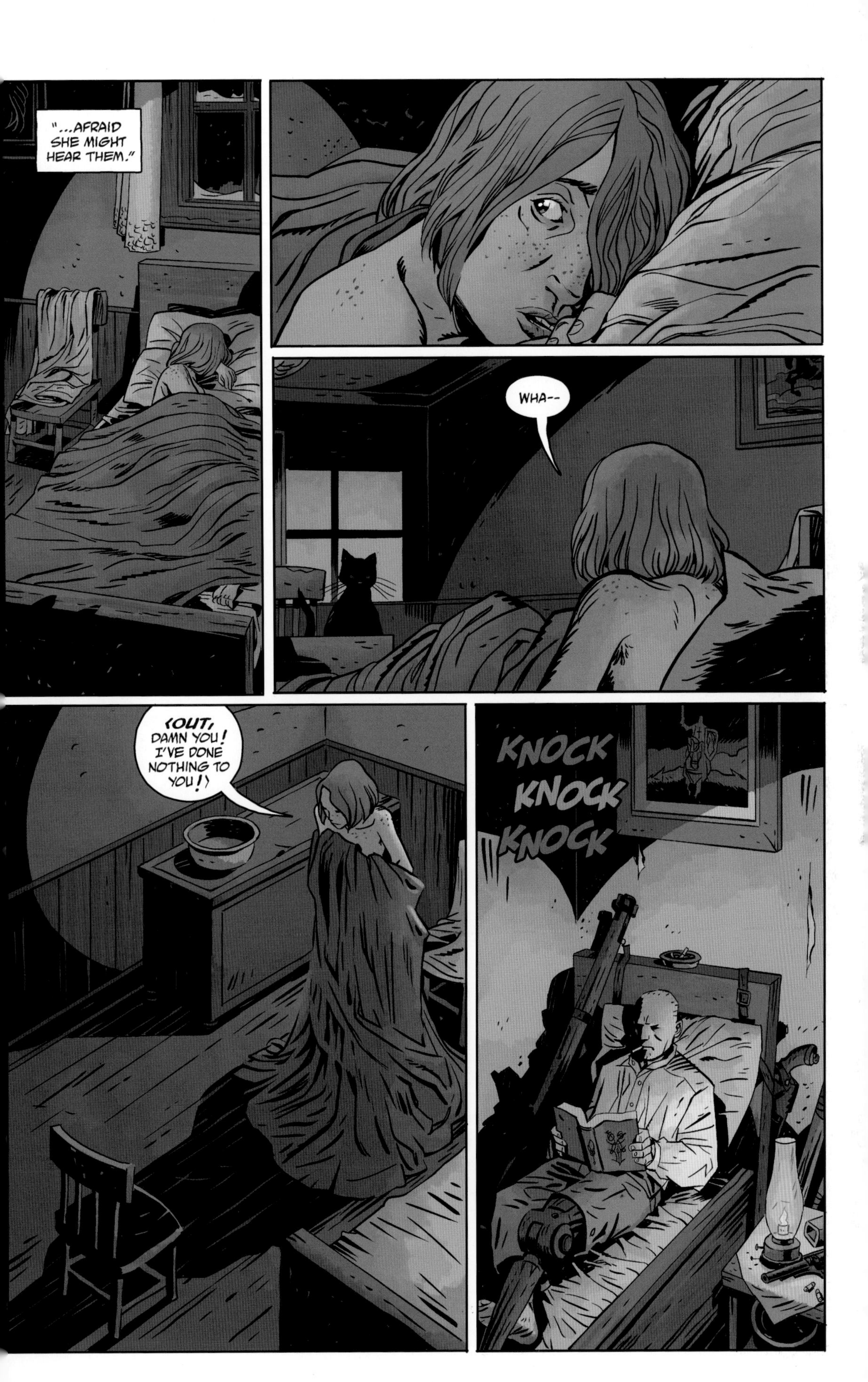
"...AFRAID SHE MIGHT HEAR THEM."
WHA--
‹OUT, DAMN YOU! I'VE DONE NOTHING TO YOU!›
KNOCK
KNOCK
KNOCK

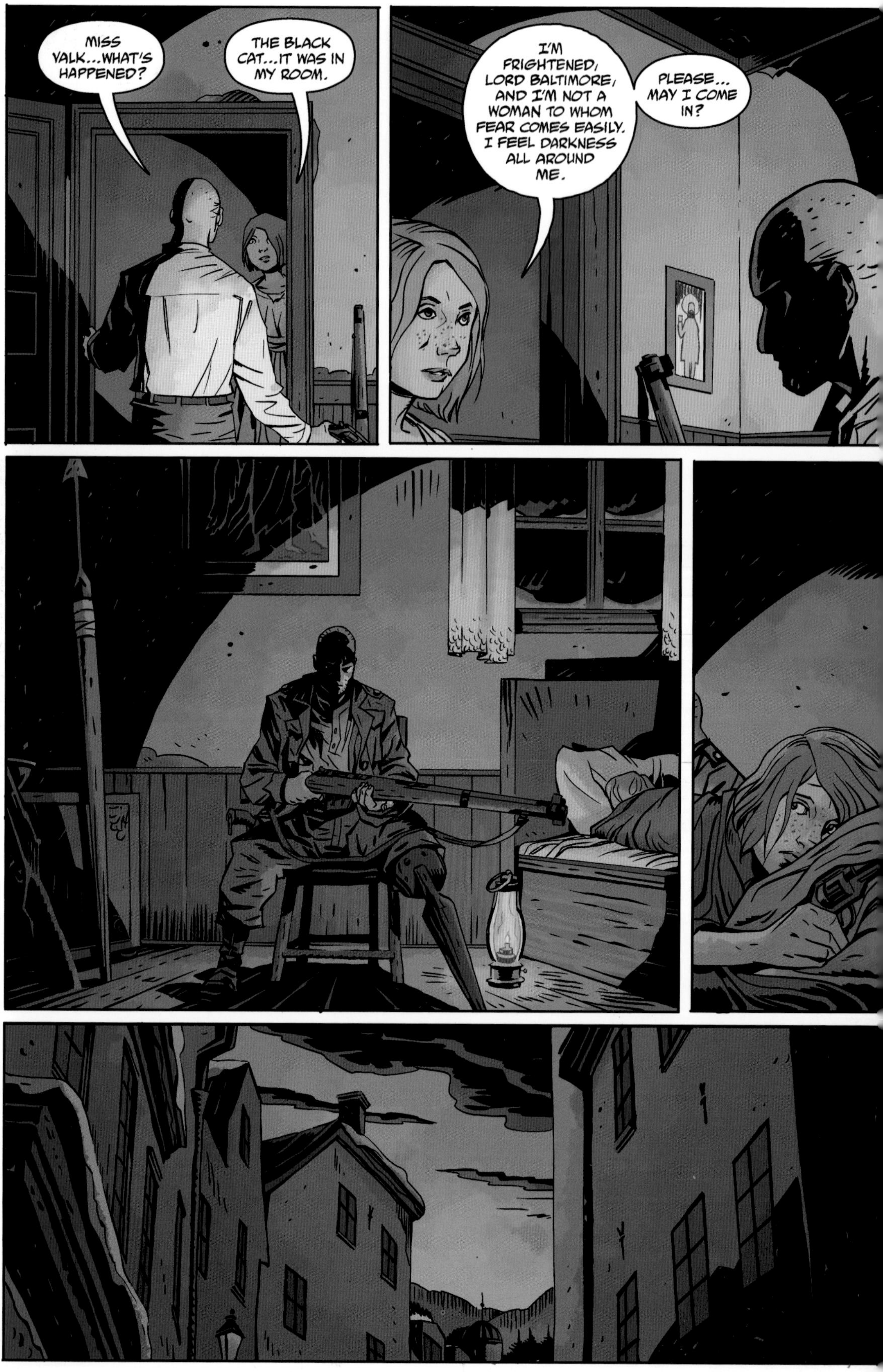
MISS VALK...WHAT'S HAPPENED?
THE BLACK CAT...IT WAS IN MY ROOM.
I'M FRIGHTENED, LORD BALTIMORE, AND I'M NOT A WOMAN TO WHOM FEAR COMES EASILY. I FEEL DARKNESS ALL AROUND ME.
PLEASE... MAY I COME IN?

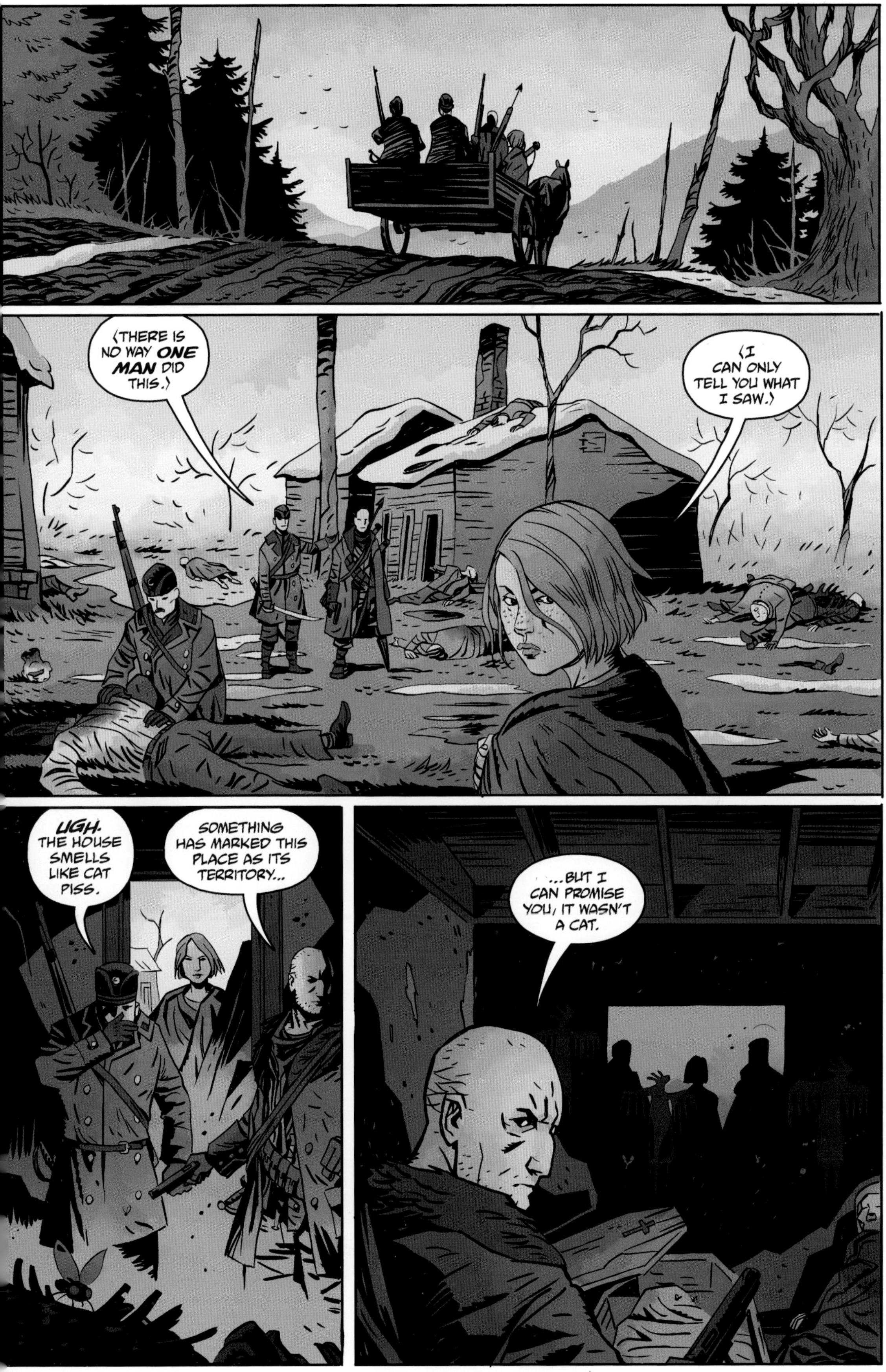

‹THERE IS NO WAY ONE MAN DID THIS.›
‹I CAN ONLY TELL YOU WHAT I SAW.›
UGH. THE HOUSE SMELLS LIKE CAT PISS.
SOMETHING HAS MARKED THIS PLACE AS ITS TERRITORY...
...BUT I CAN PROMISE YOU, IT WASN'T A CAT.

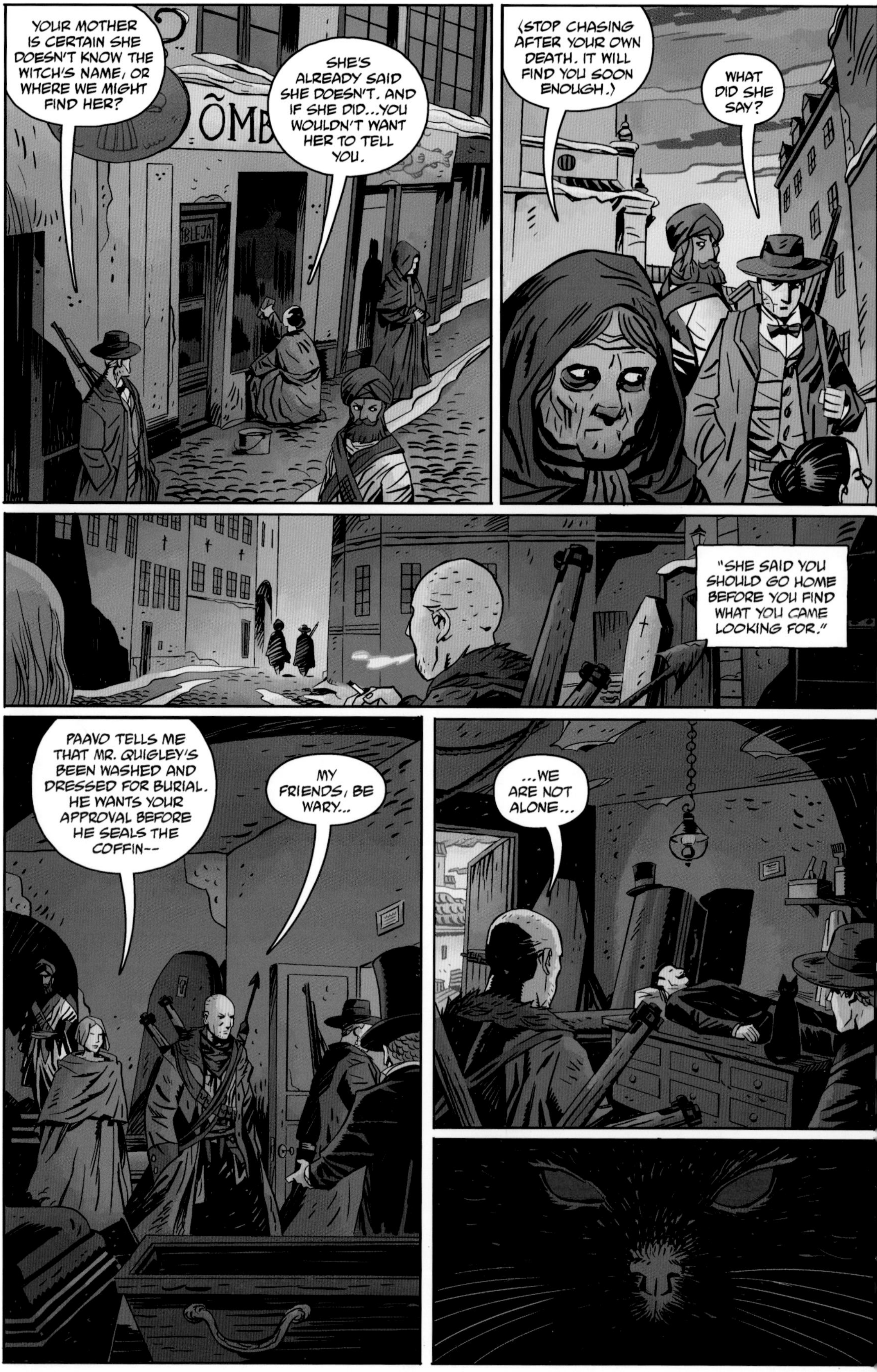
YOUR MOTHER IS CERTAIN SHE DOESN'T KNOW THE WITCH'S NAME, OR WHERE WE MIGHT FIND HER?
SHE'S ALREADY SAID SHE DOESN'T. AND IF SHE DID...YOU WOULDN'T WANT HER TO TELL YOU.
ÕMB
(STOP CHASING AFTER YOUR OWN DEATH. IT WILL FIND YOU SOON ENOUGH.)
WHAT DID SHE SAY?
"SHE SAID YOU SHOULD GO HOME BEFORE YOU FIND WHAT YOU CAME LOOKING FOR."
PAAVO TELLS ME THAT MR. QUIGLEY'S BEEN WASHED AND DRESSED FOR BURIAL. HE WANTS YOUR APPROVAL BEFORE HE SEALS THE COFFIN--
MY FRIENDS, BE WARY...
...WE ARE NOT ALONE...

# THE WITCH OF HARJU
## *Chapter Two*

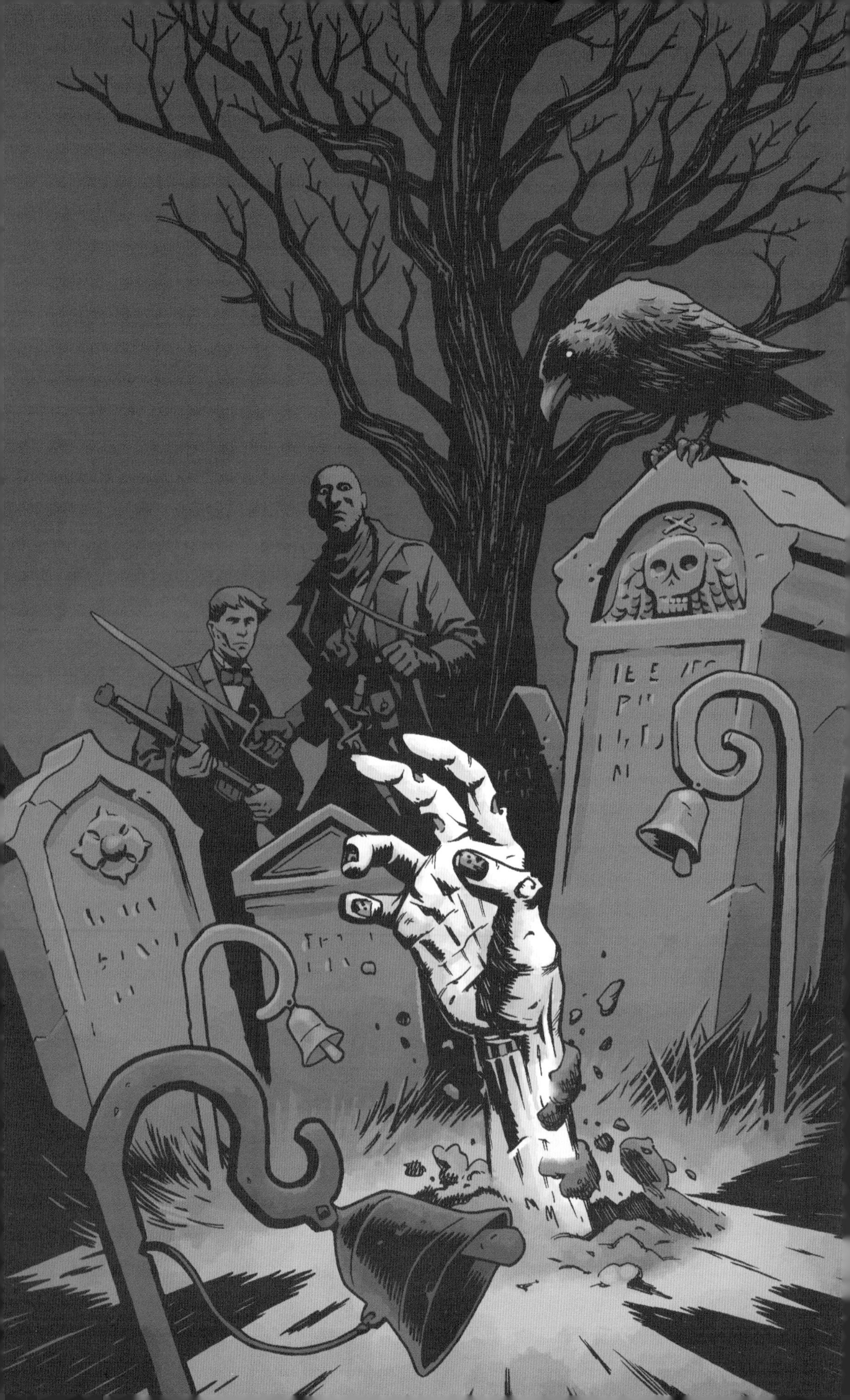

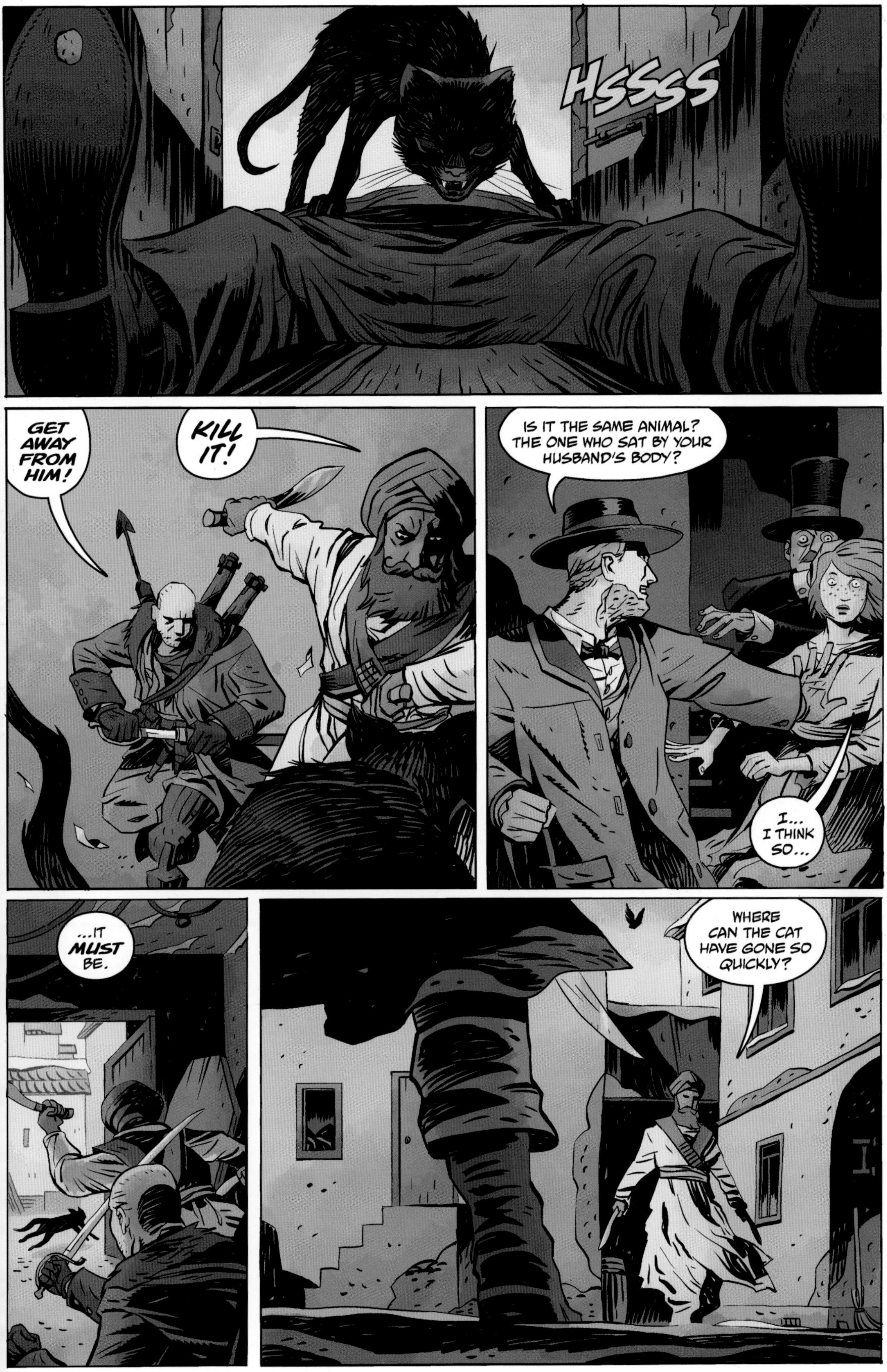
HSSSS
GET AWAY FROM HIM!
KILL IT!
IS IT THE SAME ANIMAL? THE ONE WHO SAT BY YOUR HUSBAND'S BODY?
I... I THINK SO...
...IT MUST BE.
WHERE CAN THE CAT HAVE GONE SO QUICKLY?

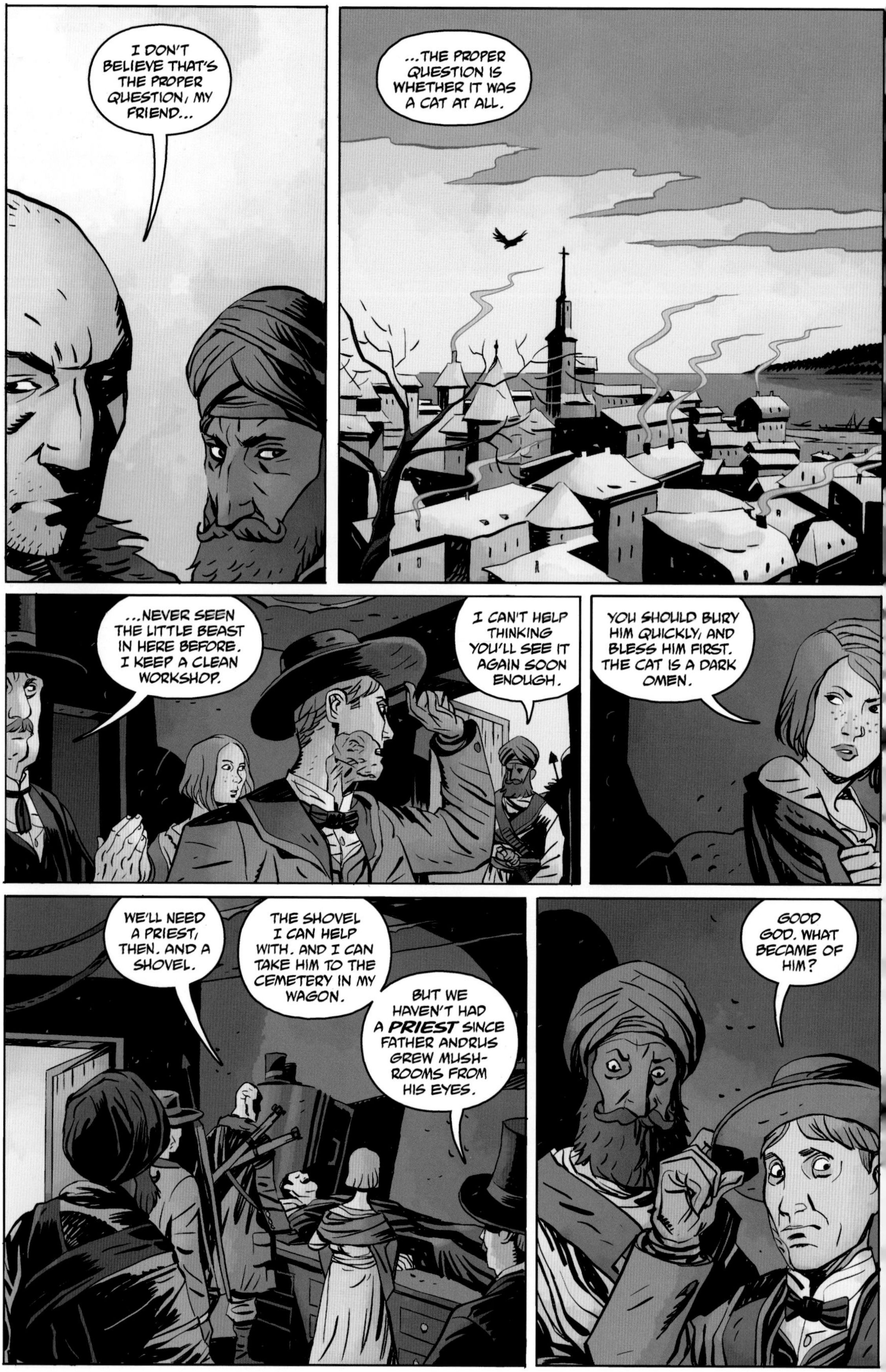
I DON'T BELIEVE THAT'S THE PROPER QUESTION, MY FRIEND...
...THE PROPER QUESTION IS WHETHER IT WAS A CAT AT ALL.
...NEVER SEEN THE LITTLE BEAST IN HERE BEFORE. I KEEP A CLEAN WORKSHOP.
I CAN'T HELP THINKING YOU'LL SEE IT AGAIN SOON ENOUGH.
YOU SHOULD BURY HIM QUICKLY, AND BLESS HIM FIRST. THE CAT IS A DARK OMEN.
WE'LL NEED A PRIEST, THEN. AND A SHOVEL.
THE SHOVEL I CAN HELP WITH. AND I CAN TAKE HIM TO THE CEMETERY IN MY WAGON.
BUT WE HAVEN'T HAD A **PRIEST** SINCE FATHER ANDRUS GREW MUSH-ROOMS FROM HIS EYES.
GOOD GOD. WHAT BECAME OF HIM?

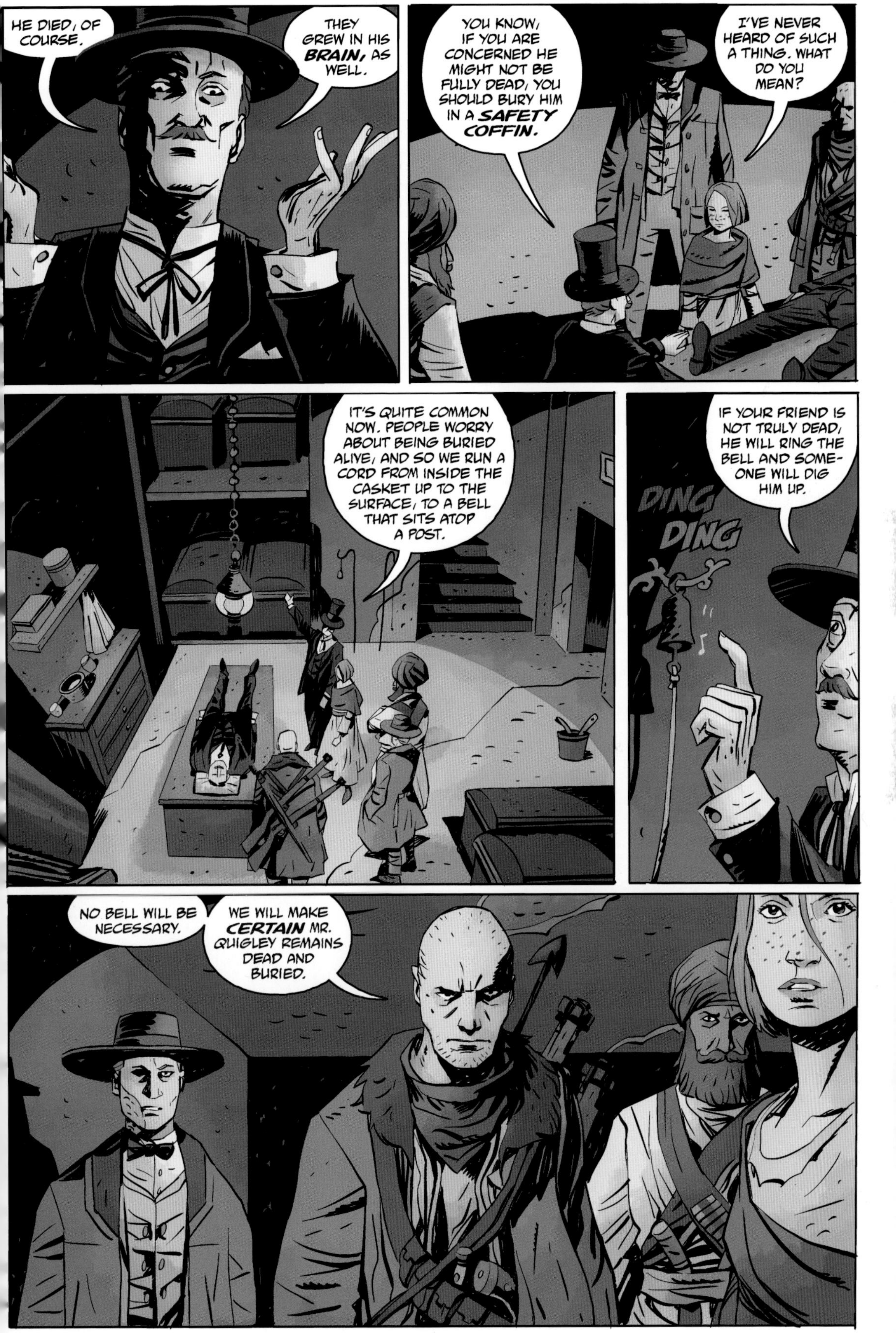
HE DIED, OF COURSE.
THEY GREW IN HIS BRAIN, AS WELL.
YOU KNOW, IF YOU ARE CONCERNED HE MIGHT NOT BE FULLY DEAD, YOU SHOULD BURY HIM IN A SAFETY COFFIN.
I'VE NEVER HEARD OF SUCH A THING. WHAT DO YOU MEAN?
IT'S QUITE COMMON NOW. PEOPLE WORRY ABOUT BEING BURIED ALIVE, AND SO WE RUN A CORD FROM INSIDE THE CASKET UP TO THE SURFACE, TO A BELL THAT SITS ATOP A POST.
DING DING
IF YOUR FRIEND IS NOT TRULY DEAD, HE WILL RING THE BELL AND SOME-ONE WILL DIG HIM UP.
NO BELL WILL BE NECESSARY.
WE WILL MAKE CERTAIN MR. QUIGLEY REMAINS DEAD AND BURIED.

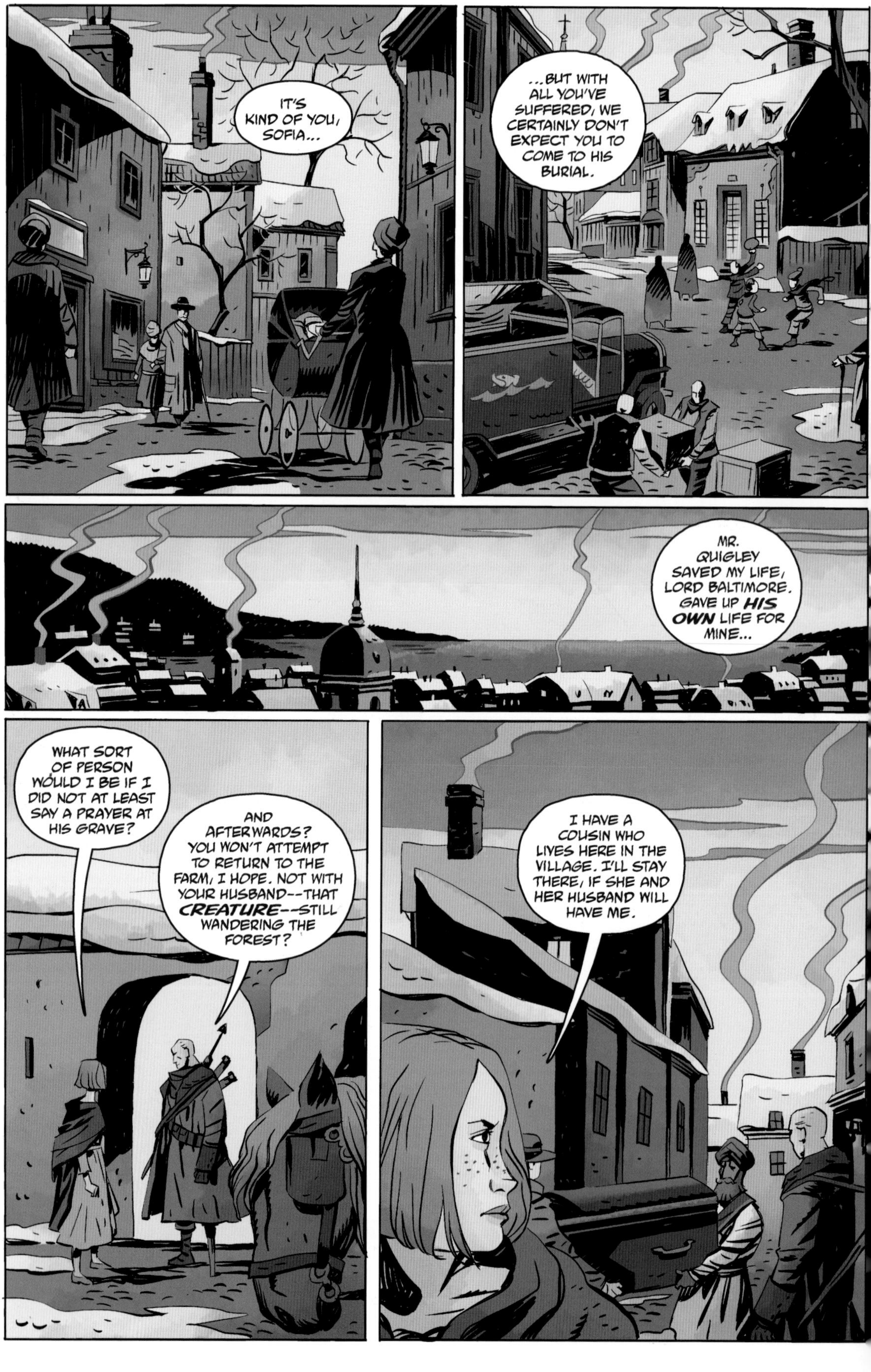
IT'S KIND OF YOU, SOFIA...
...BUT WITH ALL YOU'VE SUFFERED, WE CERTAINLY DON'T EXPECT YOU TO COME TO HIS BURIAL.
MR. QUIGLEY SAVED MY LIFE, LORD BALTIMORE. GAVE UP HIS OWN LIFE FOR MINE...
WHAT SORT OF PERSON WOULD I BE IF I DID NOT AT LEAST SAY A PRAYER AT HIS GRAVE?
AND AFTERWARDS? YOU WON'T ATTEMPT TO RETURN TO THE FARM, I HOPE. NOT WITH YOUR HUSBAND--THAT CREATURE--STILL WANDERING THE FOREST?
I HAVE A COUSIN WHO LIVES HERE IN THE VILLAGE. I'LL STAY THERE, IF SHE AND HER HUSBAND WILL HAVE ME.

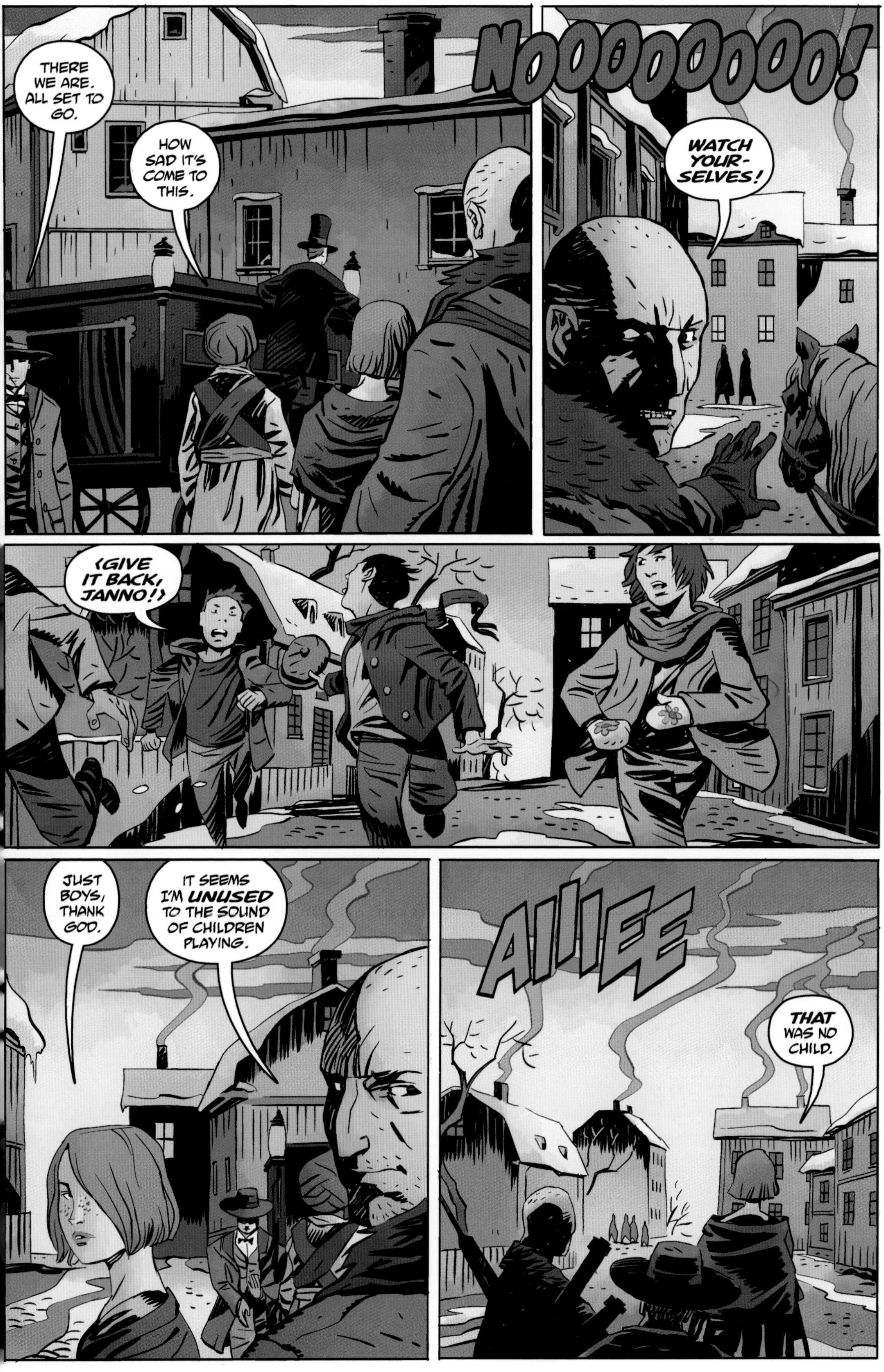
THERE WE ARE. ALL SET TO GO.
HOW SAD IT'S COME TO THIS.
NOOOOOOOOO!
WATCH YOURSELVES!
‹GIVE IT BACK, JANNO!›
JUST BOYS, THANK GOD.
IT SEEMS I'M UNUSED TO THE SOUND OF CHILDREN PLAYING.
AIIIEE
THAT WAS NO CHILD.

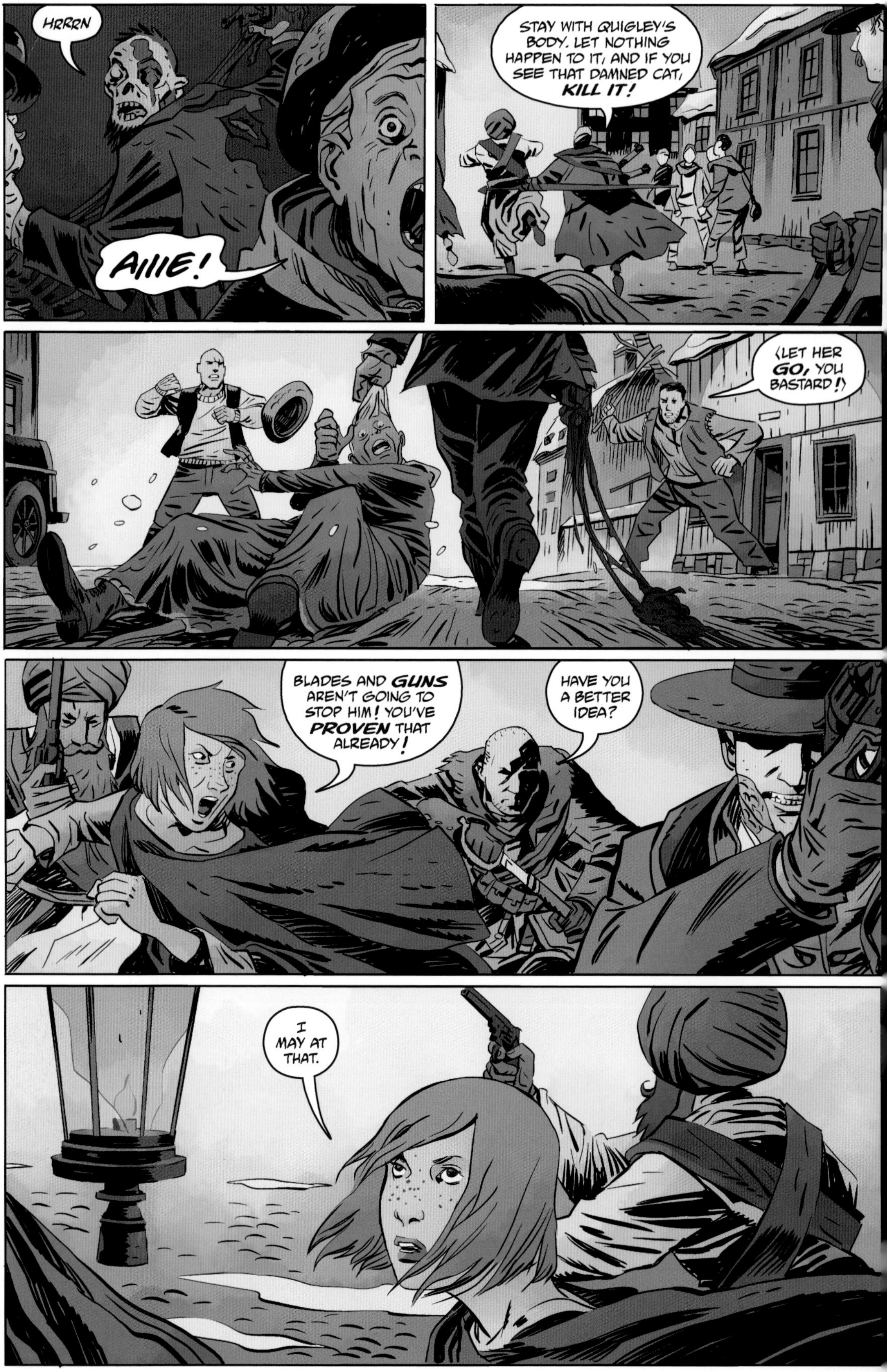
HRRRN
AIIIE!
STAY WITH QUIGLEY'S BODY. LET NOTHING HAPPEN TO IT, AND IF YOU SEE THAT DAMNED CAT, KILL IT!
‹LET HER GO, YOU BASTARD!›
BLADES AND GUNS AREN'T GOING TO STOP HIM! YOU'VE PROVEN THAT ALREADY!
HAVE YOU A BETTER IDEA?
I MAY AT THAT.

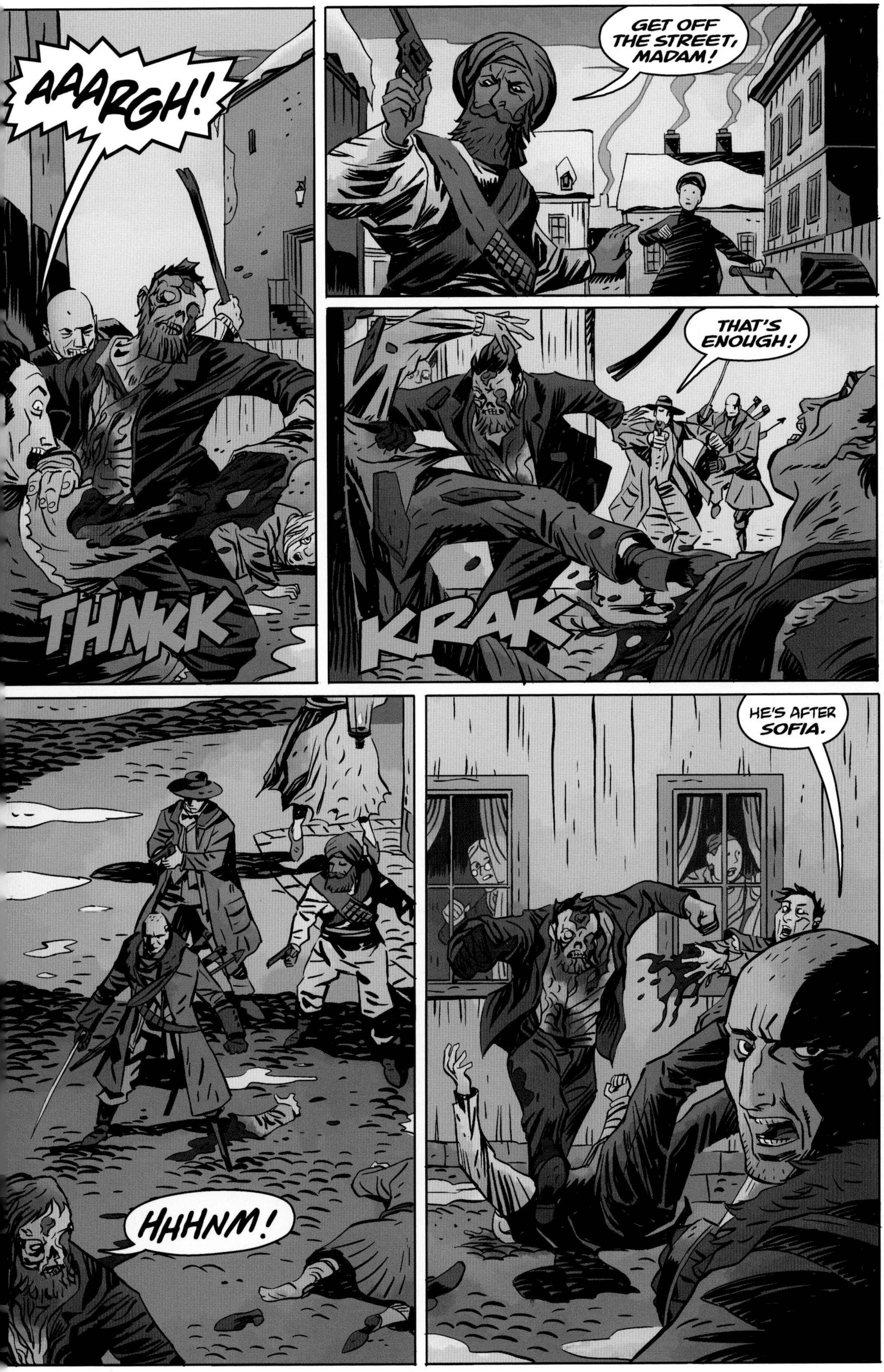
AAAARGH!
THNKK
GET OFF THE STREET, MADAM!
THAT'S ENOUGH!
KRAK
HHHNM!
HE'S AFTER SOFIA.

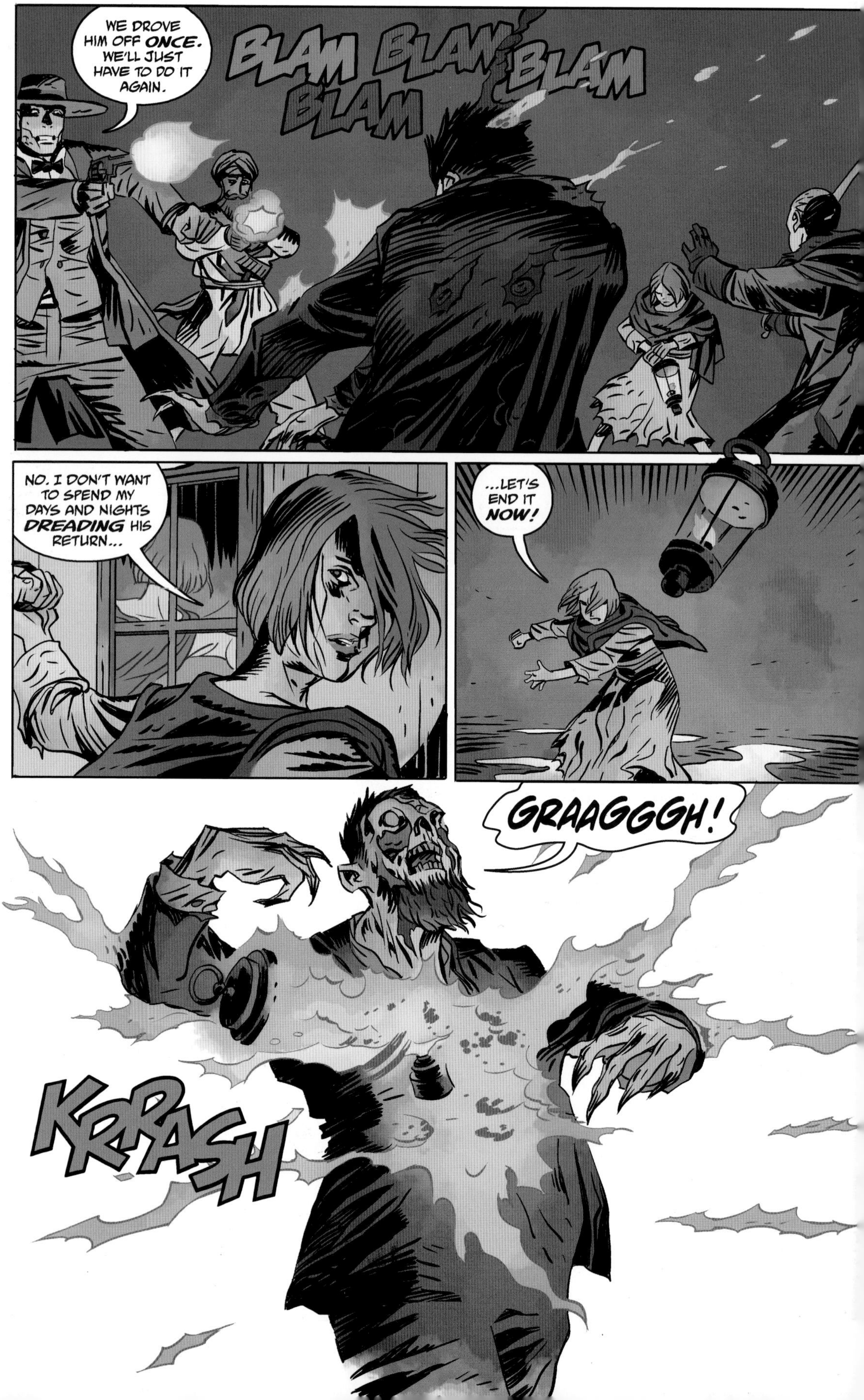
WE DROVE HIM OFF ONCE. WE'LL JUST HAVE TO DO IT AGAIN.
BLAM BLAM BLAM BLAM
NO. I DON'T WANT TO SPEND MY DAYS AND NIGHTS DREADING HIS RETURN...
...LET'S END IT NOW!
GRAAGGGH!
KRRASH

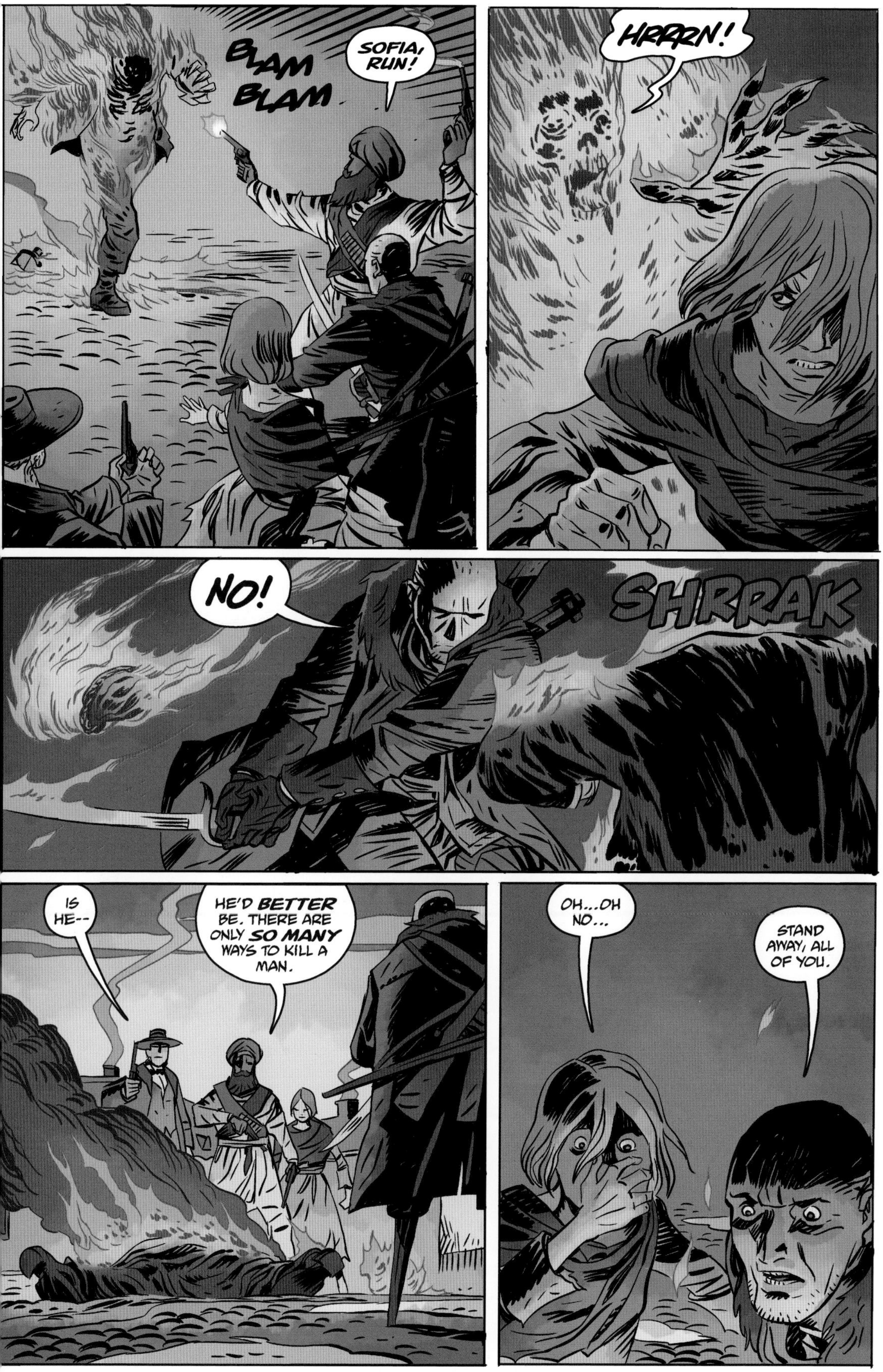
BLAM
BLAM
SOFIA, RUN!
HRRRN!
NO!
SHRRAK
IS HE--
HE'D BETTER BE. THERE ARE ONLY SO MANY WAYS TO KILL A MAN.
OH...OH NO...
STAND AWAY, ALL OF YOU.

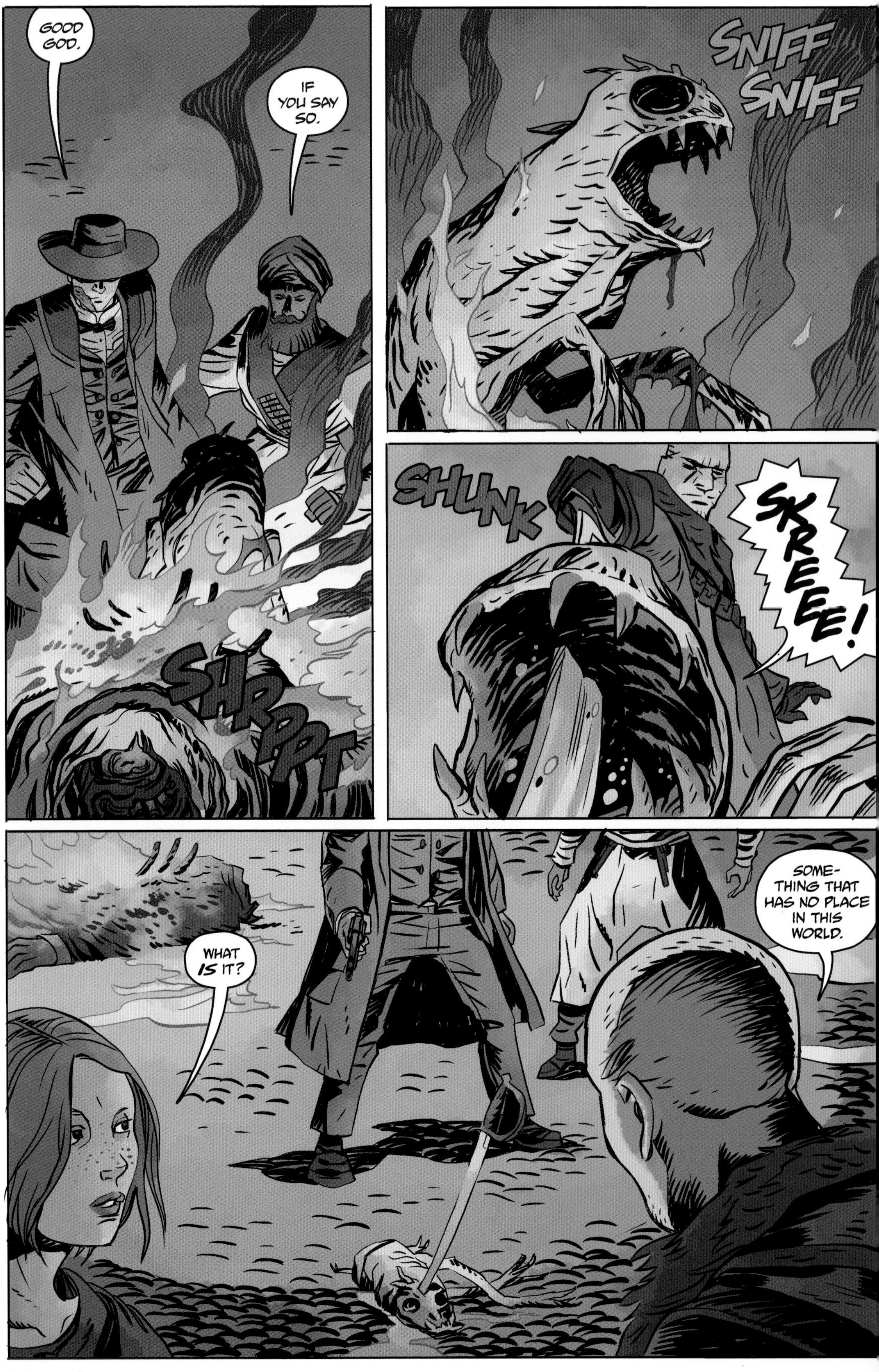
GOOD GOD.
IF YOU SAY SO.
SHRPPT
SNIFF SNIFF
SHUNK
SKREEEE!
WHAT IS IT?
SOME-THING THAT HAS NO PLACE IN THIS WORLD.

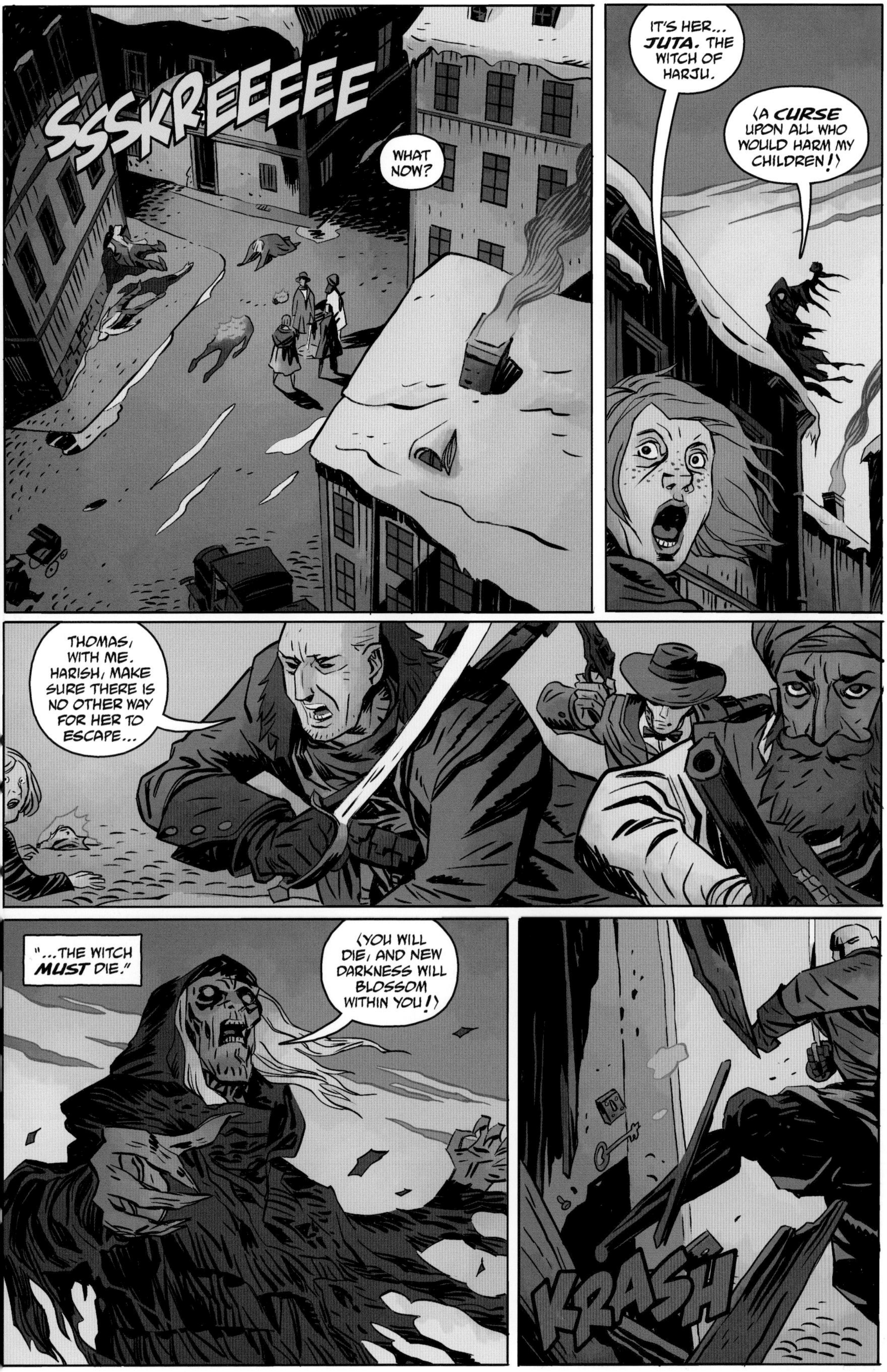
SSSKREEEEE
WHAT NOW?
IT'S HER... JUTA. THE WITCH OF HARJU.
‹A CURSE UPON ALL WHO WOULD HARM MY CHILDREN!›
THOMAS, WITH ME. HARISH, MAKE SURE THERE IS NO OTHER WAY FOR HER TO ESCAPE...
"...THE WITCH MUST DIE."
‹YOU WILL DIE, AND NEW DARKNESS WILL BLOSSOM WITHIN YOU!›
KRASH

‹TRANSLATED FROM ESTONIAN›

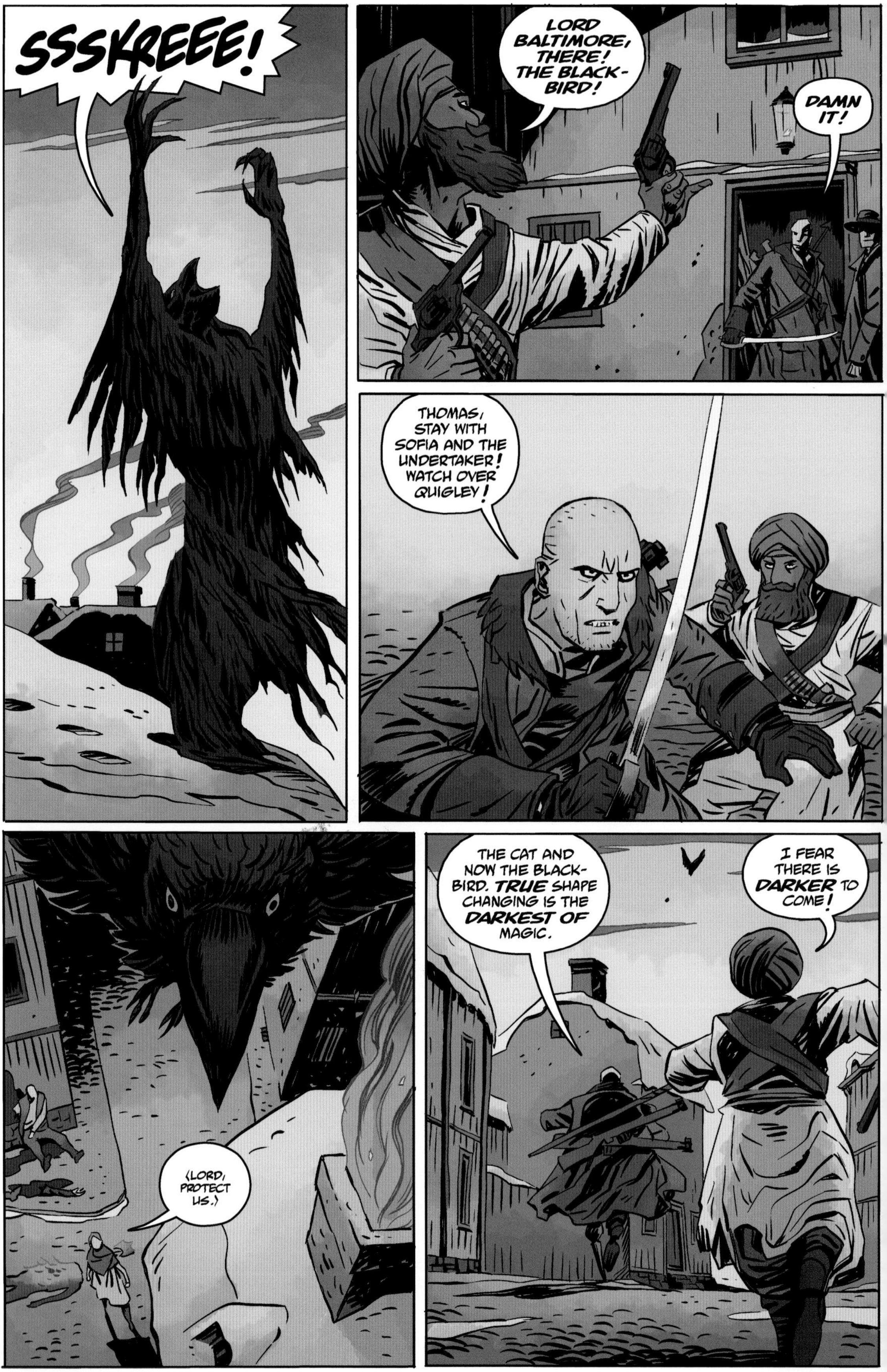
SSSKREEE!
LORD BALTIMORE, THERE! THE BLACK-BIRD!
DAMN IT!
THOMAS, STAY WITH SOFIA AND THE UNDERTAKER! WATCH OVER QUIGLEY!
‹LORD, PROTECT US.›
THE CAT AND NOW THE BLACK-BIRD. TRUE SHAPE CHANGING IS THE DARKEST OF MAGIC.
I FEAR THERE IS DARKER TO COME!

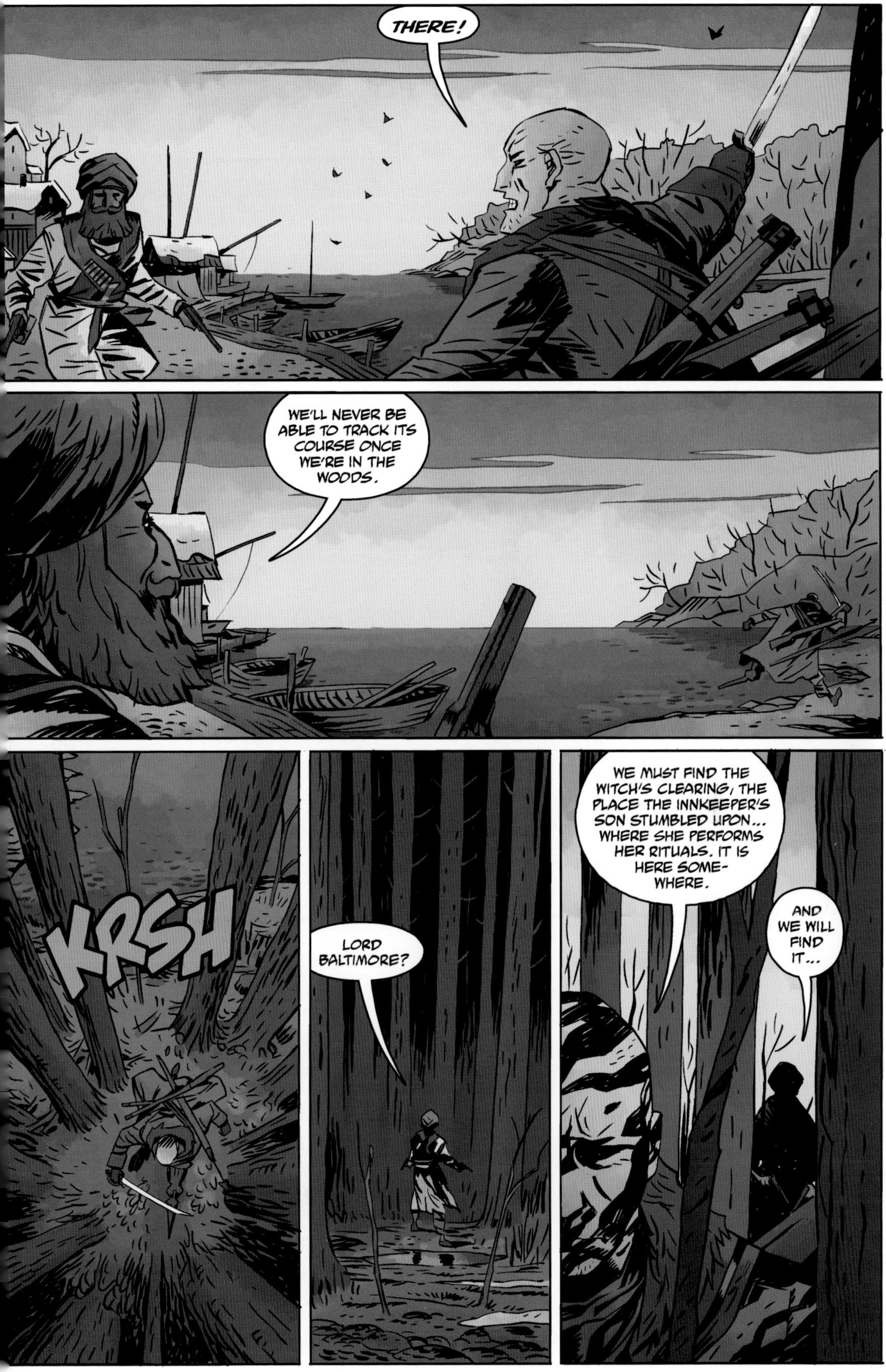
THERE!
WE'LL NEVER BE ABLE TO TRACK ITS COURSE ONCE WE'RE IN THE WOODS.
KRSH
LORD BALTIMORE?
WE MUST FIND THE WITCH'S CLEARING, THE PLACE THE INNKEEPER'S SON STUMBLED UPON... WHERE SHE PERFORMS HER RITUALS. IT IS HERE SOME-WHERE.
AND WE WILL FIND IT...

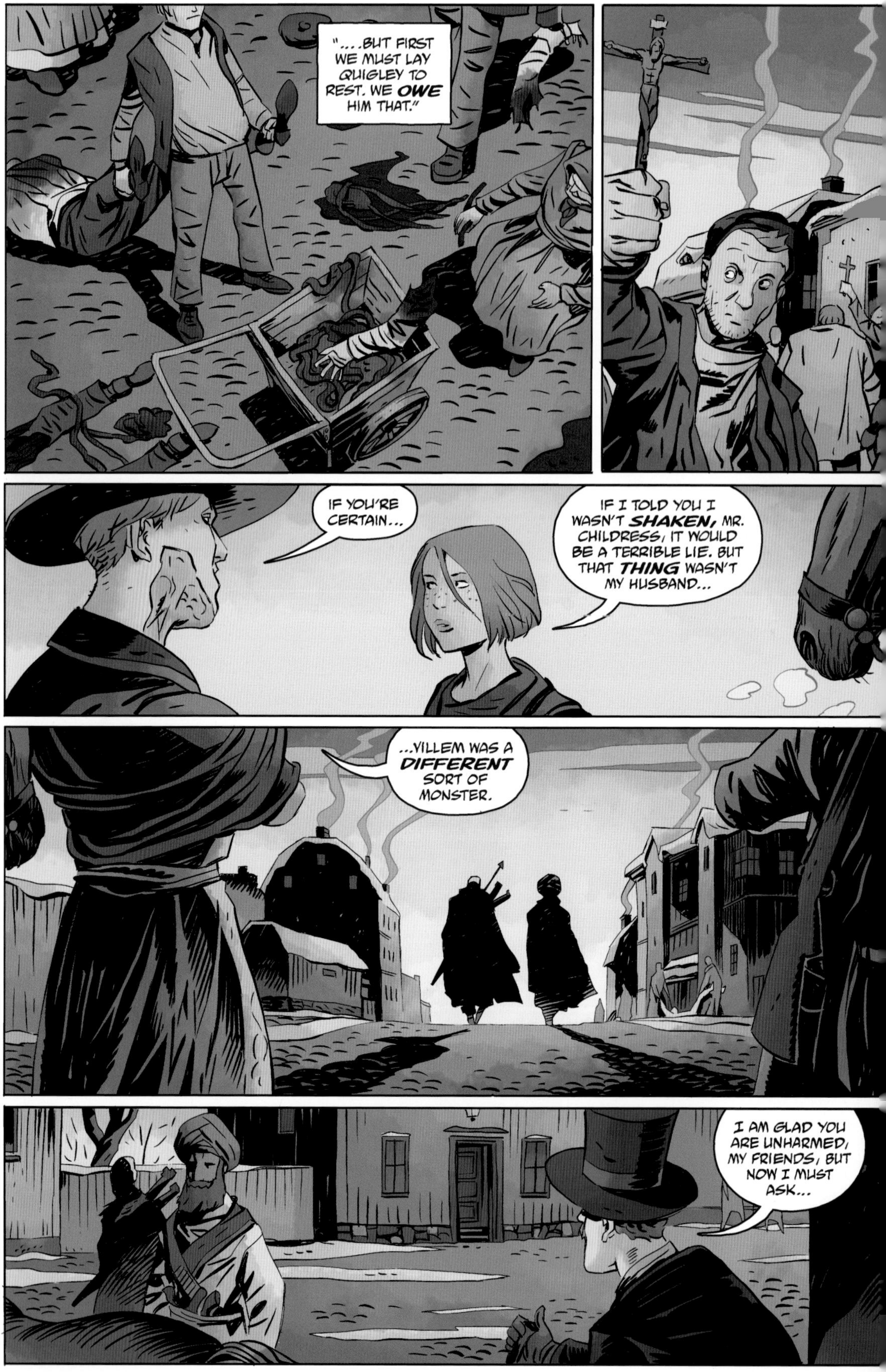
"....BUT FIRST WE MUST LAY QUIGLEY TO REST. WE OWE HIM THAT."
IF YOU'RE CERTAIN...
IF I TOLD YOU I WASN'T SHAKEN, MR. CHILDRESS, IT WOULD BE A TERRIBLE LIE. BUT THAT THING WASN'T MY HUSBAND...
...VILLEM WAS A DIFFERENT SORT OF MONSTER.
I AM GLAD YOU ARE UNHARMED, MY FRIENDS, BUT NOW I MUST ASK...

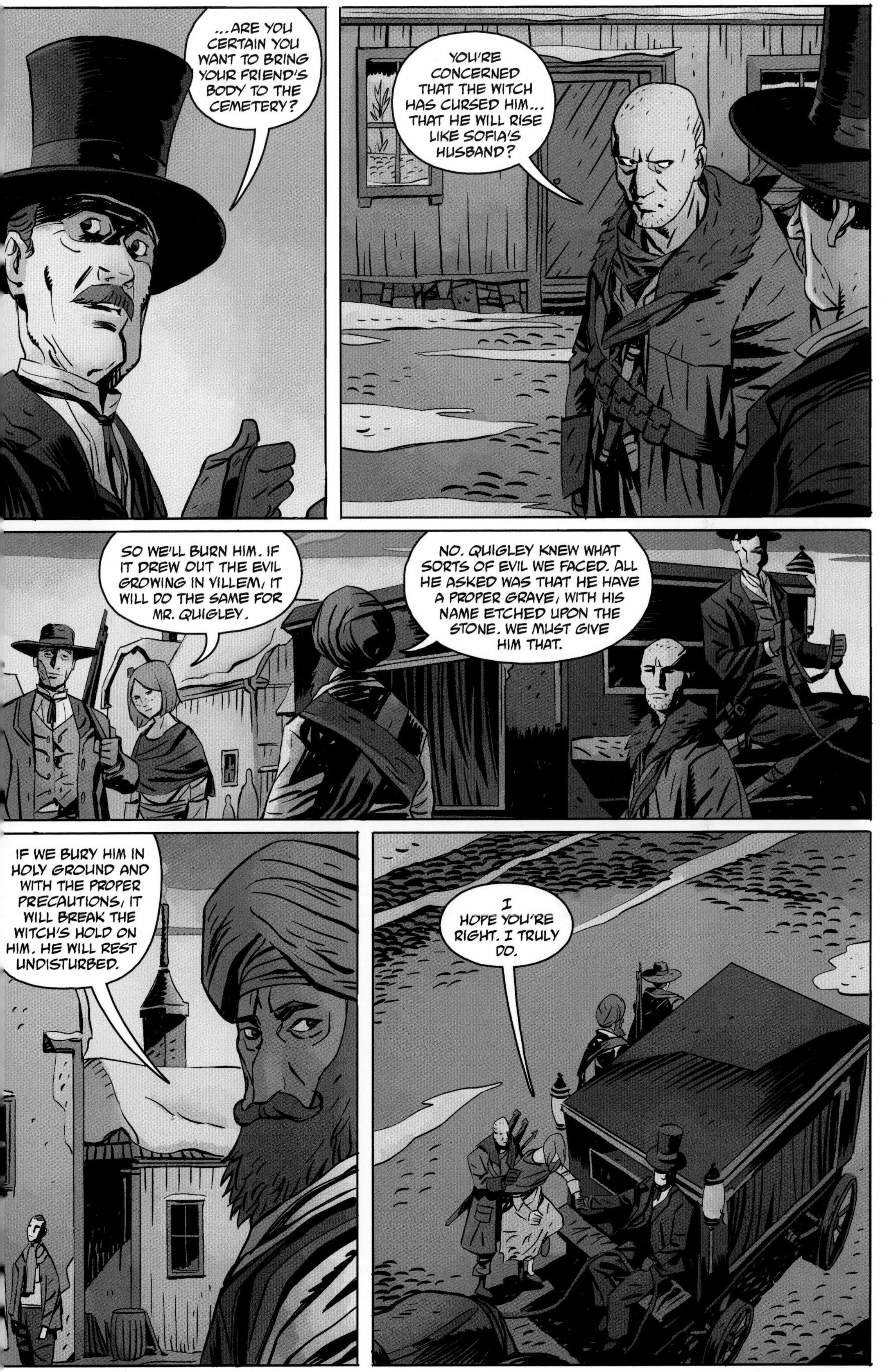
...ARE YOU CERTAIN YOU WANT TO BRING YOUR FRIEND'S BODY TO THE CEMETERY?
YOU'RE CONCERNED THAT THE WITCH HAS CURSED HIM... THAT HE WILL RISE LIKE SOFIA'S HUSBAND?
SO WE'LL BURN HIM. IF IT DREW OUT THE EVIL GROWING IN VILLEM, IT WILL DO THE SAME FOR MR. QUIGLEY.
NO. QUIGLEY KNEW WHAT SORTS OF EVIL WE FACED. ALL HE ASKED WAS THAT HE HAVE A PROPER GRAVE, WITH HIS NAME ETCHED UPON THE STONE. WE MUST GIVE HIM THAT.
IF WE BURY HIM IN HOLY GROUND AND WITH THE PROPER PRECAUTIONS, IT WILL BREAK THE WITCH'S HOLD ON HIM. HE WILL REST UNDISTURBED.
I HOPE YOU'RE RIGHT. I TRULY DO.

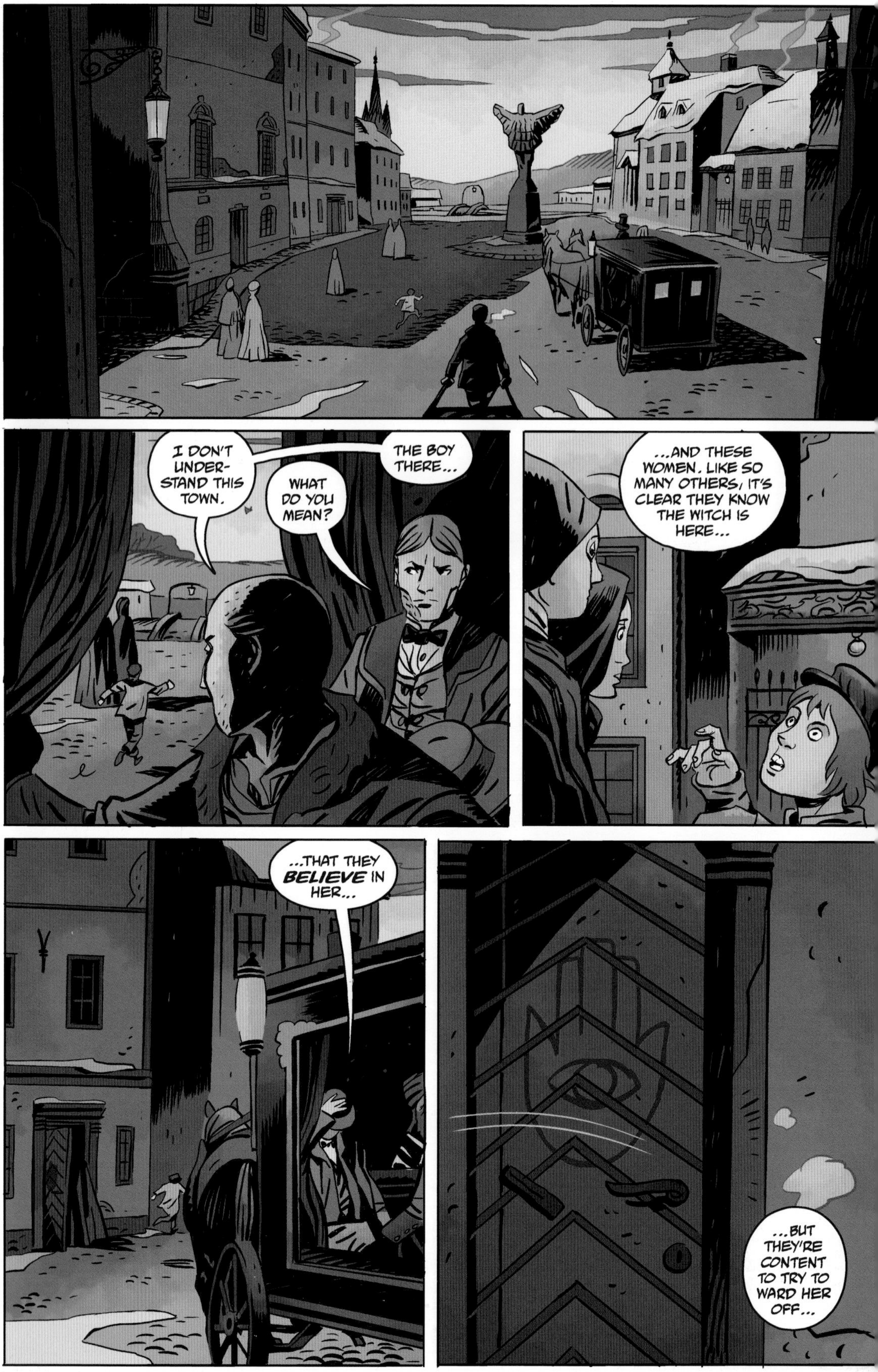
I DON'T UNDER-STAND THIS TOWN.
THE BOY THERE...
WHAT DO YOU MEAN?
...AND THESE WOMEN. LIKE SO MANY OTHERS, IT'S CLEAR THEY KNOW THE WITCH IS HERE...
...THAT THEY *BELIEVE* IN HER...
...BUT THEY'RE CONTENT TO TRY TO WARD HER OFF...

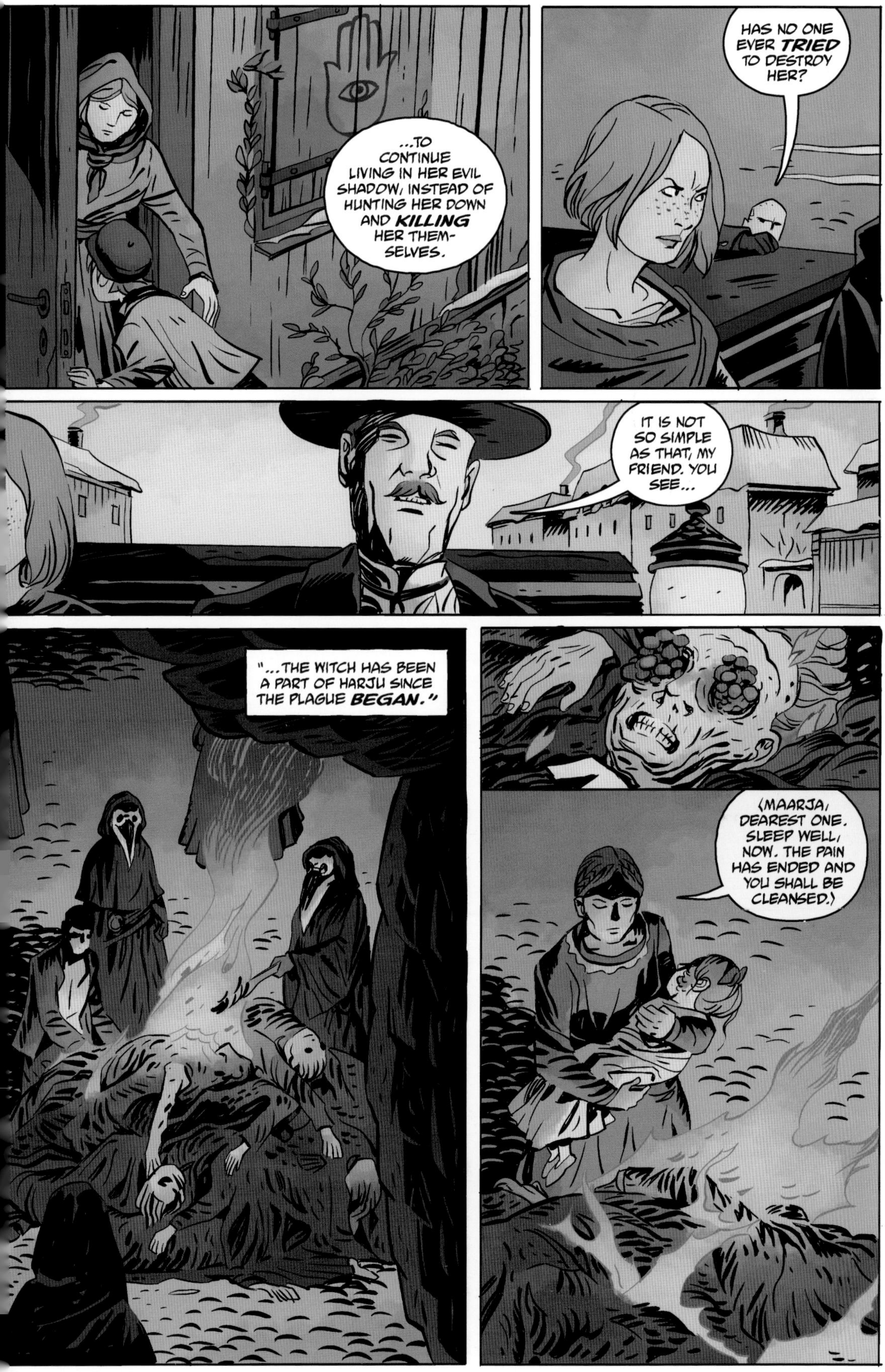
...TO CONTINUE LIVING IN HER EVIL SHADOW, INSTEAD OF HUNTING HER DOWN AND KILLING HER THEM-SELVES.
HAS NO ONE EVER TRIED TO DESTROY HER?
IT IS NOT SO SIMPLE AS THAT, MY FRIEND. YOU SEE...
"...THE WITCH HAS BEEN A PART OF HARJU SINCE THE PLAGUE BEGAN."
(MAARJA, DEAREST ONE. SLEEP WELL, NOW. THE PAIN HAS ENDED AND YOU SHALL BE CLEANSED.)

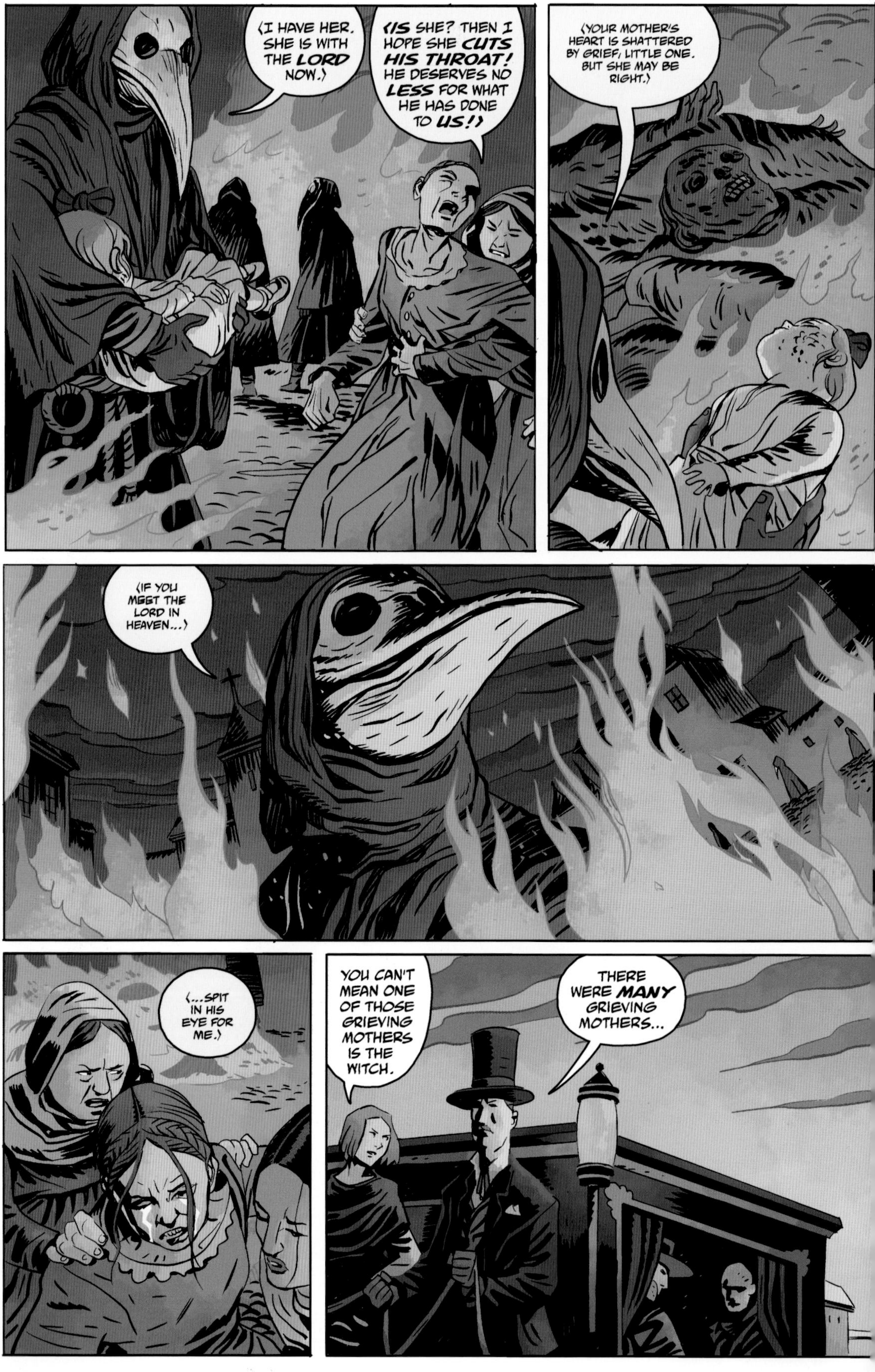

⟨I HAVE HER. SHE IS WITH THE LORD NOW.⟩
⟨IS SHE? THEN I HOPE SHE CUTS HIS THROAT! HE DESERVES NO LESS FOR WHAT HE HAS DONE TO US!⟩
⟨YOUR MOTHER'S HEART IS SHATTERED BY GRIEF, LITTLE ONE. BUT SHE MAY BE RIGHT.⟩
⟨IF YOU MEET THE LORD IN HEAVEN...⟩
⟨...SPIT IN HIS EYE FOR ME.⟩
YOU CAN'T MEAN ONE OF THOSE GRIEVING MOTHERS IS THE WITCH.
THERE WERE MANY GRIEVING MOTHERS...

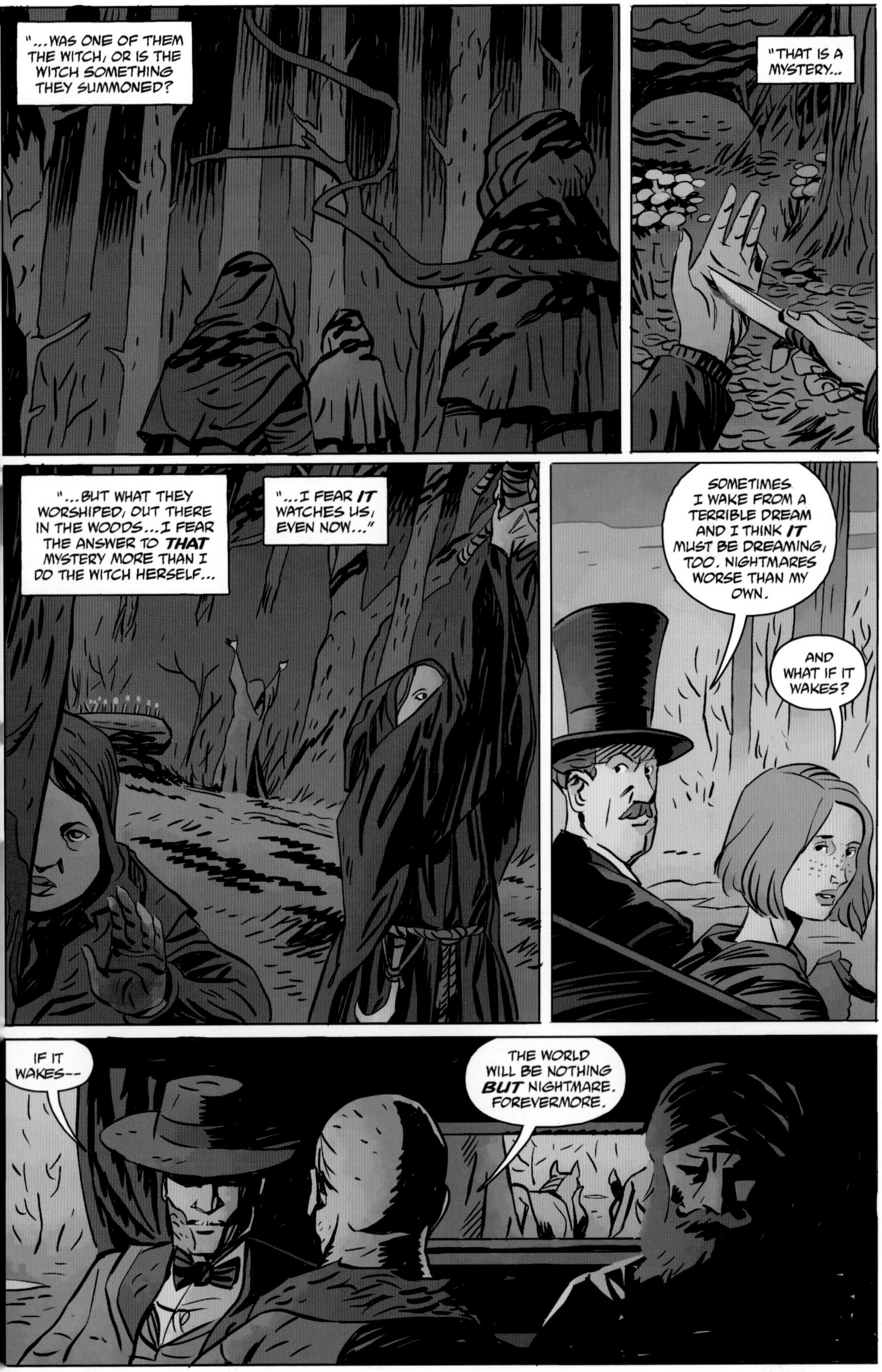
"...WAS ONE OF THEM THE WITCH, OR IS THE WITCH SOMETHING THEY SUMMONED?
"THAT IS A MYSTERY...
"...BUT WHAT THEY WORSHIPED, OUT THERE IN THE WOODS...I FEAR THE ANSWER TO **THAT** MYSTERY MORE THAN I DO THE WITCH HERSELF...
"...I FEAR **IT** WATCHES US, EVEN NOW..."
SOMETIMES I WAKE FROM A TERRIBLE DREAM AND I THINK **IT** MUST BE DREAMING, TOO. NIGHTMARES WORSE THAN MY OWN.
AND WHAT IF IT WAKES?
IF IT WAKES--
THE WORLD WILL BE NOTHING **BUT** NIGHTMARE. FOREVERMORE.

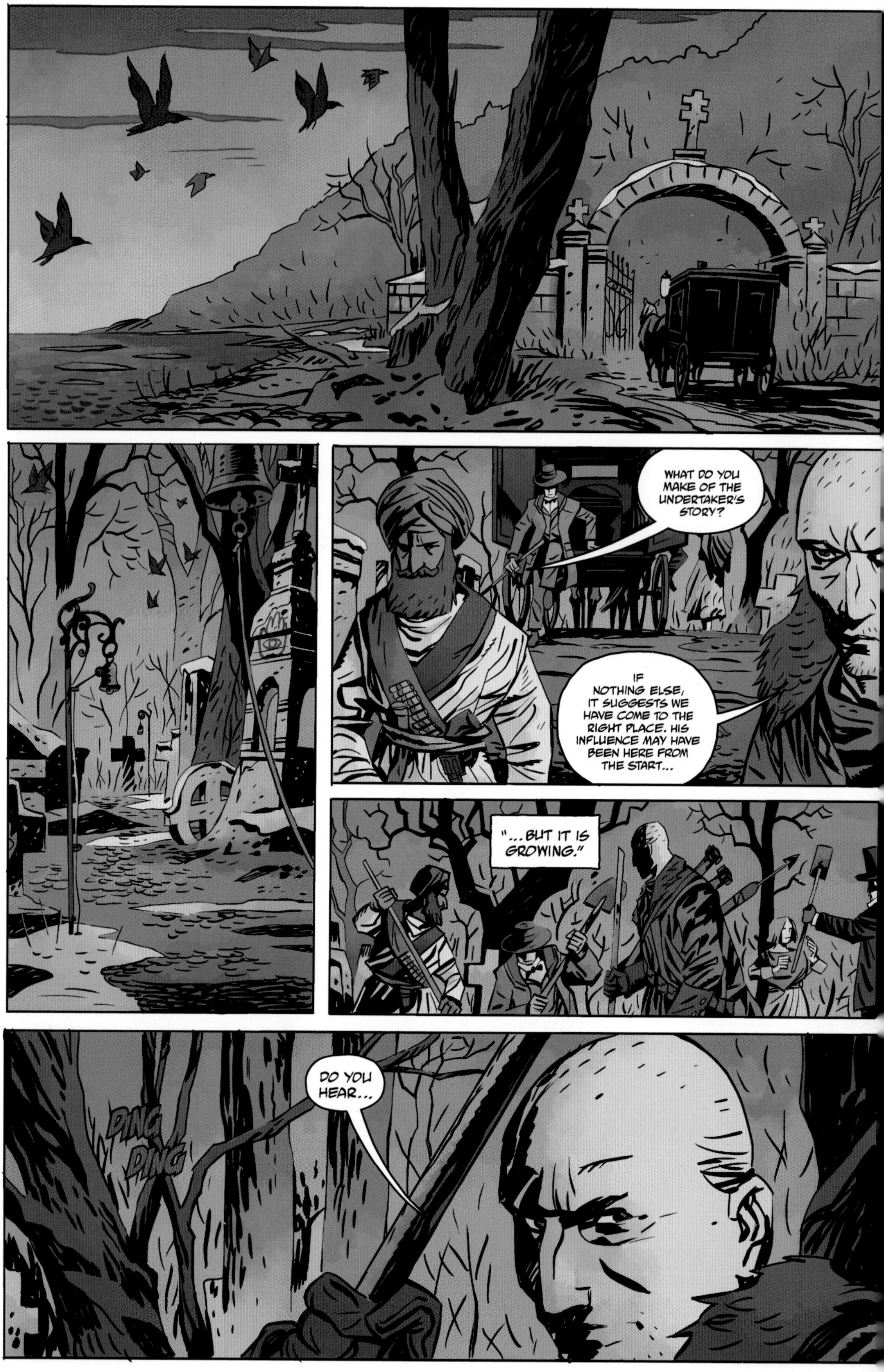
WHAT DO YOU MAKE OF THE UNDERTAKER'S STORY?
IF NOTHING ELSE, IT SUGGESTS WE HAVE COME TO THE RIGHT PLACE. HIS INFLUENCE MAY HAVE BEEN HERE FROM THE START...
"...BUT IT IS GROWING."
DING DING
DO YOU HEAR...

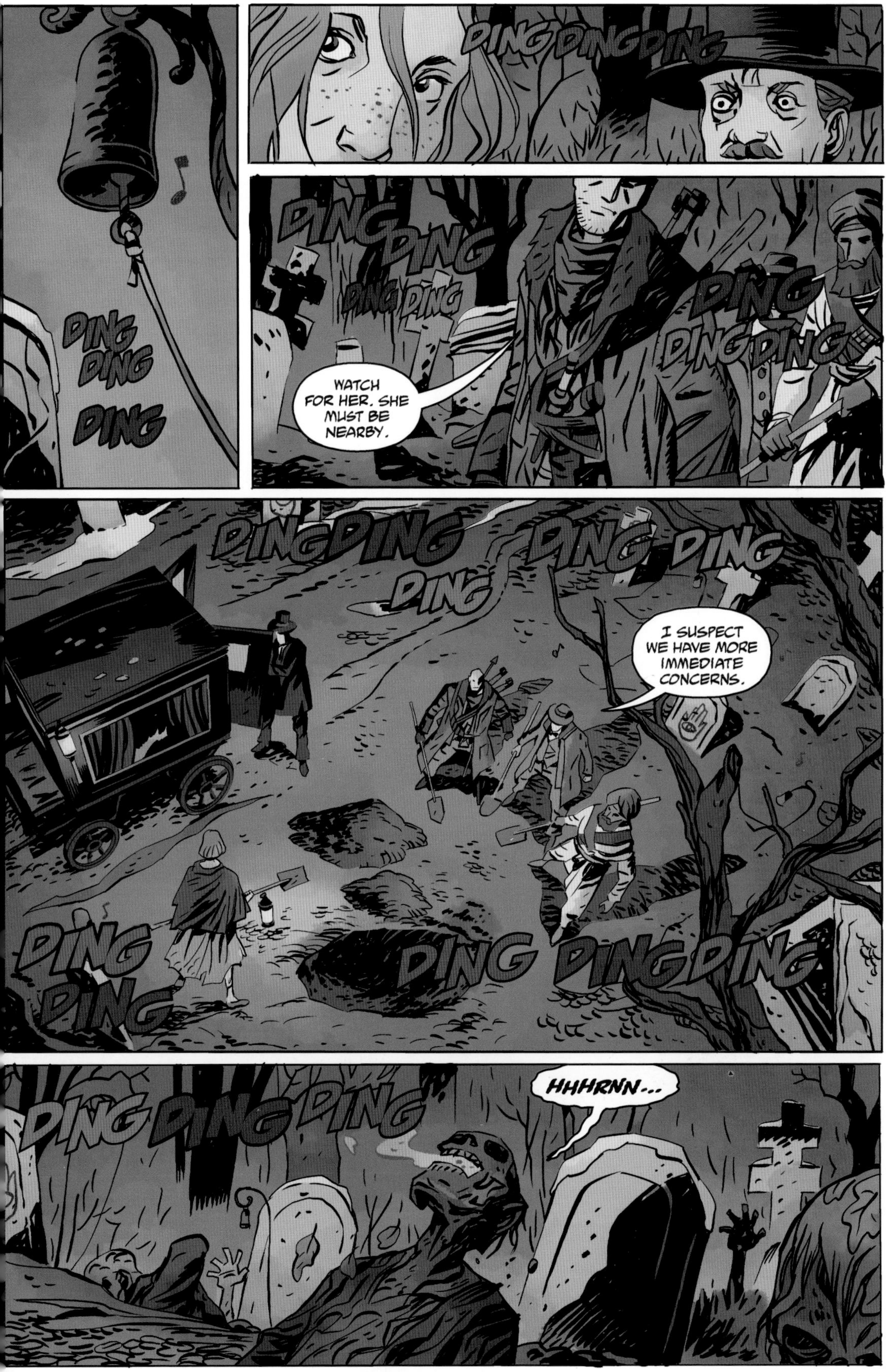
DING DING DING
DINGDINGDING
DING DING DING DING
WATCH FOR HER. SHE MUST BE NEARBY.
DING DINGDINGDING
DINGDING DING DING DING
I SUSPECT WE HAVE MORE IMMEDIATE CONCERNS.
DING DING DING DINGDING
DINGDINGDINGDING
HHHRNN...

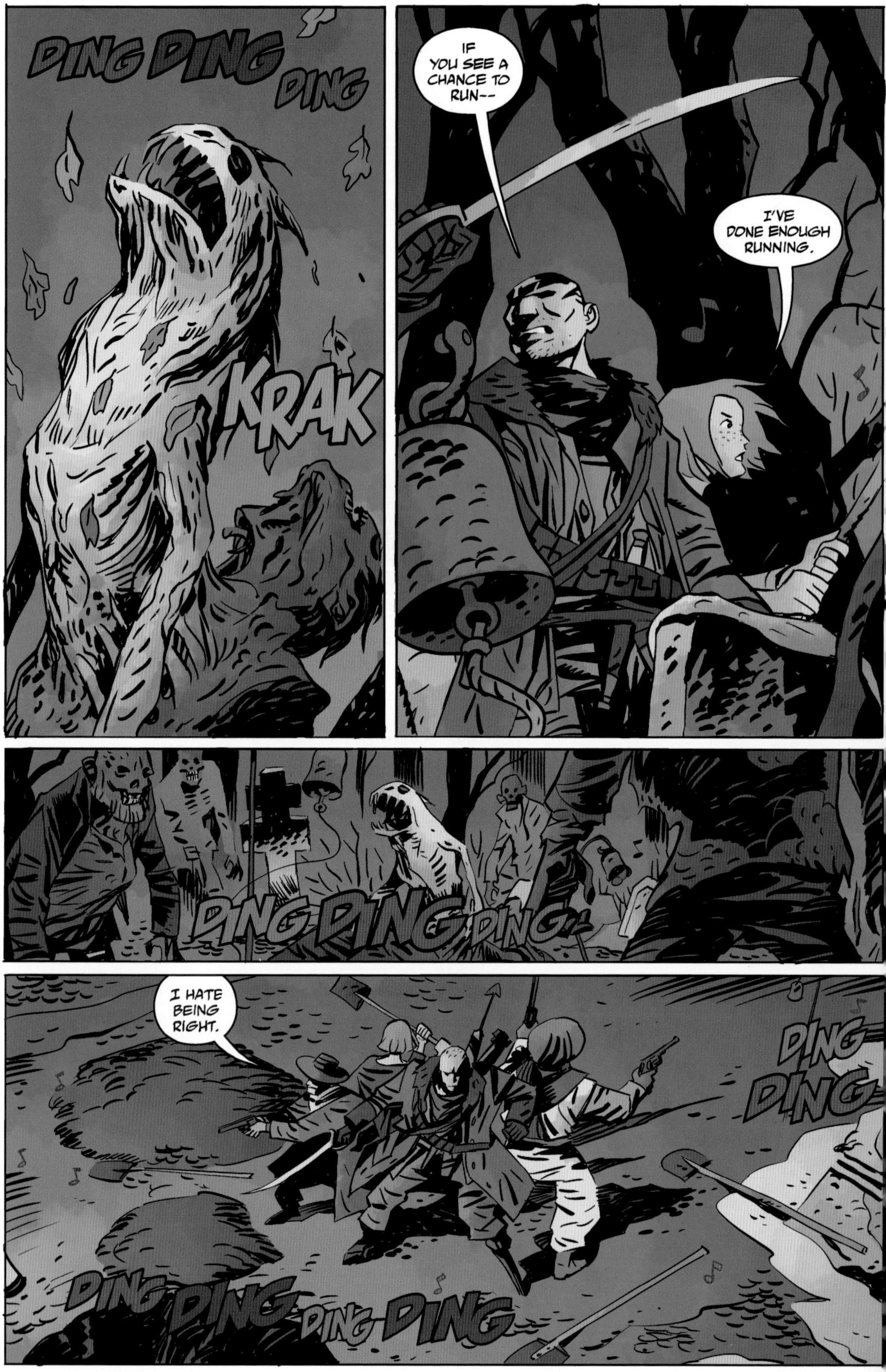
DING DING DING
KRAK
IF YOU SEE A CHANCE TO RUN--
I'VE DONE ENOUGH RUNNING.
DING DING DING..
I HATE BEING RIGHT.
DING DING
DING DING DING DING

# THE WITCH OF HARJU
*Chapter Three*

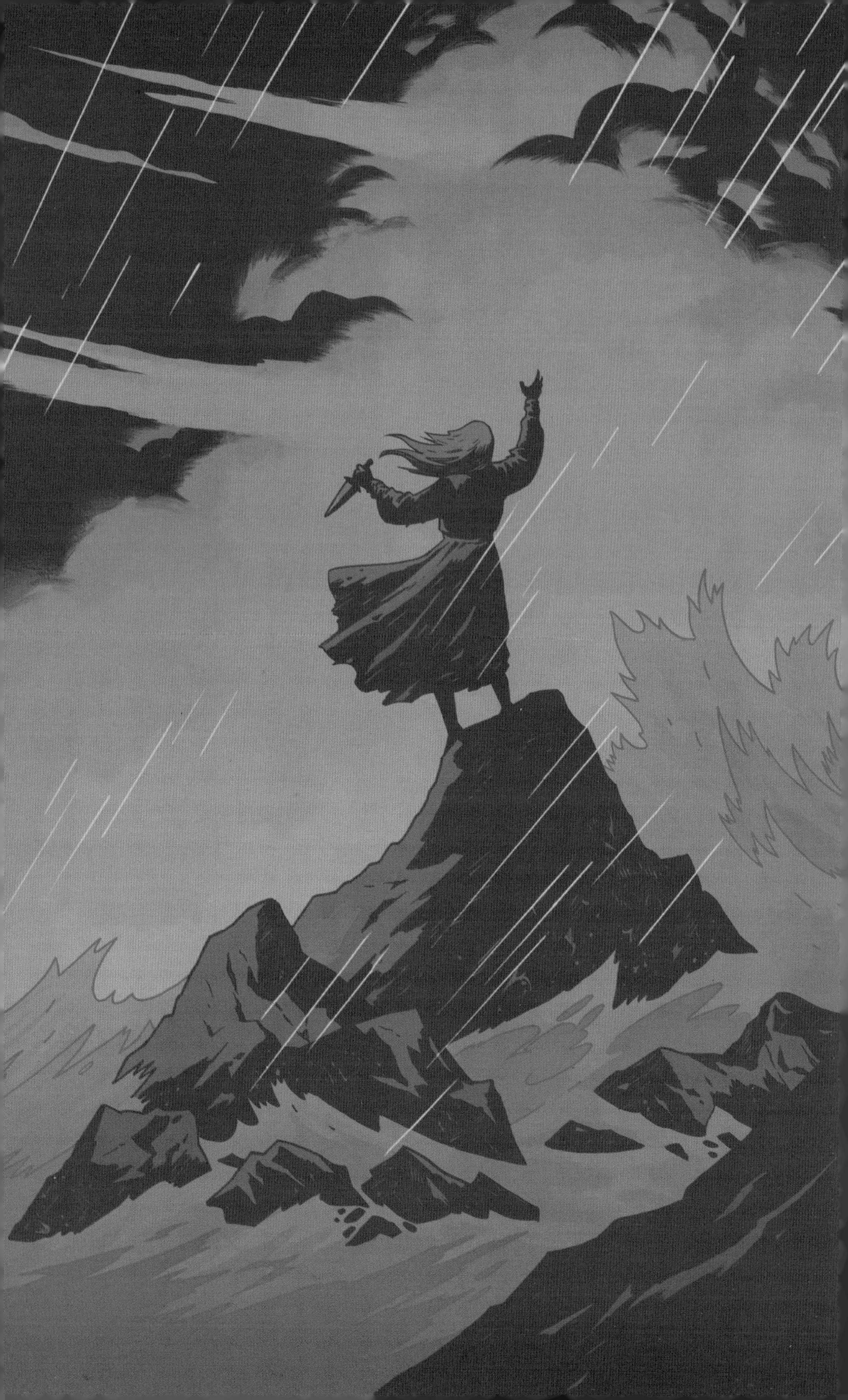

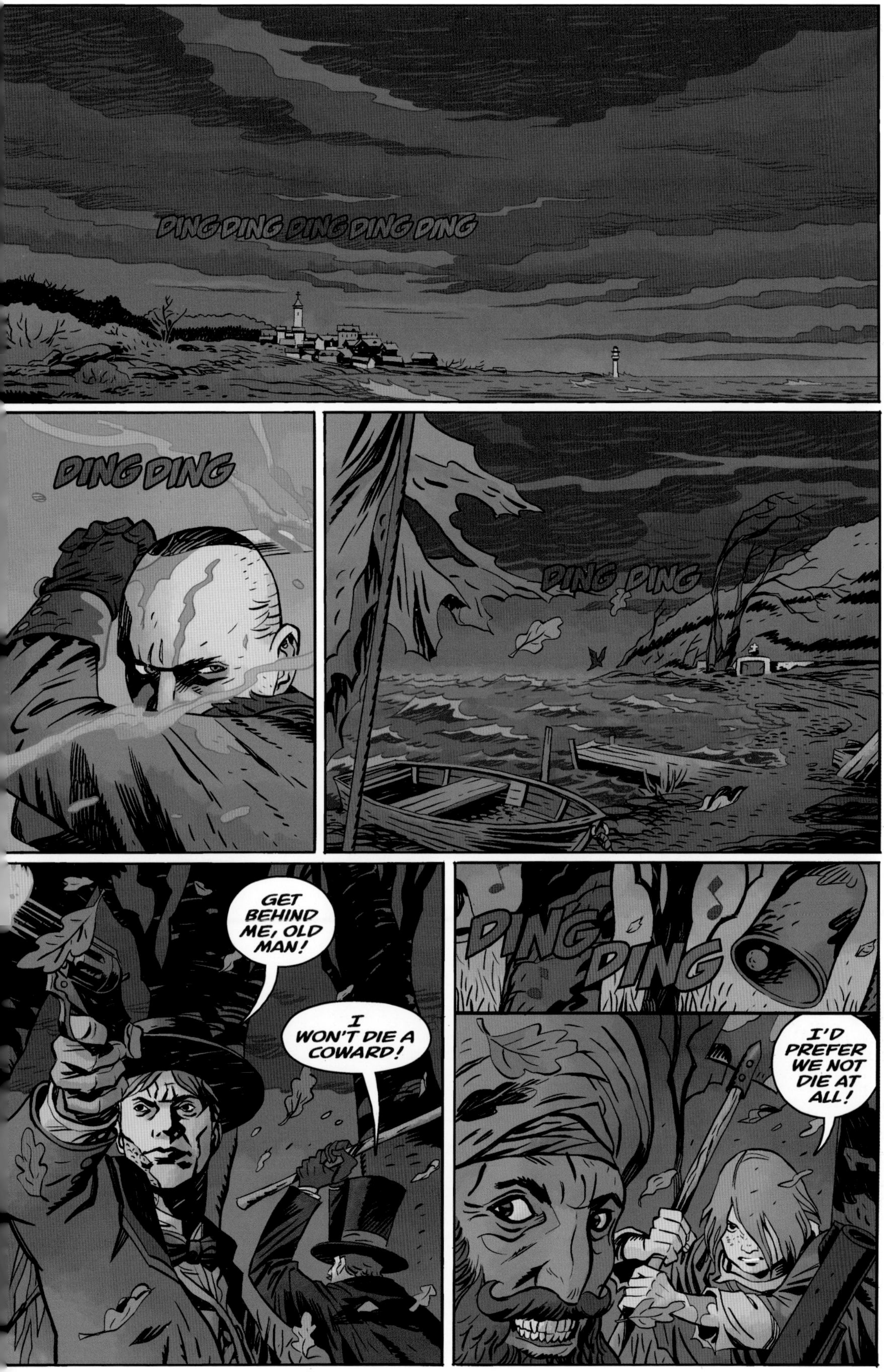
DING DING DING DING DING
DING DING
DING DING
GET BEHIND ME, OLD MAN!
I WON'T DIE A COWARD!
DING DING
I'D PREFER WE NOT DIE AT ALL!

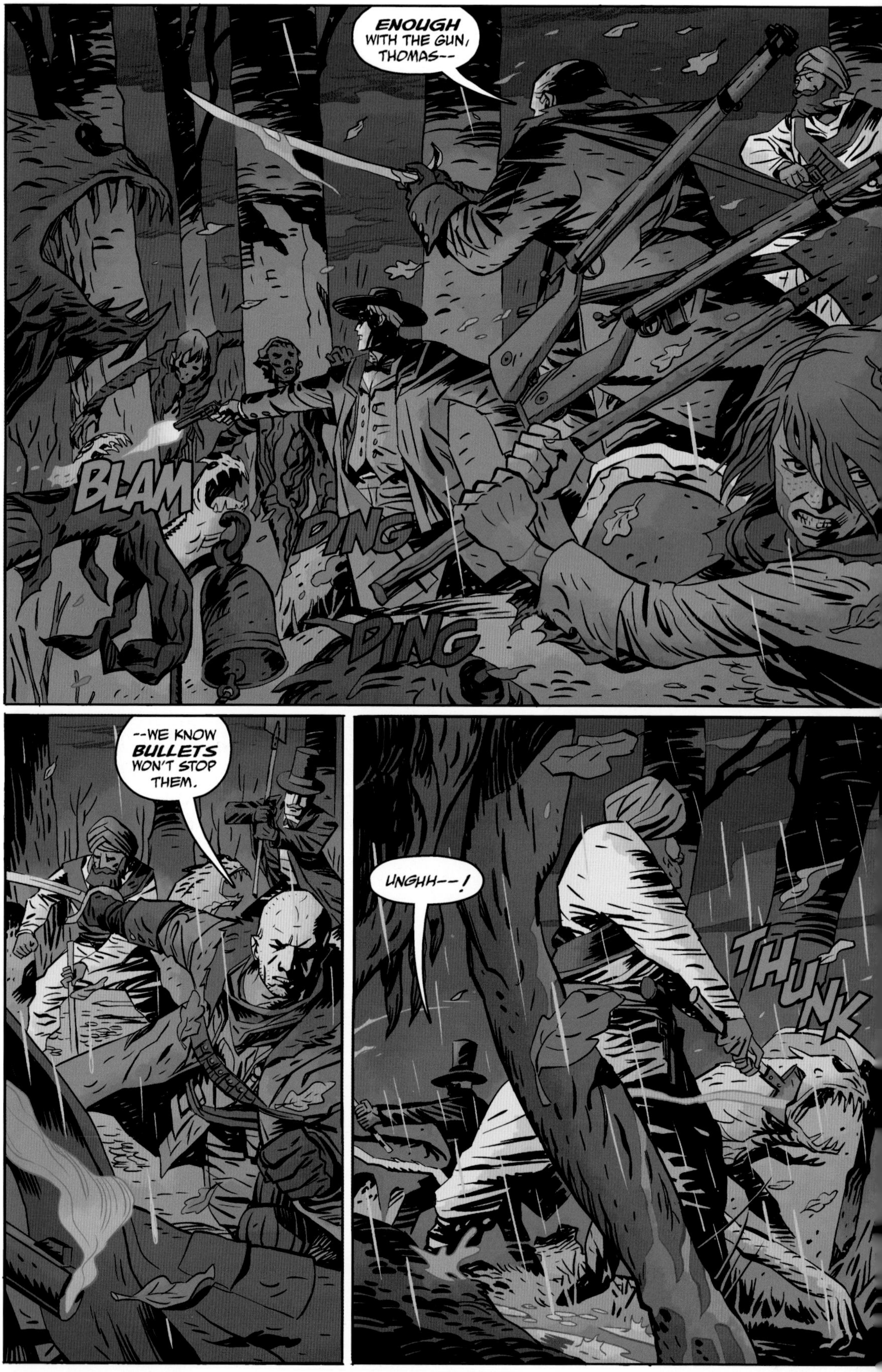
ENOUGH WITH THE GUN, THOMAS--
BLAM
DING
DING
--WE KNOW BULLETS WON'T STOP THEM.
UNGHH--!
THUNK

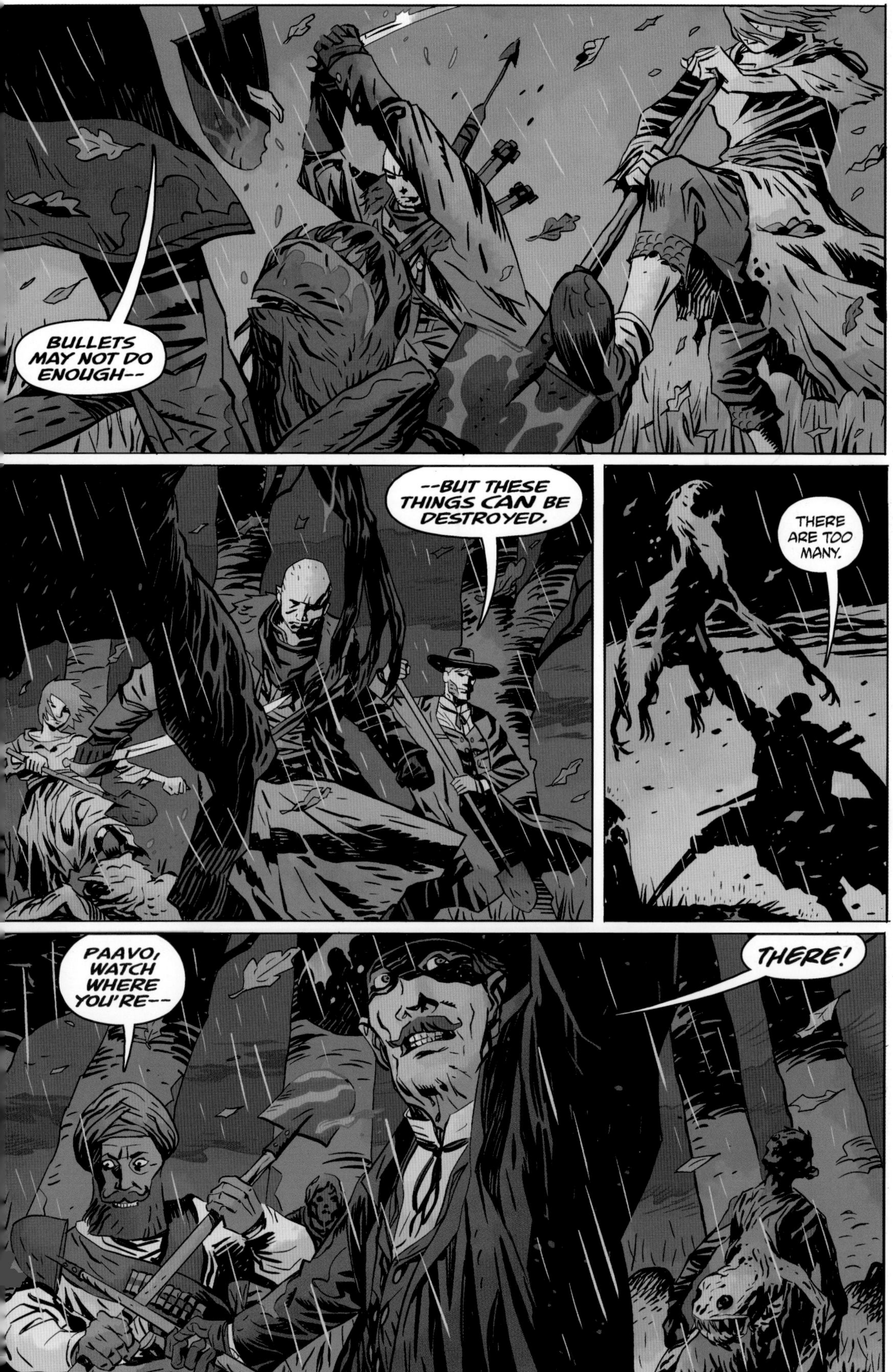
BULLETS MAY NOT DO ENOUGH--
--BUT THESE THINGS CAN BE DESTROYED.
THERE ARE TOO MANY.
PAAVO, WATCH WHERE YOU'RE--
THERE!

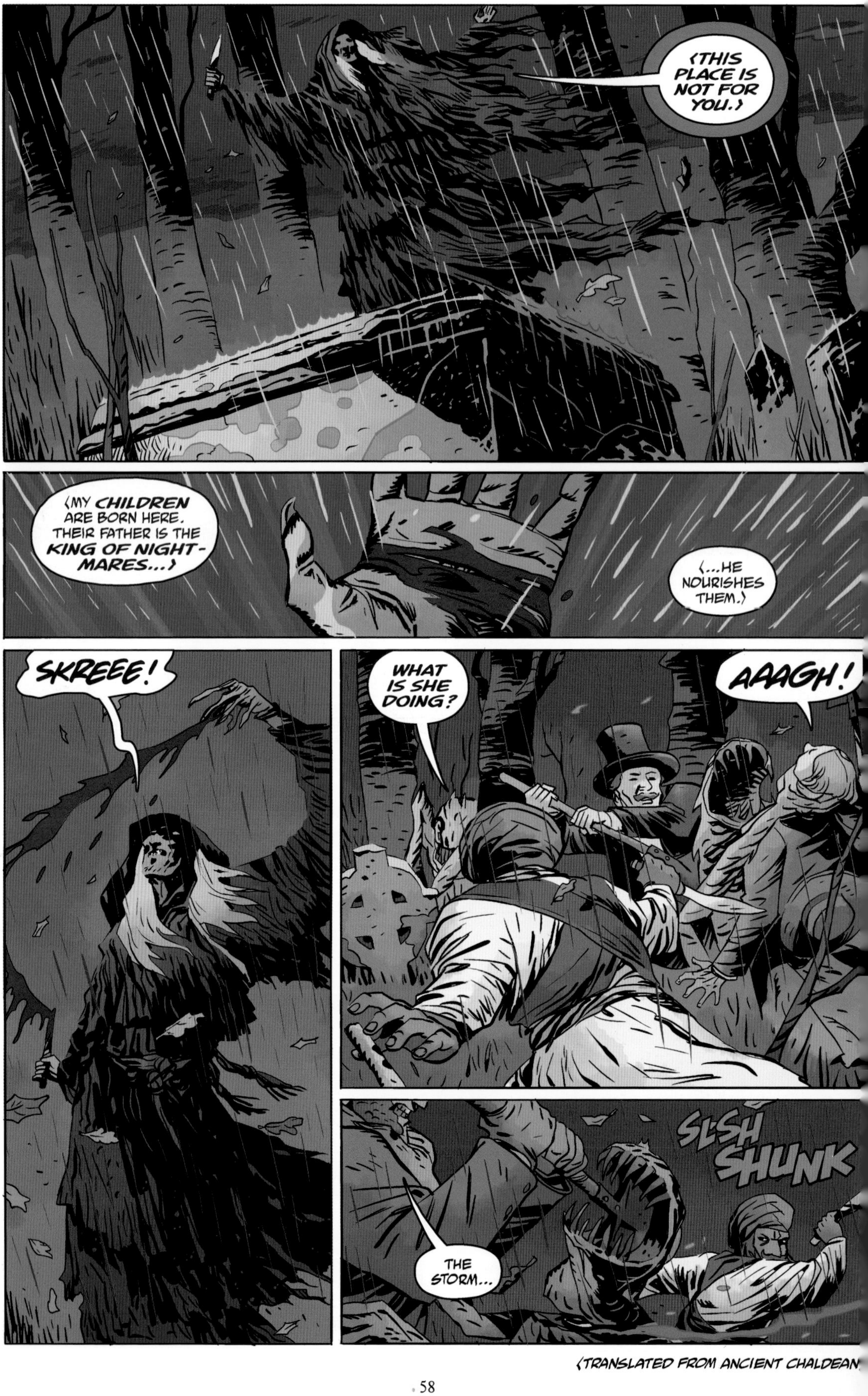

‹THIS PLACE IS NOT FOR YOU.›
‹MY CHILDREN ARE BORN HERE. THEIR FATHER IS THE KING OF NIGHTMARES...›
‹...HE NOURISHES THEM.›
SKREEE!
WHAT IS SHE DOING?
AAAGH!
SLSH SHUNK
THE STORM...


‹TRANSLATED FROM ANCIENT CHALDEAN

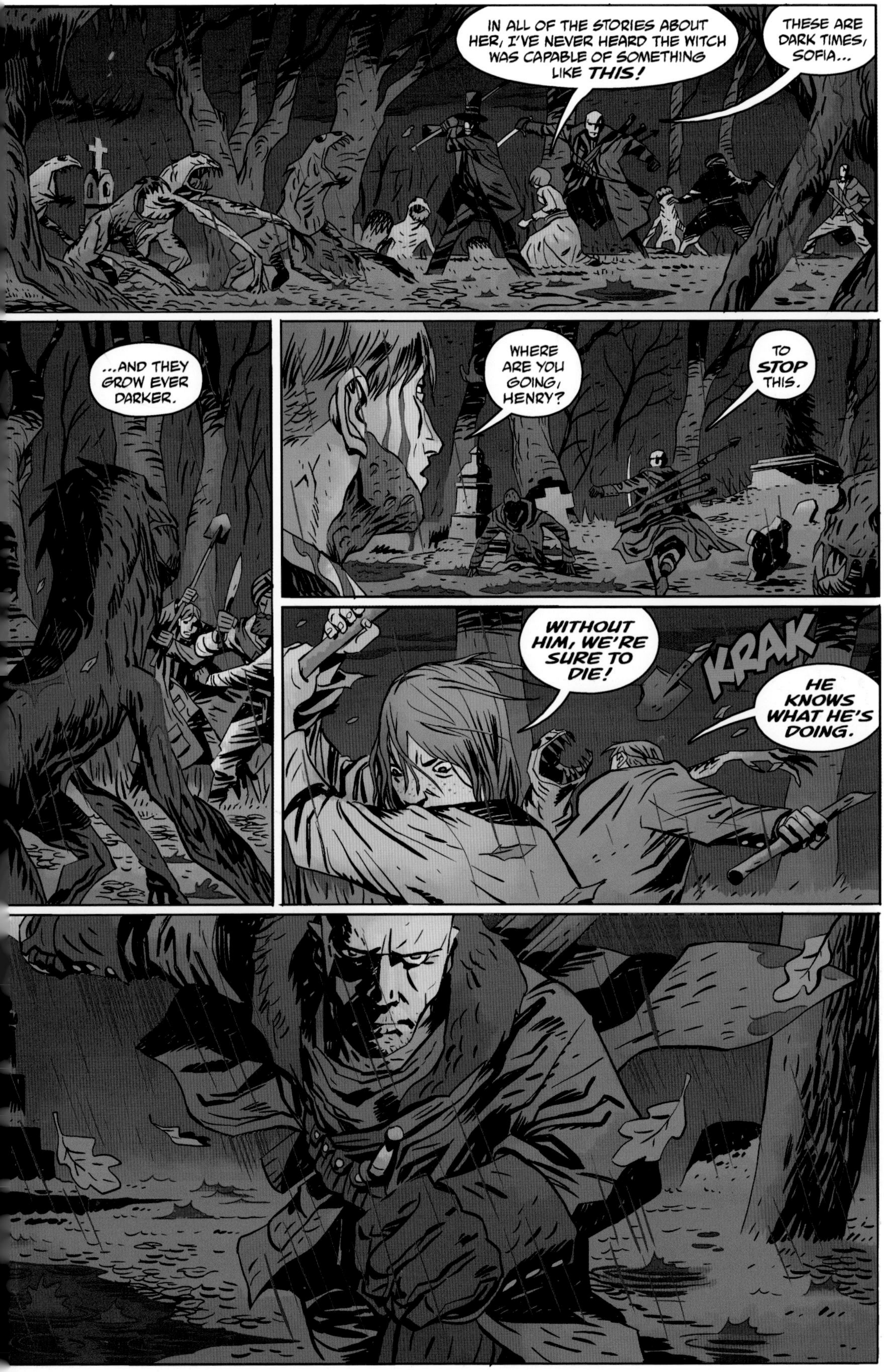
IN ALL OF THE STORIES ABOUT HER, I'VE NEVER HEARD THE WITCH WAS CAPABLE OF SOMETHING LIKE THIS!
THESE ARE DARK TIMES, SOFIA...
...AND THEY GROW EVER DARKER.
WHERE ARE YOU GOING, HENRY?
TO STOP THIS.
WITHOUT HIM, WE'RE SURE TO DIE!
KRAK
HE KNOWS WHAT HE'S DOING.

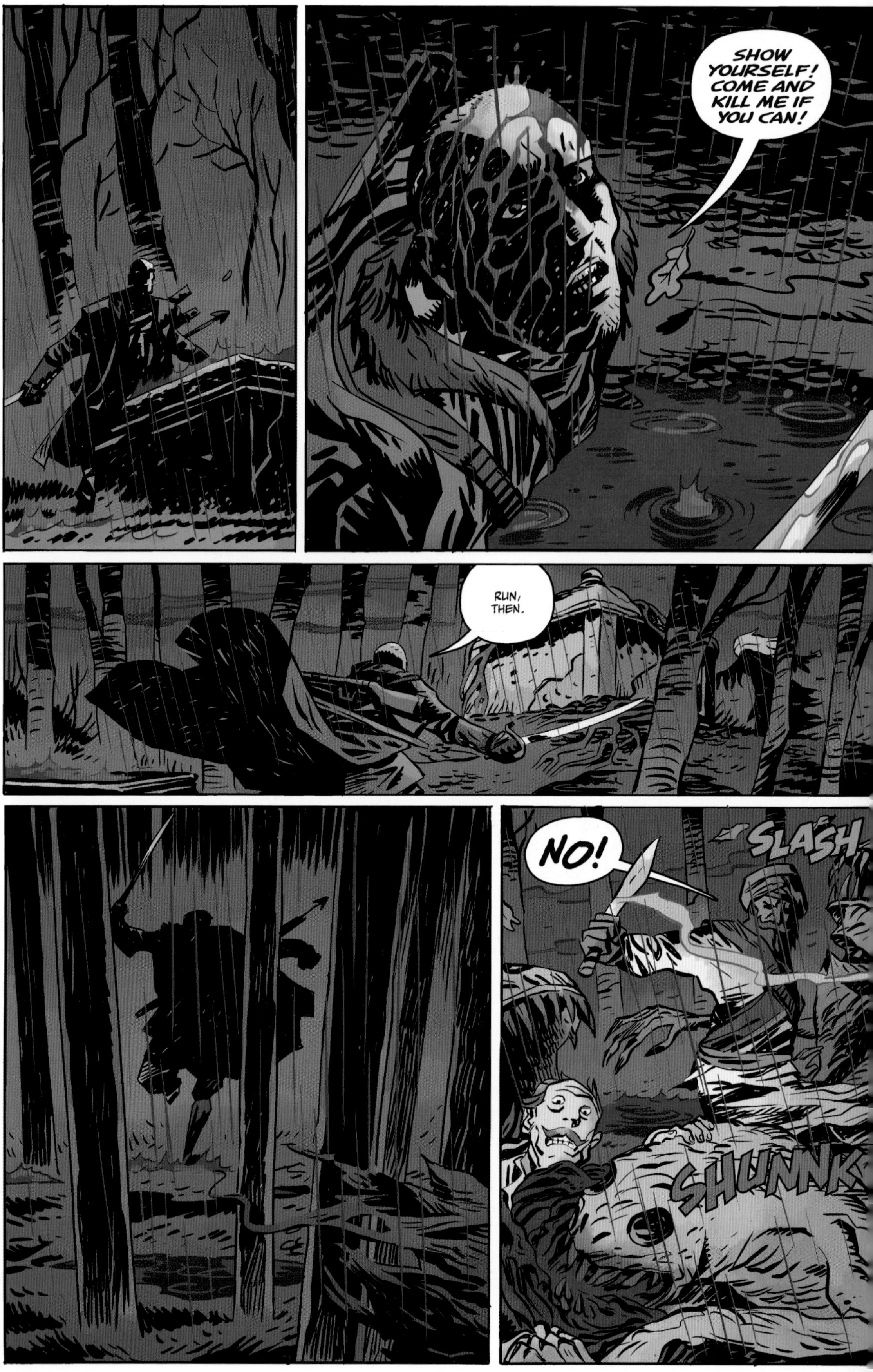
SHOW YOURSELF! COME AND KILL ME IF YOU CAN!
RUN, THEN.
NO!
SLASH
SHUNNK

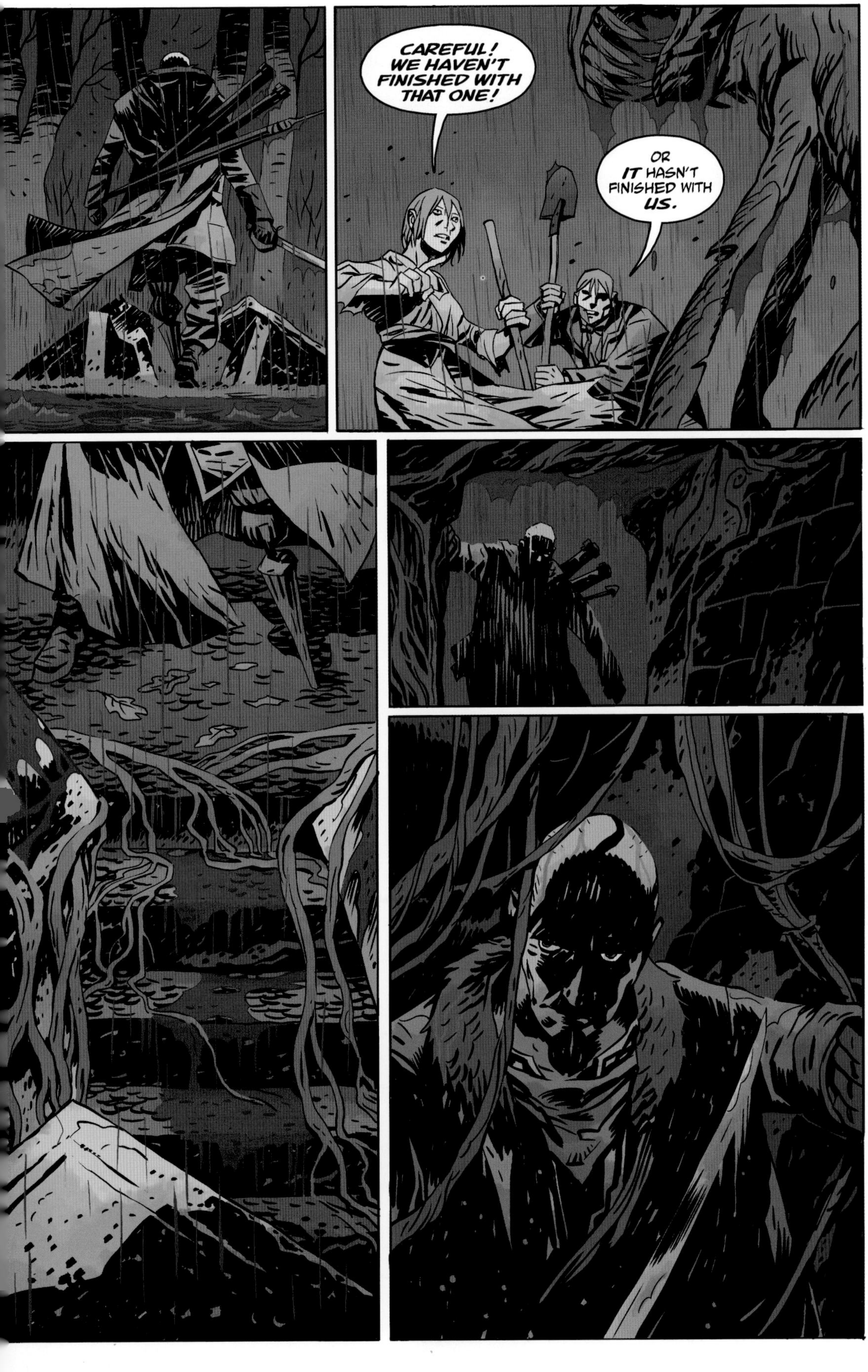
CAREFUL! WE HAVEN'T FINISHED WITH THAT ONE!
OR IT HASN'T FINISHED WITH US.

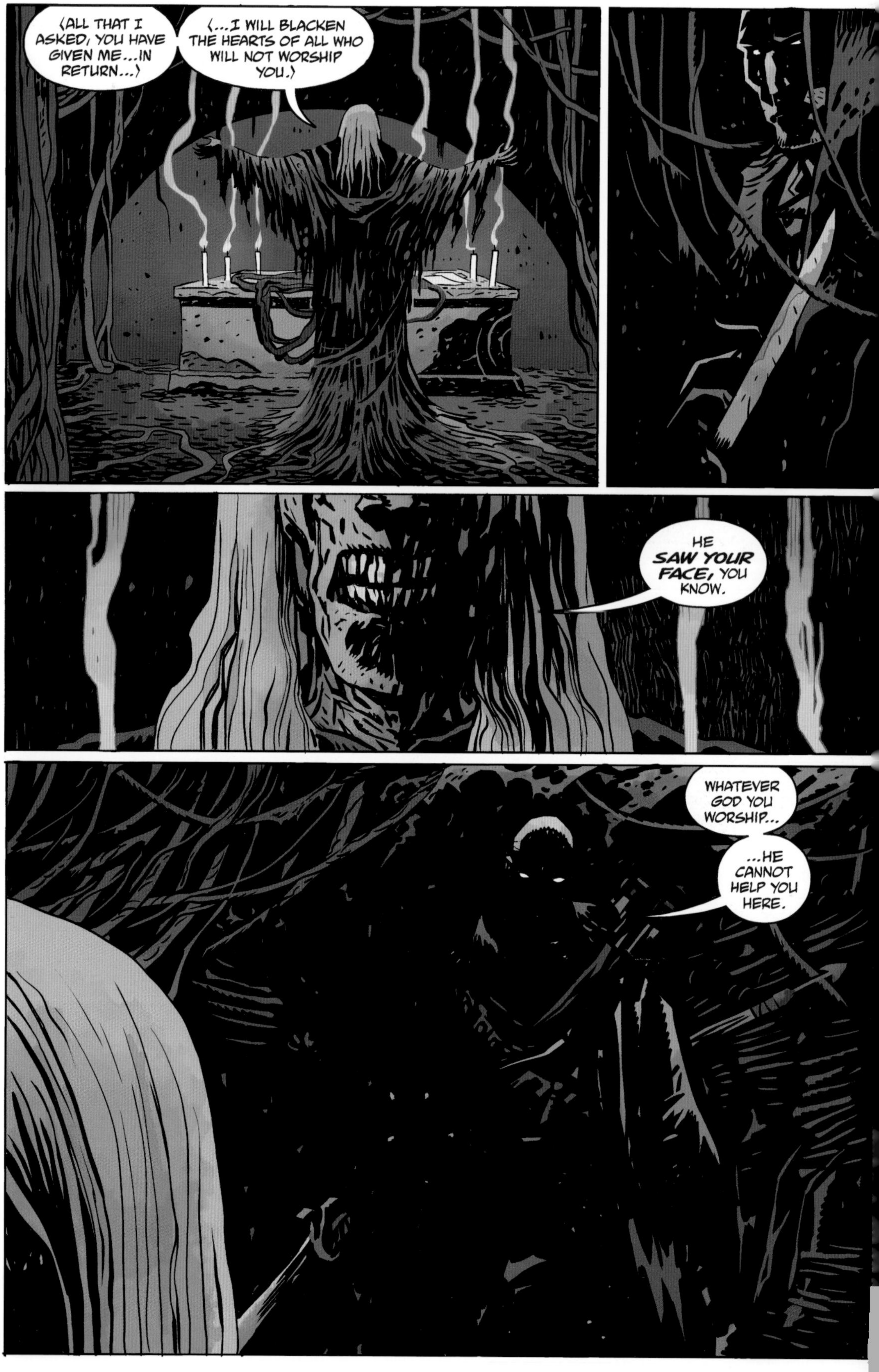

‹ALL THAT I ASKED, YOU HAVE GIVEN ME...IN RETURN...›
‹...I WILL BLACKEN THE HEARTS OF ALL WHO WILL NOT WORSHIP YOU.›
HE SAW YOUR FACE, YOU KNOW.
WHATEVER GOD YOU WORSHIP...
...HE CANNOT HELP YOU HERE.

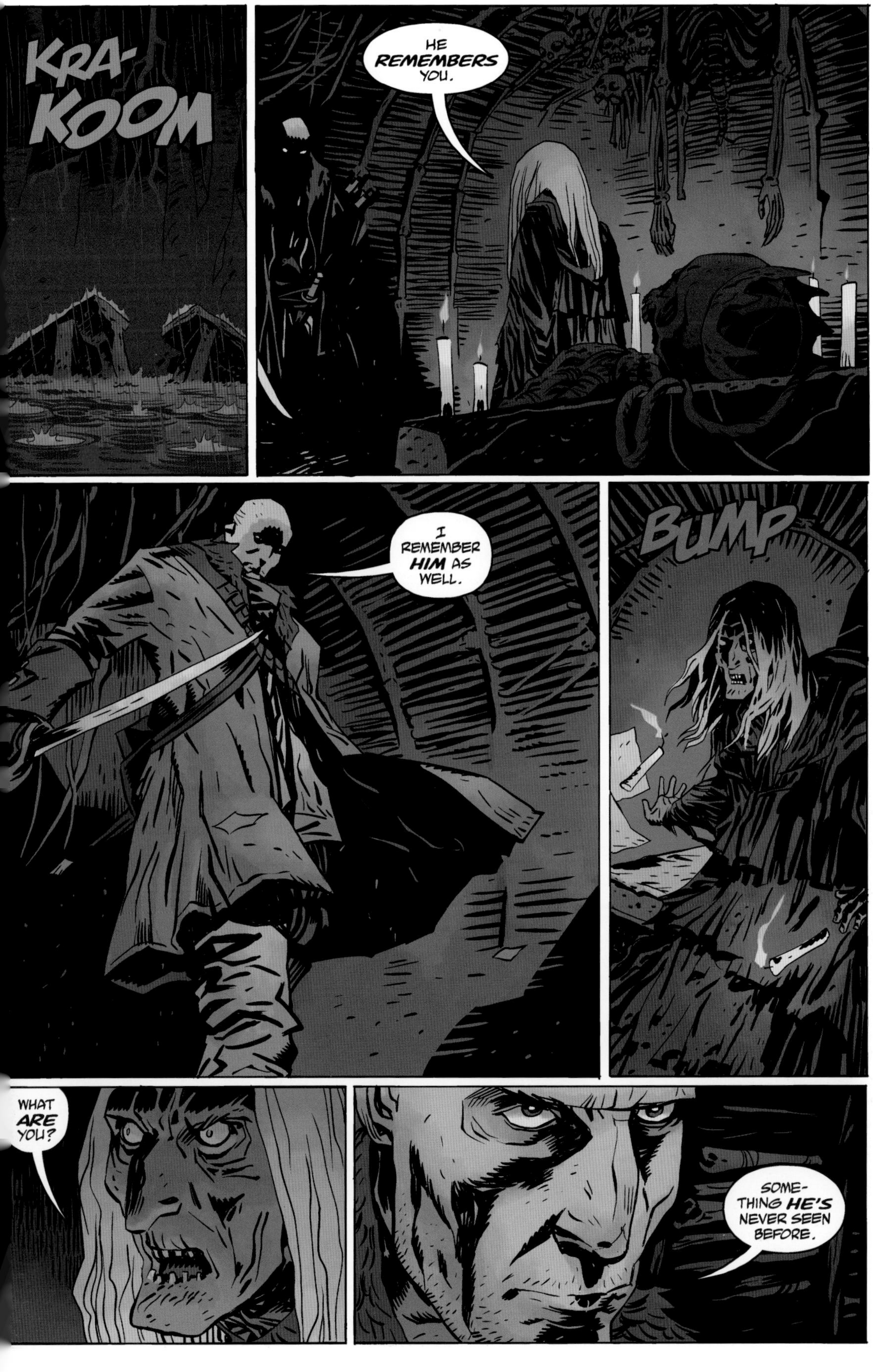
KRA-KOOM
HE REMEMBERS YOU.
I REMEMBER HIM AS WELL.
BUMP
WHAT ARE YOU?
SOME-THING HE'S NEVER SEEN BEFORE.

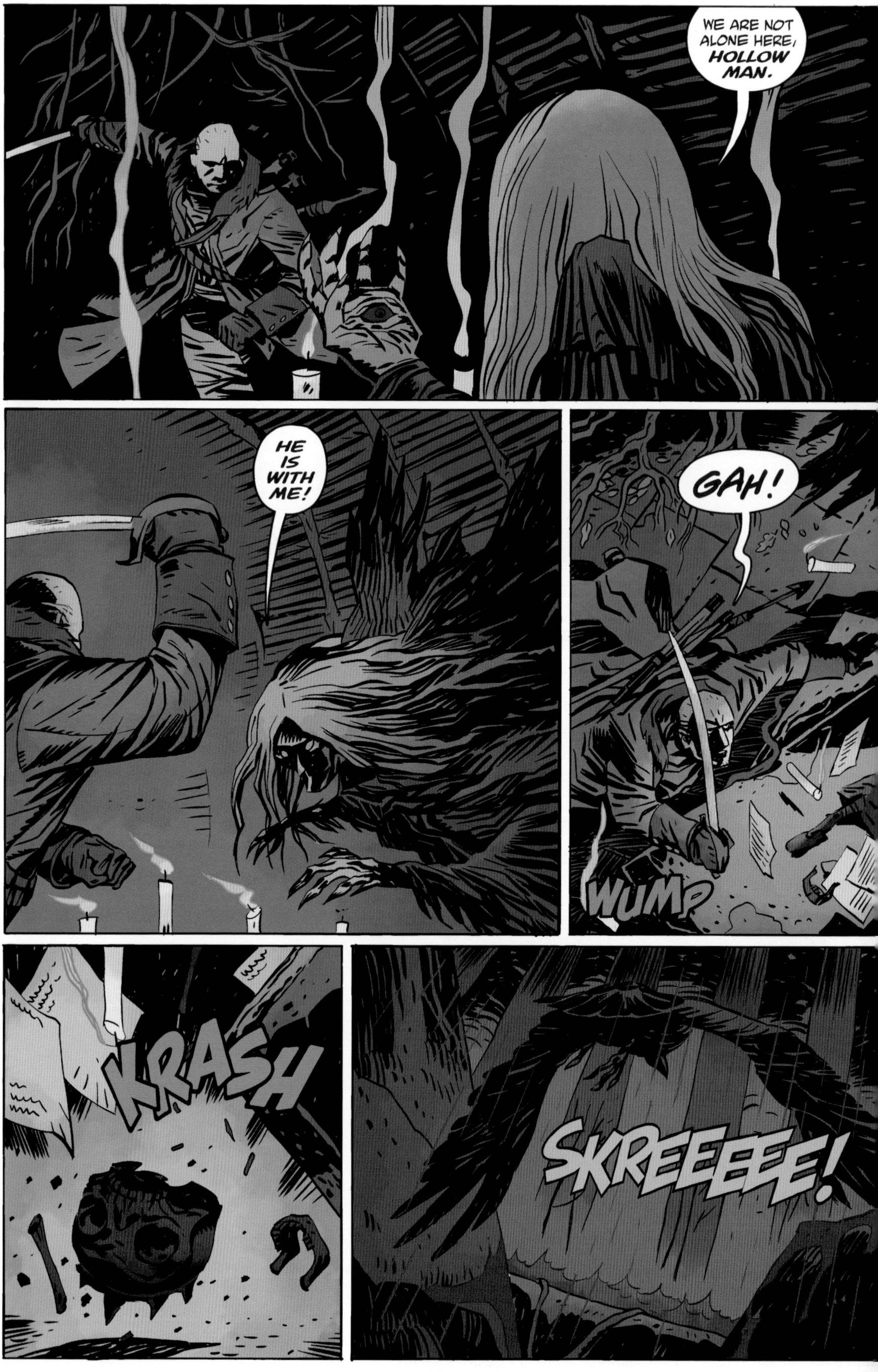
WE ARE NOT ALONE HERE, HOLLOW MAN.
HE IS WITH ME!
GAH!
WUMP
KRASH
SKREEEEEE!

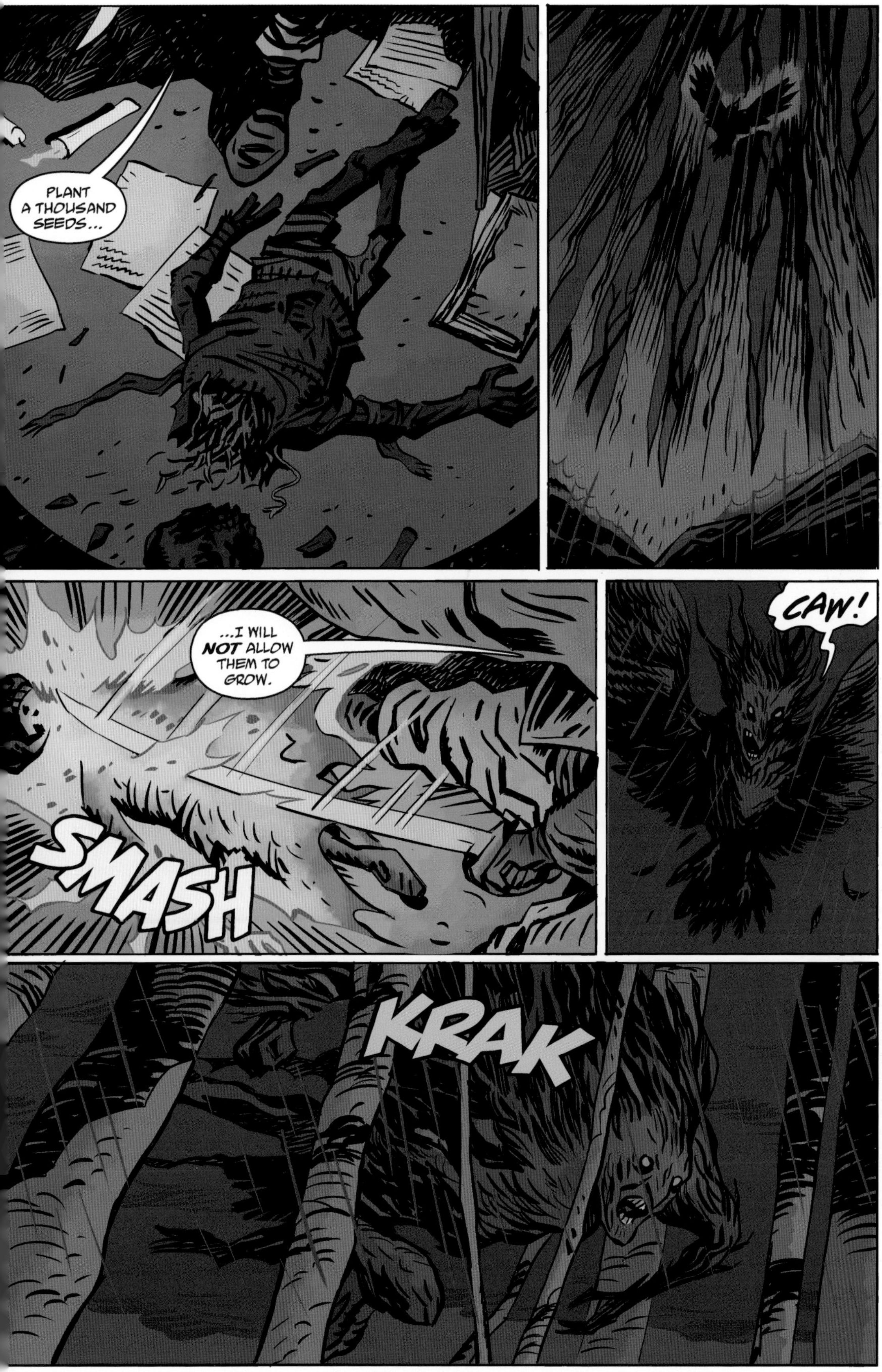
PLANT A THOUSAND SEEDS...
...I WILL NOT ALLOW THEM TO GROW.
SMASH
CAW!
KRAK

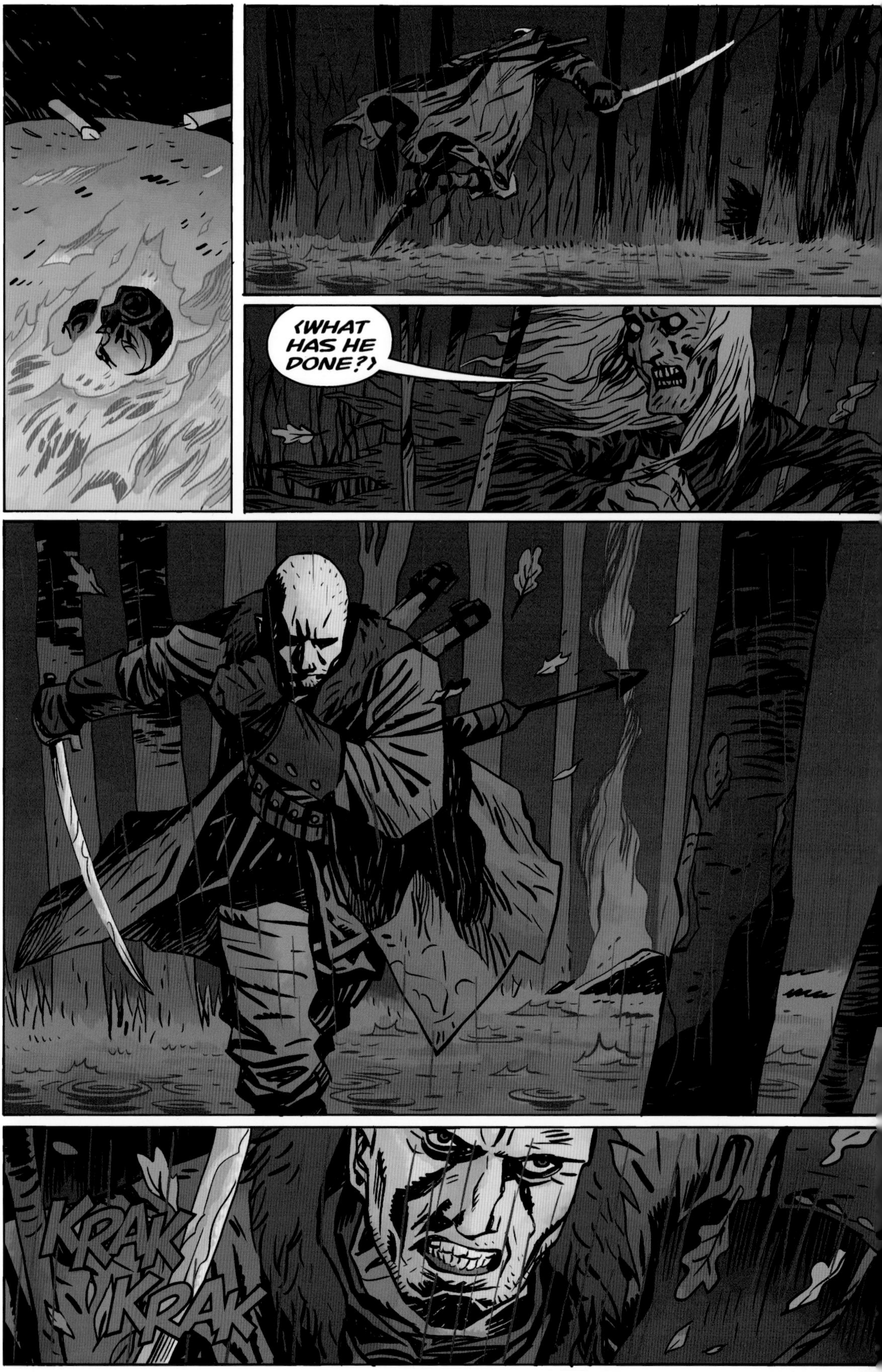
‹WHAT HAS HE DONE?›
KRAK KRAK

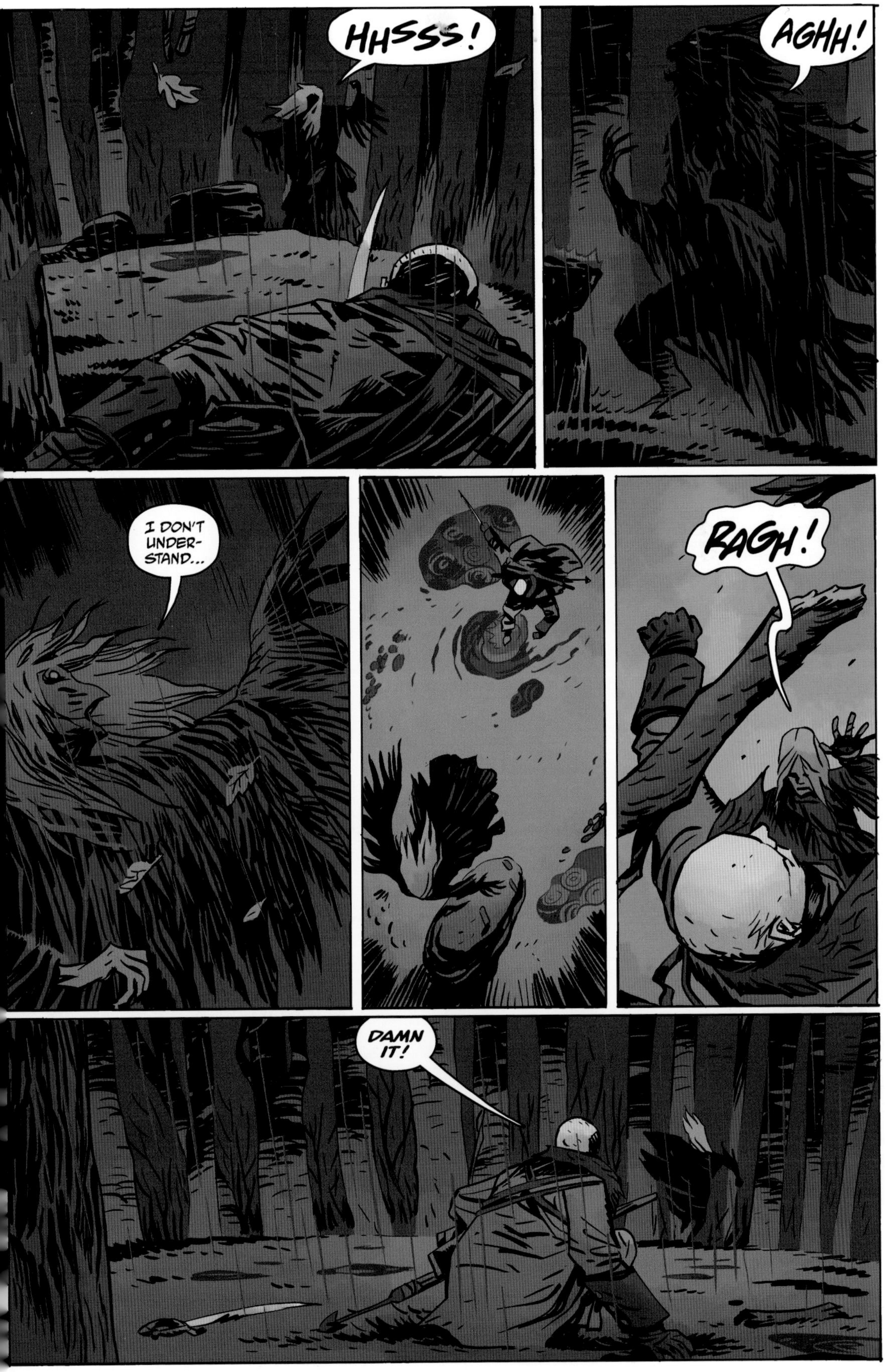
HHSSS!
AGHH!
I DON'T UNDER-STAND...
RAGH!
DAMN IT!

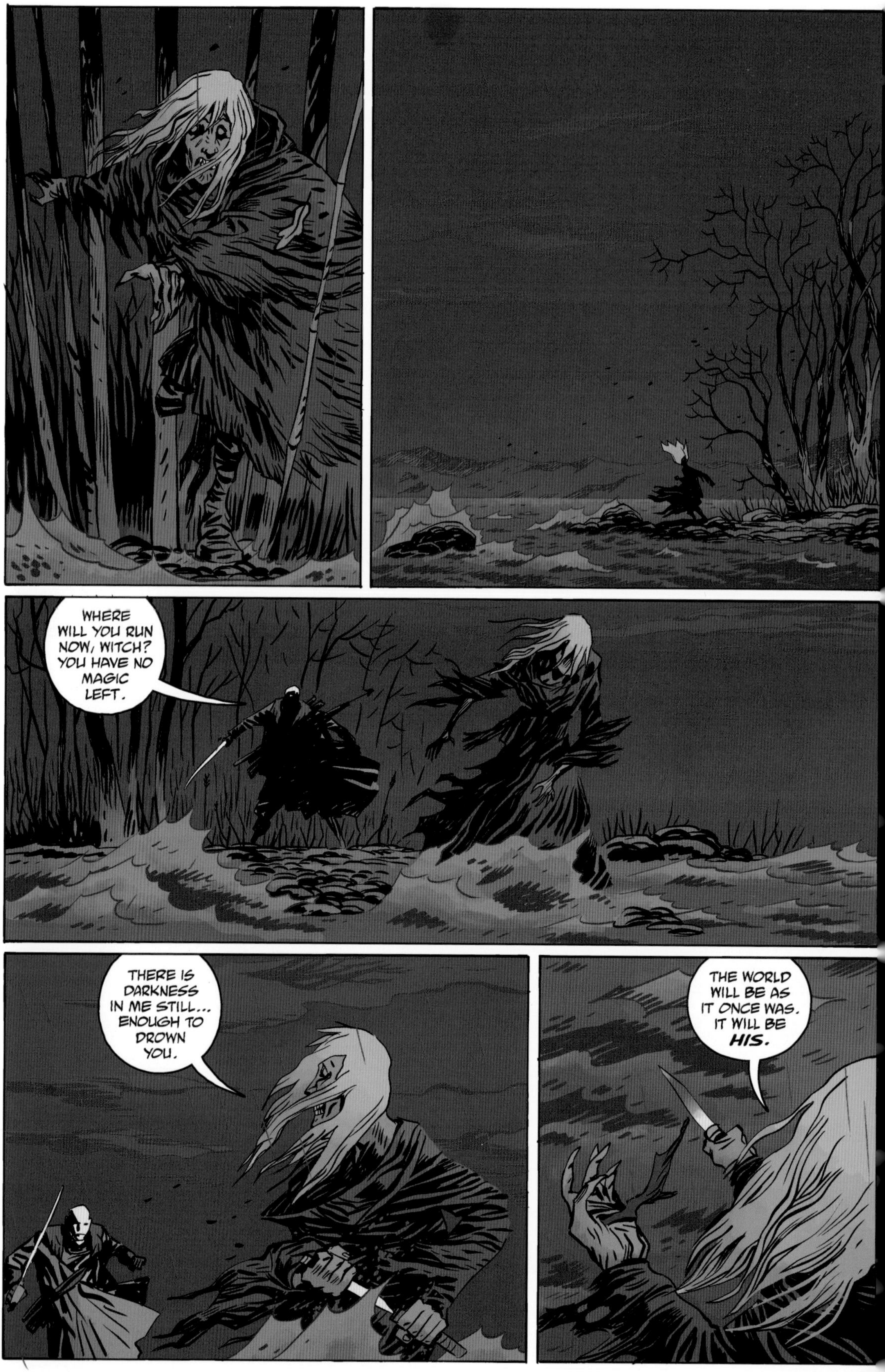
WHERE WILL YOU RUN NOW, WITCH? YOU HAVE NO MAGIC LEFT.
THERE IS DARKNESS IN ME STILL... ENOUGH TO DROWN YOU.
THE WORLD WILL BE AS IT ONCE WAS. IT WILL BE **HIS.**

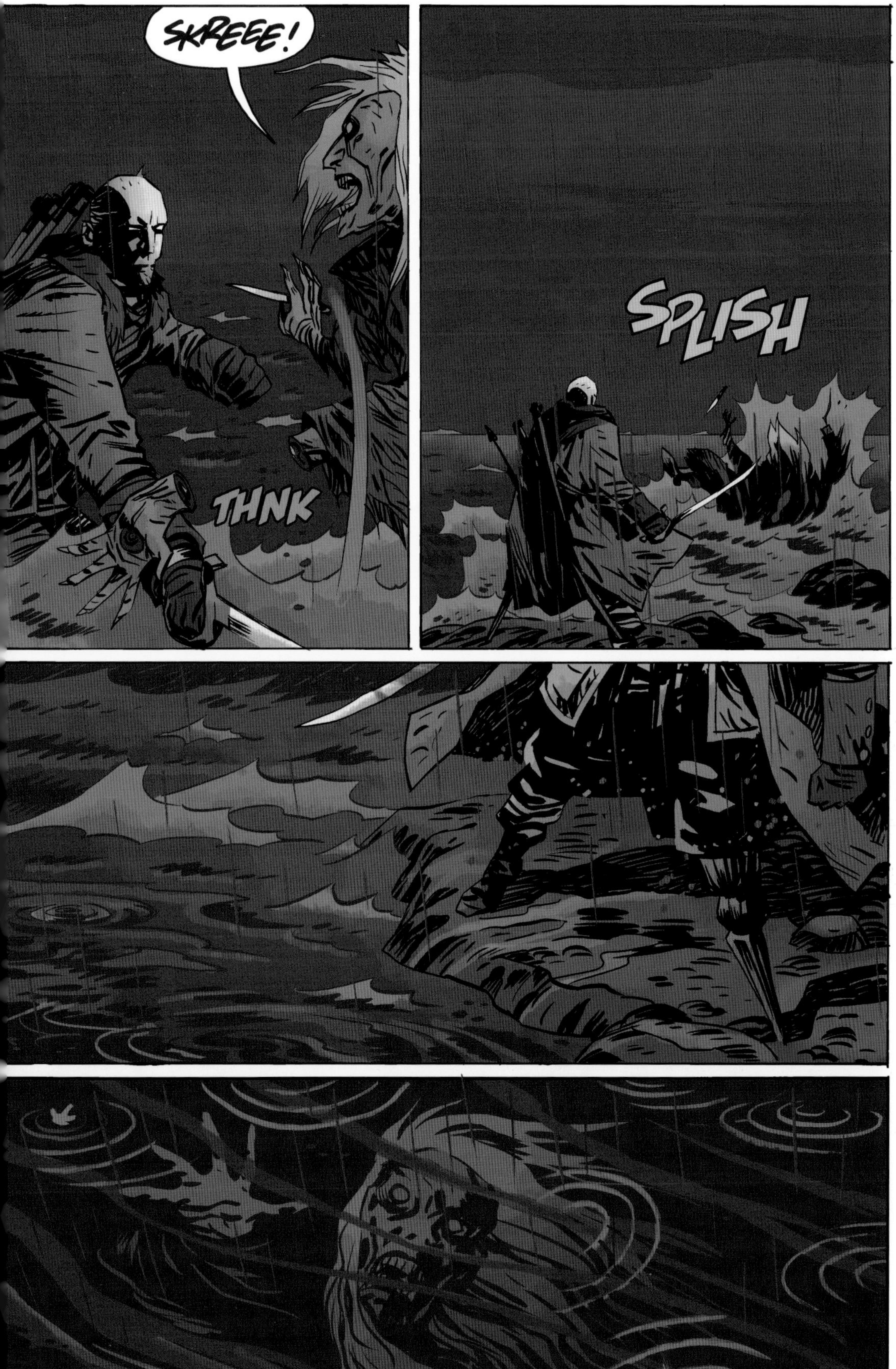
SKREEE!
THNK
SPLISH

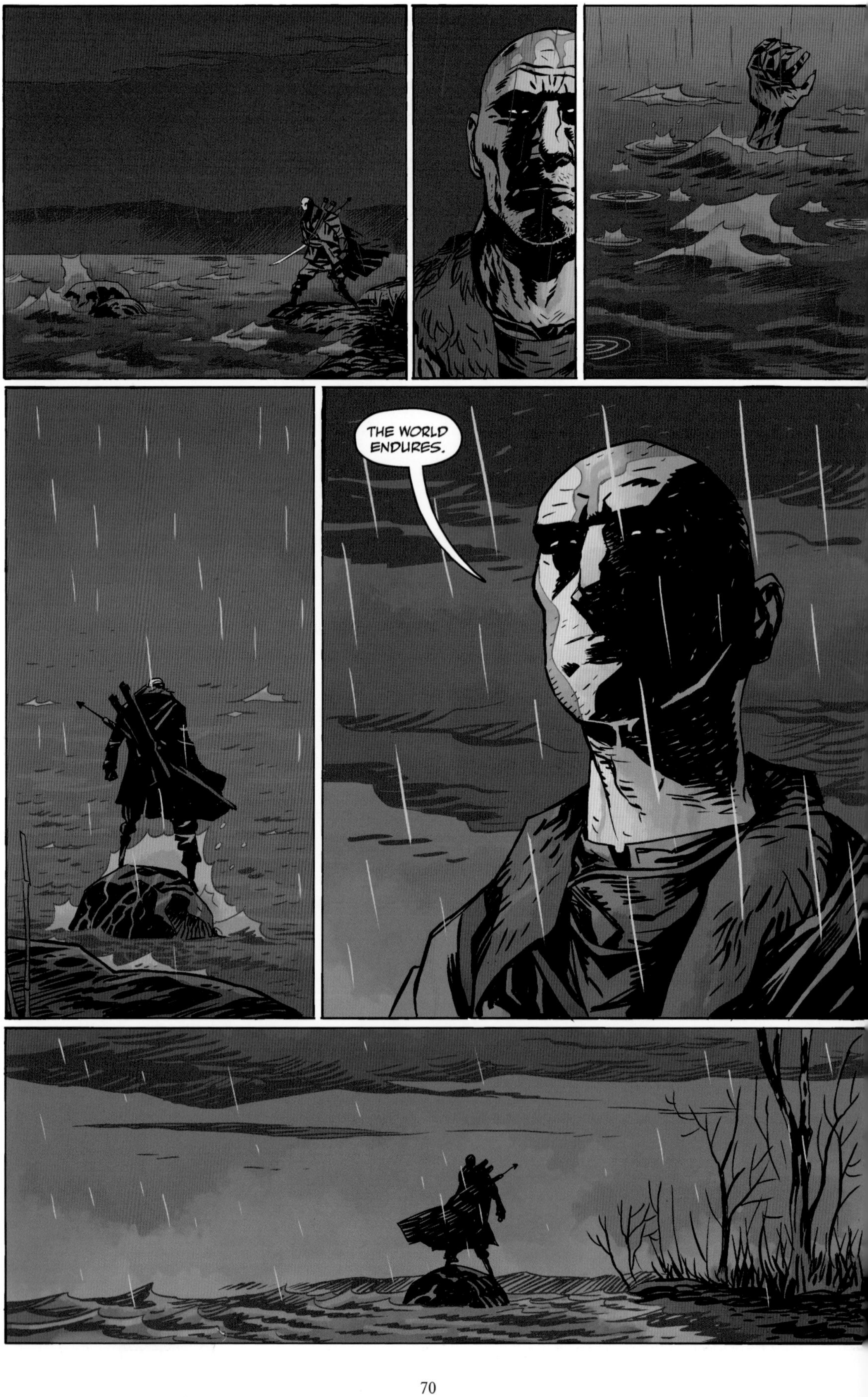
THE WORLD ENDURES.

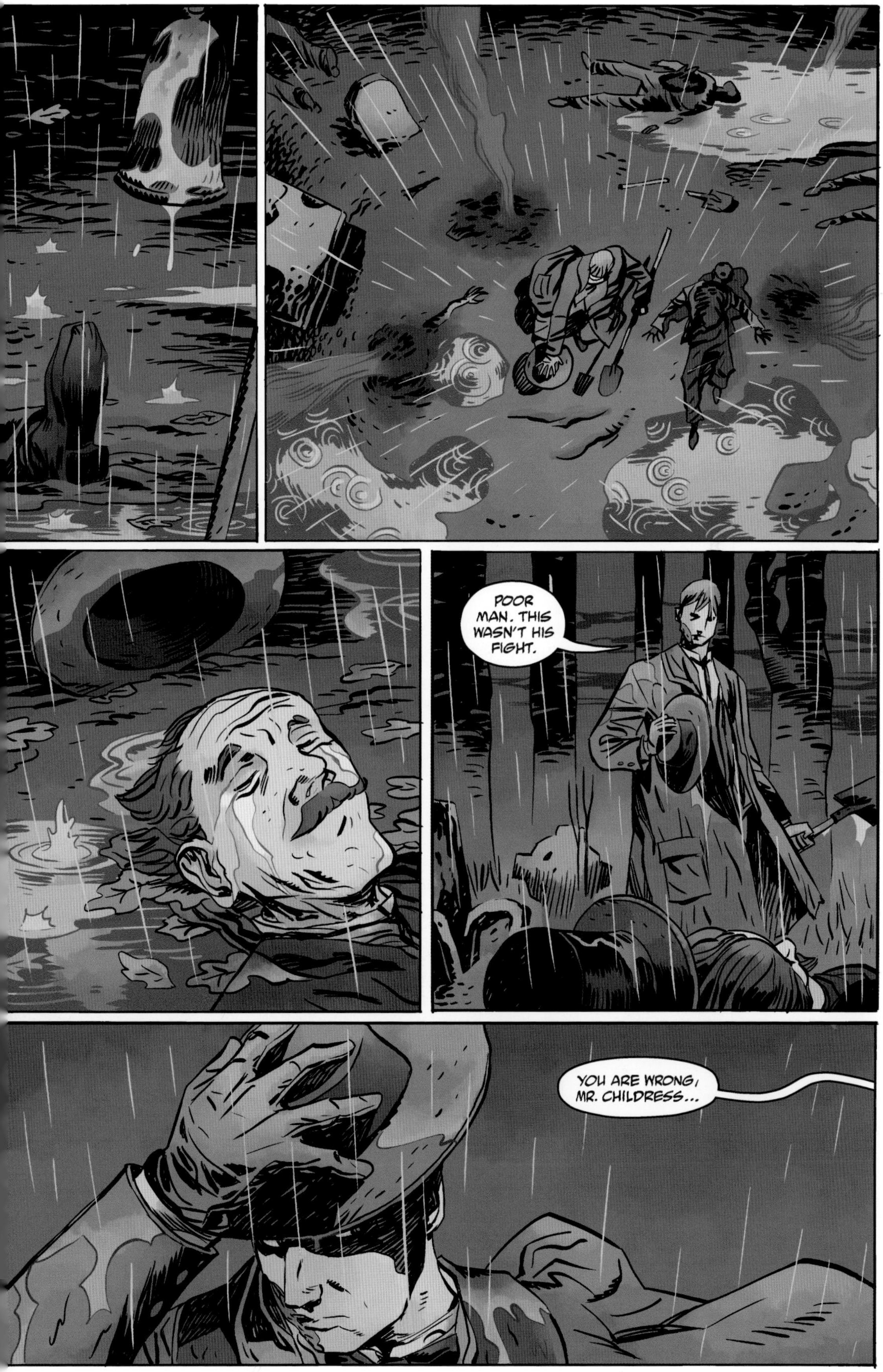
POOR MAN. THIS WASN'T HIS FIGHT.
YOU ARE WRONG, MR. CHILDRESS...

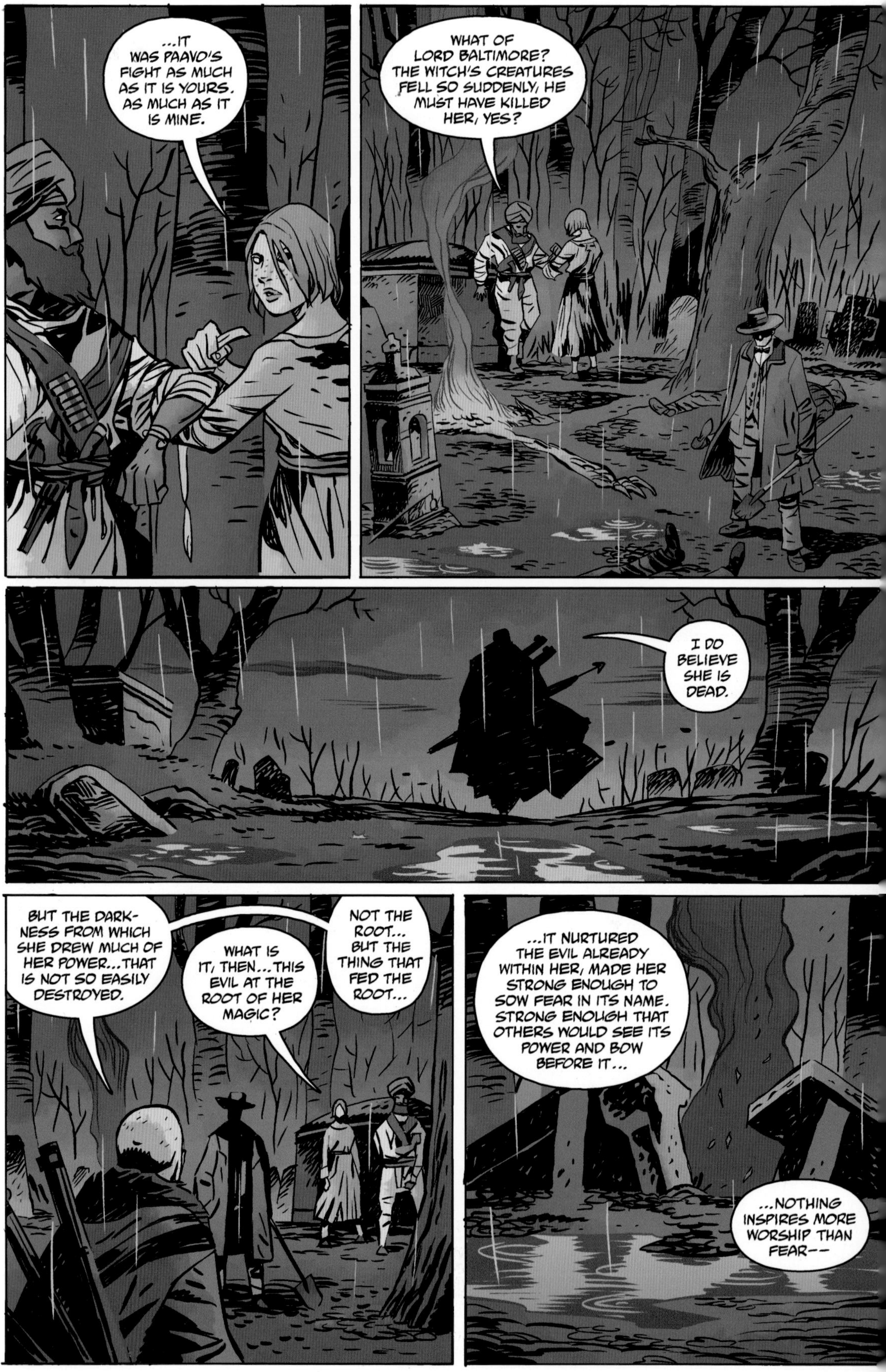
...IT WAS PAAVO'S FIGHT AS MUCH AS IT IS YOURS. AS MUCH AS IT IS MINE.
WHAT OF LORD BALTIMORE? THE WITCH'S CREATURES FELL SO SUDDENLY, HE MUST HAVE KILLED HER, YES?
I DO BELIEVE SHE IS DEAD.
BUT THE DARKNESS FROM WHICH SHE DREW MUCH OF HER POWER...THAT IS NOT SO EASILY DESTROYED.
WHAT IS IT, THEN...THIS EVIL AT THE ROOT OF HER MAGIC?
NOT THE ROOT... BUT THE THING THAT FED THE ROOT...
...IT NURTURED THE EVIL ALREADY WITHIN HER, MADE HER STRONG ENOUGH TO SOW FEAR IN ITS NAME. STRONG ENOUGH THAT OTHERS WOULD SEE ITS POWER AND BOW BEFORE IT...
...NOTHING INSPIRES MORE WORSHIP THAN FEAR--

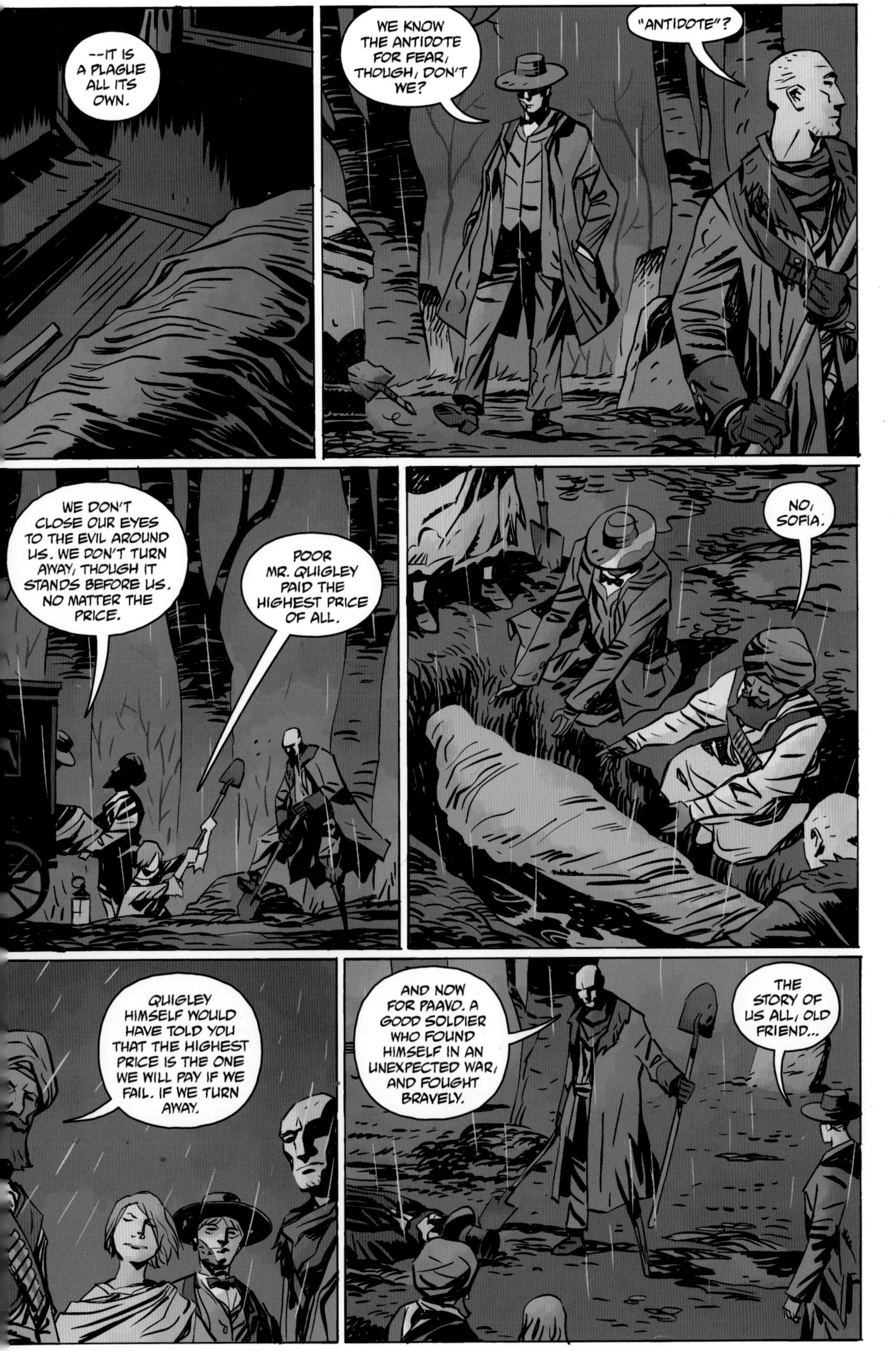
--IT IS A PLAGUE ALL ITS OWN.
WE KNOW THE ANTIDOTE FOR FEAR, THOUGH, DON'T WE?
"ANTIDOTE"?
WE DON'T CLOSE OUR EYES TO THE EVIL AROUND US. WE DON'T TURN AWAY, THOUGH IT STANDS BEFORE US. NO MATTER THE PRICE.
POOR MR. QUIGLEY PAID THE HIGHEST PRICE OF ALL.
NO, SOFIA.
QUIGLEY HIMSELF WOULD HAVE TOLD YOU THAT THE HIGHEST PRICE IS THE ONE WE WILL PAY IF WE FAIL. IF WE TURN AWAY.
AND NOW FOR PAAVO. A GOOD SOLDIER WHO FOUND HIMSELF IN AN UNEXPECTED WAR, AND FOUGHT BRAVELY.
THE STORY OF US ALL, OLD FRIEND...

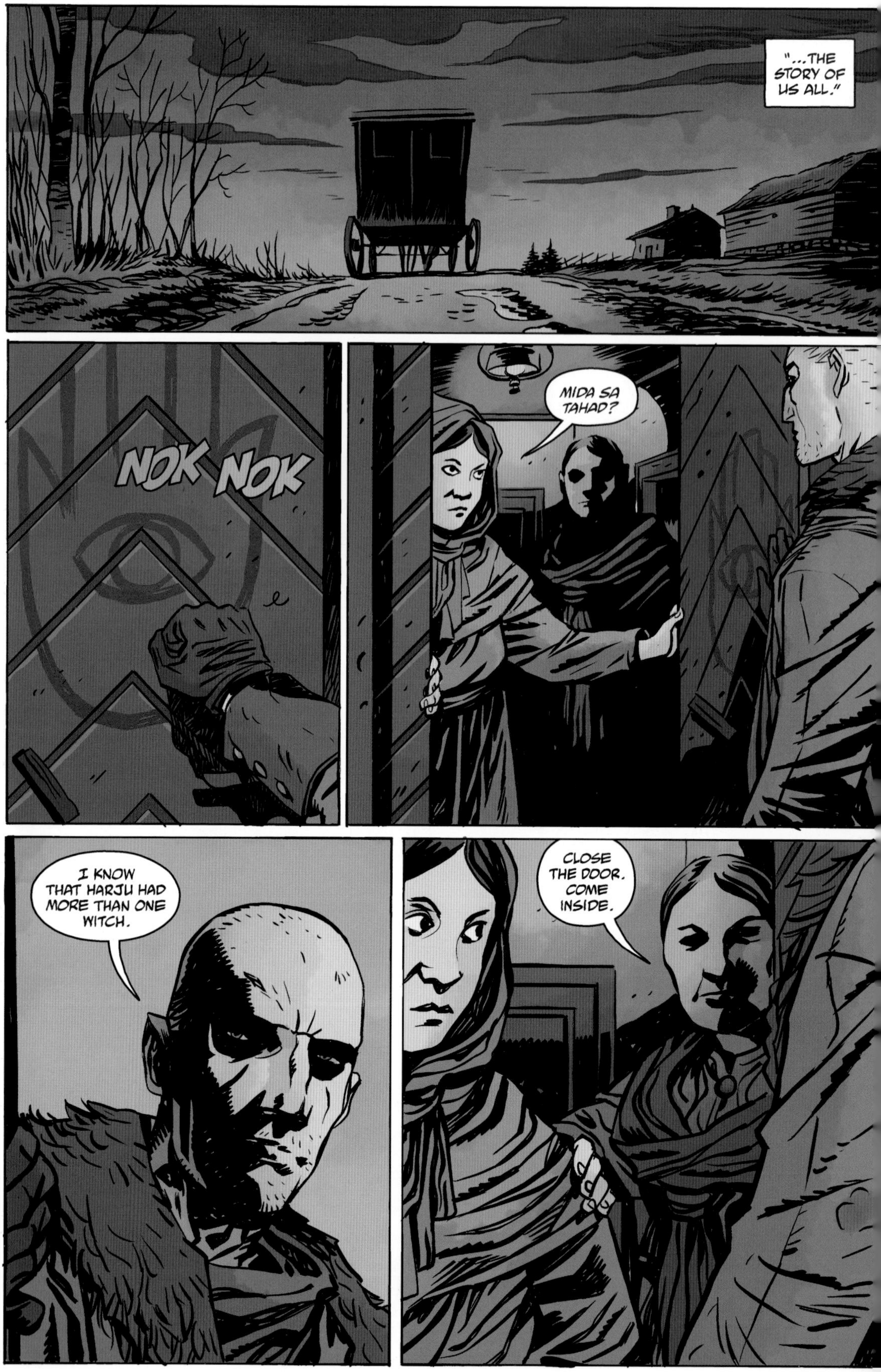
"...THE STORY OF US ALL."
NOK NOK
MIDA SA TAHAD?
I KNOW THAT HARJU HAD MORE THAN ONE WITCH.
CLOSE THE DOOR. COME INSIDE.

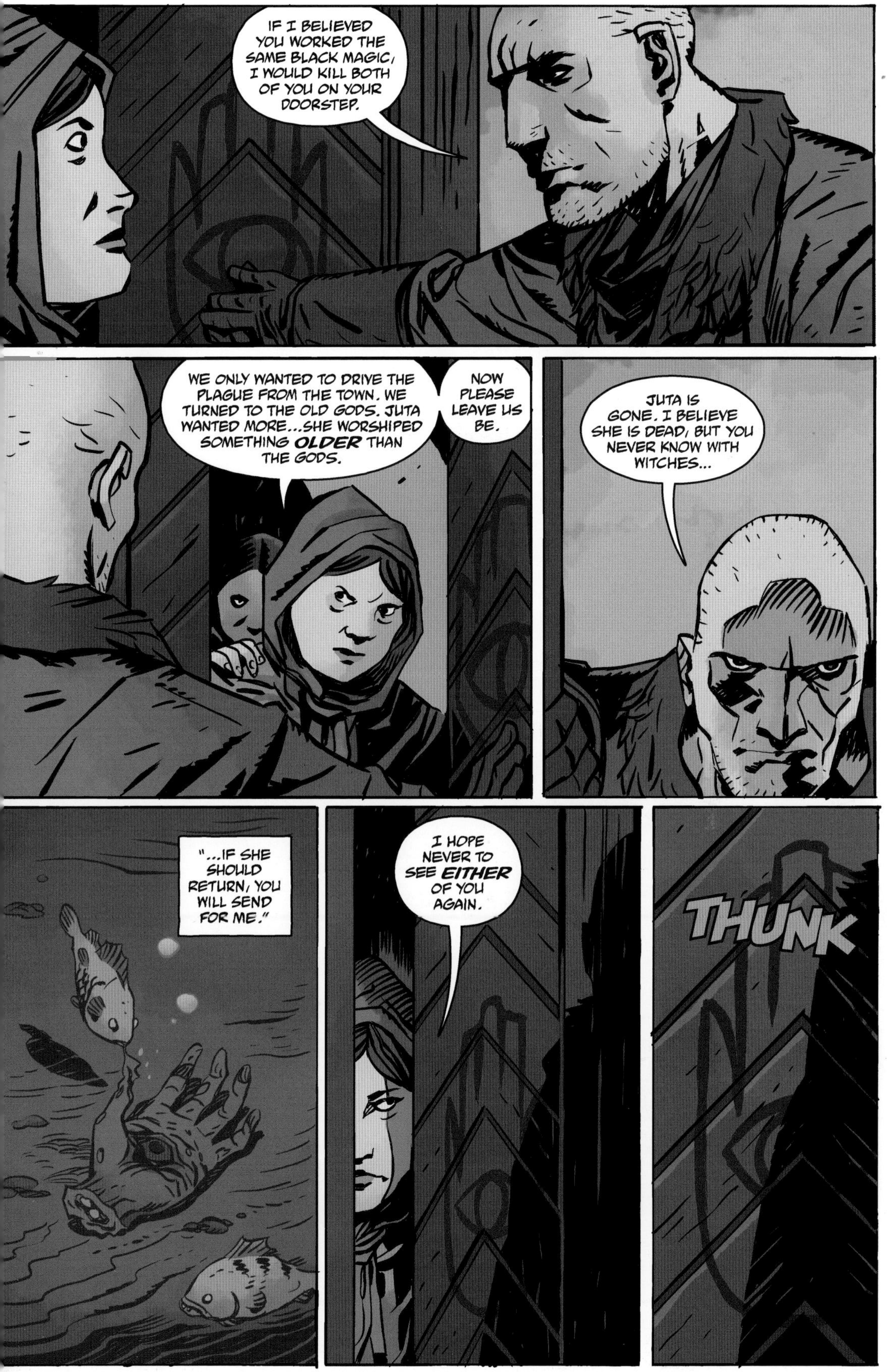
IF I BELIEVED YOU WORKED THE SAME BLACK MAGIC, I WOULD KILL BOTH OF YOU ON YOUR DOORSTEP.
WE ONLY WANTED TO DRIVE THE PLAGUE FROM THE TOWN. WE TURNED TO THE OLD GODS. JUTA WANTED MORE...SHE WORSHIPED SOMETHING OLDER THAN THE GODS.
NOW PLEASE LEAVE US BE.
JUTA IS GONE. I BELIEVE SHE IS DEAD, BUT YOU NEVER KNOW WITH WITCHES...
"...IF SHE SHOULD RETURN, YOU WILL SEND FOR ME."
I HOPE NEVER TO SEE EITHER OF YOU AGAIN.
THUNK

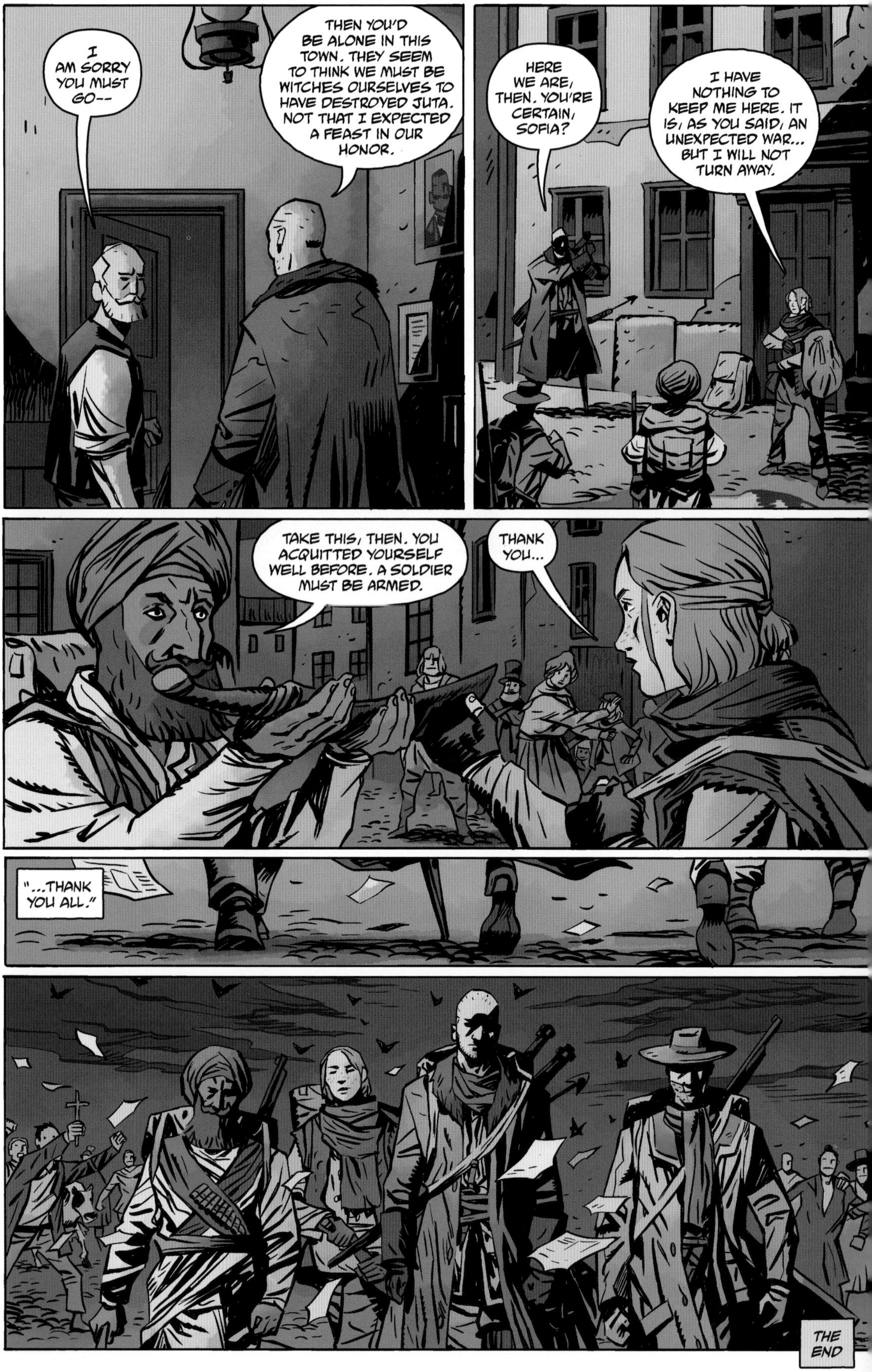
I AM SORRY YOU MUST GO--
THEN YOU'D BE ALONE IN THIS TOWN. THEY SEEM TO THINK WE MUST BE WITCHES OURSELVES TO HAVE DESTROYED JUTA. NOT THAT I EXPECTED A FEAST IN OUR HONOR.
HERE WE ARE, THEN. YOU'RE CERTAIN, SOFIA?
I HAVE NOTHING TO KEEP ME HERE. IT IS, AS YOU SAID, AN UNEXPECTED WAR... BUT I WILL NOT TURN AWAY.
TAKE THIS, THEN. YOU ACQUITTED YOURSELF WELL BEFORE. A SOLDIER MUST BE ARMED.
THANK YOU...
"...THANK YOU ALL."
THE END

# THE WOLF AND THE APOSTLE
## *Chapter One*

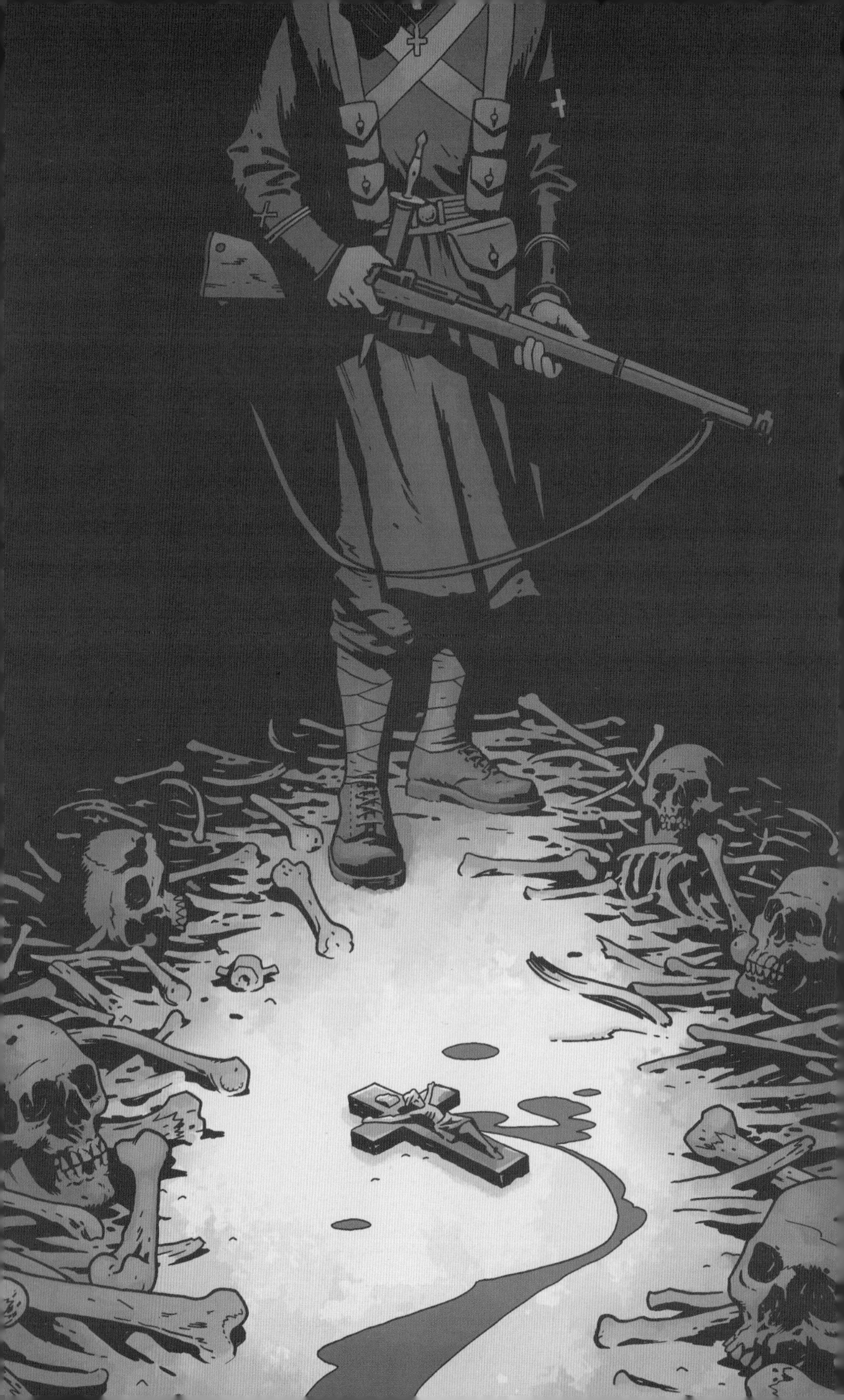

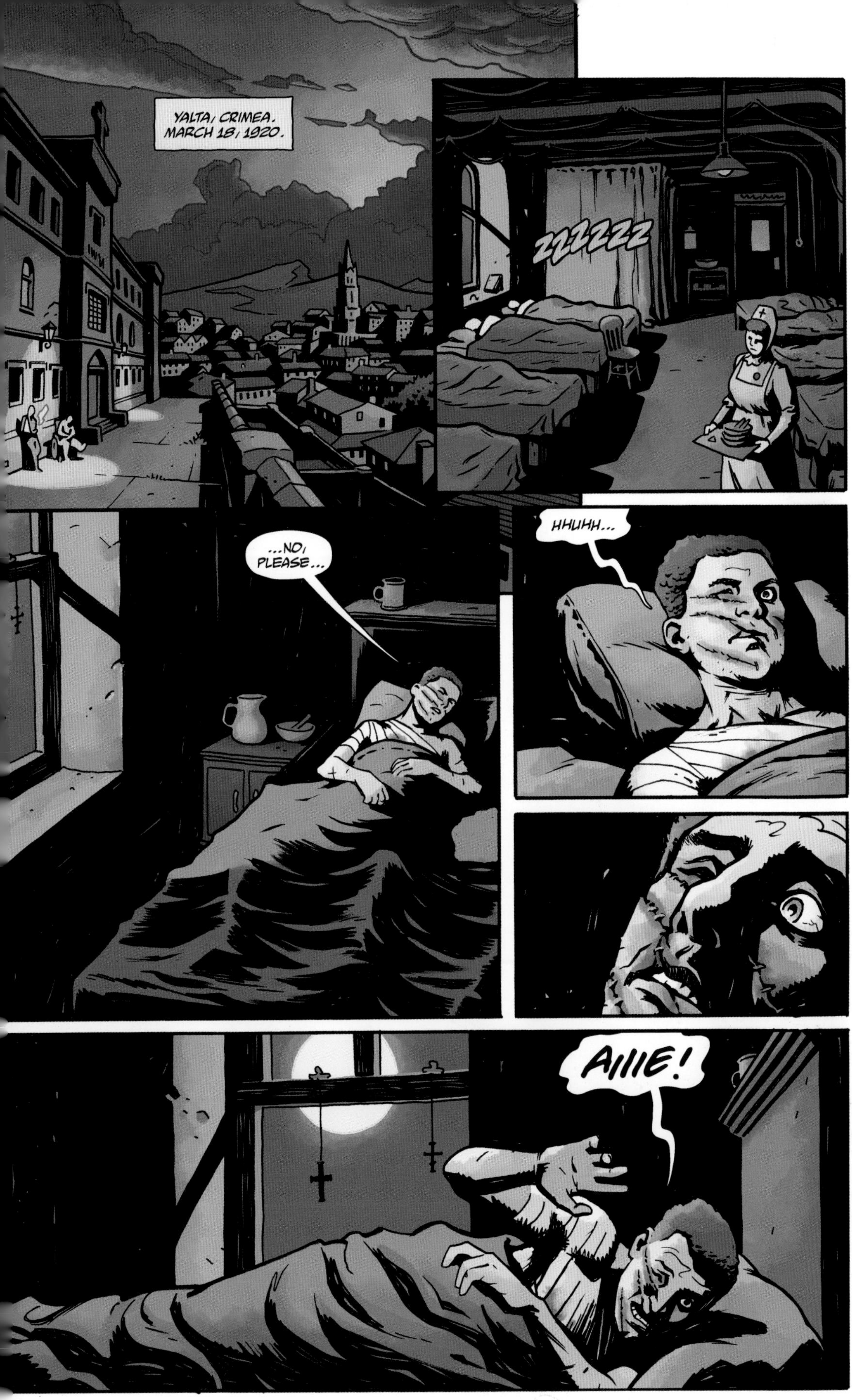
YALTA, CRIMEA. MARCH 18, 1920.
ZZZZZZ
...NO, PLEASE...
HHUHH...
AIIIE!

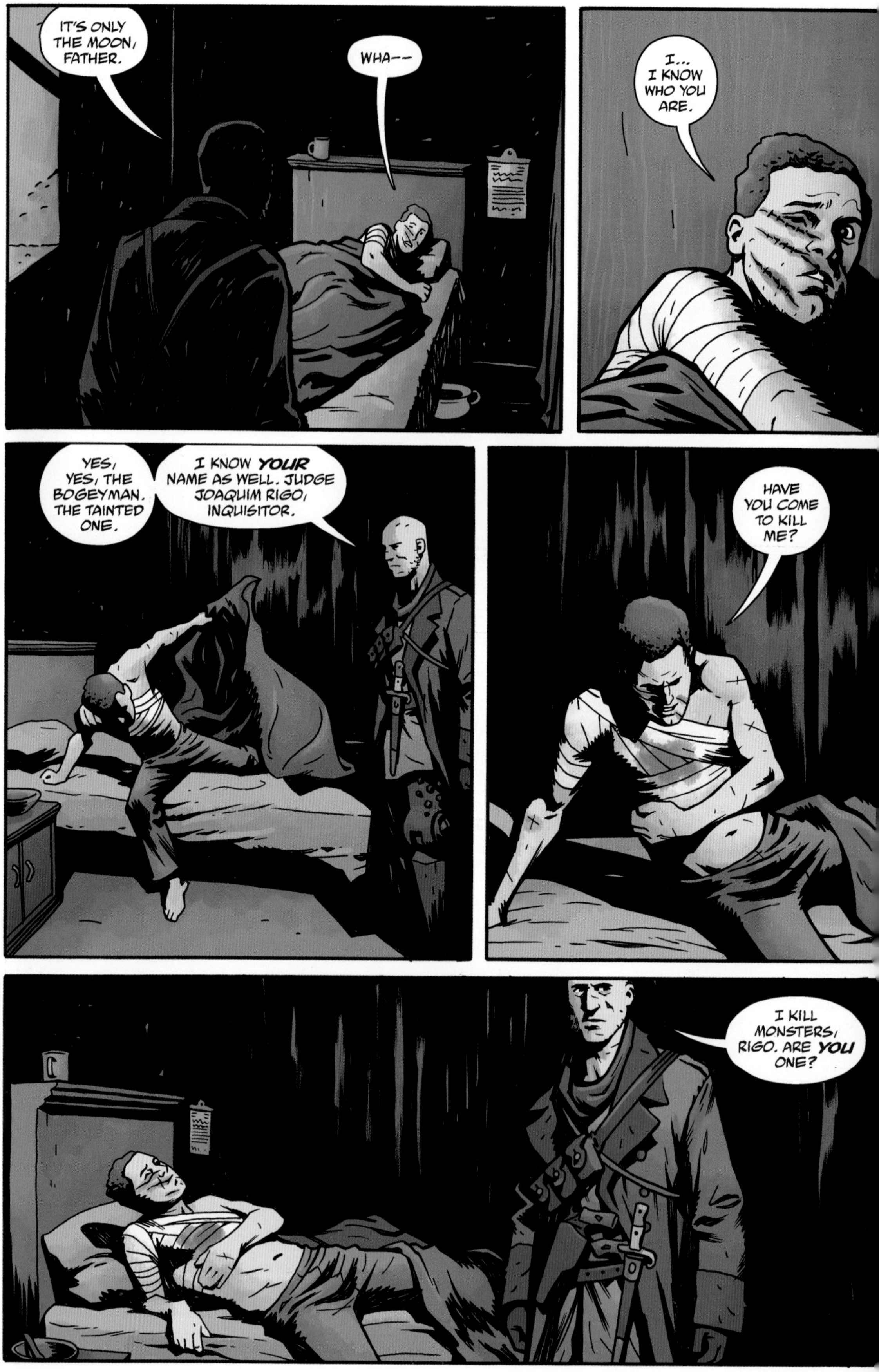

IT'S ONLY THE MOON, FATHER.
WHA--
I... I KNOW WHO YOU ARE.
YES, YES, THE BOGEYMAN. THE TAINTED ONE.
I KNOW YOUR NAME AS WELL. JUDGE JOAQUIM RIGO, INQUISITOR.
HAVE YOU COME TO KILL ME?
I KILL MONSTERS, RIGO. ARE YOU ONE?

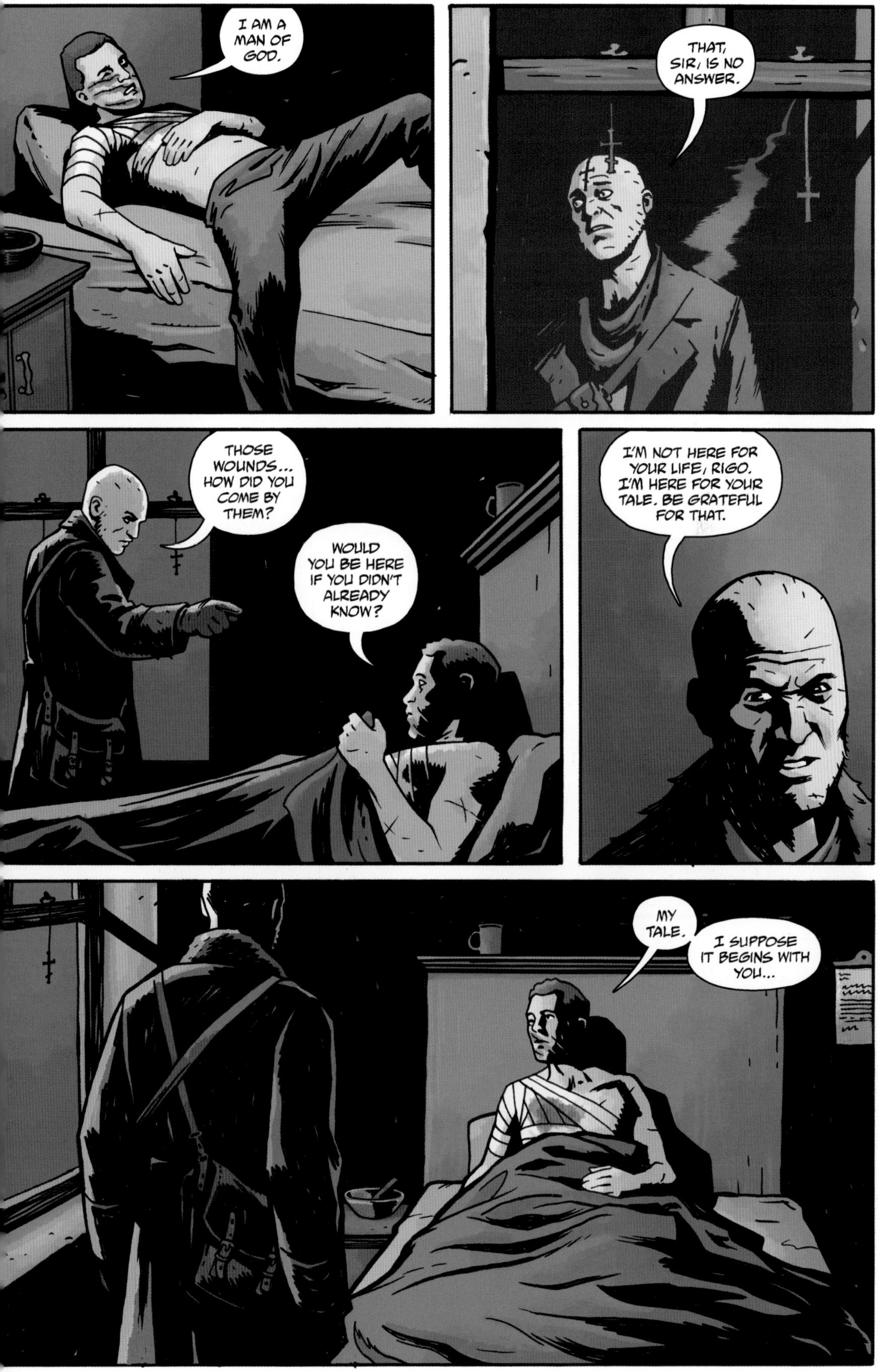
I AM A MAN OF GOD.
THAT, SIR, IS NO ANSWER.
THOSE WOUNDS... HOW DID YOU COME BY THEM?
WOULD YOU BE HERE IF YOU DIDN'T ALREADY KNOW?
I'M NOT HERE FOR YOUR LIFE, RIGO. I'M HERE FOR YOUR TALE. BE GRATEFUL FOR THAT.
MY TALE.
I SUPPOSE IT BEGINS WITH YOU...

"...AND THE TRAIN THAT DERAILED OUTSIDE BUDAPEST.

"THE INQUISITION'S INVESTIGATION REVEALED THAT BOTH YOU AND JUDGE DUVIC BOARDED THE TRAIN...

"YOU WERE THE ONLY SURVIVOR OF THE CRASH, BUT THERE WERE VERY FEW BODIES, SINCE MOST ONBOARD WERE NOT HUMAN TO BEGIN WITH.

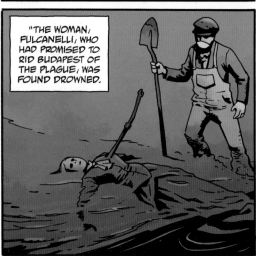

"THE WOMAN, FULCANELLI, WHO HAD PROMISED TO RID BUDAPEST OF THE PLAGUE, WAS FOUND DROWNED.

"THEY DID FIND ONE MAN STILL ALIVE NOT FAR FROM THE WRECKAGE-- A MONK..."

⟨HERE! THIS ONE IS STILL BREATHING!⟩

⟨TRANSLATED FROM HUNGARIAN

82

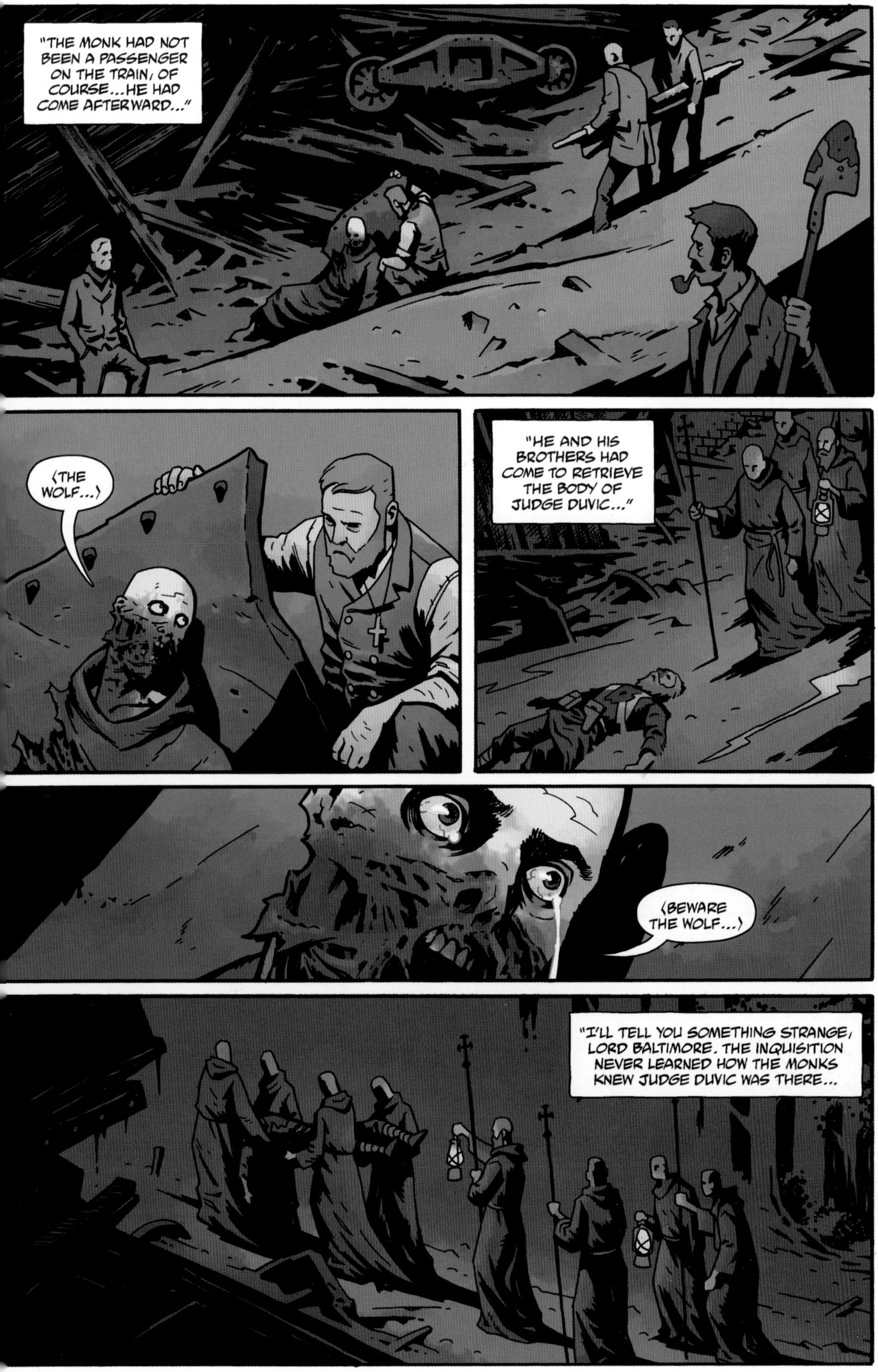
"THE MONK HAD NOT BEEN A PASSENGER ON THE TRAIN, OF COURSE...HE HAD COME AFTERWARD..."
‹THE WOLF...›
"HE AND HIS BROTHERS HAD COME TO RETRIEVE THE BODY OF JUDGE DUVIC..."
‹BEWARE THE WOLF...›
"I'LL TELL YOU SOMETHING STRANGE, LORD BALTIMORE. THE INQUISITION NEVER LEARNED HOW THE MONKS KNEW JUDGE DUVIC WAS THERE...

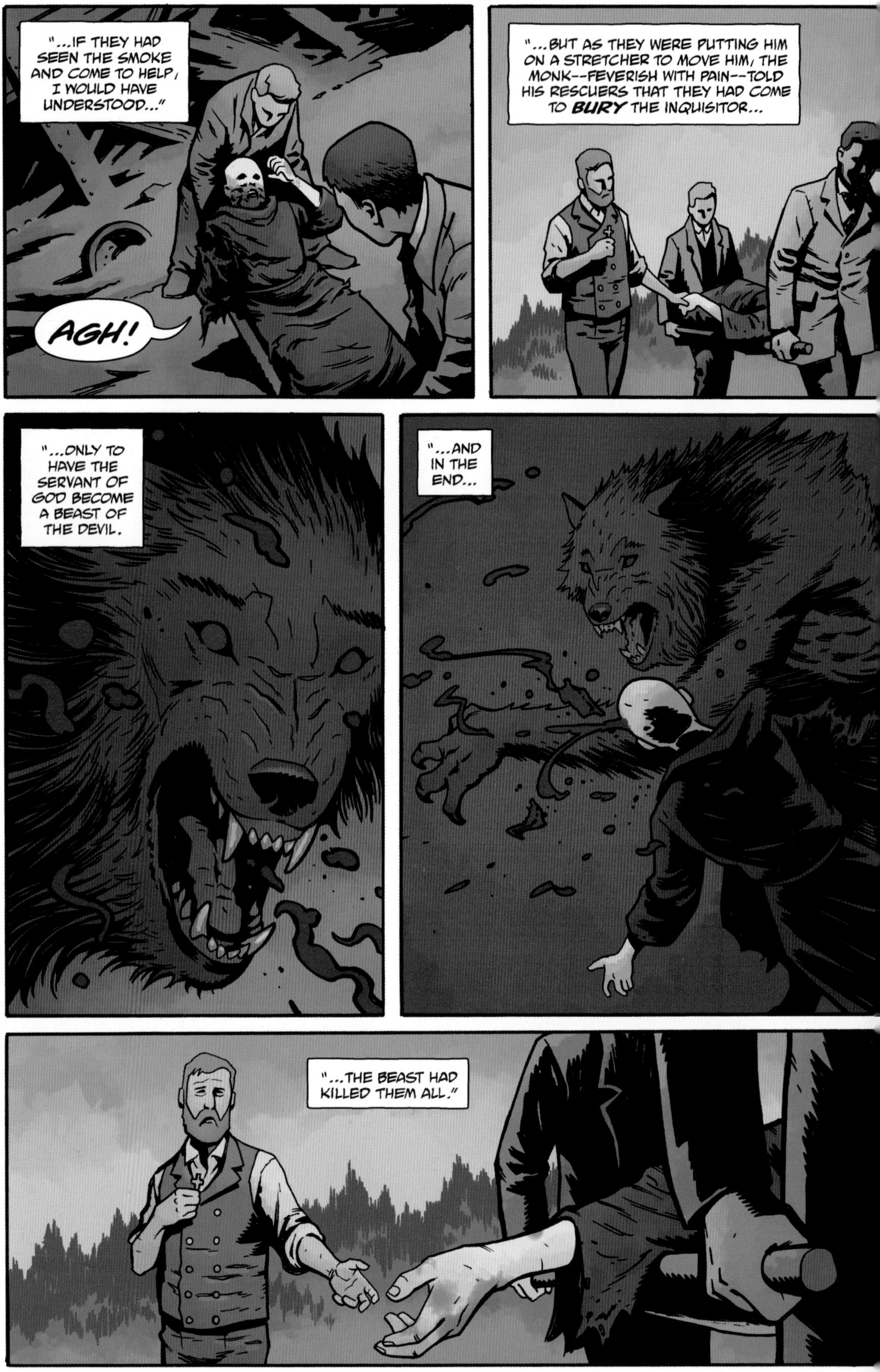
"...IF THEY HAD SEEN THE SMOKE AND COME TO HELP, I WOULD HAVE UNDERSTOOD..."
AGH!
"...BUT AS THEY WERE PUTTING HIM ON A STRETCHER TO MOVE HIM, THE MONK--FEVERISH WITH PAIN--TOLD HIS RESCUERS THAT THEY HAD COME TO BURY THE INQUISITOR...
"...ONLY TO HAVE THE SERVANT OF GOD BECOME A BEAST OF THE DEVIL.
"...AND IN THE END...
"...THE BEAST HAD KILLED THEM ALL."

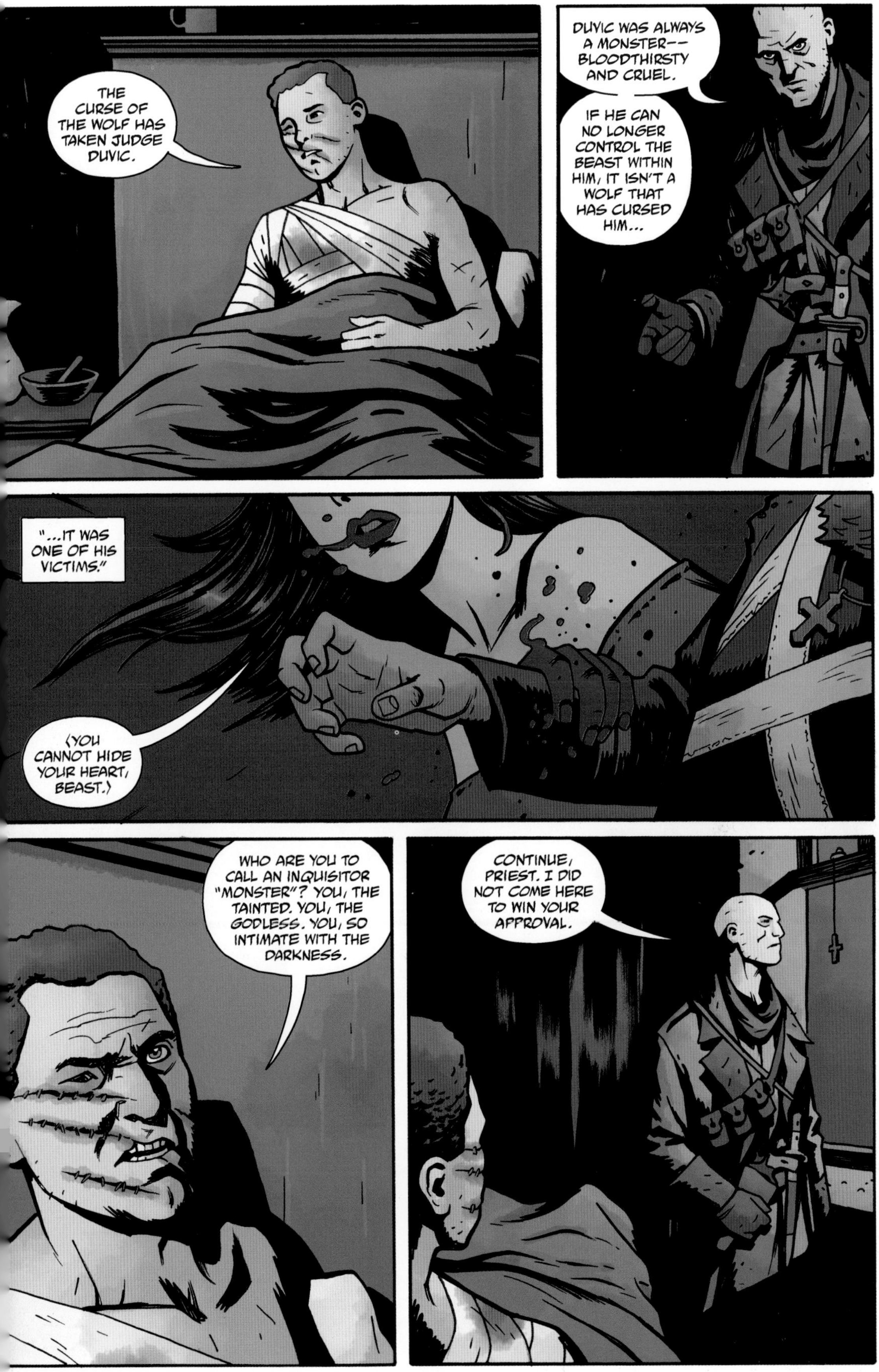

THE CURSE OF THE WOLF HAS TAKEN JUDGE DUVIC.
DUVIC WAS ALWAYS A MONSTER-- BLOODTHIRSTY AND CRUEL.
IF HE CAN NO LONGER CONTROL THE BEAST WITHIN HIM, IT ISN'T A WOLF THAT HAS CURSED HIM...
"...IT WAS ONE OF HIS VICTIMS."
‹YOU CANNOT HIDE YOUR HEART, BEAST.›
WHO ARE YOU TO CALL AN INQUISITOR "MONSTER"? YOU, THE TAINTED. YOU, THE GODLESS. YOU, SO INTIMATE WITH THE DARKNESS.
CONTINUE, PRIEST. I DID NOT COME HERE TO WIN YOUR APPROVAL.

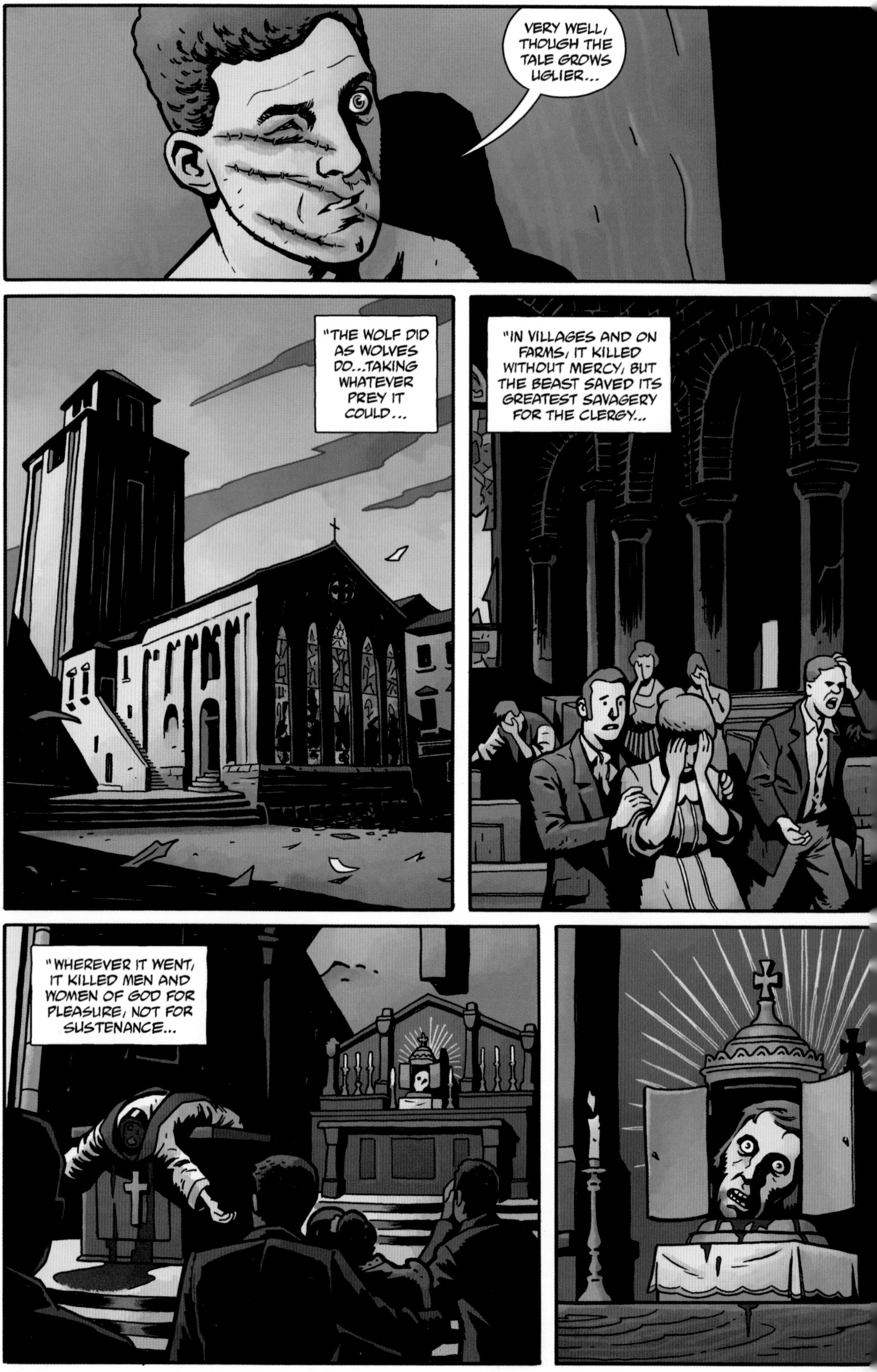
VERY WELL, THOUGH THE TALE GROWS UGLIER...
"THE WOLF DID AS WOLVES DO...TAKING WHATEVER PREY IT COULD...
"IN VILLAGES AND ON FARMS, IT KILLED WITHOUT MERCY, BUT THE BEAST SAVED ITS GREATEST SAVAGERY FOR THE CLERGY...
"WHEREVER IT WENT, IT KILLED MEN AND WOMEN OF GOD FOR PLEASURE, NOT FOR SUSTENANCE...

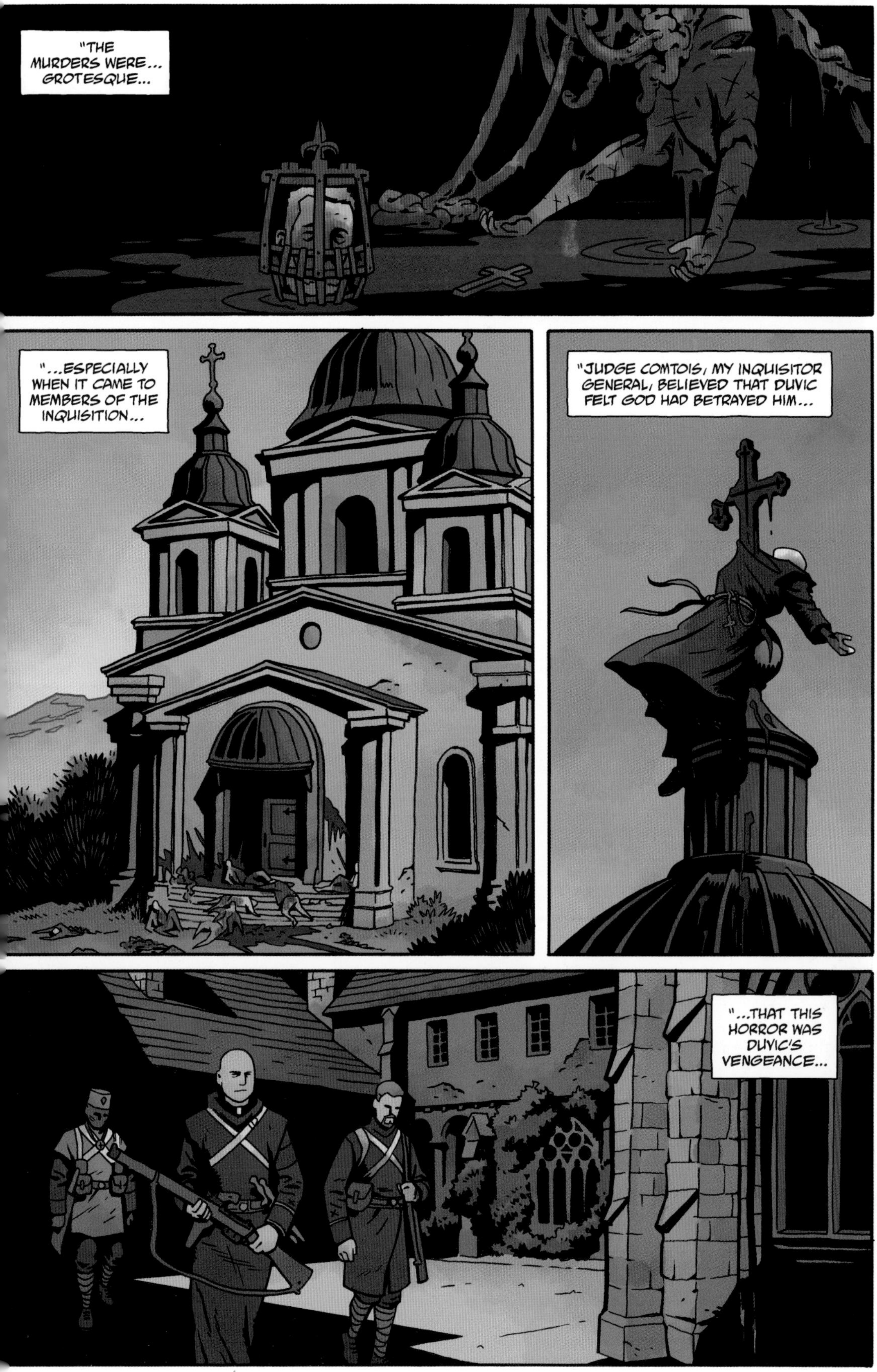
"THE MURDERS WERE... GROTESQUE...
"...ESPECIALLY WHEN IT CAME TO MEMBERS OF THE INQUISITION...
"JUDGE COMTOIS, MY INQUISITOR GENERAL, BELIEVED THAT DUVIC FELT GOD HAD BETRAYED HIM...
"...THAT THIS HORROR WAS DUVIC'S VENGEANCE...

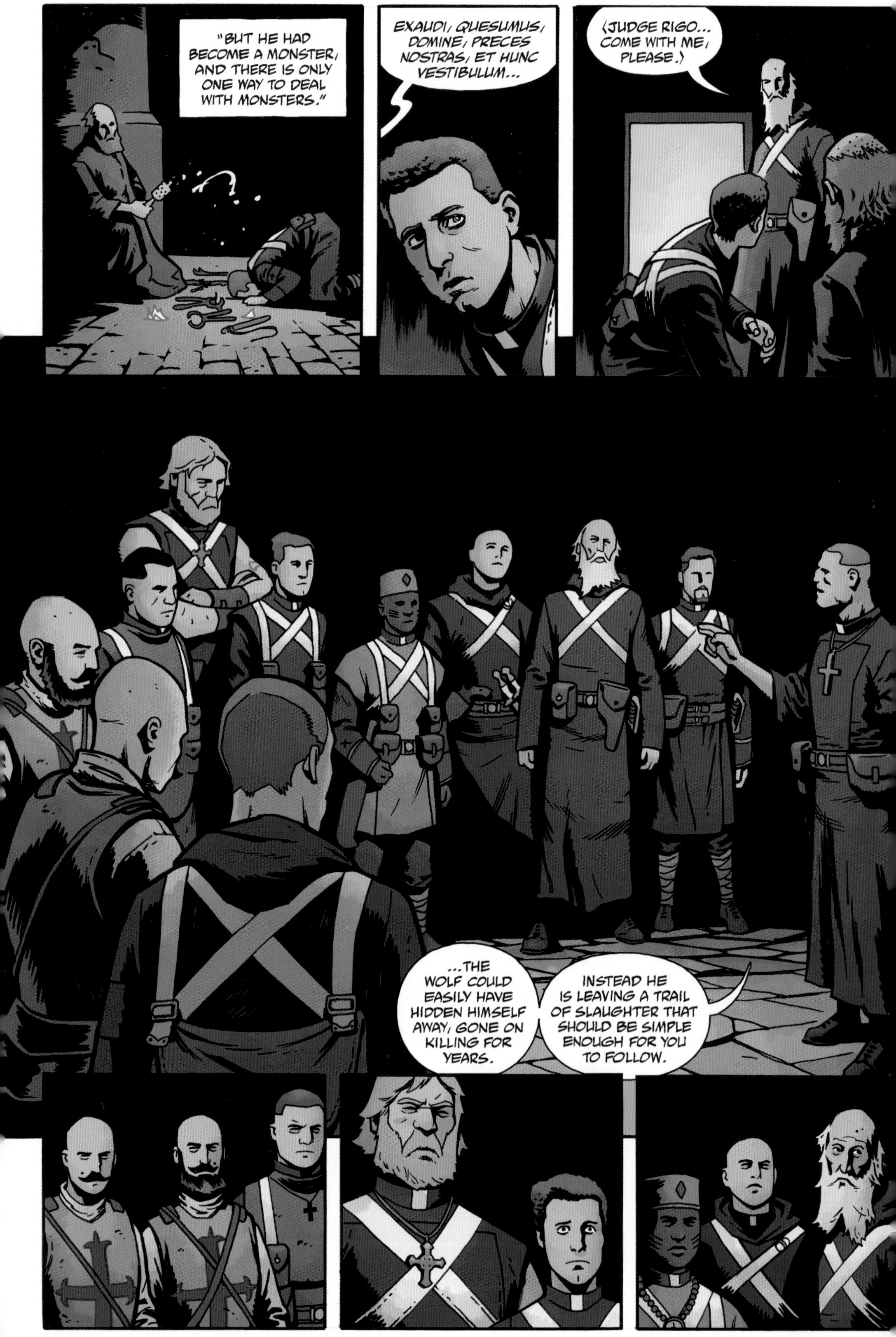
"BUT HE HAD BECOME A MONSTER, AND THERE IS ONLY ONE WAY TO DEAL WITH MONSTERS."
EXAUDI, QUESUMUS, DOMINE, PRECES NOSTRAS, ET HUNC VESTIBULUM...
(JUDGE RIGO... COME WITH ME, PLEASE.)
...THE WOLF COULD EASILY HAVE HIDDEN HIMSELF AWAY, GONE ON KILLING FOR YEARS.
INSTEAD HE IS LEAVING A TRAIL OF SLAUGHTER THAT SHOULD BE SIMPLE ENOUGH FOR YOU TO FOLLOW.

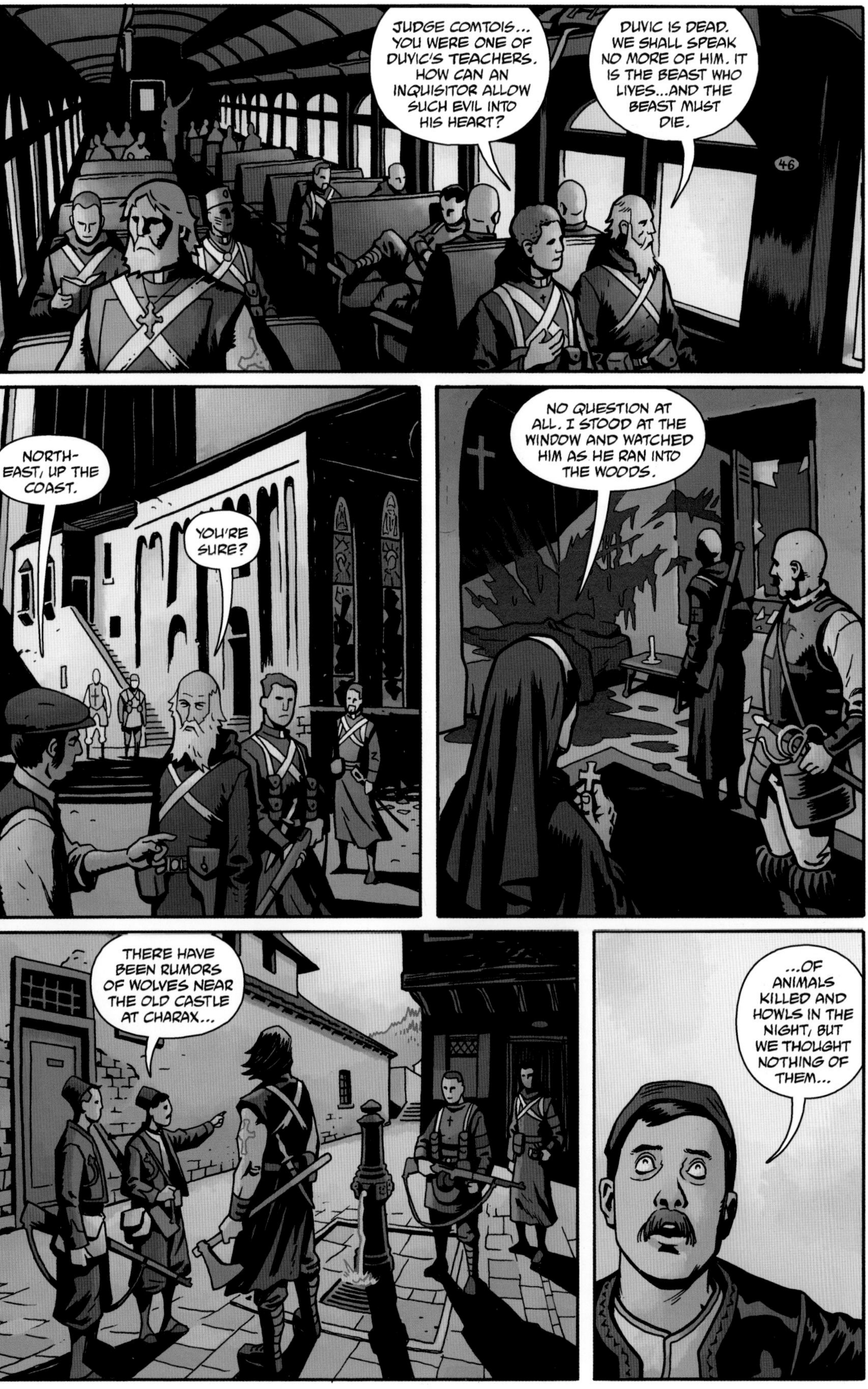
JUDGE COMTOIS... YOU WERE ONE OF DUVIC'S TEACHERS. HOW CAN AN INQUISITOR ALLOW SUCH EVIL INTO HIS HEART?
DUVIC IS DEAD. WE SHALL SPEAK NO MORE OF HIM. IT IS THE BEAST WHO LIVES...AND THE BEAST MUST DIE.
46
NORTH-EAST, UP THE COAST.
YOU'RE SURE?
NO QUESTION AT ALL. I STOOD AT THE WINDOW AND WATCHED HIM AS HE RAN INTO THE WOODS.
THERE HAVE BEEN RUMORS OF WOLVES NEAR THE OLD CASTLE AT CHARAX...
...OF ANIMALS KILLED AND HOWLS IN THE NIGHT, BUT WE THOUGHT NOTHING OF THEM...

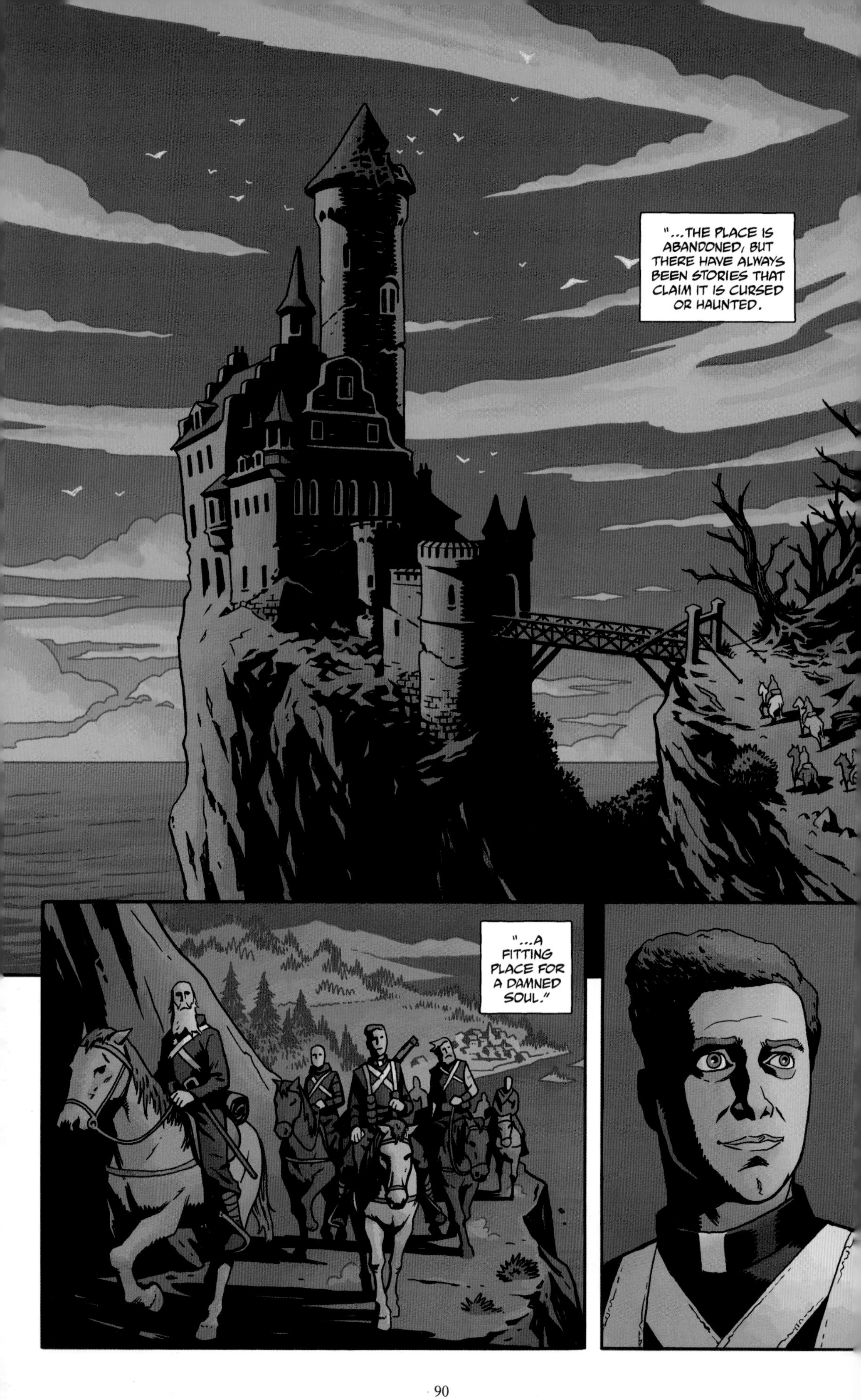
"...THE PLACE IS ABANDONED, BUT THERE HAVE ALWAYS BEEN STORIES THAT CLAIM IT IS CURSED OR HAUNTED.
"...A FITTING PLACE FOR A DAMNED SOUL."

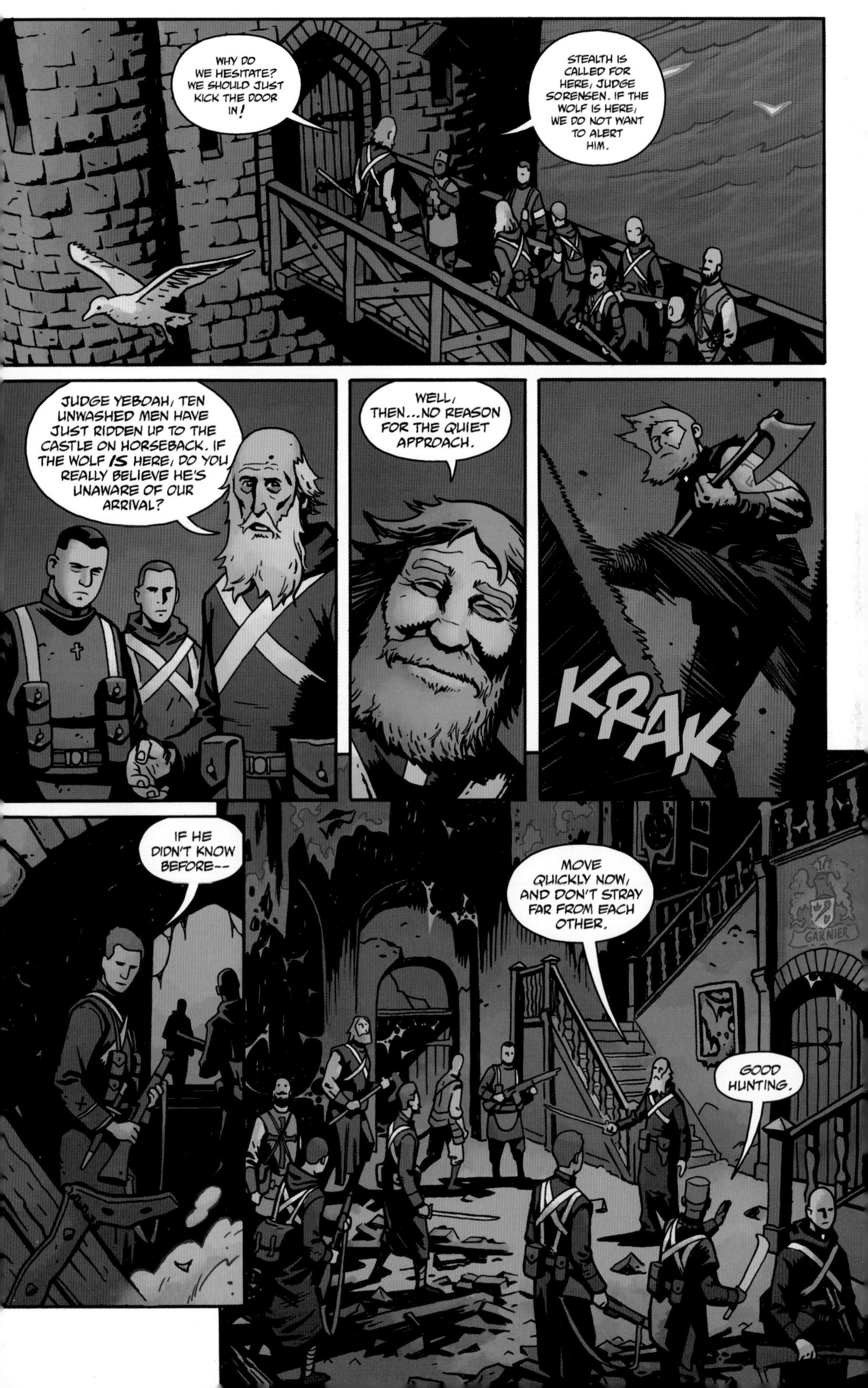
WHY DO WE HESITATE? WE SHOULD JUST KICK THE DOOR IN!
STEALTH IS CALLED FOR HERE, JUDGE SORENSEN. IF THE WOLF IS HERE, WE DO NOT WANT TO ALERT HIM.
JUDGE YEBOAH, TEN UNWASHED MEN HAVE JUST RIDDEN UP TO THE CASTLE ON HORSEBACK. IF THE WOLF *IS* HERE, DO YOU REALLY BELIEVE HE'S UNAWARE OF OUR ARRIVAL?
WELL, THEN...NO REASON FOR THE QUIET APPROACH.
KRAK
IF HE DIDN'T KNOW BEFORE--
MOVE QUICKLY NOW, AND DON'T STRAY FAR FROM EACH OTHER.
GARNIER
GOOD HUNTING.

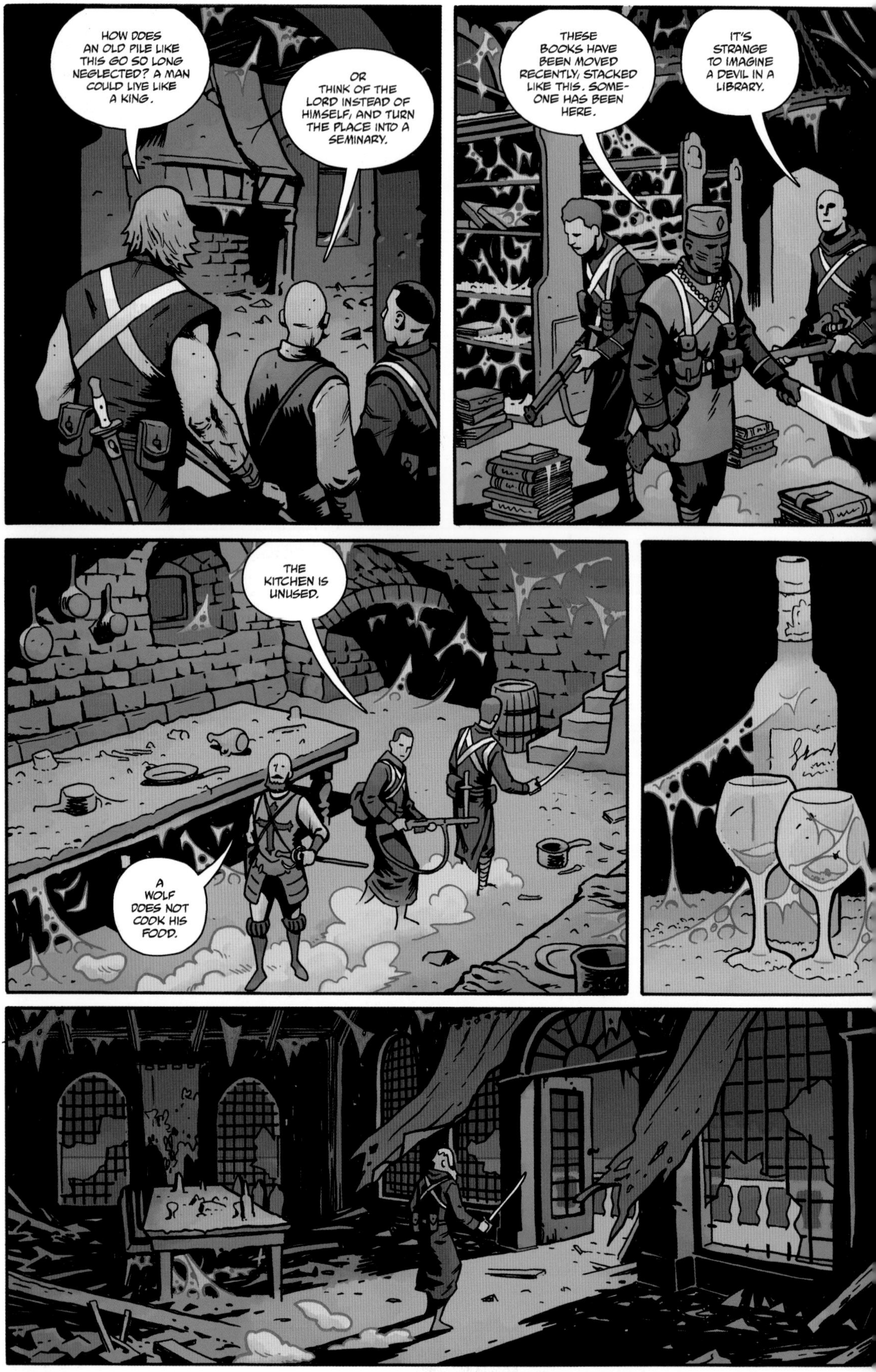
HOW DOES AN OLD PILE LIKE THIS GO SO LONG NEGLECTED? A MAN COULD LIVE LIKE A KING.
OR THINK OF THE LORD INSTEAD OF HIMSELF, AND TURN THE PLACE INTO A SEMINARY.
THESE BOOKS HAVE BEEN MOVED RECENTLY, STACKED LIKE THIS. SOME-ONE HAS BEEN HERE.
IT'S STRANGE TO IMAGINE A DEVIL IN A LIBRARY.
THE KITCHEN IS UNUSED.
A WOLF DOES NOT COOK HIS FOOD.

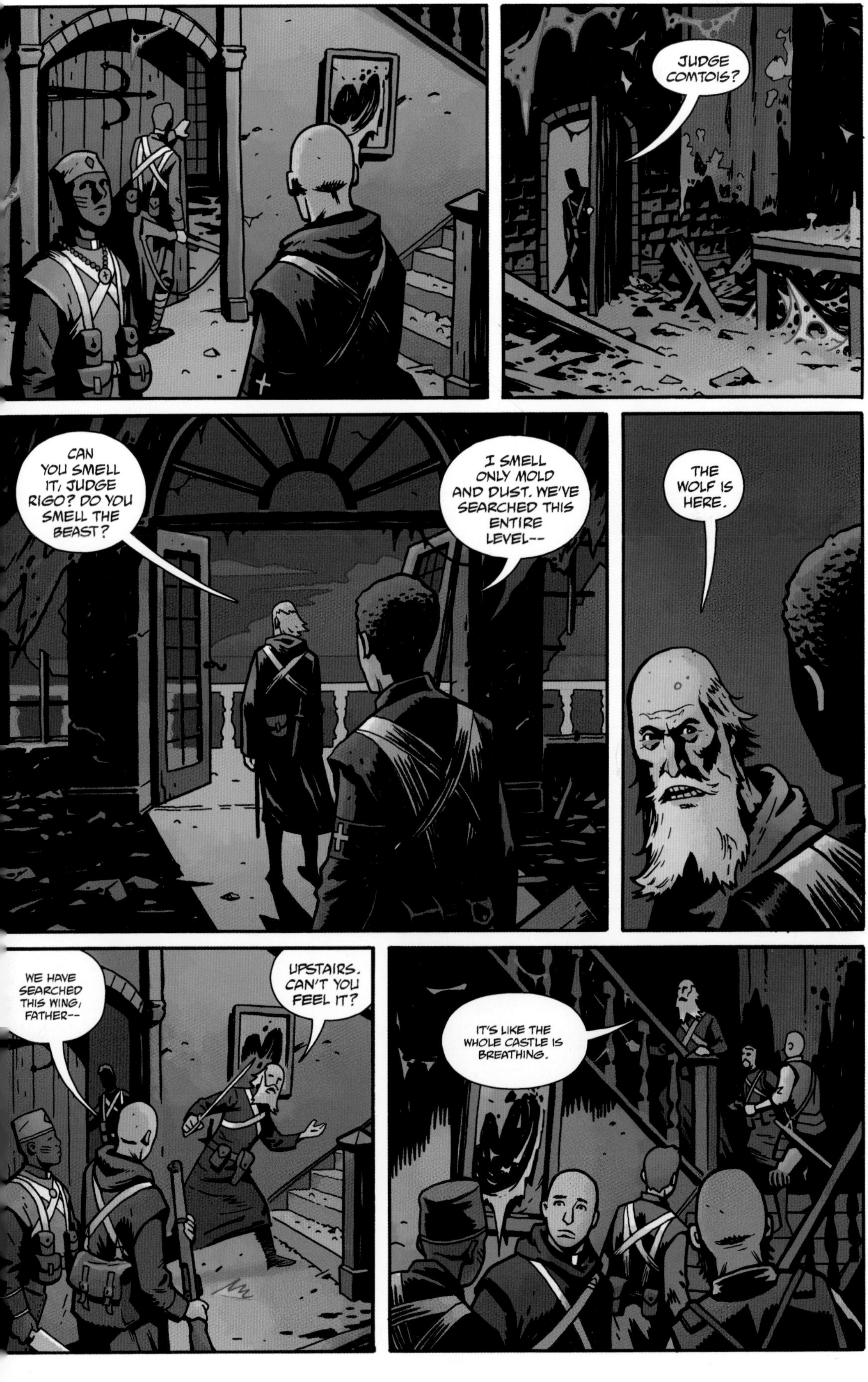
JUDGE COMTOIS?
CAN YOU SMELL IT, JUDGE RIGO? DO YOU SMELL THE BEAST?
I SMELL ONLY MOLD AND DUST. WE'VE SEARCHED THIS ENTIRE LEVEL--
THE WOLF IS HERE.
WE HAVE SEARCHED THIS WING, FATHER--
UPSTAIRS. CAN'T YOU FEEL IT?
IT'S LIKE THE WHOLE CASTLE IS BREATHING.

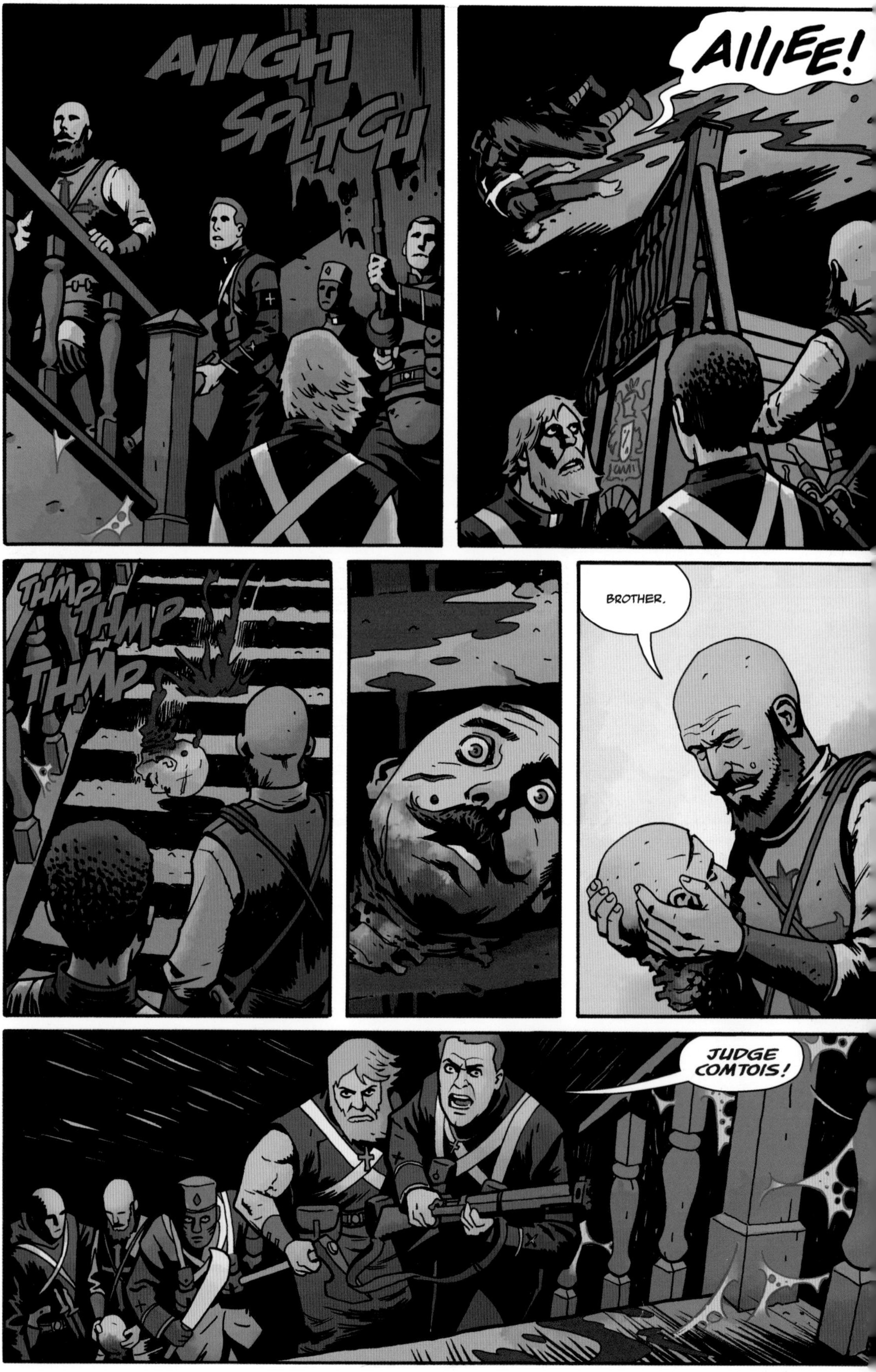
AIIIGH
SPLTCH
AIIIEE!
THMP THMP THMP
BROTHER.
JUDGE COMTOIS!

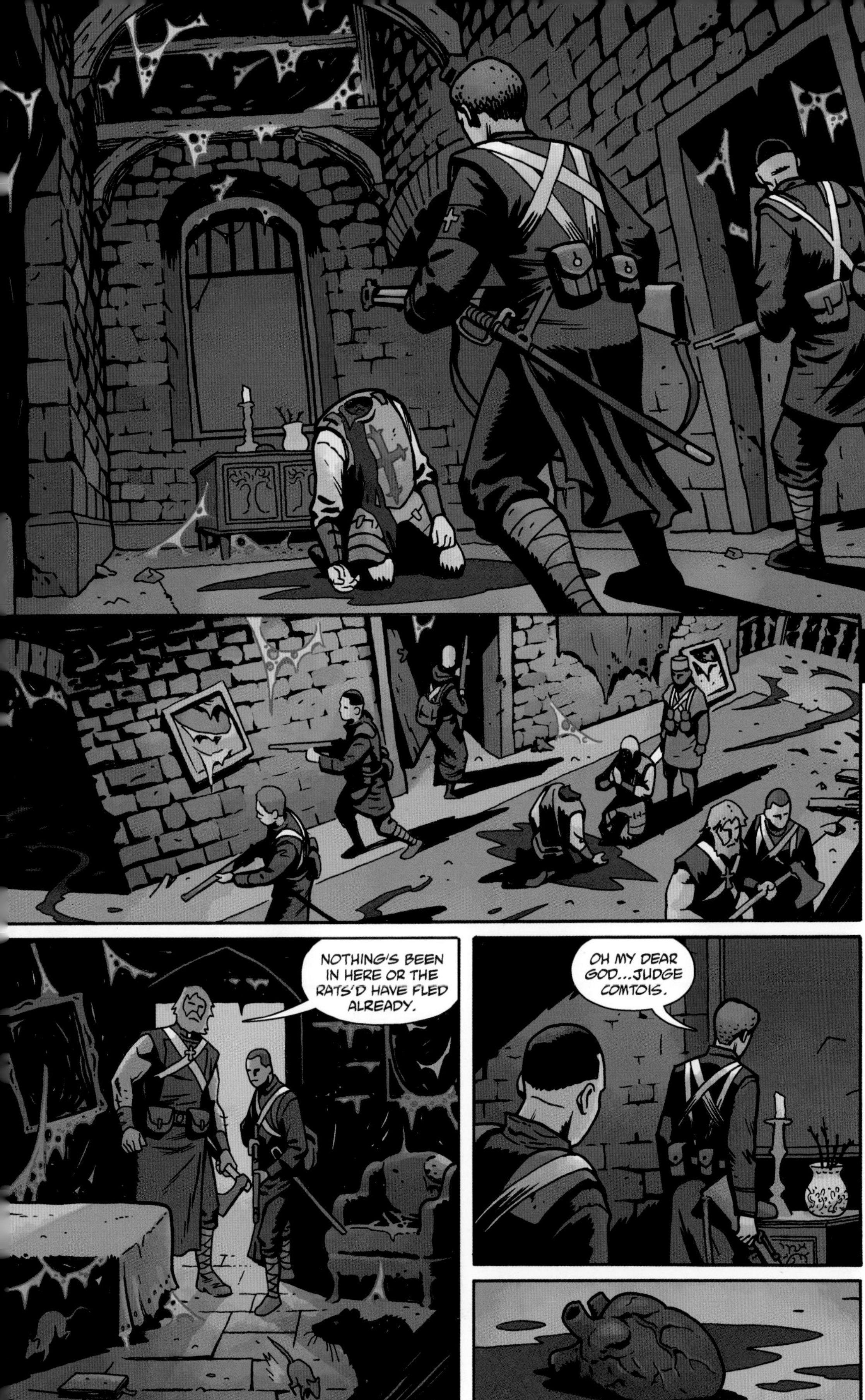
NOTHING'S BEEN IN HERE OR THE RATS'D HAVE FLED ALREADY.
OH MY DEAR GOD...JUDGE COMTOIS.

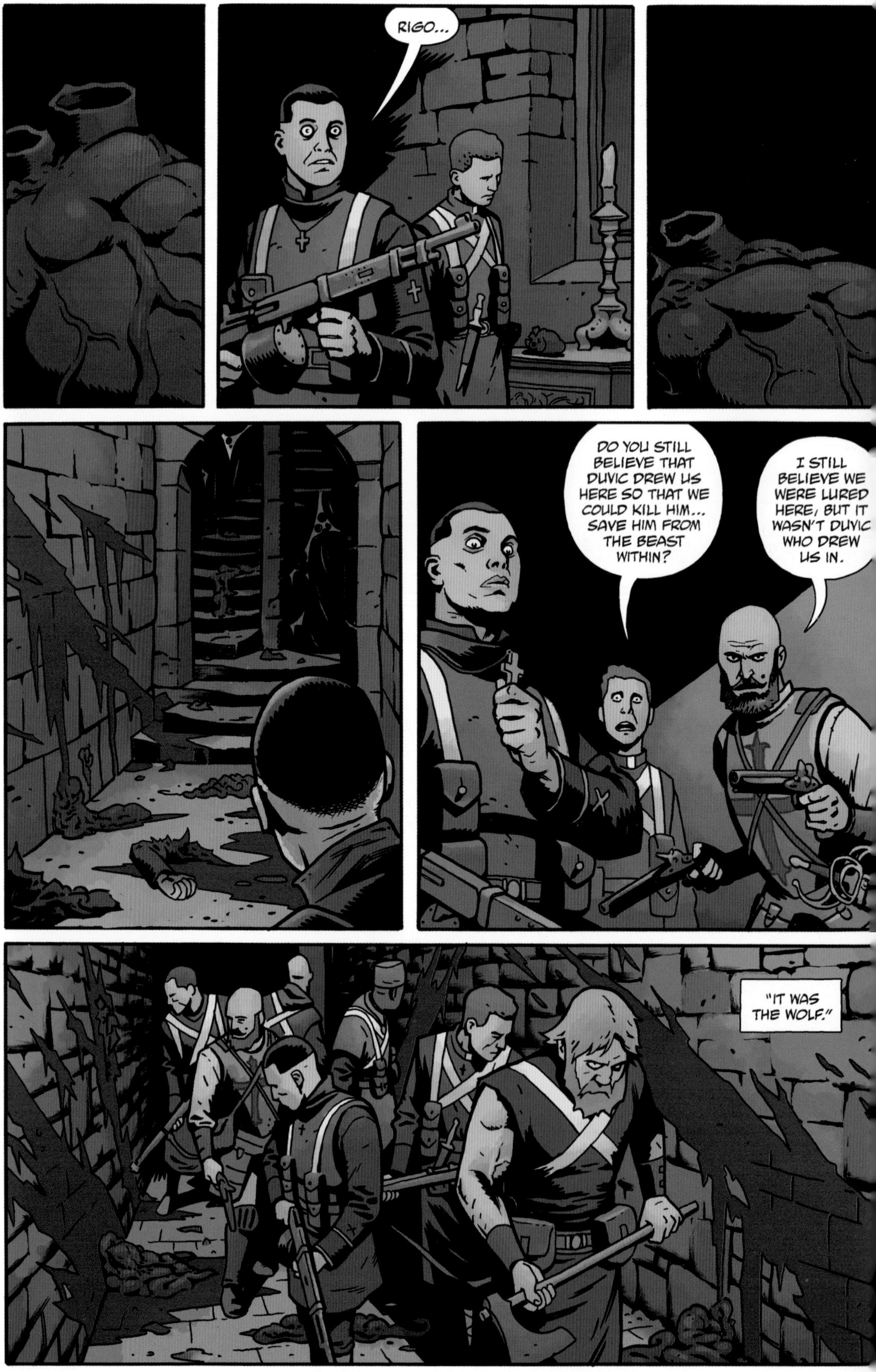
RIGO...
DO YOU STILL BELIEVE THAT DUVIC DREW US HERE SO THAT WE COULD KILL HIM... SAVE HIM FROM THE BEAST WITHIN?
I STILL BELIEVE WE WERE LURED HERE, BUT IT WASN'T DUVIC WHO DREW US IN.
"IT WAS THE WOLF."

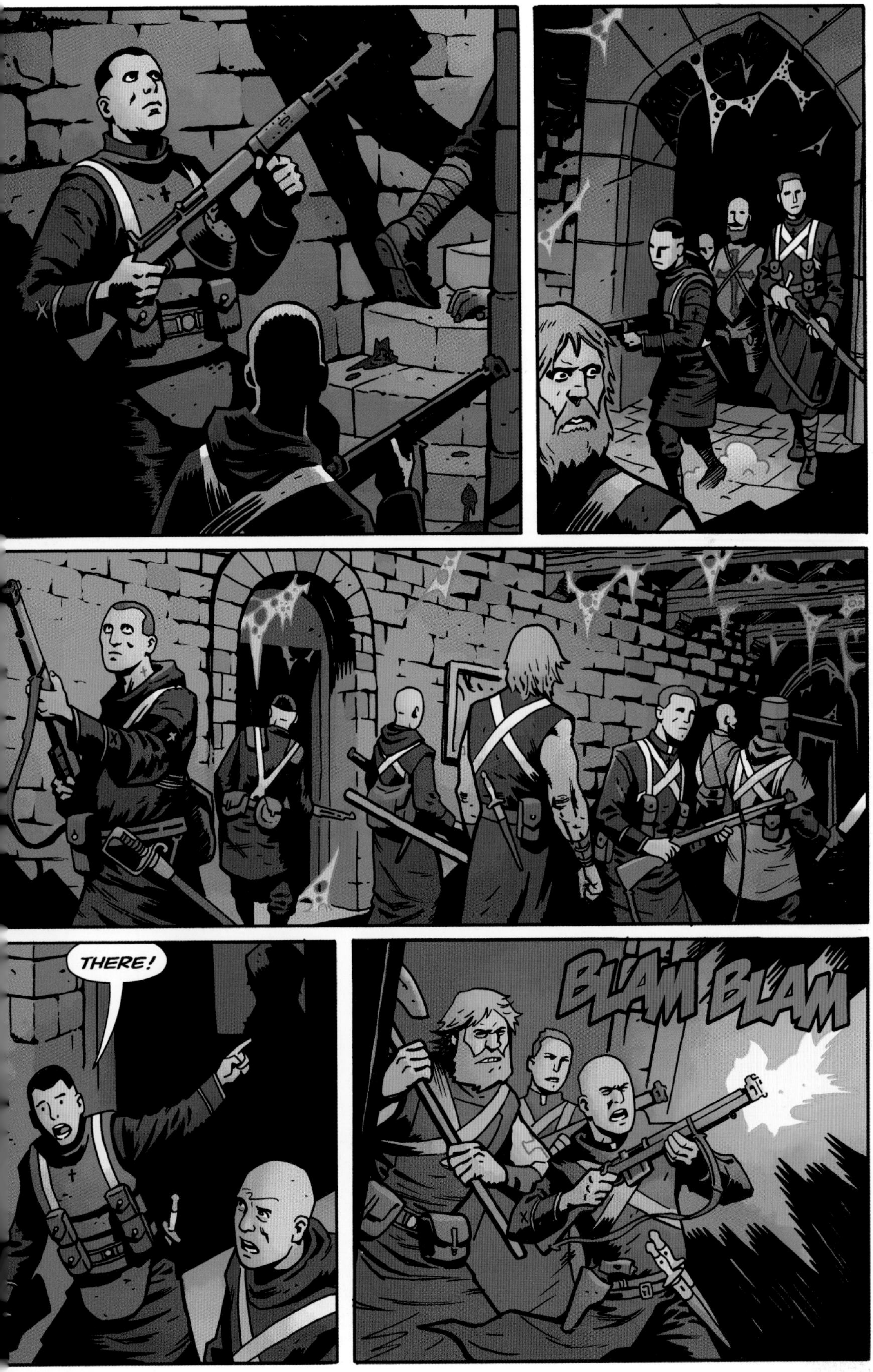
THERE!
BLAM BLAM

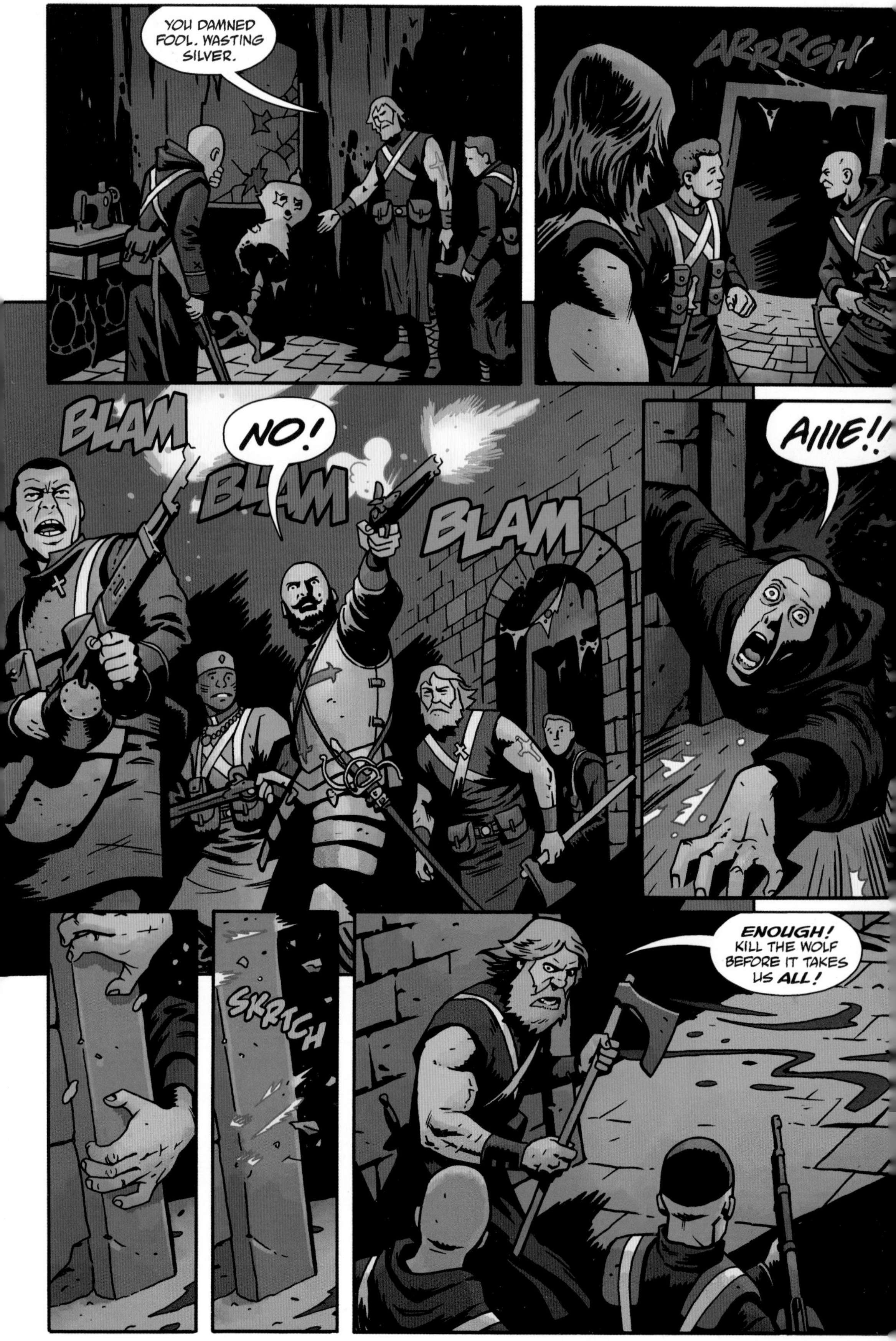

YOU DAMNED FOOL. WASTING SILVER.
ARRRGH
BLAM
NO!
BLAM
BLAM
AIIIE!!
SKRTCH
ENOUGH! KILL THE WOLF BEFORE IT TAKES US ALL!

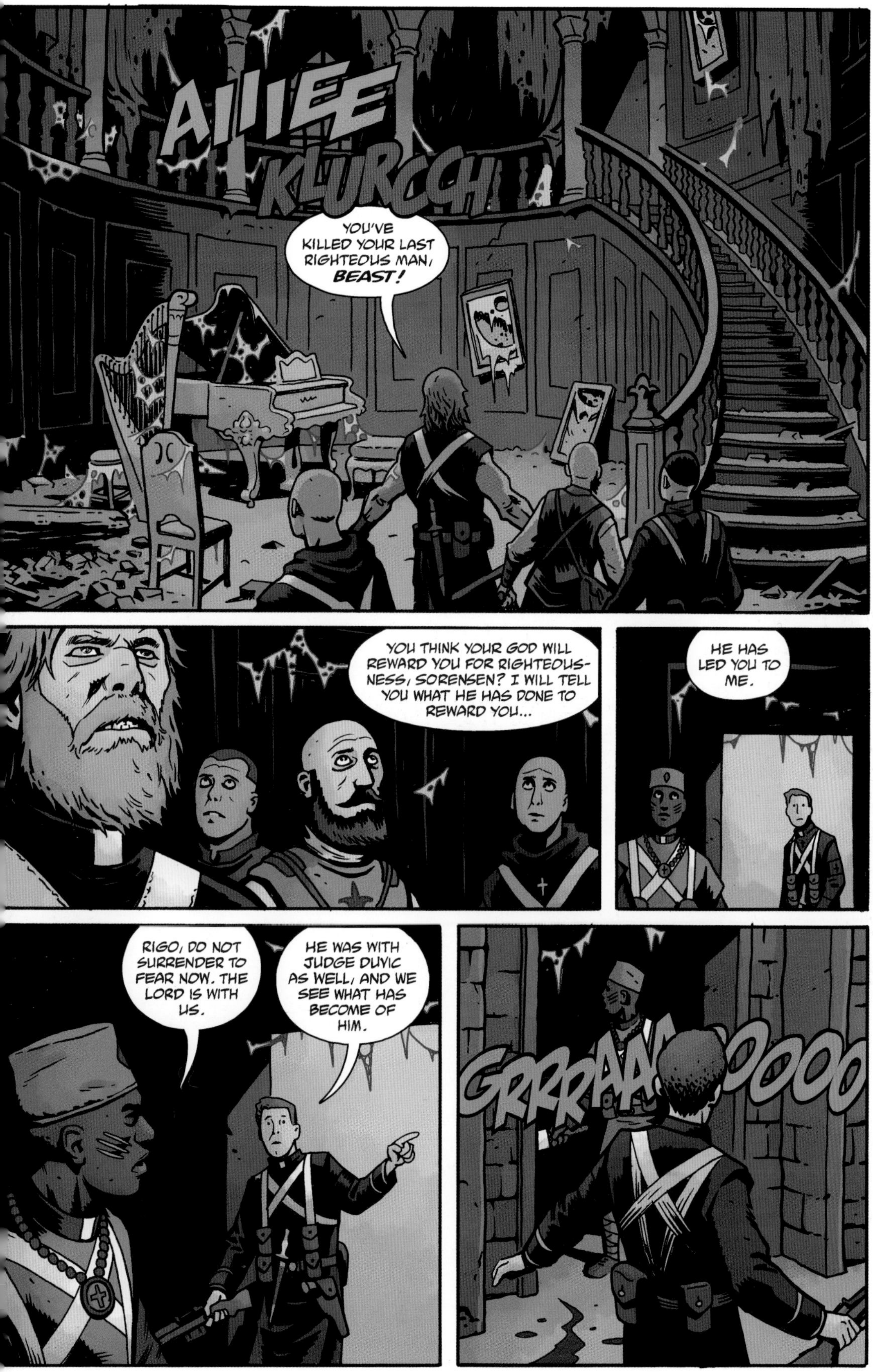
AIIIEE
KLURCCH
YOU'VE KILLED YOUR LAST RIGHTEOUS MAN, BEAST!
YOU THINK YOUR GOD WILL REWARD YOU FOR RIGHTEOUSNESS, SORENSEN? I WILL TELL YOU WHAT HE HAS DONE TO REWARD YOU...
HE HAS LED YOU TO ME.
RIGO, DO NOT SURRENDER TO FEAR NOW. THE LORD IS WITH US.
HE WAS WITH JUDGE DUVIC AS WELL, AND WE SEE WHAT HAS BECOME OF HIM.
GRRRAAAOOOOO

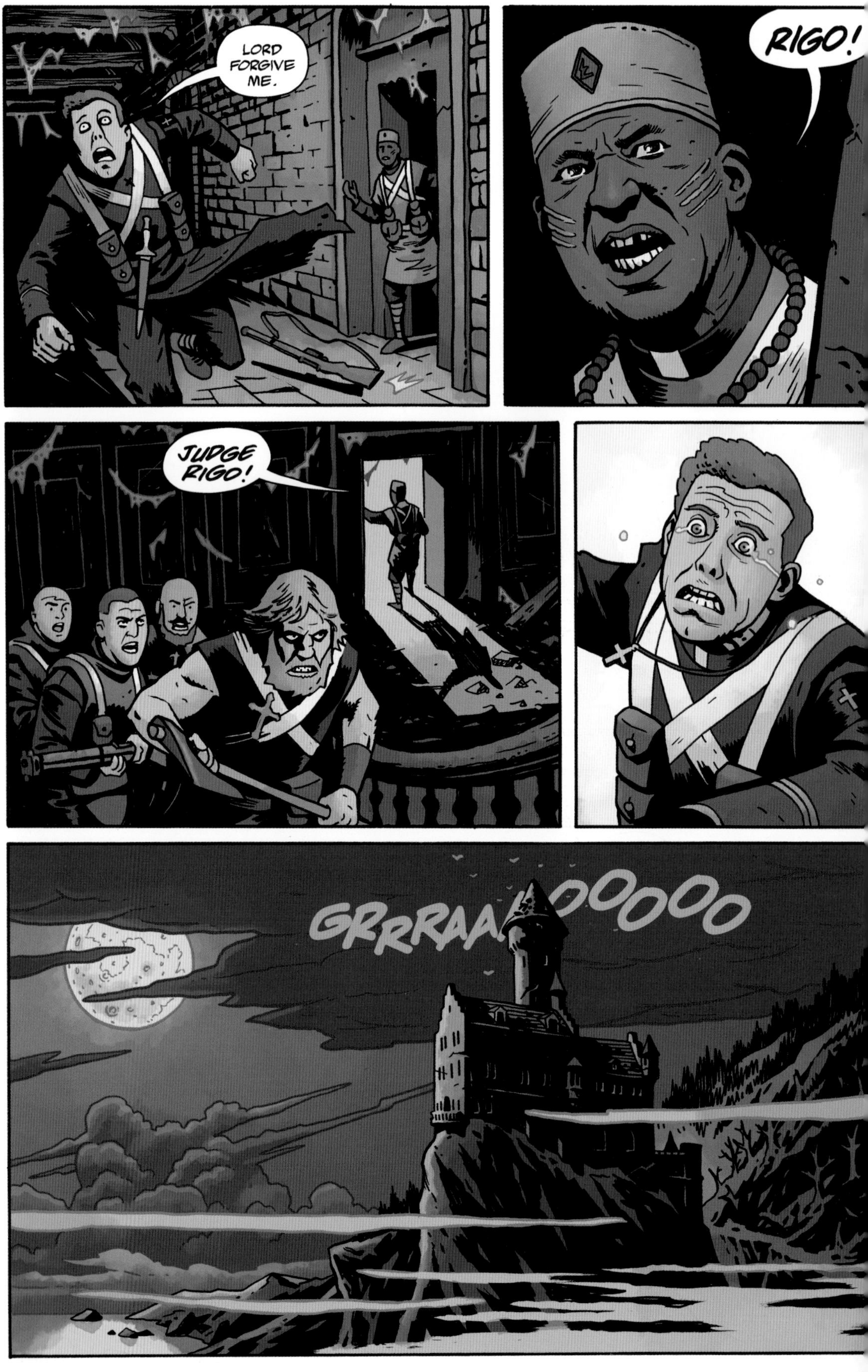
LORD FORGIVE ME.
RIGO!
JUDGE RIGO!
GRRRAAOOOOOO

# THE WOLF AND THE APOSTLE
## *Chapter Two*

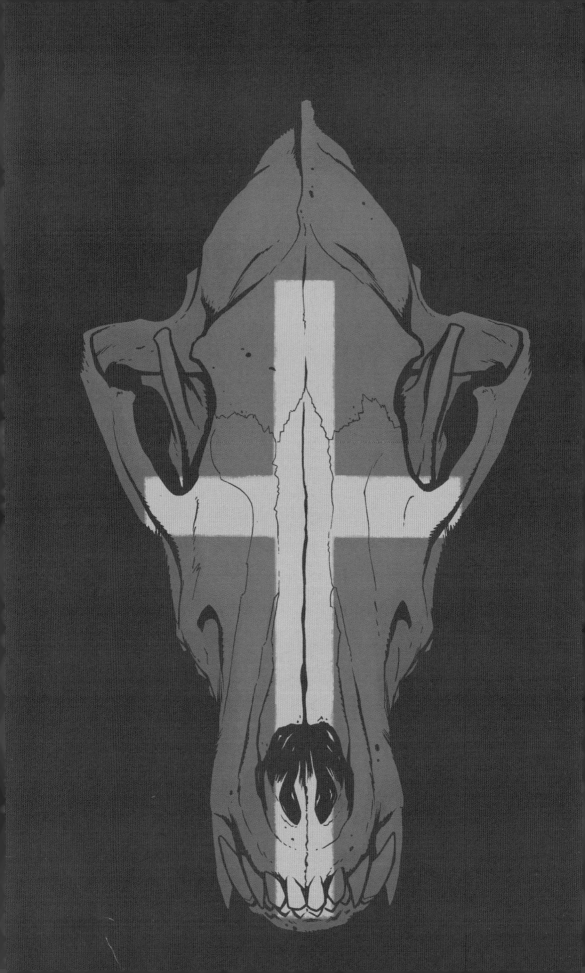

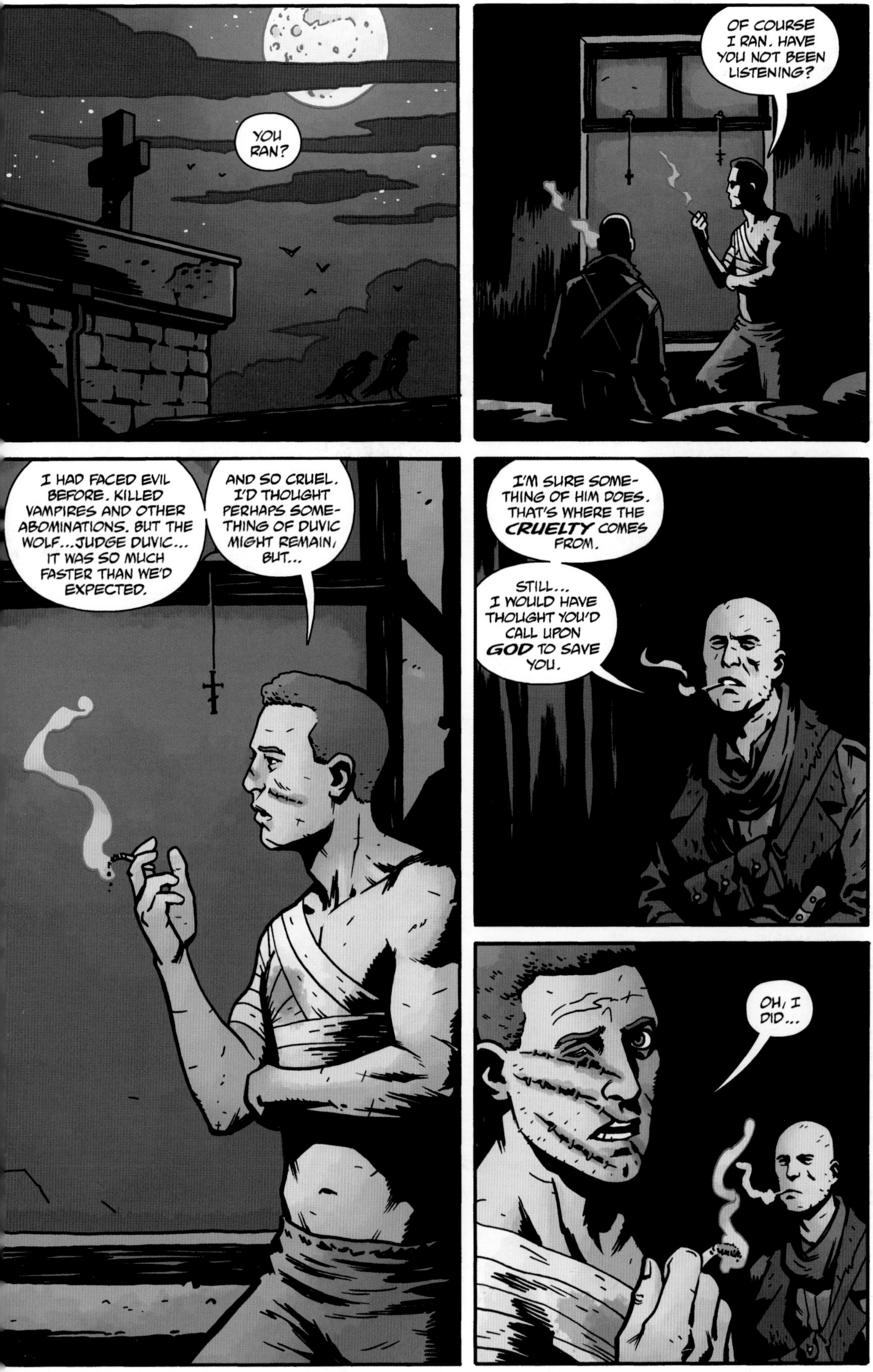
YOU RAN?
OF COURSE I RAN. HAVE YOU NOT BEEN LISTENING?
I HAD FACED EVIL BEFORE. KILLED VAMPIRES AND OTHER ABOMINATIONS. BUT THE WOLF...JUDGE DUVIC... IT WAS SO MUCH FASTER THAN WE'D EXPECTED.
AND SO CRUEL. I'D THOUGHT PERHAPS SOMETHING OF DUVIC MIGHT REMAIN, BUT...
I'M SURE SOMETHING OF HIM DOES. THAT'S WHERE THE CRUELTY COMES FROM.
STILL... I WOULD HAVE THOUGHT YOU'D CALL UPON GOD TO SAVE YOU.
OH, I DID...

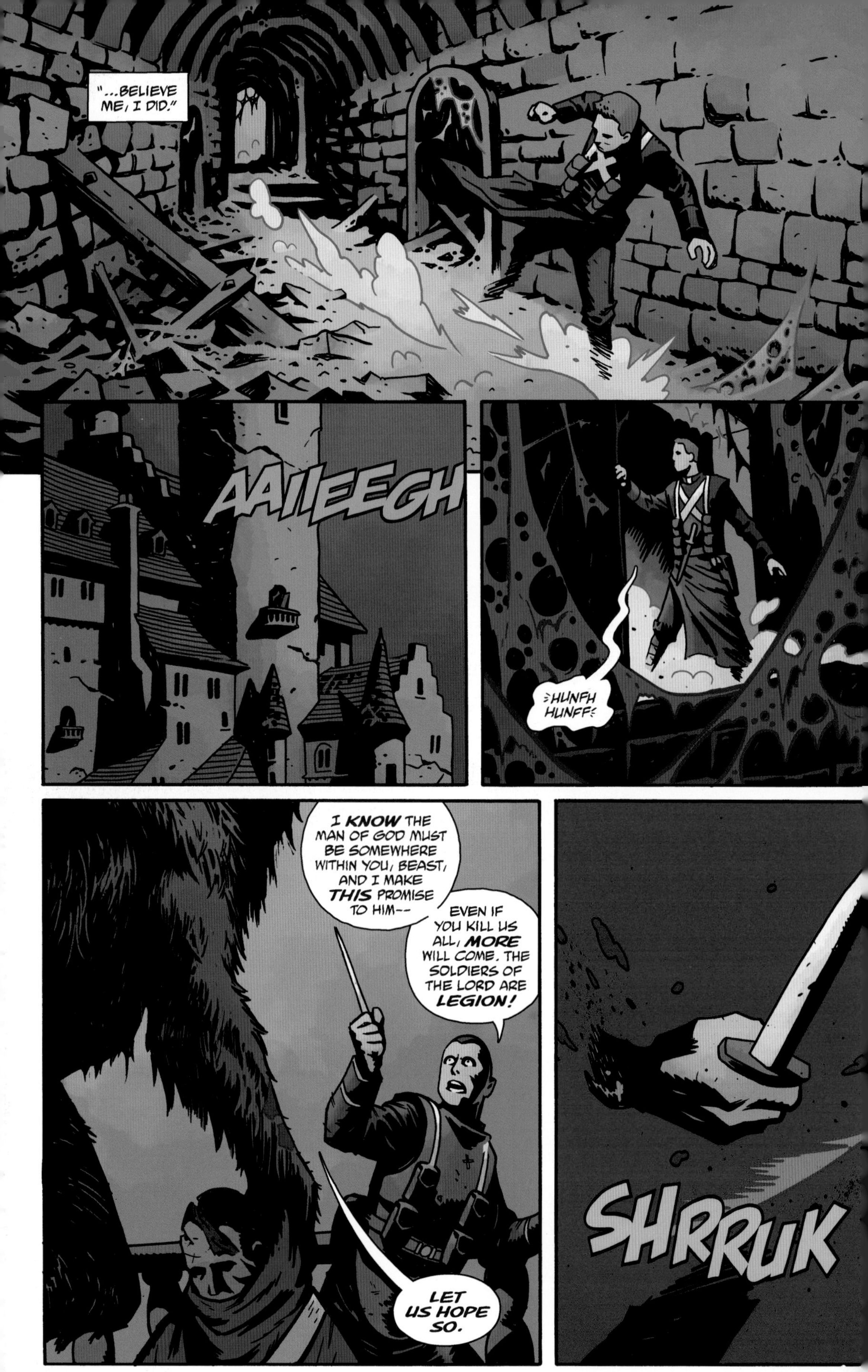
"...BELIEVE ME, I DID."
AAIIEEGH
=HUNFH HUNFF=
I KNOW THE MAN OF GOD MUST BE SOMEWHERE WITHIN YOU, BEAST, AND I MAKE THIS PROMISE TO HIM--
EVEN IF YOU KILL US ALL, MORE WILL COME. THE SOLDIERS OF THE LORD ARE LEGION!
LET US HOPE SO.
SHRRUK

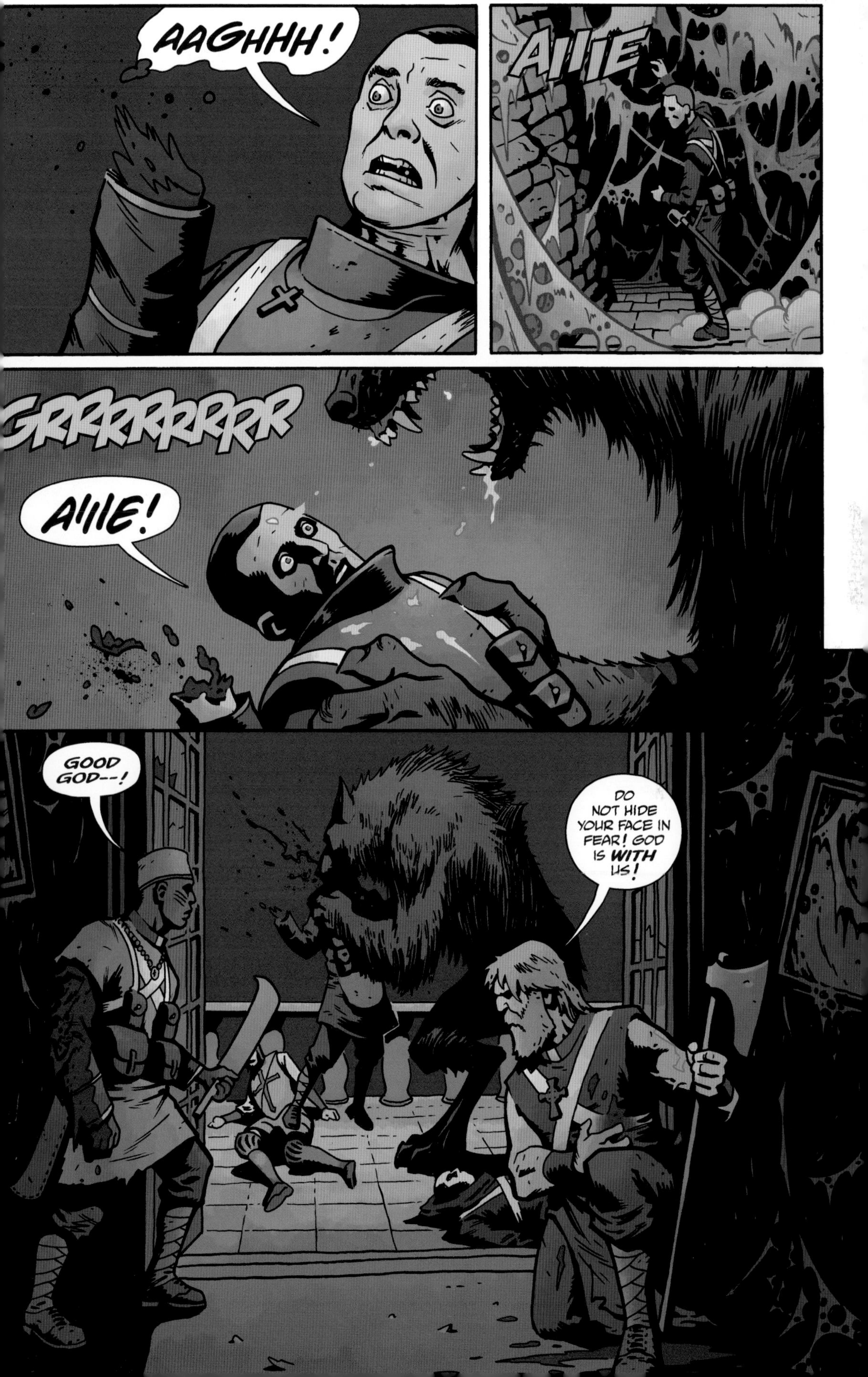
AAGHHH!
AIIIE
GRRRRRRRRR
AIIIE!
GOOD GOD--!
DO NOT HIDE YOUR FACE IN FEAR! GOD IS WITH US!

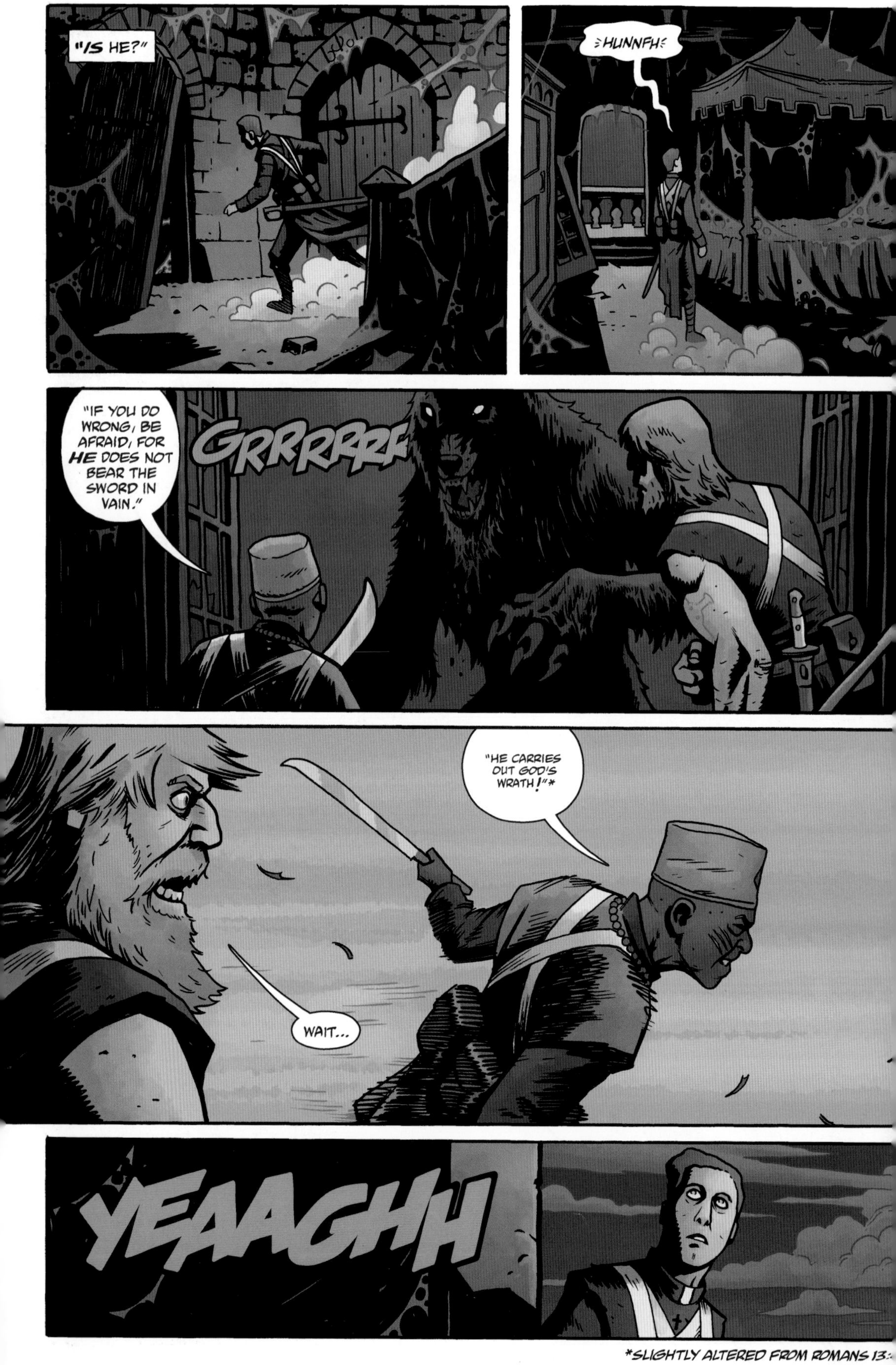
"IS HE?"
HUNNFH
GRRRRRR
"IF YOU DO WRONG, BE AFRAID, FOR HE DOES NOT BEAR THE SWORD IN VAIN."
"HE CARRIES OUT GOD'S WRATH!"*
WAIT...
YEAAGHH

*SLIGHTLY ALTERED FROM ROMANS 13:4

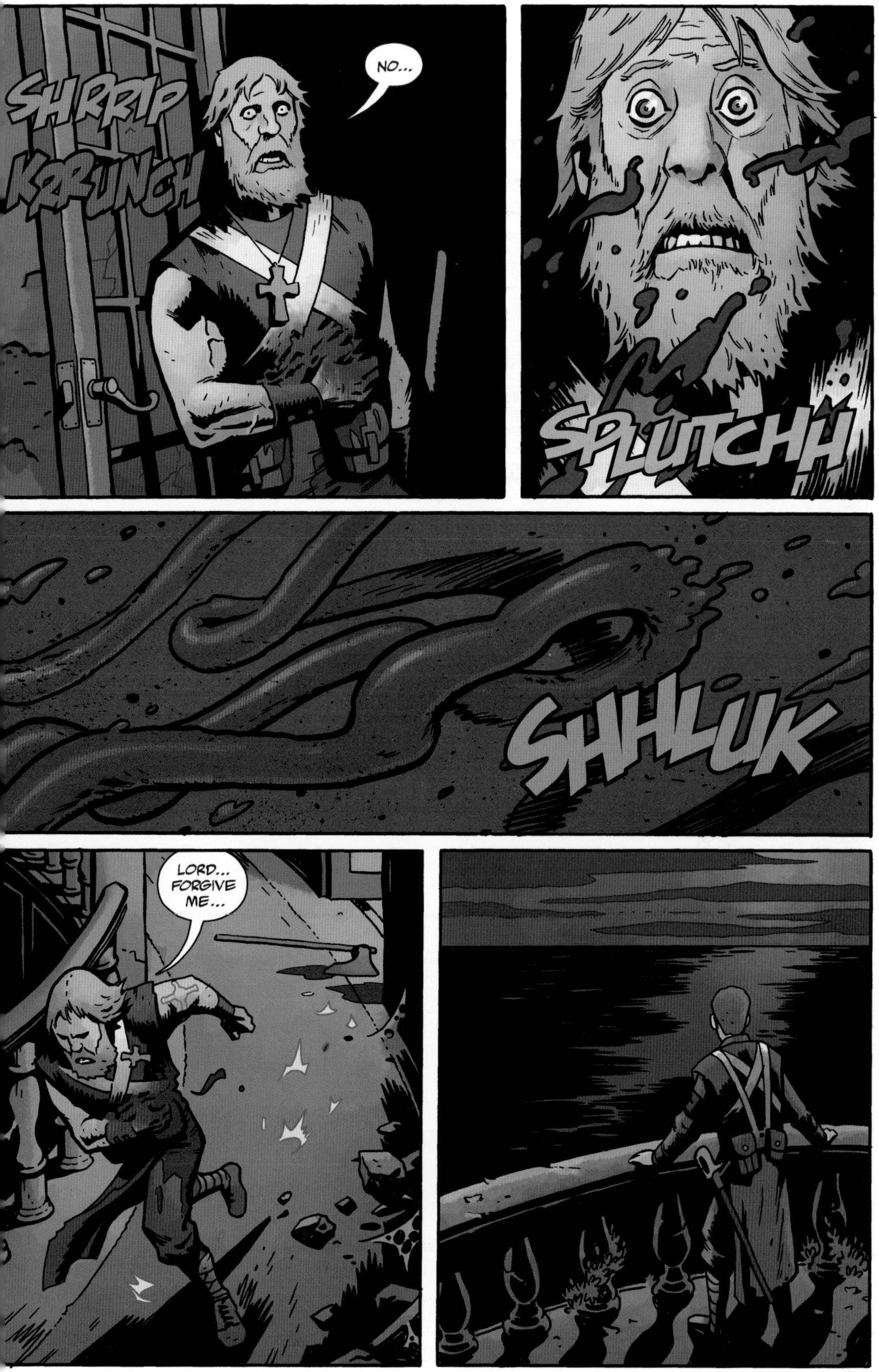
SHRRIP
KRRUNCH
NO...
SPLUTCHH
SHHLUK
LORD... FORGIVE ME...

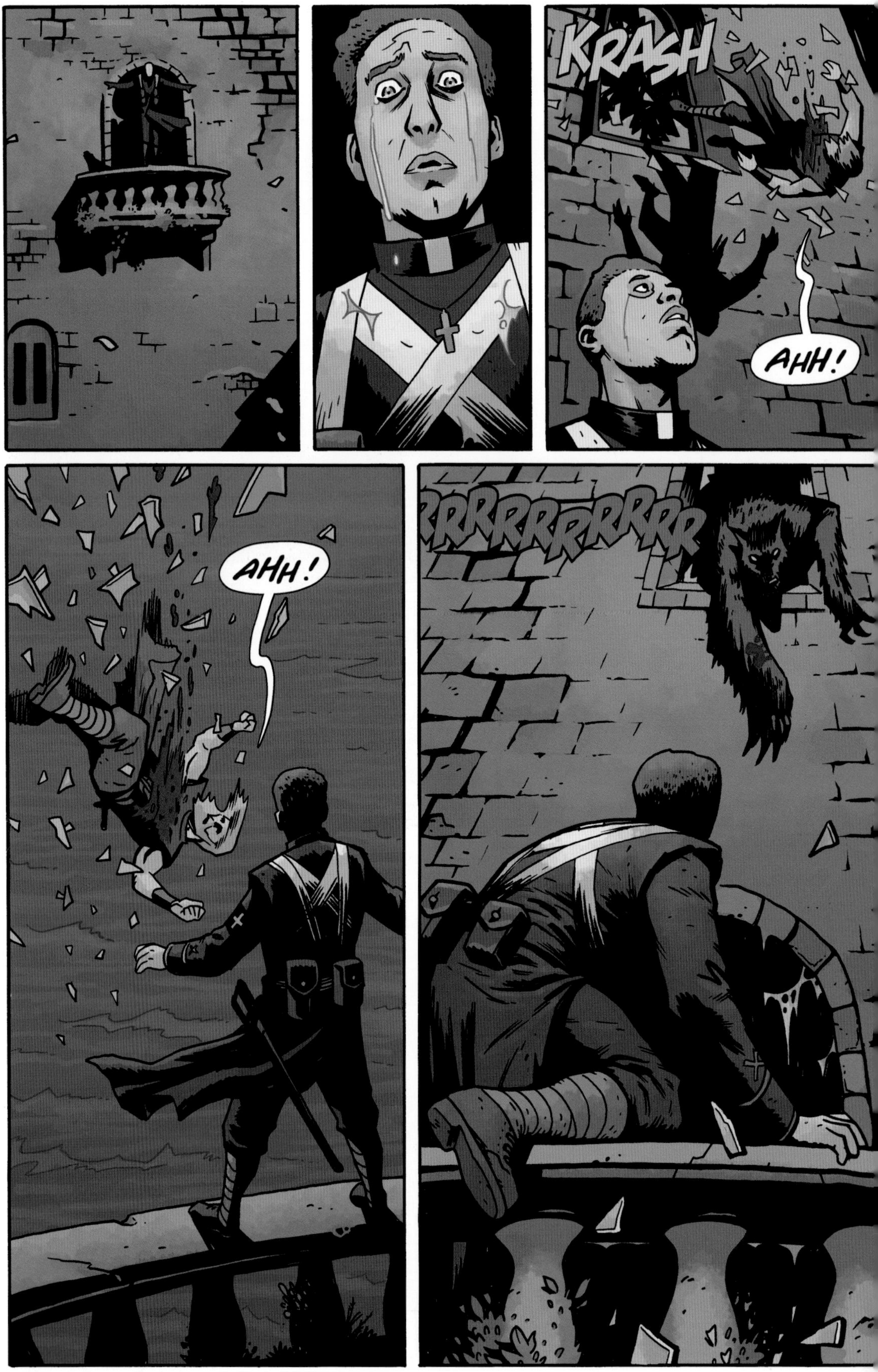
KRASH
AHH!
AHH!
RRRRRRRRRRRR

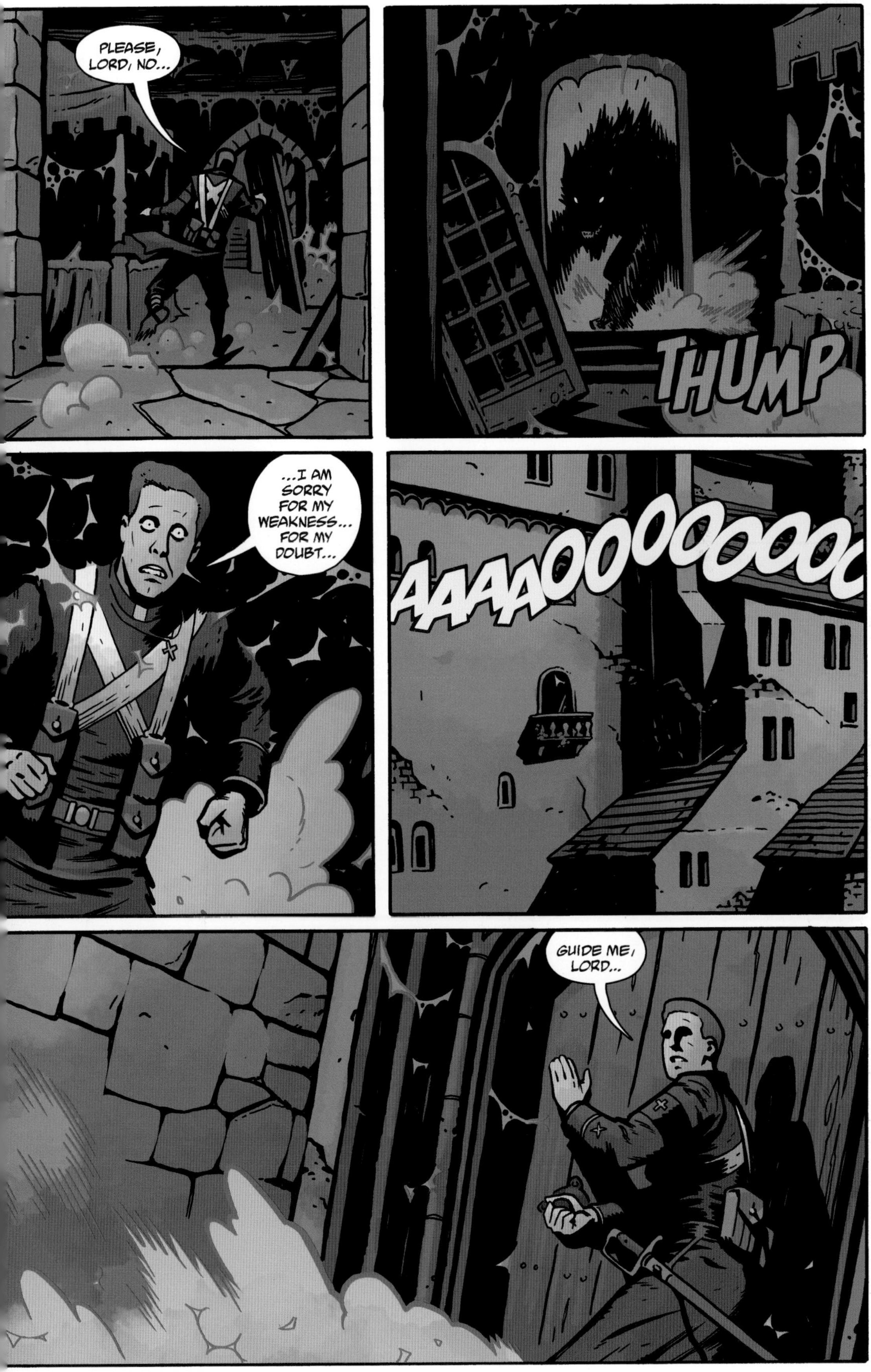

PLEASE, LORD, NO...
THUMP
...I AM SORRY FOR MY WEAKNESS... FOR MY DOUBT...
AAAAOOOOOOOOO
GUIDE ME, LORD...

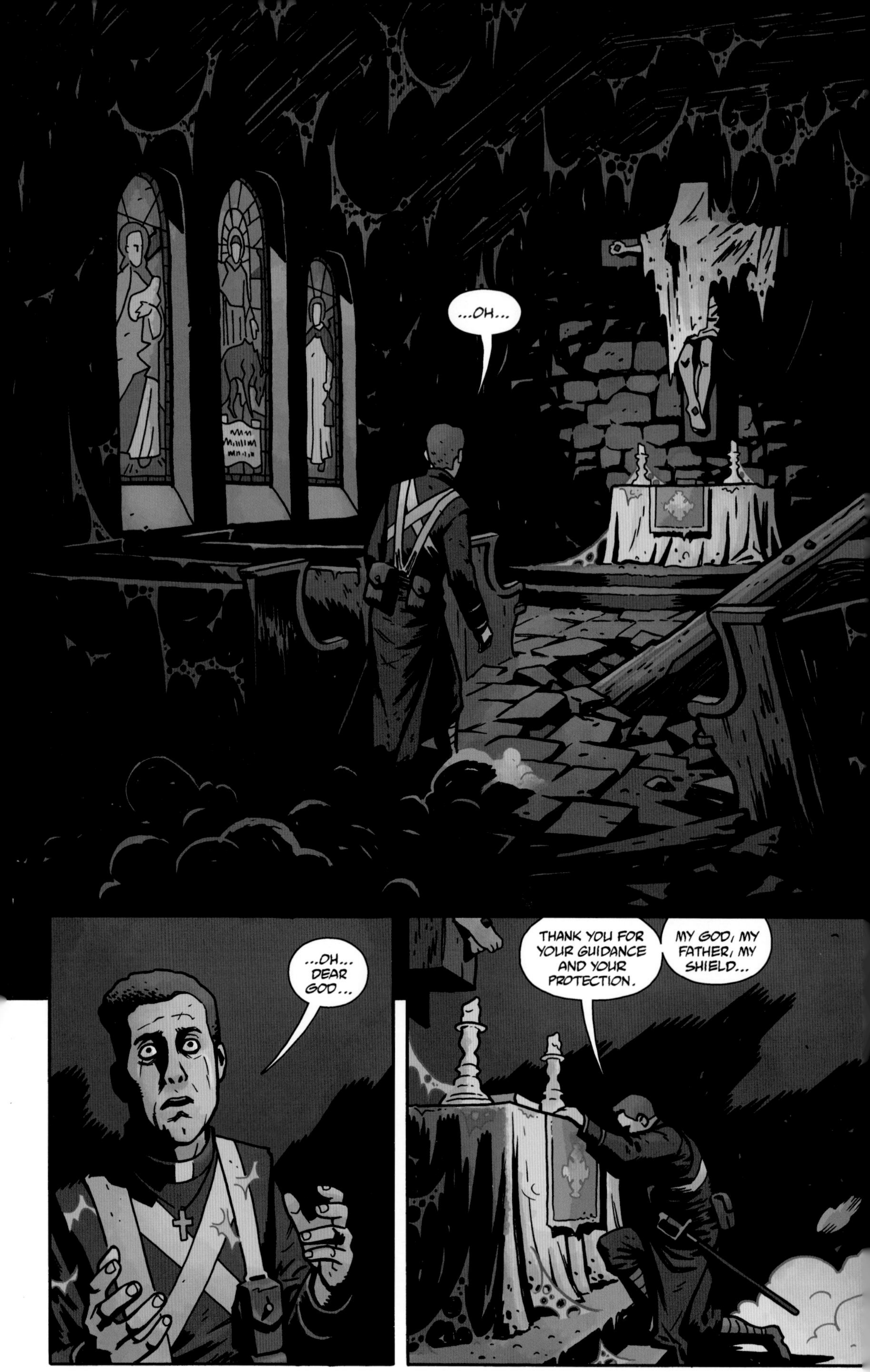
...OH...
...OH... DEAR GOD...
THANK YOU FOR YOUR GUIDANCE AND YOUR PROTECTION.
MY GOD, MY FATHER, MY SHIELD...

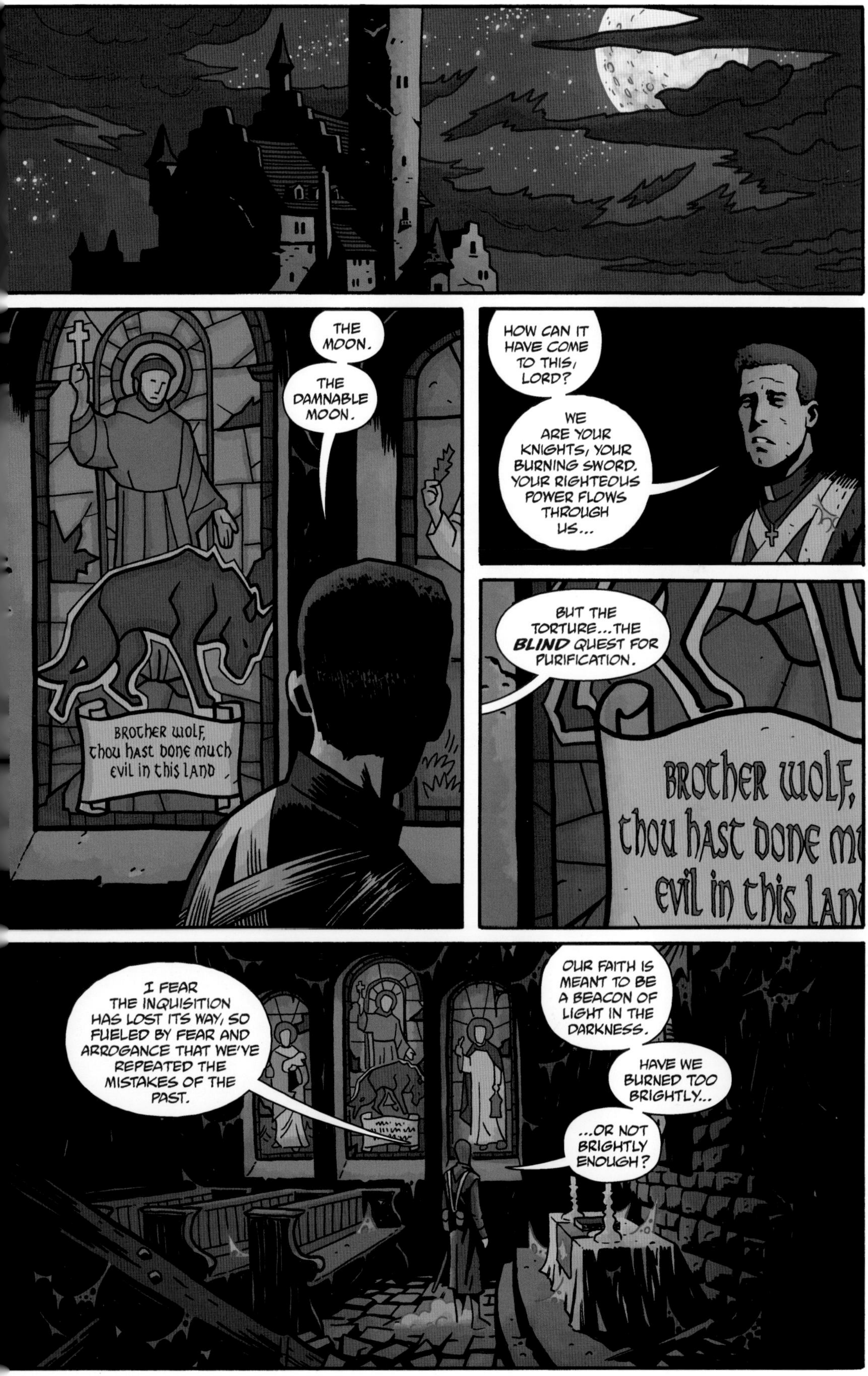
THE MOON.
THE DAMNABLE MOON.
BROTHER WOLF, THOU HAST DONE MUCH EVIL IN THIS LAND
HOW CAN IT HAVE COME TO THIS, LORD?
WE ARE YOUR KNIGHTS, YOUR BURNING SWORD. YOUR RIGHTEOUS POWER FLOWS THROUGH US...
BUT THE TORTURE...THE *BLIND* QUEST FOR PURIFICATION.
I FEAR THE INQUISITION HAS LOST ITS WAY, SO FUELED BY FEAR AND ARROGANCE THAT WE'VE REPEATED THE MISTAKES OF THE PAST.
OUR FAITH IS MEANT TO BE A BEACON OF LIGHT IN THE DARKNESS.
HAVE WE BURNED TOO BRIGHTLY...
...OR NOT BRIGHTLY ENOUGH?

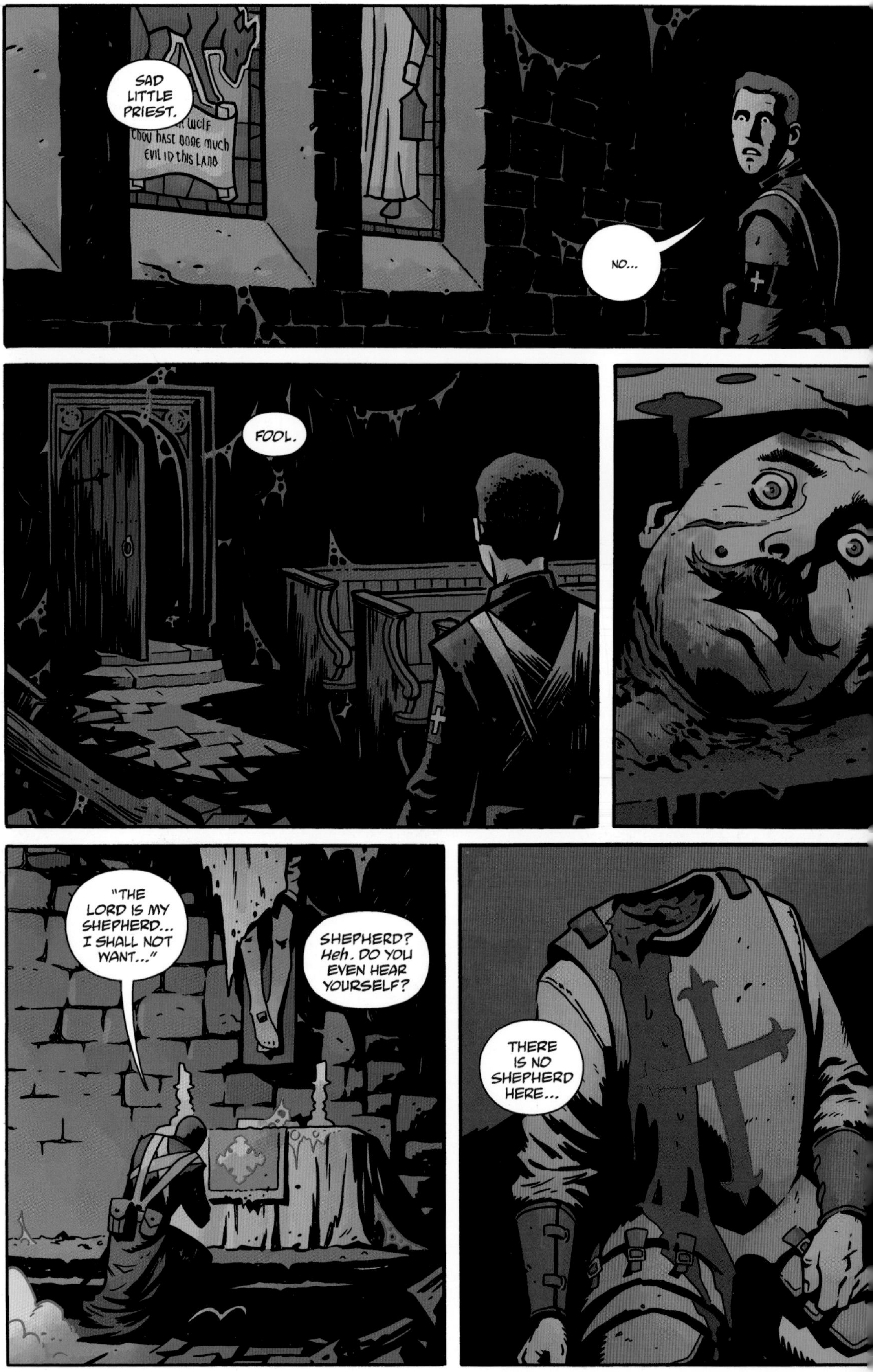
SAD LITTLE PRIEST.
...wolf thou hast done much evil in this land
NO...
FOOL.
"THE LORD IS MY SHEPHERD... I SHALL NOT WANT..."
SHEPHERD? Heh. DO YOU EVEN HEAR YOURSELF?
THERE IS NO SHEPHERD HERE...

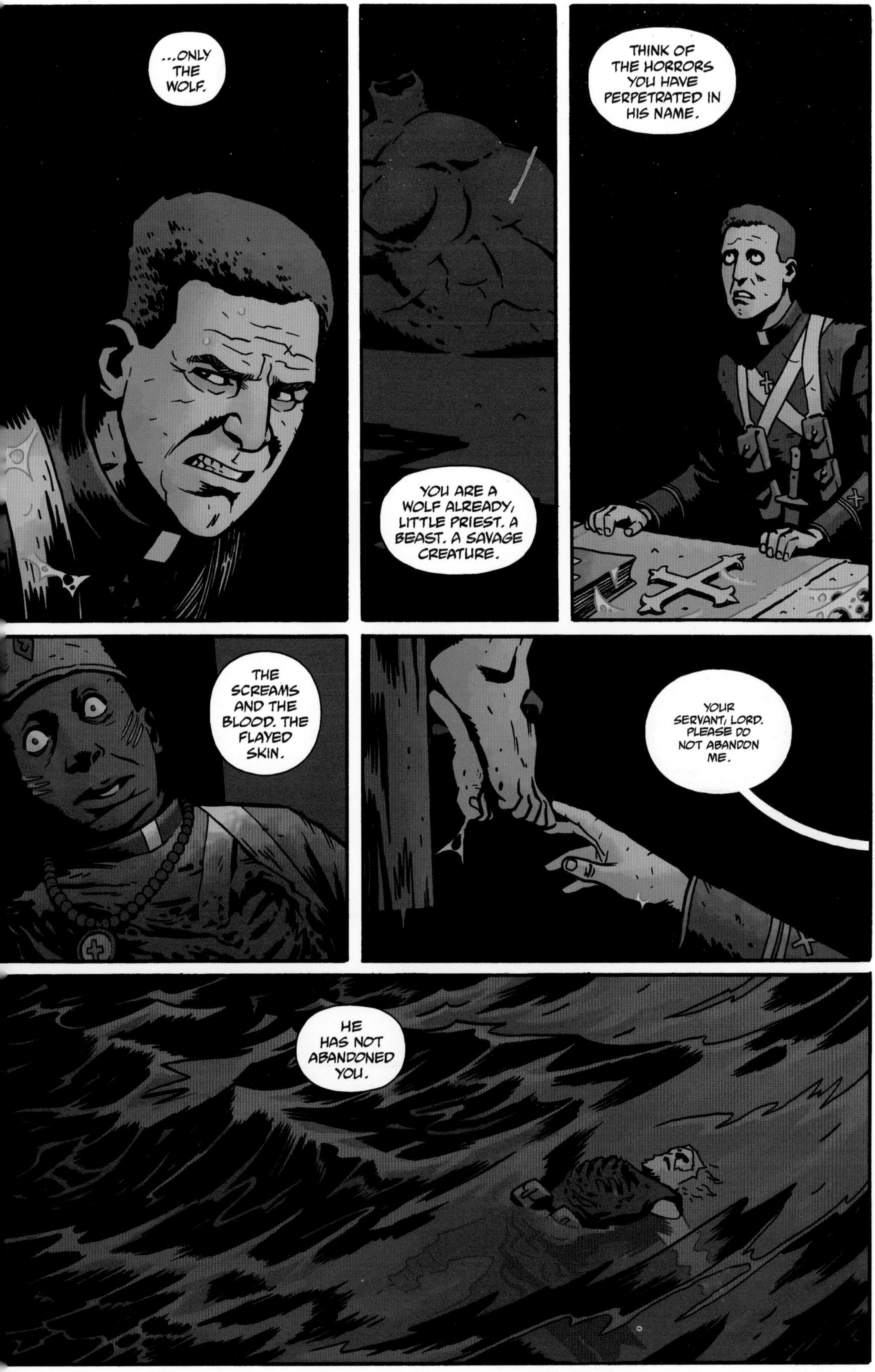
...ONLY THE WOLF.
THINK OF THE HORRORS YOU HAVE PERPETRATED IN HIS NAME.
YOU ARE A WOLF ALREADY, LITTLE PRIEST. A BEAST. A SAVAGE CREATURE.
THE SCREAMS AND THE BLOOD. THE FLAYED SKIN.
YOUR SERVANT, LORD. PLEASE DO NOT ABANDON ME.
HE HAS NOT ABANDONED YOU.

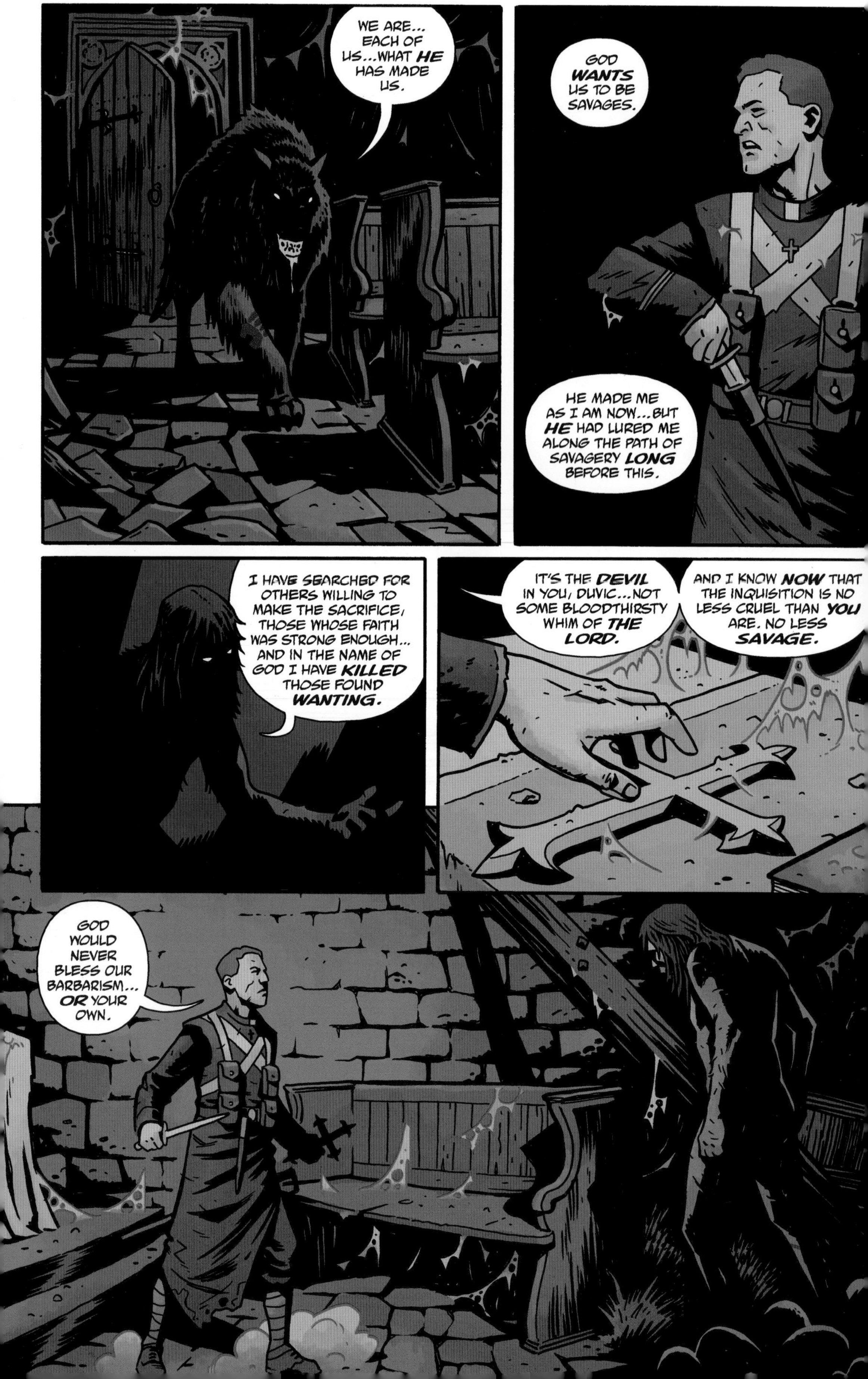
WE ARE... EACH OF US...WHAT HE HAS MADE US.
GOD WANTS US TO BE SAVAGES.
HE MADE ME AS I AM NOW...BUT HE HAD LURED ME ALONG THE PATH OF SAVAGERY LONG BEFORE THIS.
I HAVE SEARCHED FOR OTHERS WILLING TO MAKE THE SACRIFICE, THOSE WHOSE FAITH WAS STRONG ENOUGH... AND IN THE NAME OF GOD I HAVE KILLED THOSE FOUND WANTING.
IT'S THE DEVIL IN YOU, DUVIC...NOT SOME BLOODTHIRSTY WHIM OF THE LORD.
AND I KNOW NOW THAT THE INQUISITION IS NO LESS CRUEL THAN YOU ARE. NO LESS SAVAGE.
GOD WOULD NEVER BLESS OUR BARBARISM... OR YOUR OWN.

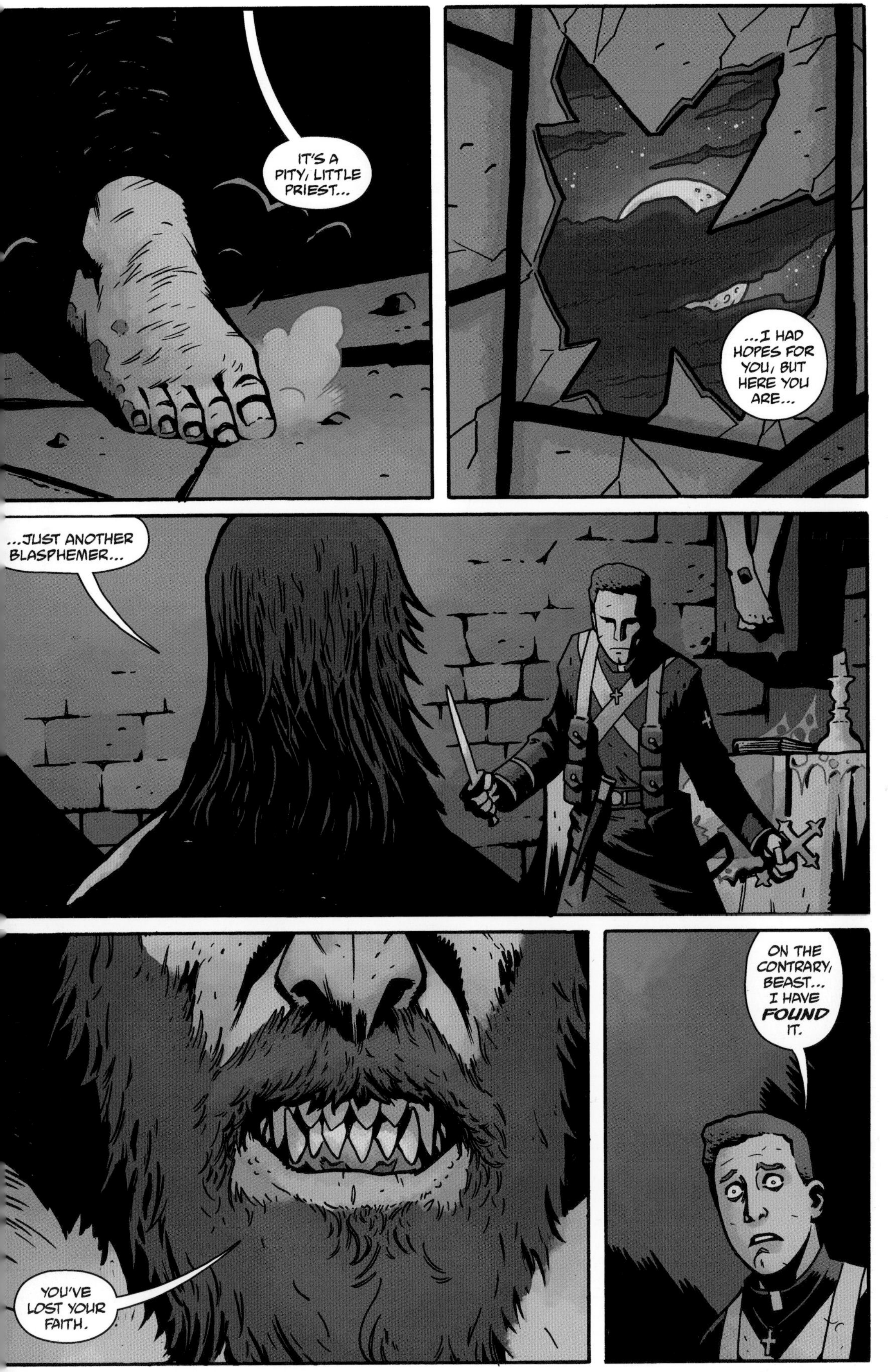
IT'S A PITY, LITTLE PRIEST...
...I HAD HOPES FOR YOU, BUT HERE YOU ARE...
...JUST ANOTHER BLASPHEMER...
YOU'VE LOST YOUR FAITH.
ON THE CONTRARY, BEAST... I HAVE FOUND IT.

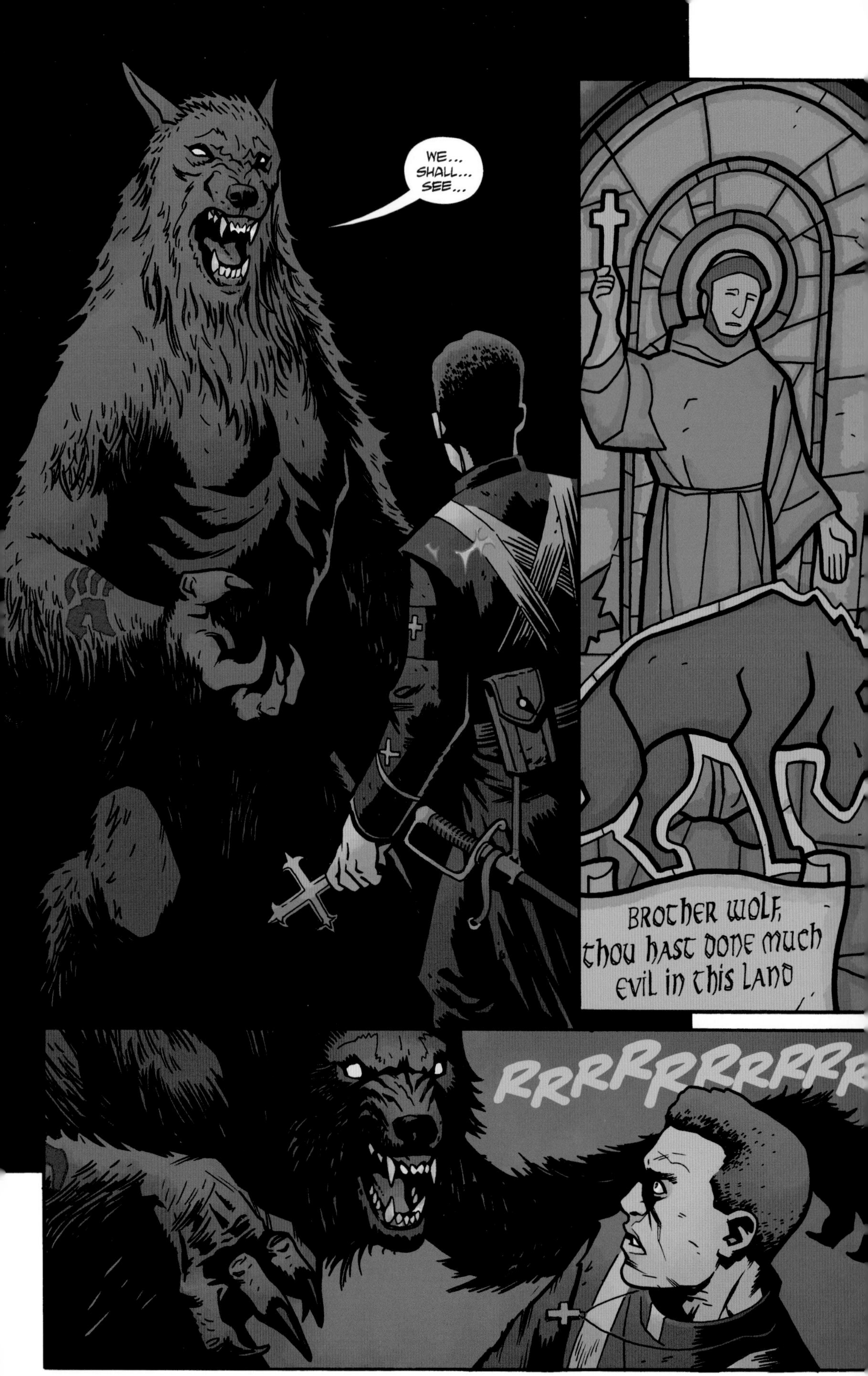
WE... SHALL... SEE...
BROTHER WOLF, thou hast done much evil in this land
RRRRRRRRRR

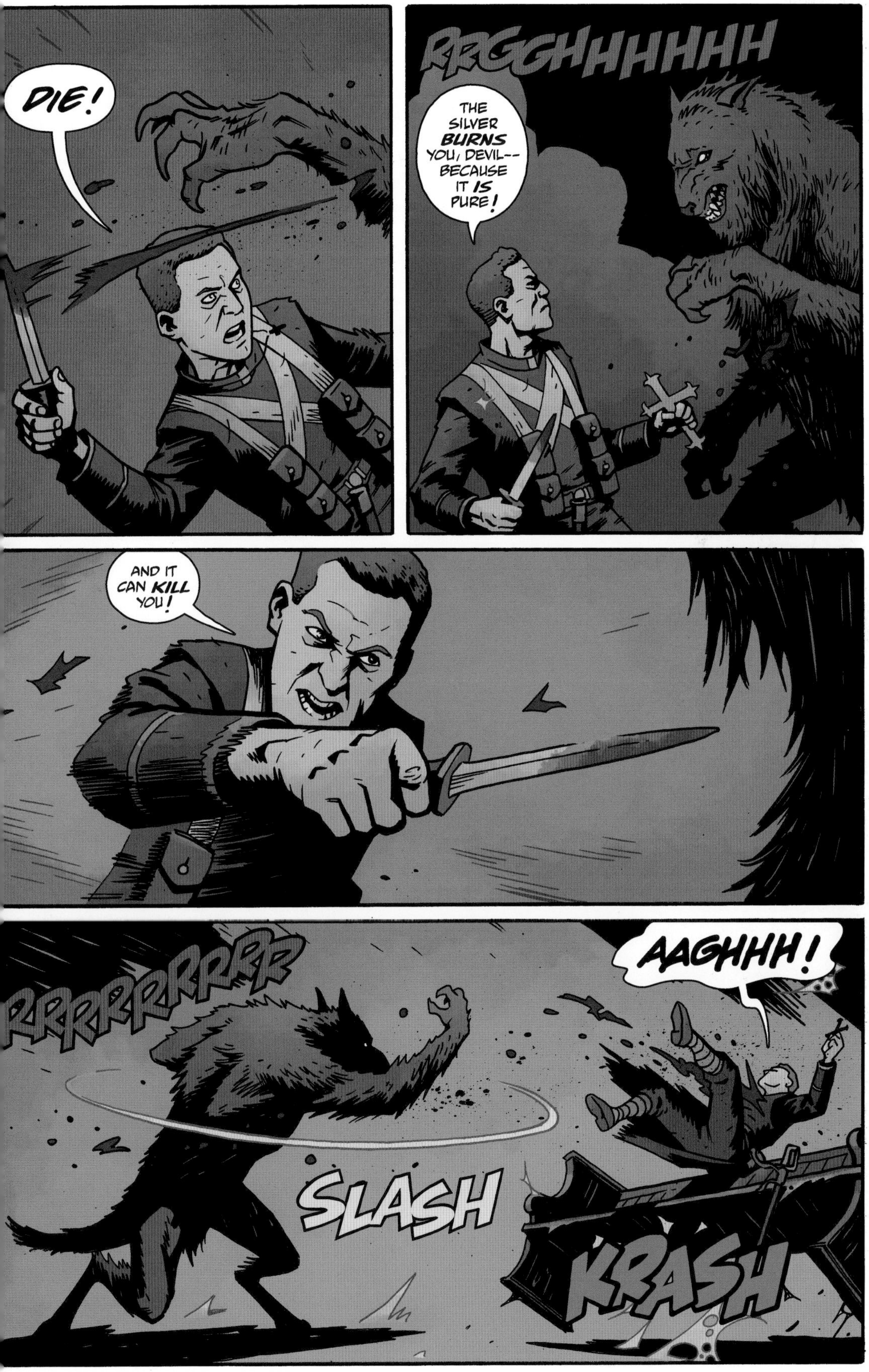
DIE!
RRGGHHHHHH
THE SILVER BURNS YOU, DEVIL-- BECAUSE IT IS PURE!
AND IT CAN KILL YOU!
RRRRRRRRR
AAGHHH!
SLASH
KRASH

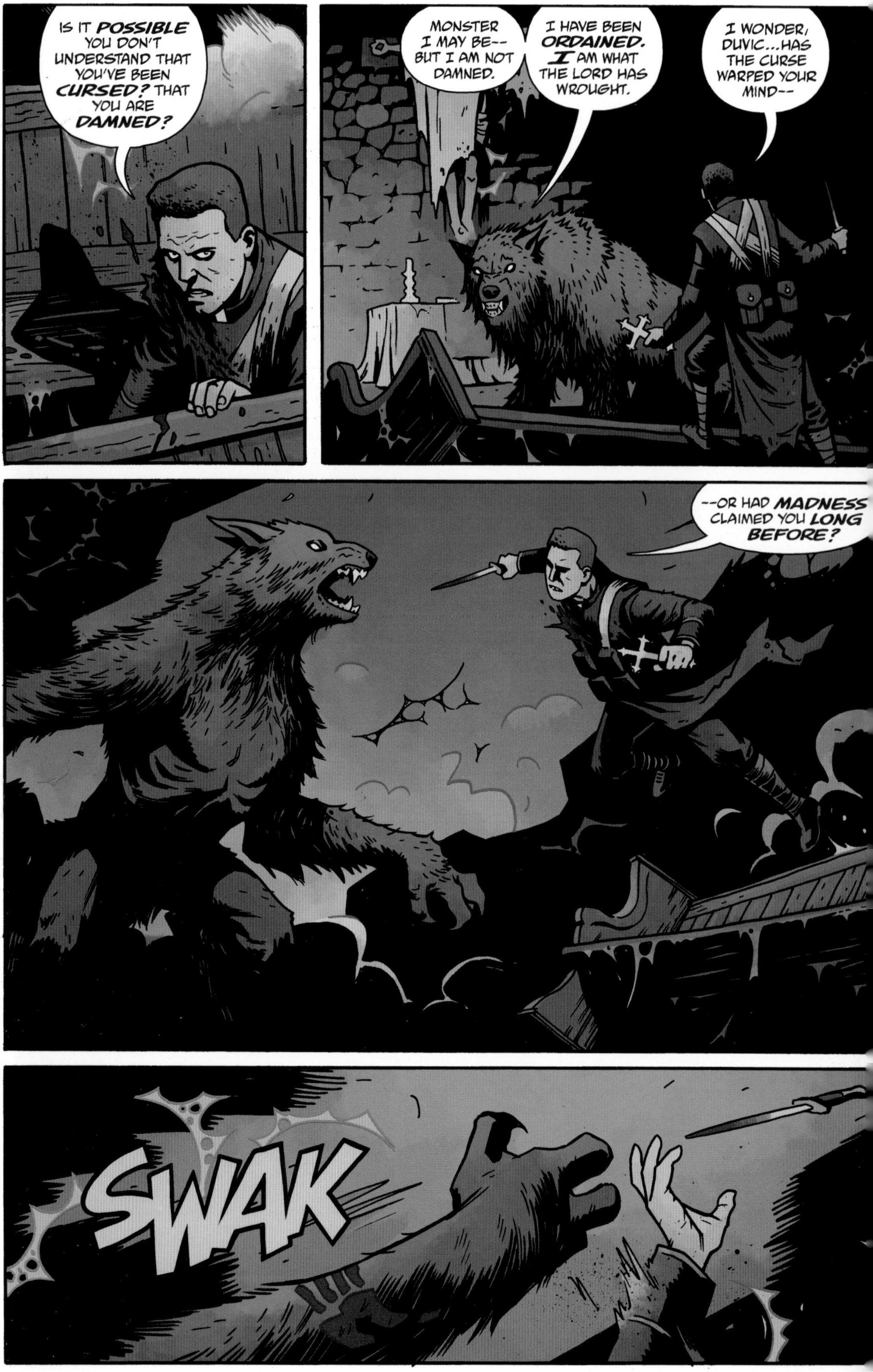
IS IT POSSIBLE YOU DON'T UNDERSTAND THAT YOU'VE BEEN CURSED? THAT YOU ARE DAMNED?
MONSTER I MAY BE-- BUT I AM NOT DAMNED.
I HAVE BEEN ORDAINED. I AM WHAT THE LORD HAS WROUGHT.
I WONDER, DUVIC...HAS THE CURSE WARPED YOUR MIND--
--OR HAD MADNESS CLAIMED YOU LONG BEFORE?
SWAK

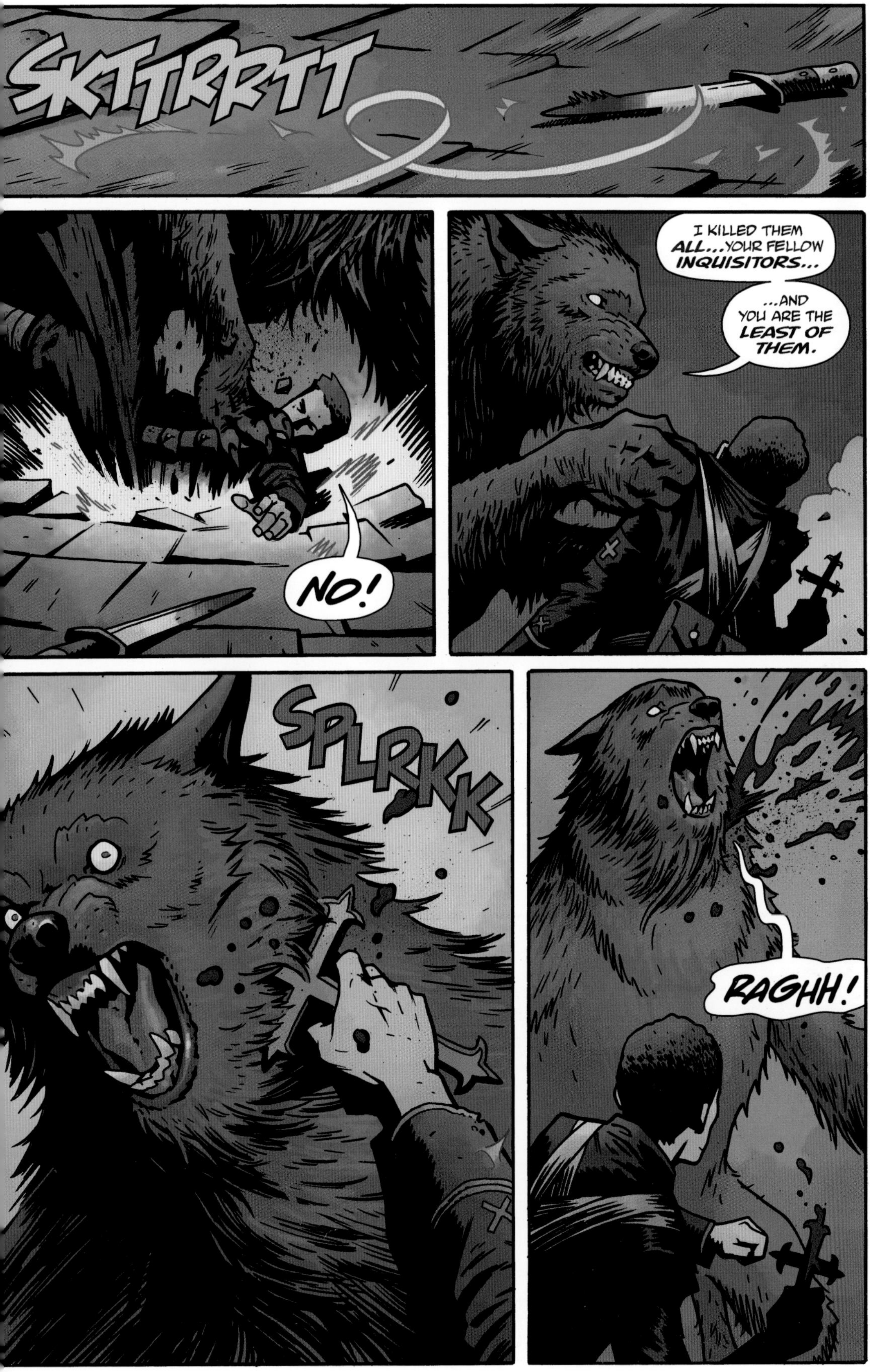

SKTTRRTT
NO!
I KILLED THEM ALL...YOUR FELLOW INQUISITORS...
...AND YOU ARE THE LEAST OF THEM.
SPLRKKK
RAGHH!

UNGHH...

RRRK GGH

RRRGHHH

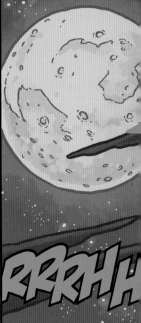

RRRHH

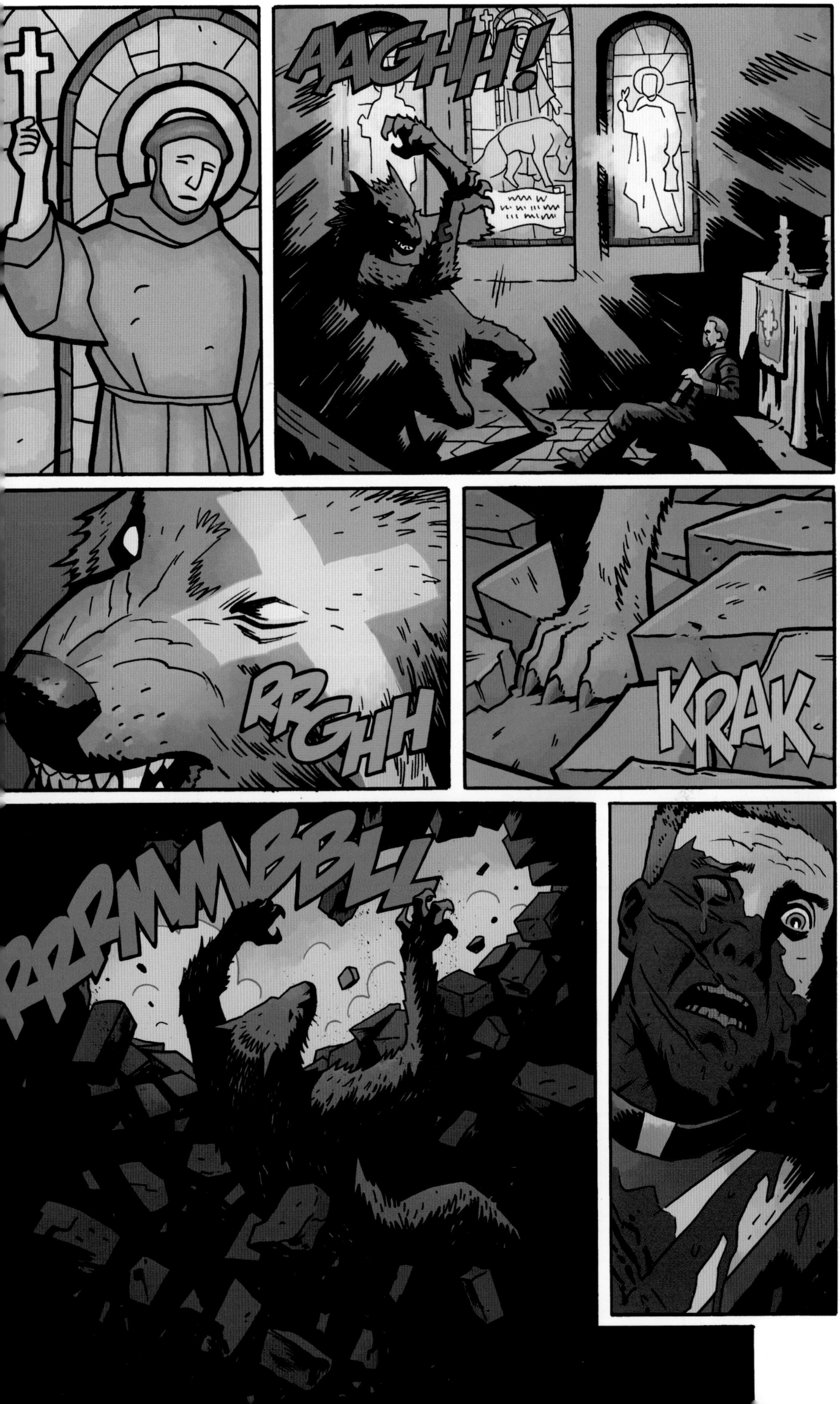
AAGHH!
RRGHH
KRAK
RRRMMBBLL

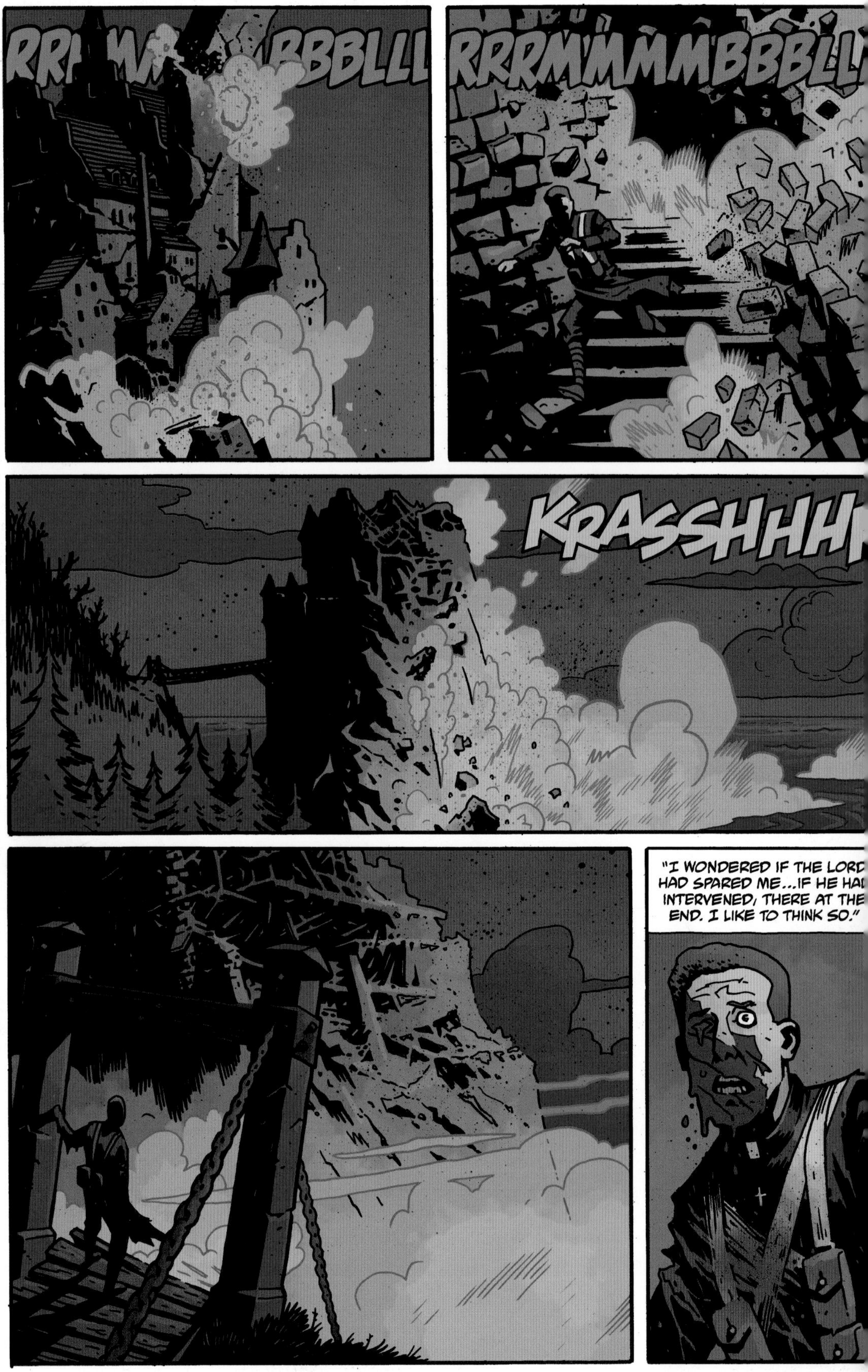
RRRMMMMMBBBLLL
RRRMMMMMBBBLLL
KRASSHHH
"I WONDERED IF THE LORD HAD SPARED ME...IF HE HAD INTERVENED, THERE AT THE END. I LIKE TO THINK SO."

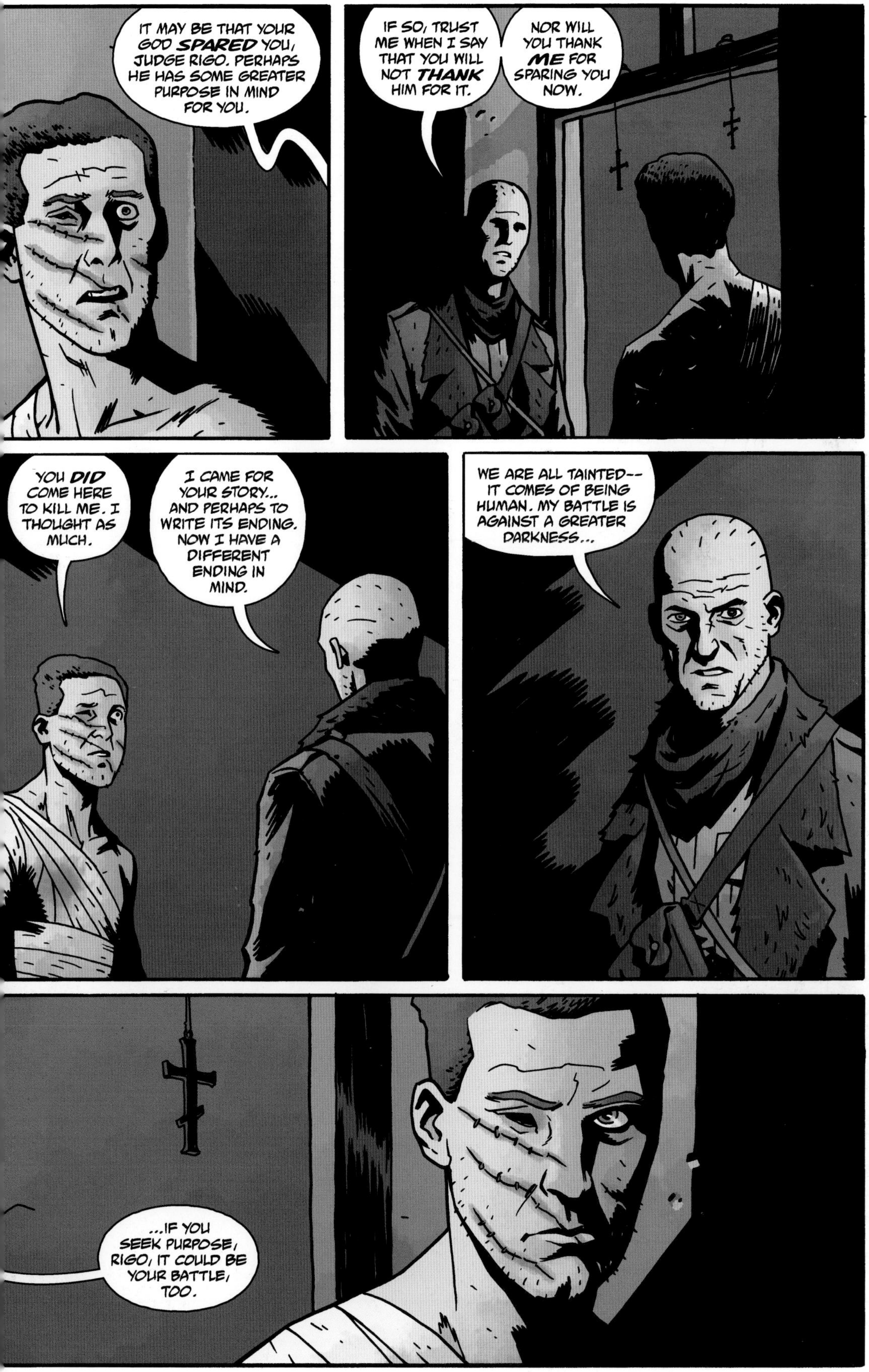
IT MAY BE THAT YOUR GOD SPARED YOU, JUDGE RIGO. PERHAPS HE HAS SOME GREATER PURPOSE IN MIND FOR YOU.
IF SO, TRUST ME WHEN I SAY THAT YOU WILL NOT THANK HIM FOR IT.
NOR WILL YOU THANK ME FOR SPARING YOU NOW.
YOU DID COME HERE TO KILL ME. I THOUGHT AS MUCH.
I CAME FOR YOUR STORY... AND PERHAPS TO WRITE ITS ENDING. NOW I HAVE A DIFFERENT ENDING IN MIND.
WE ARE ALL TAINTED-- IT COMES OF BEING HUMAN. MY BATTLE IS AGAINST A GREATER DARKNESS...
...IF YOU SEEK PURPOSE, RIGO, IT COULD BE YOUR BATTLE, TOO.

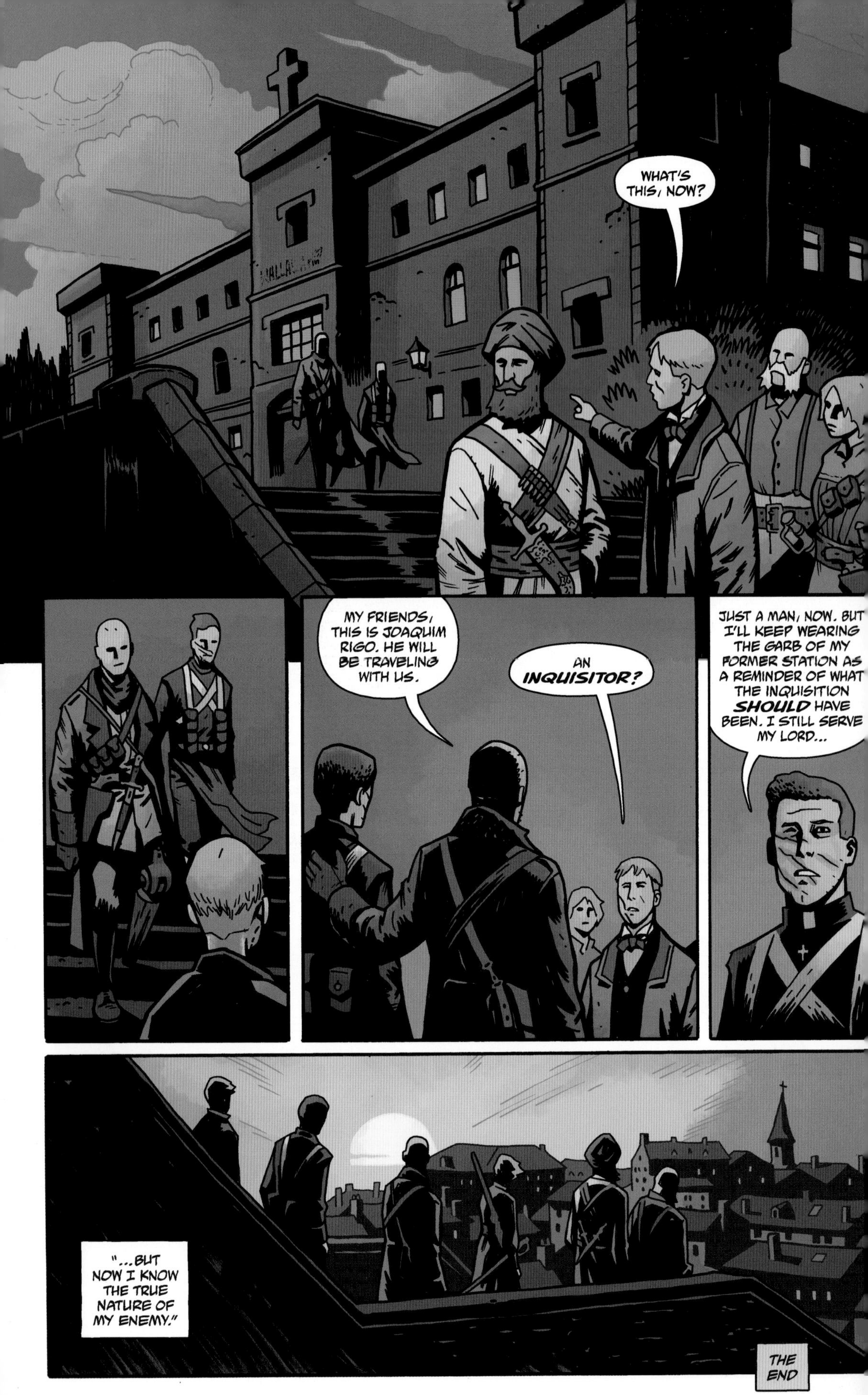

WHAT'S THIS, NOW?
MY FRIENDS, THIS IS JOAQUIM RIGO. HE WILL BE TRAVELING WITH US.
AN INQUISITOR?
JUST A MAN, NOW. BUT I'LL KEEP WEARING THE GARB OF MY FORMER STATION AS A REMINDER OF WHAT THE INQUISITION SHOULD HAVE BEEN. I STILL SERVE MY LORD...
"...BUT NOW I KNOW THE TRUE NATURE OF MY ENEMY."
THE END

# BALTIMORE

## THE APOSTLE AND THE WITCH OF HARJU

## SKETCHBOOK

*Notes by Peter Bergting and Ben Stenbeck*

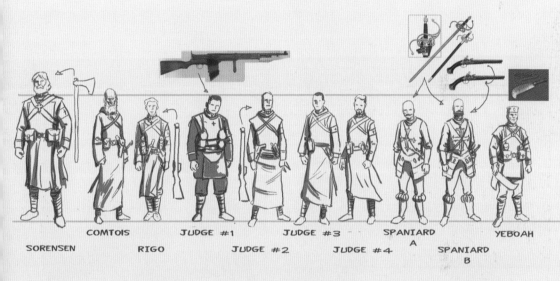

SORENSEN    COMTOIS    RIGO    JUDGE #1    JUDGE #2    JUDGE #3    JUDGE #4    SPANIARD A    SPANIARD B    YEBOAH

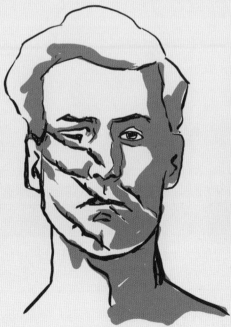

*Ben Stenbeck:* Part of the idea for *The Wolf and the Apostle* came from that group shot of the Inquisition we did in *The Inquisitor.* Judges 2, 3, and 4 above are in that scene. Originally I wanted them all to be in full suits of armor, but settled for armor on only a few of them.

*Left:* Rigo. I should have kept his hair as big as this. I had great reference for that eye, with no other wound touching it, almost like the sheer blunt force of the werewolf hitting him is what popped his eye out. Gross.

1
DARK HORSE COMICS
BALTIMORE
THE PLAGUE SHIPS
2 OF 5
2
DARK HORSE COMICS
BALTIMORE
Bones
3
DARK HORSE COMICS
BALTIMORE
THE PLAGUE SHIPS
2 OF 5
Bones
4
DARK HORSE COMICS
BALTIMORE
THE PLAGUE SHIPS
2 OF 5
crying

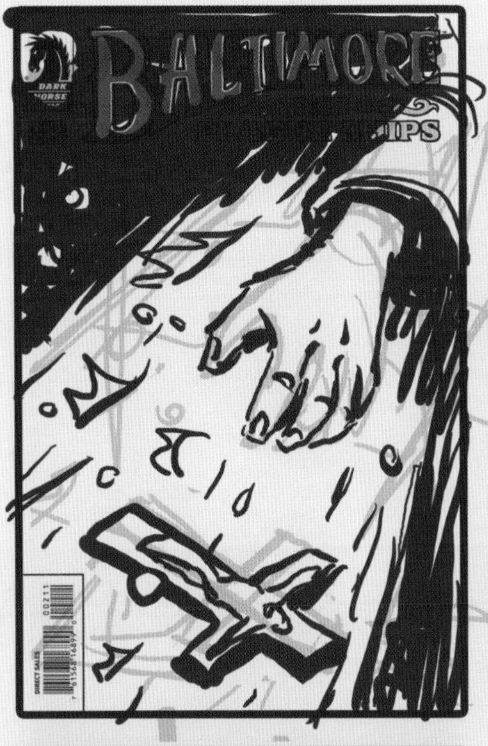
BALTIMORE

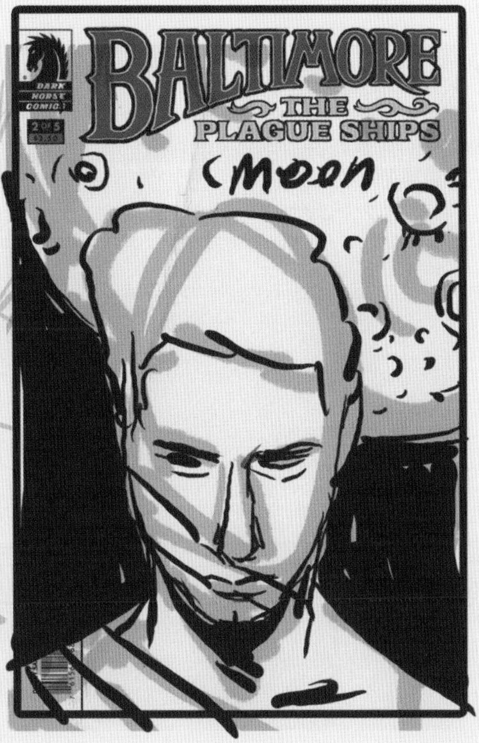
DARK HORSE COMICS
BALTIMORE
THE PLAGUE SHIPS
2 of 5
MOON

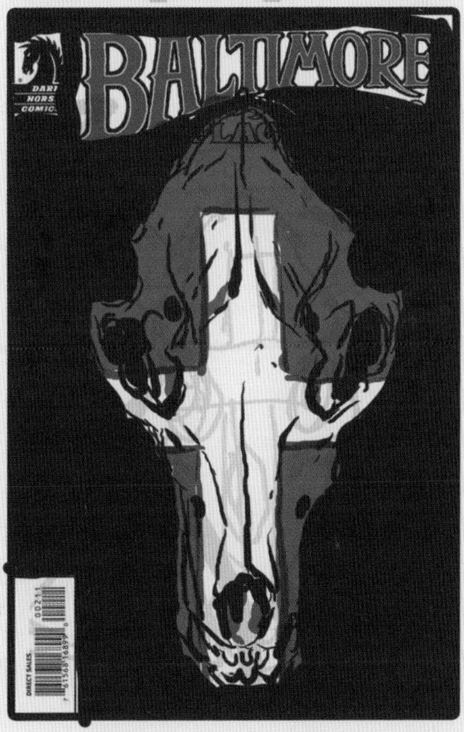
BALTIMORE

*BS:* These cover sketches were all done digitally—very fast. The *Witch of Harju* covers on the following pages were tough because the scripts weren't written when I drew these, which is why my witch isn't nearly as cool as Peter's.

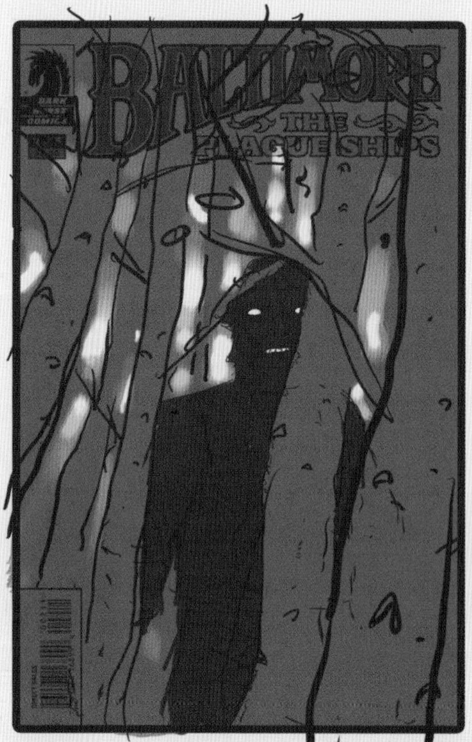
BALTIMORE
THE
PLAGUE SHIPS

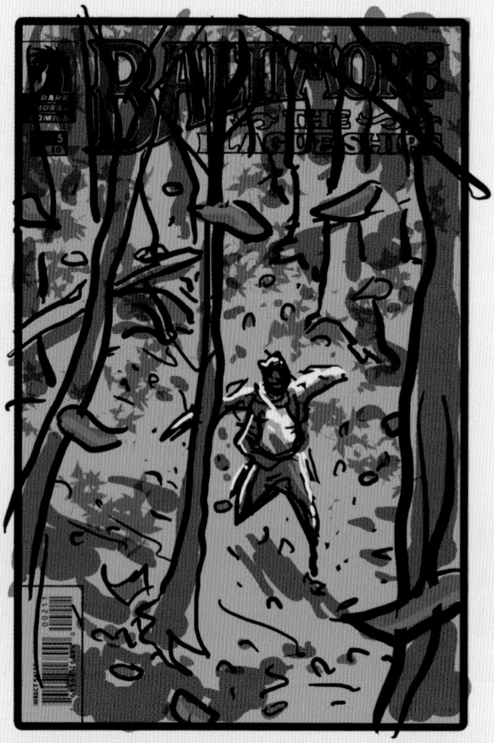
BALTIMORE
THE
PLAGUE SHIPS

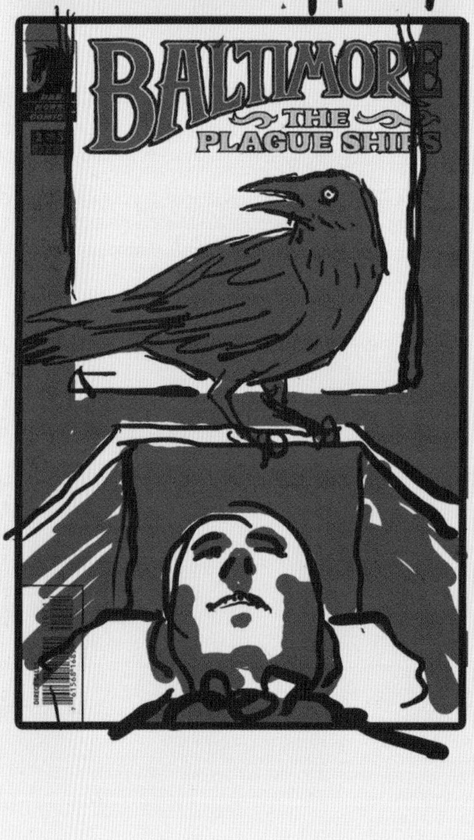
BALTIMORE
THE
PLAGUE SHIPS

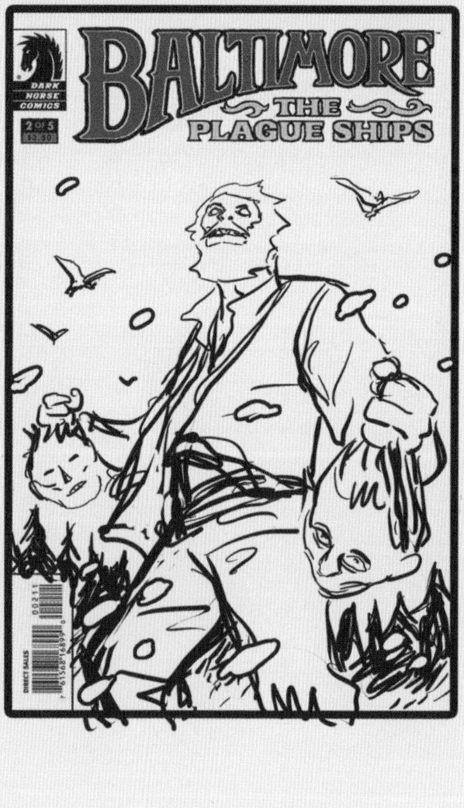
BALTIMORE
THE
PLAGUE SHIPS
DARK
HORSE
COMICS
2 OF 5
$3.50
DIRECT SALES

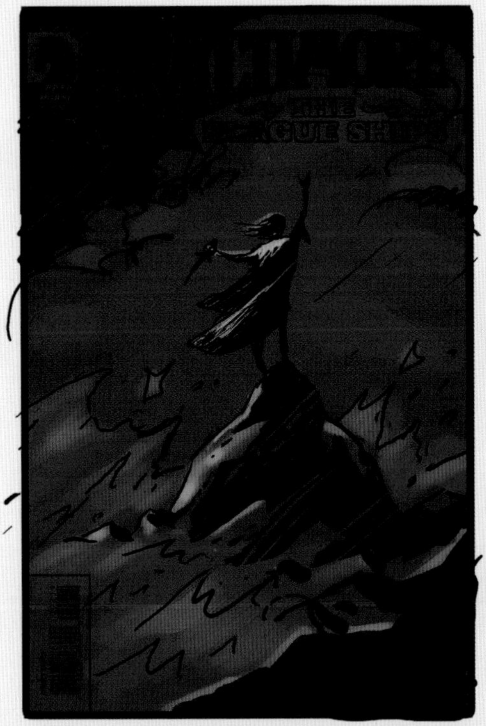

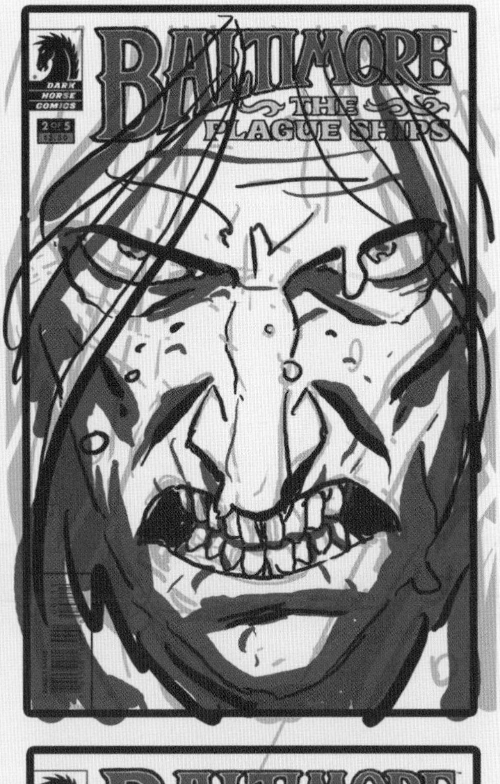
DARK HORSE COMICS
BALTIMORE
THE PLAGUE SHIPS
2 OF 5

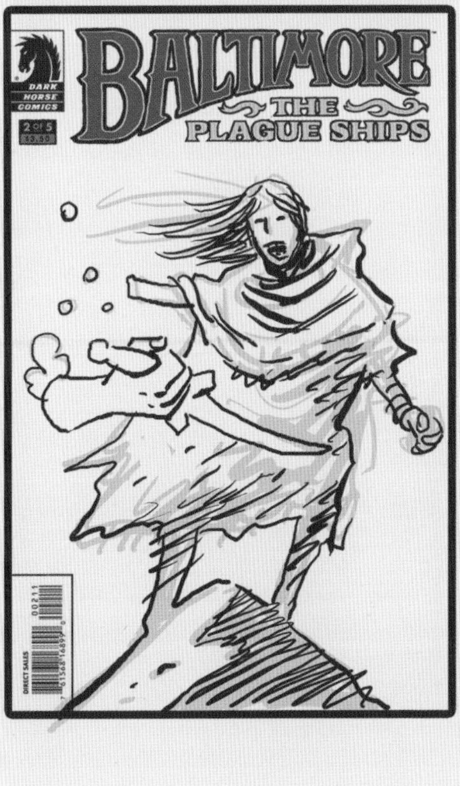
DARK HORSE COMICS
BALTIMORE
THE PLAGUE SHIPS
2 OF 5
DIRECT SALES

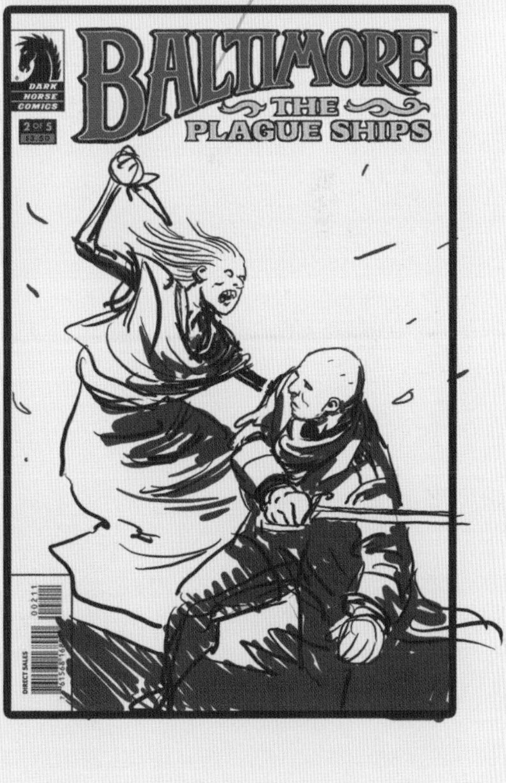
DARK HORSE COMICS
BALTIMORE
THE PLAGUE SHIPS
2 OF 5
DIRECT SALES

*Peter Bergting:* I was in the middle of working on *The Portent: Ashes* and had no idea Dark Horse wanted me for *Baltimore* when my *Portent* editor, Daniel Chabon, asked me for a test page. I was anxious to get everything right and there was a lot of back and forth until it started to gel. I redid panel 2 because the expression was off. This being a test page, I could draw what I wanted, so I pitted Baltimore against two famous Swedish writers that would make awesome vampires. I had no idea that Dave Stewart would be coloring it, so I added my own colors. When I do my own stuff the colors make up perhaps 75 percent of my art, but I was never nervous about handing my work over to Dave. He is, after all, the master.

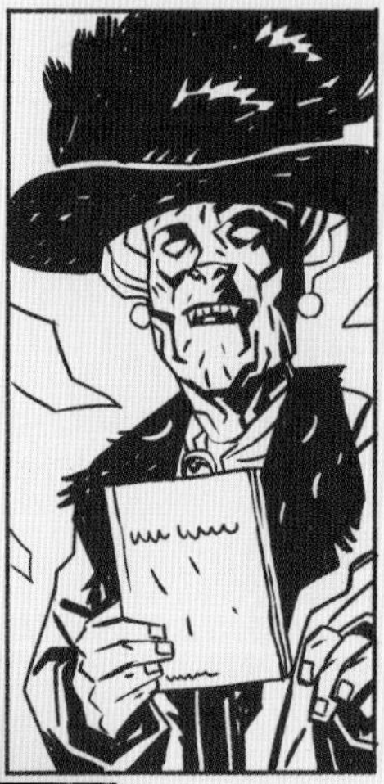

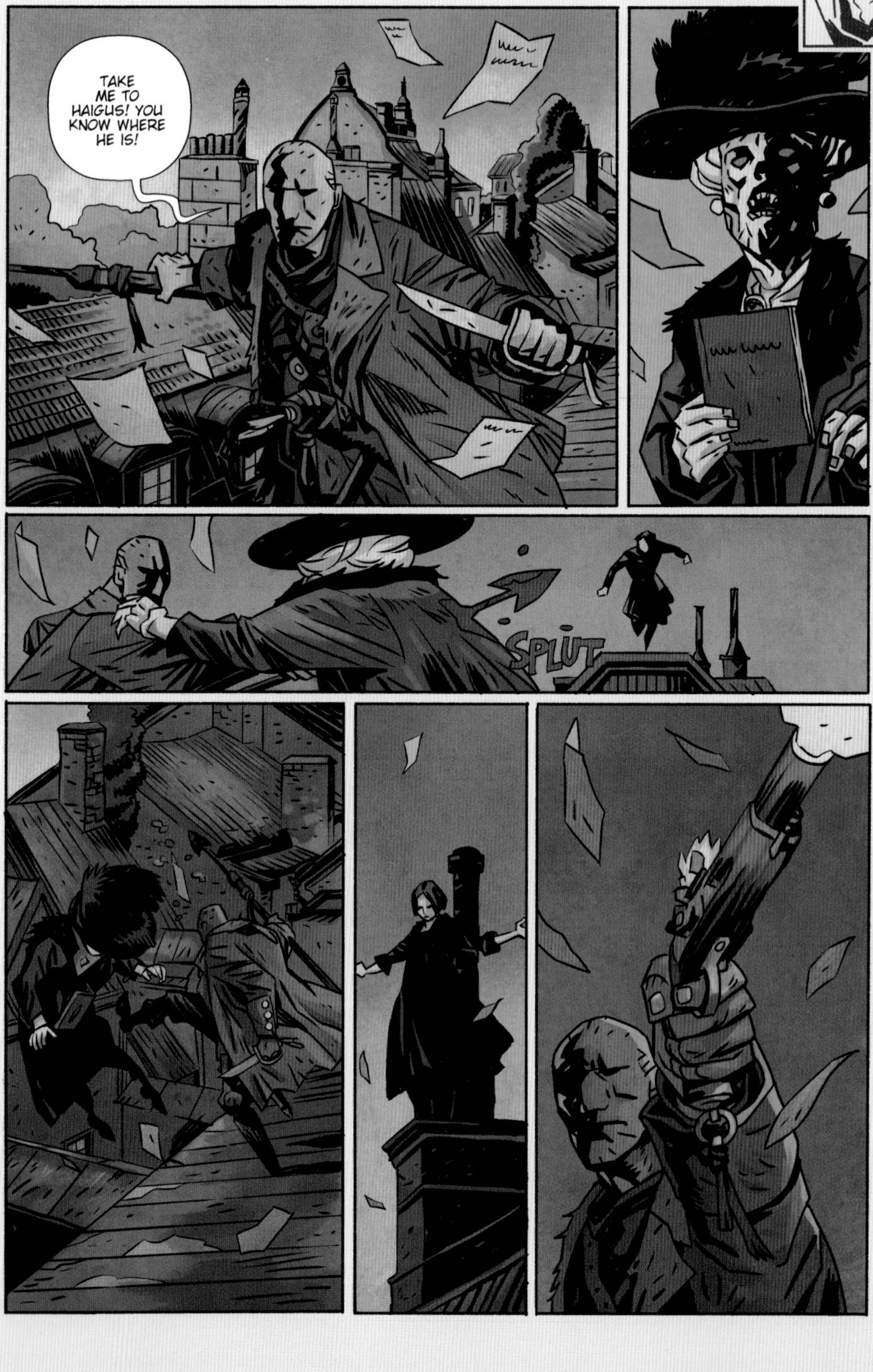
TAKE ME TO HAIGUS! YOU KNOW WHERE HE IS!
SPLUT

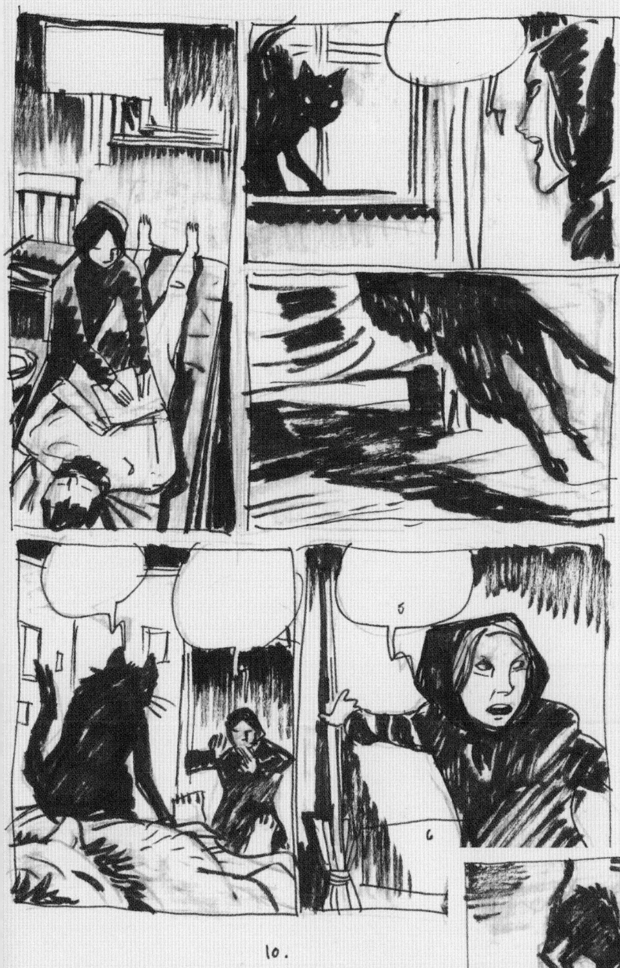
10.

This was a fun scene in my first issue with the foulmouthed cat. The layout changed considerably in the inking stage. When I do my own books I usually skip the pencils. Working digitally allows me to meld the process, constantly redrawing until I'm happy instead of handing in pencils for approval and then inking them. I try to keep my pencils as loose as I can get away with so I can experiment more when inking.

I love drawing cats. Later I added one or two even when they weren't in the script. But at this stage on the book I was very reverential of the script, not having the guts to offer input. I'm getting more confident now. Scott and Shantel, the editors, have been great with that, pushing me to not only deliver better stuff, but also to be more confident.

*Following pages:* This was the preview page that was supposed to sell the book. I immediately started second guessing myself. What did Dark Horse want, what would Mike say, and so on. I got so nervous that I started aping Mignola's style, resulting in a few interesting back-and-forths between the editors and me. They kept asking for more Bergting, and I kept sending in Mignola pastiches. I think I found my stride at the end of the first series. The preview page ended up looking nothing like the finished page.

Chris writes awesome scripts. There are moody passages that just beg to be illustrated and quiet character beats that could look boring, but thanks to the dialogue, always come out fabulous.

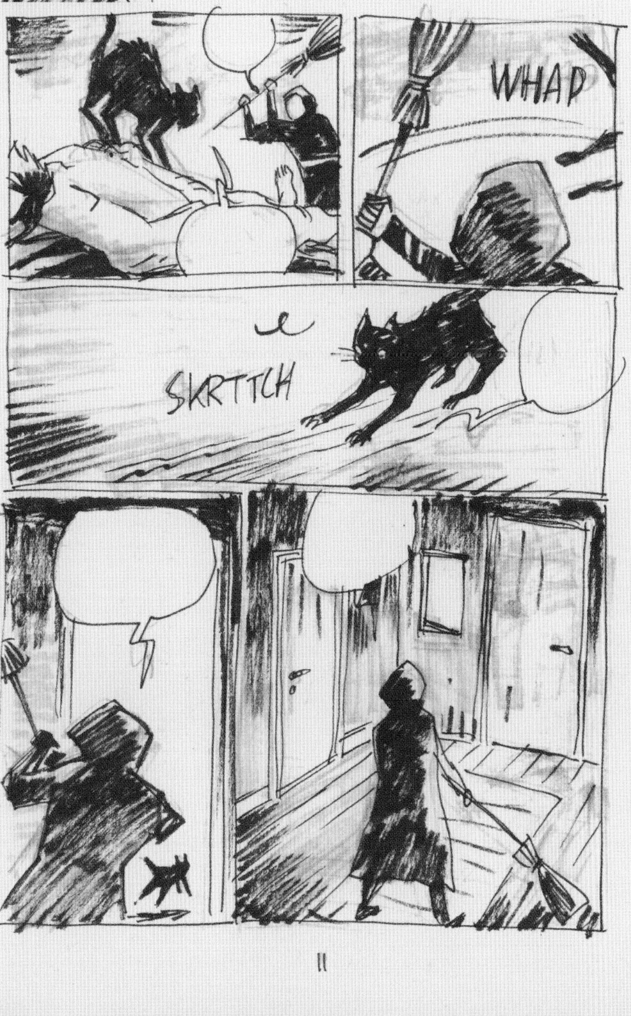
WHAP
SKRTTCH
11

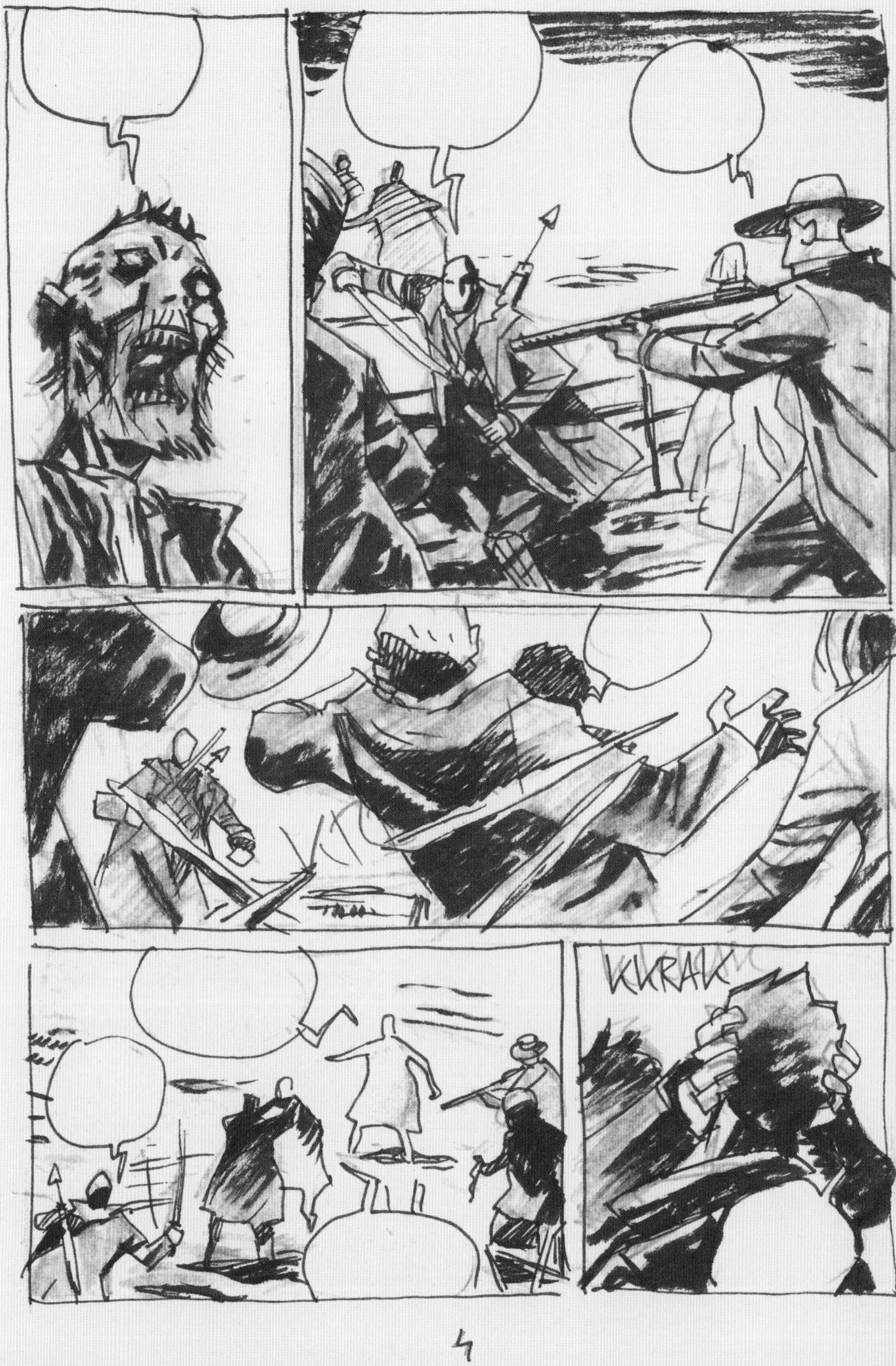
KKRAK

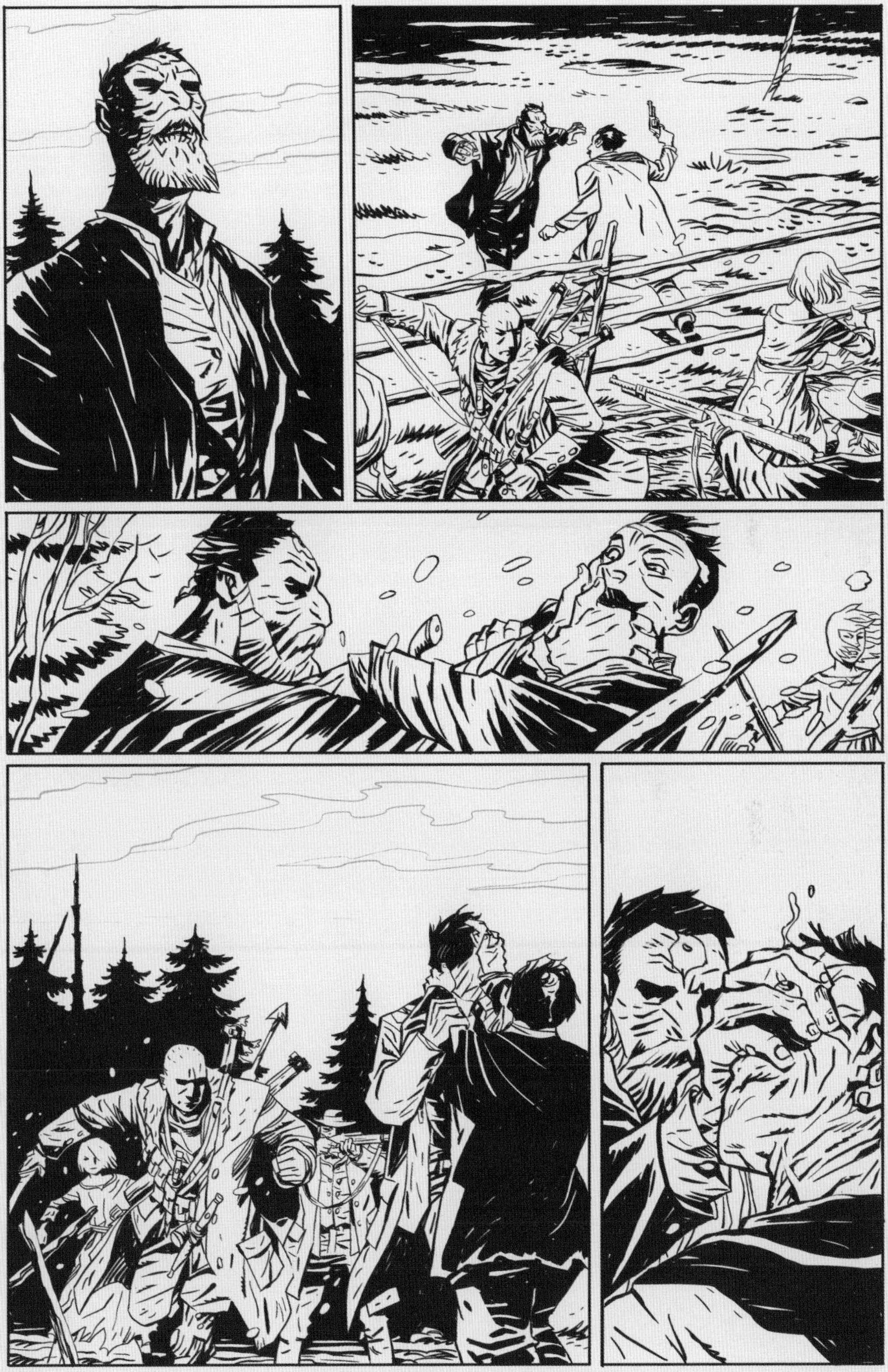

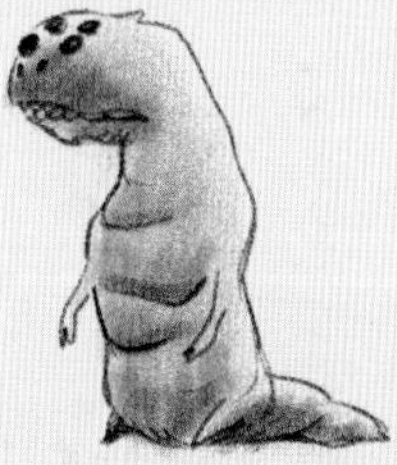

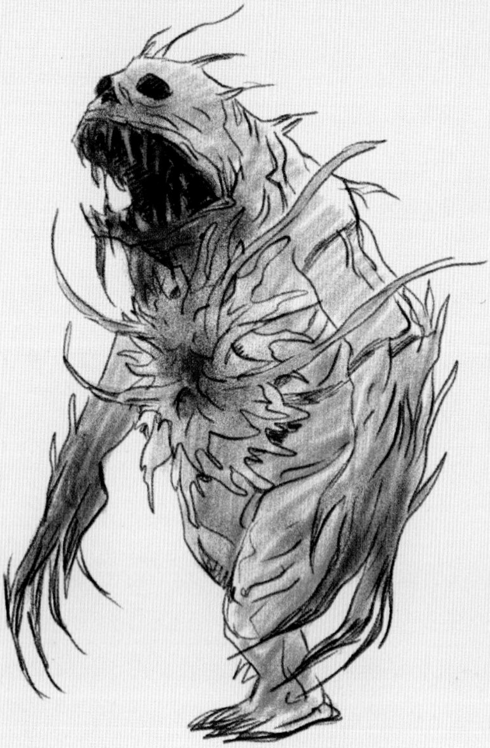

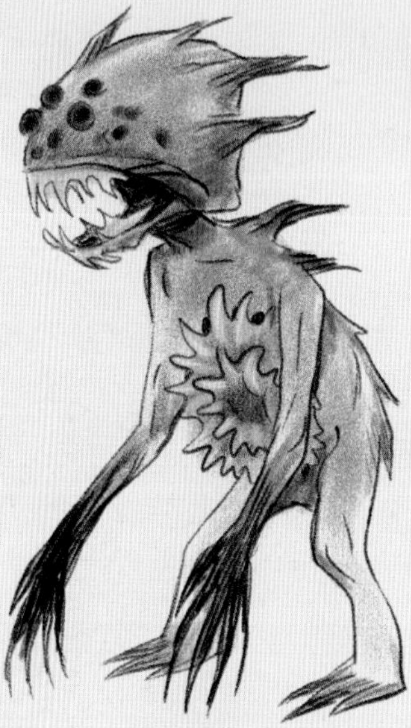

*PB:* Chris had a really fun description and some specific references. The trick was coming up with something original and fun and scary, then having Mike put his filter on it. No one does monsters like Mike does. No one. It was thrilling to see my critters come back, looking awesome. One look at Mike's drawing and you go, "Yeah, that's how it's supposed to look." It's like being back in school.

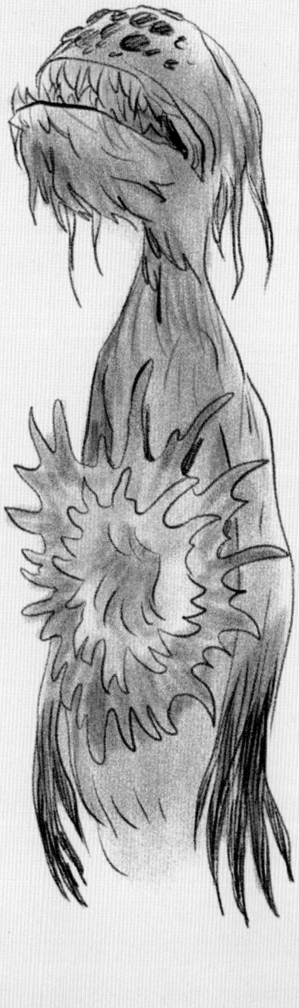

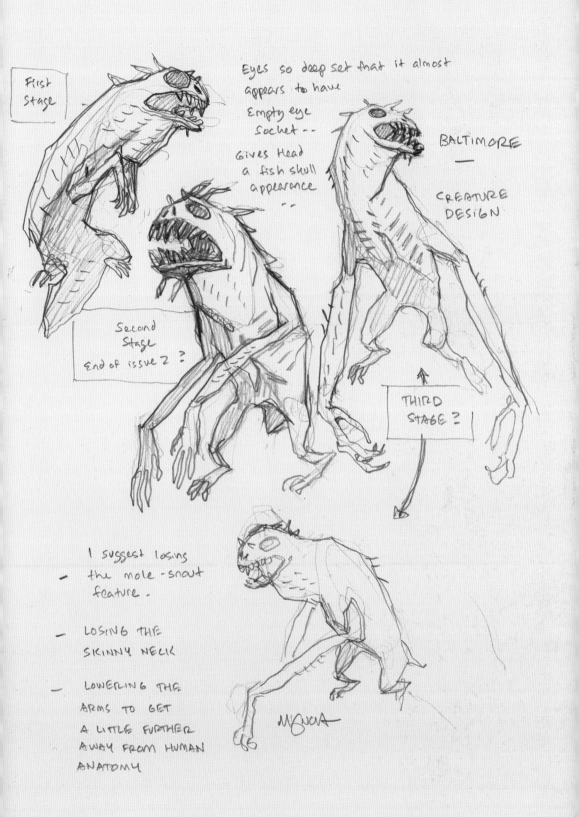

First Stage

Eyes so deep set that it almost appears to have Empty eye Socket --

Gives Head a fish skull appearance --

BALTIMORE
—

CREATURE DESIGN

Second Stage
End of issue 2 ?

THIRD STAGE ?

- I suggest losing
- the mole-snout feature.

- LOSING THE SKINNY NECK

- LOWERING THE ARMS TO GET A LITTLE FURTHER AWAY FROM HUMAN ANATOMY

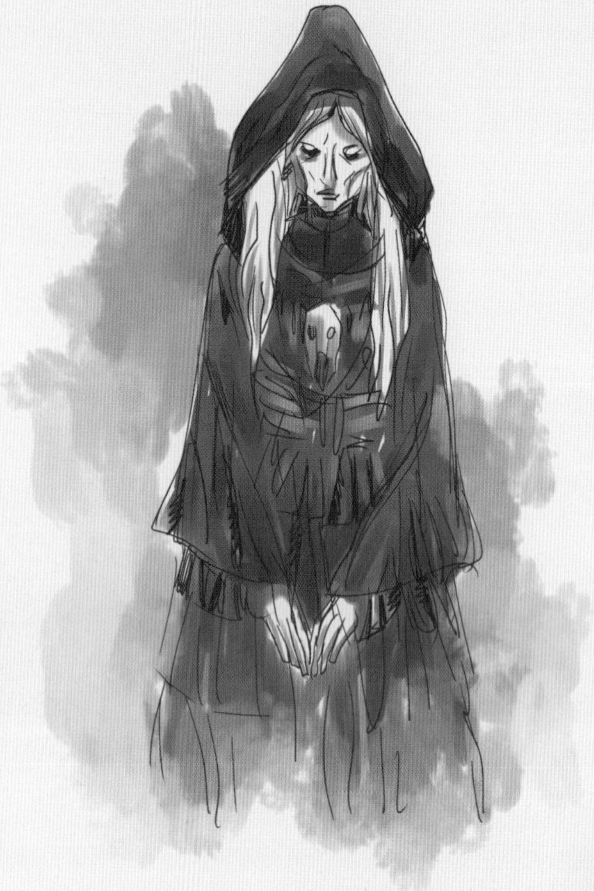

*PB:* Again, another design that went through Mike. The witch was supposed to end up on the cover of the trade. She didn't, but there was a specific design we needed to come up with, a symbol Mike could use, so I took her bird-like features and put that idea in the tattered clothes.

*Following pages:* I do a lot of sketches while working and to keep myself busy while dragging kids around. Some of these are done while at riding school, others at the breakfast table. The one at the end of this section, the portrait of Baltimore, is my way of getting under his skin. Just finding the mood. Little pieces like this help remind me who the characters are.

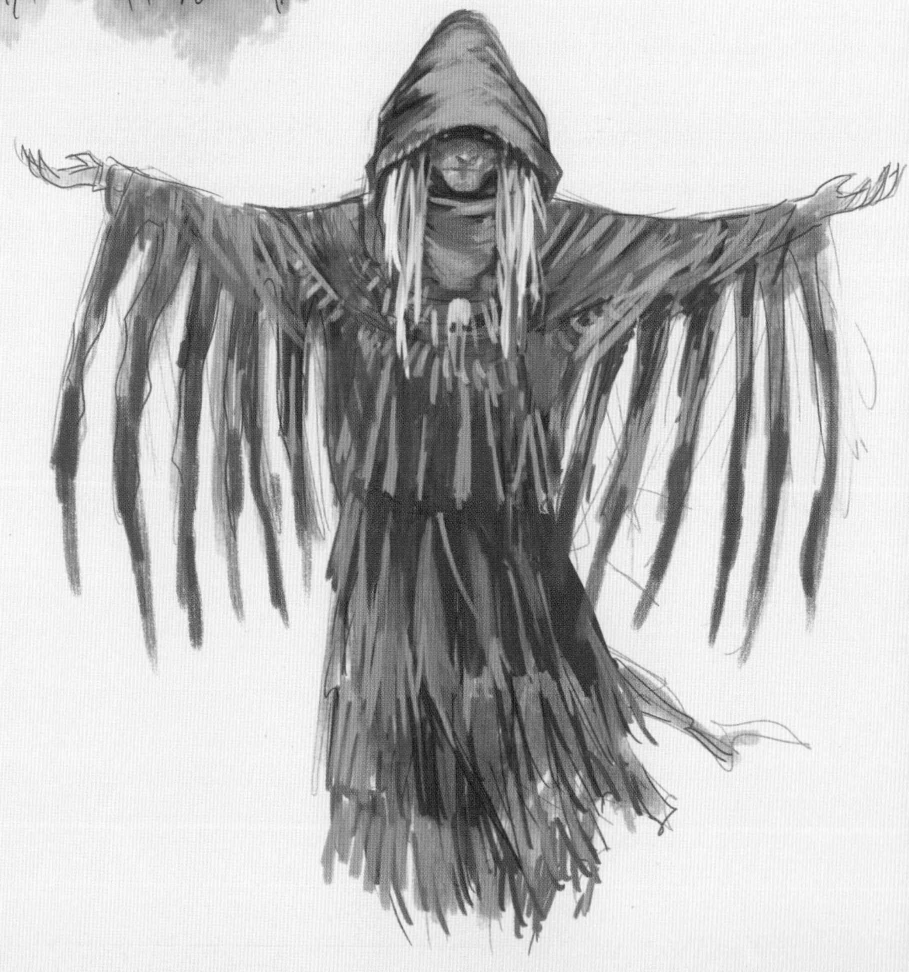

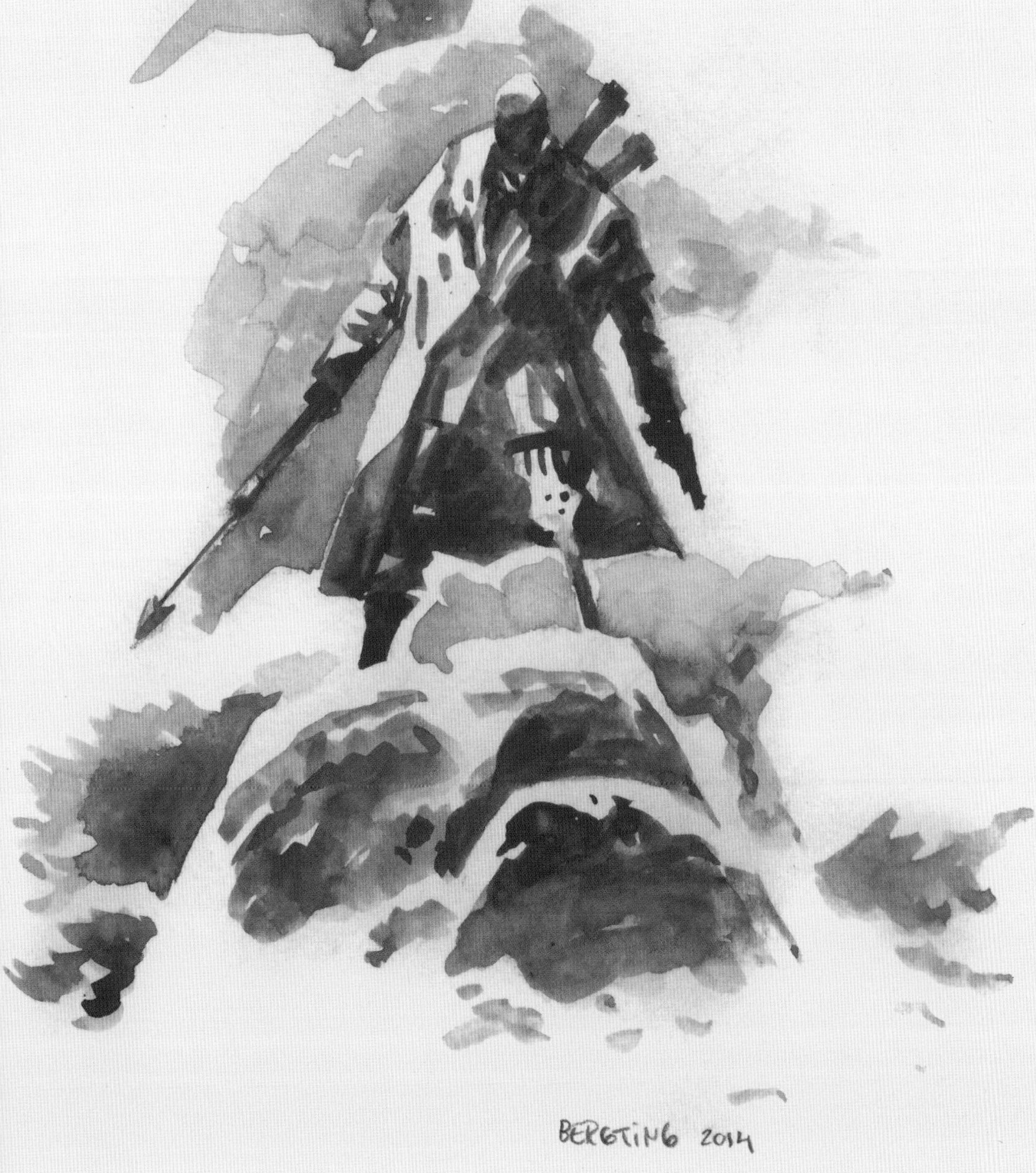
BERGTING 2014

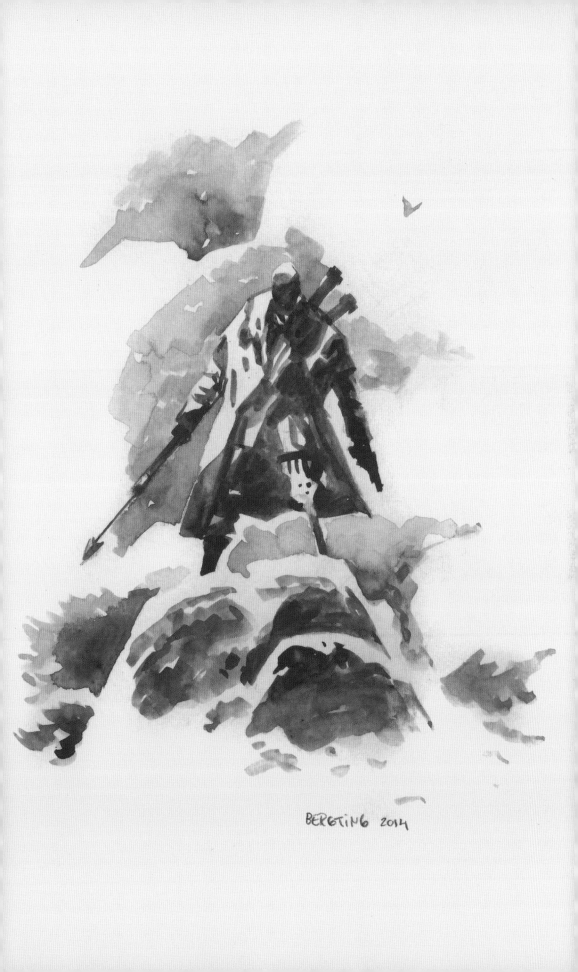

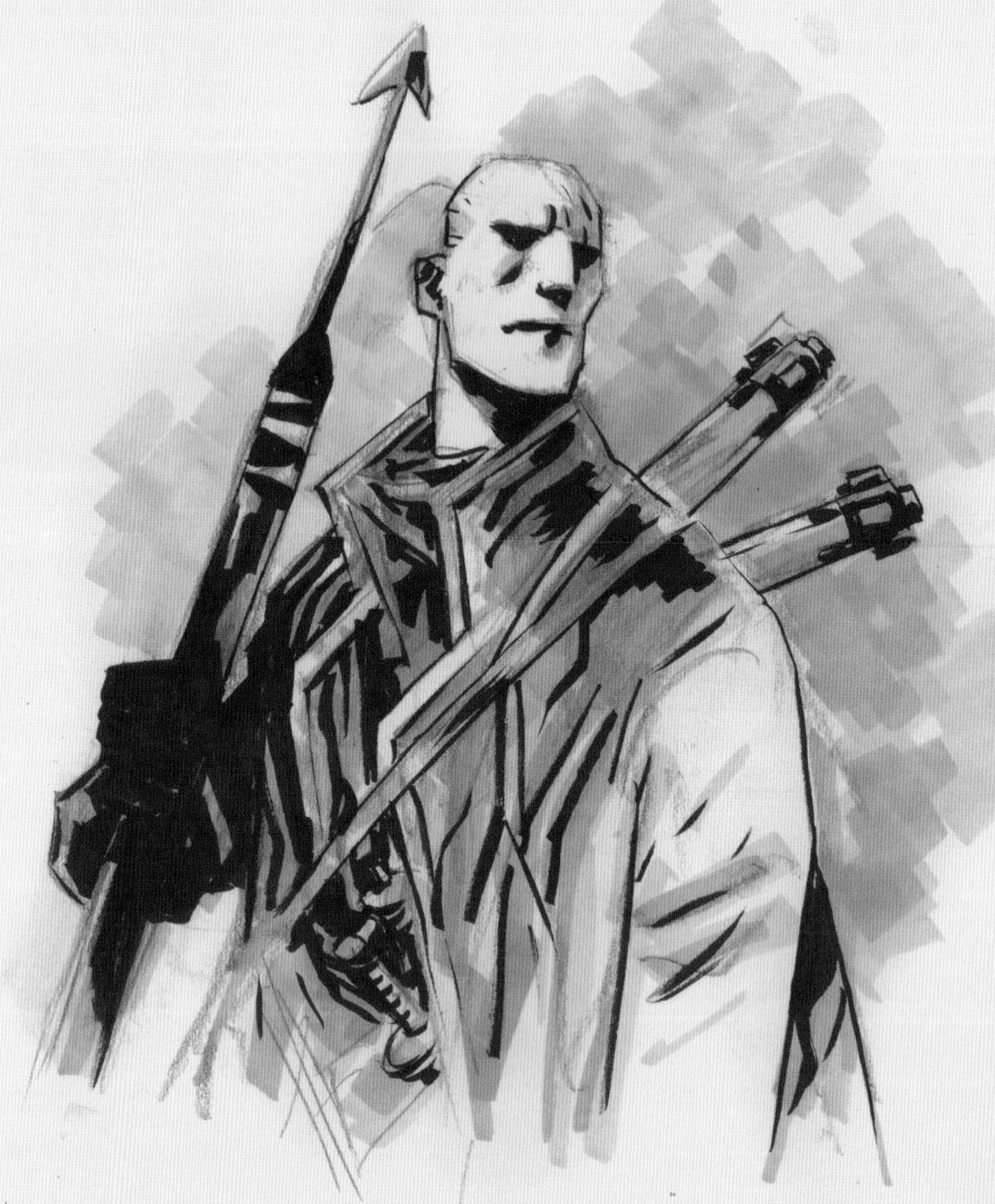

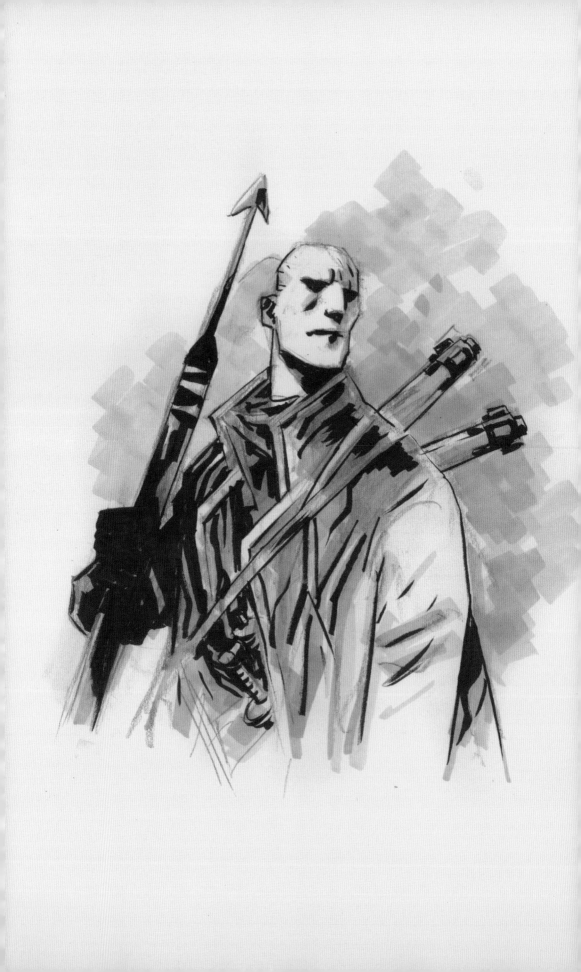

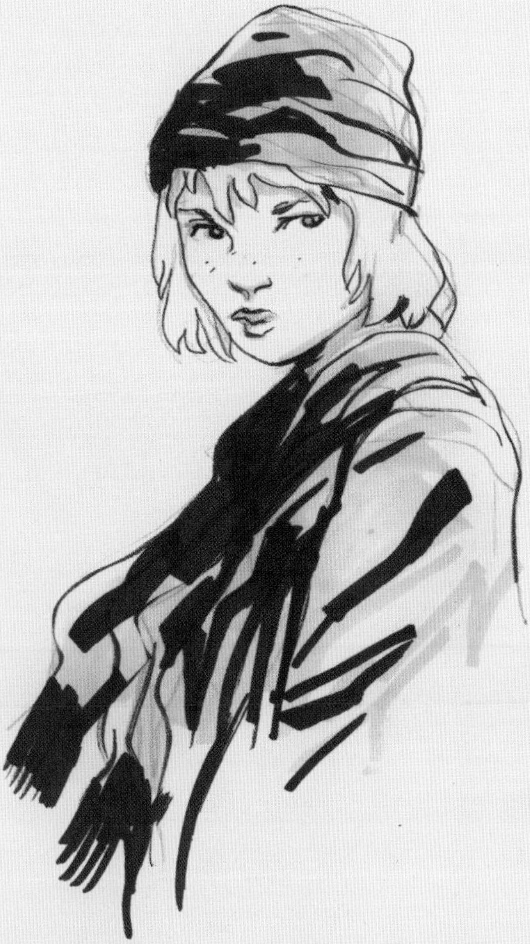

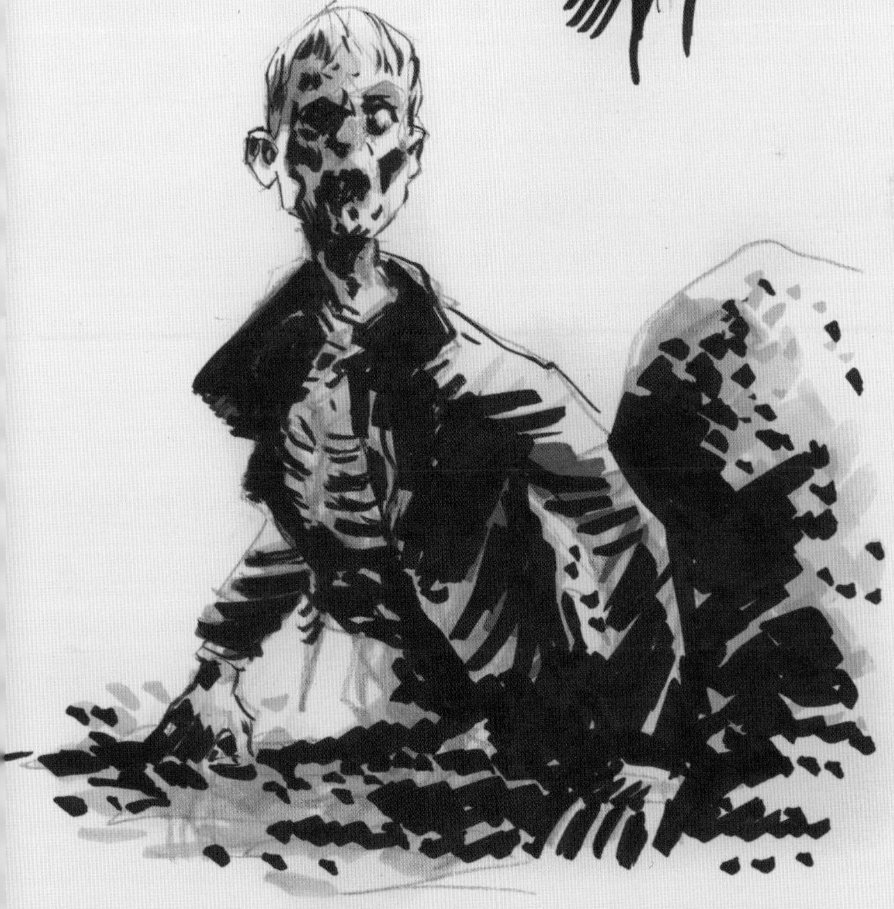

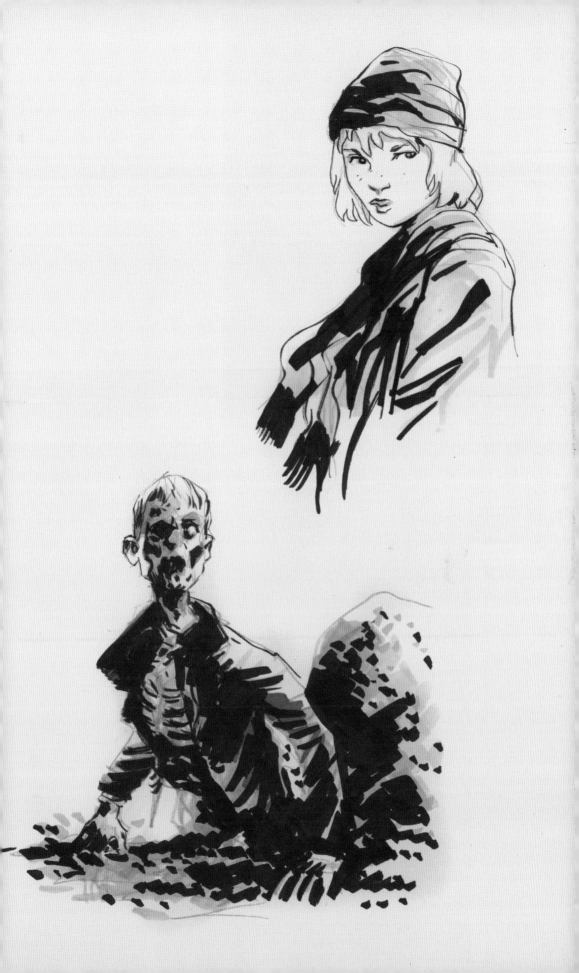

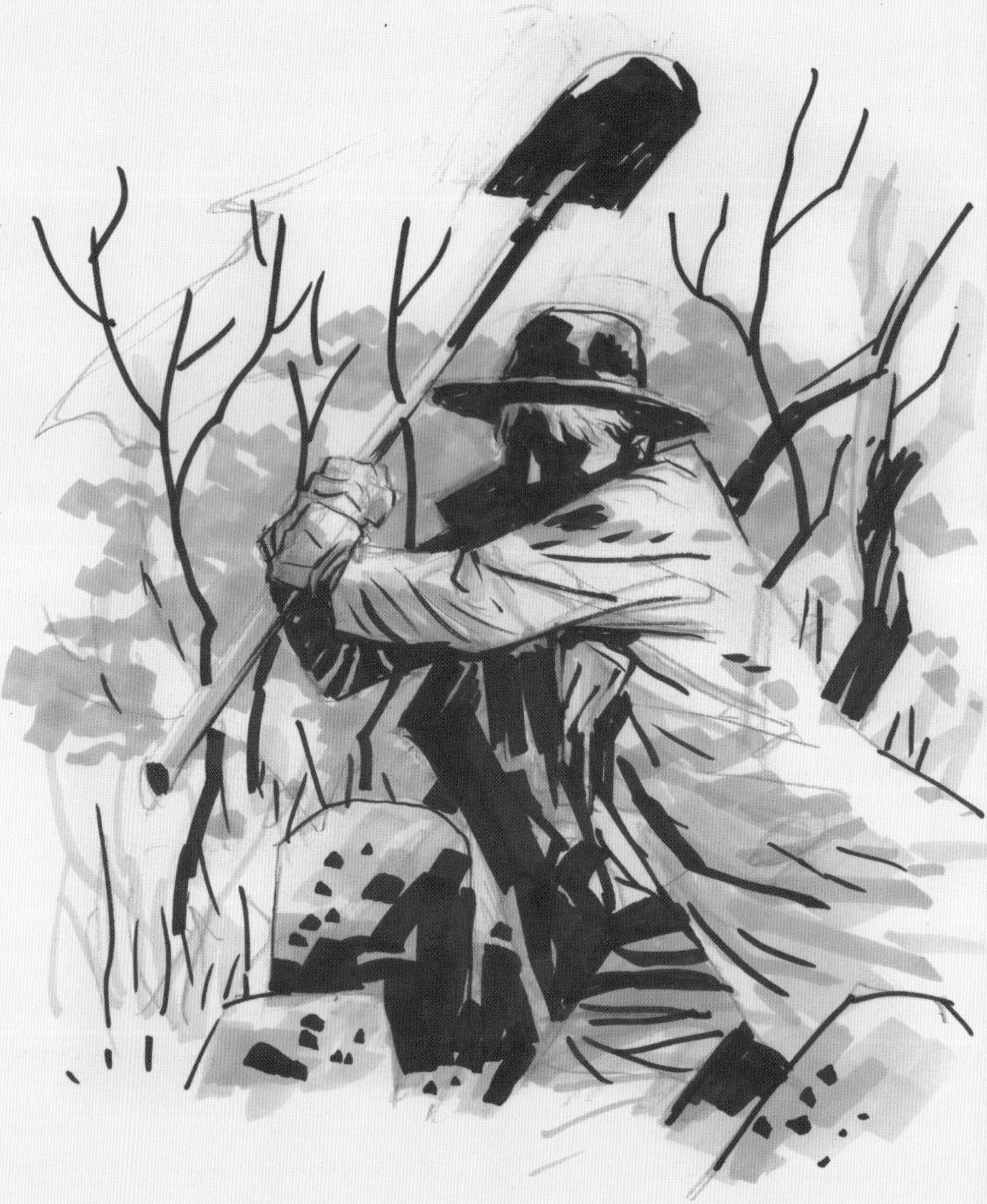

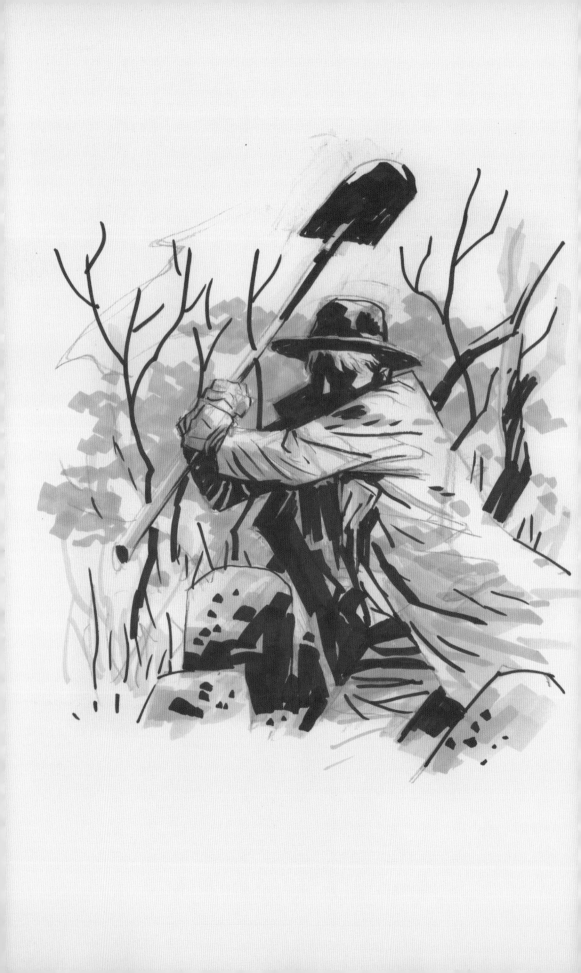

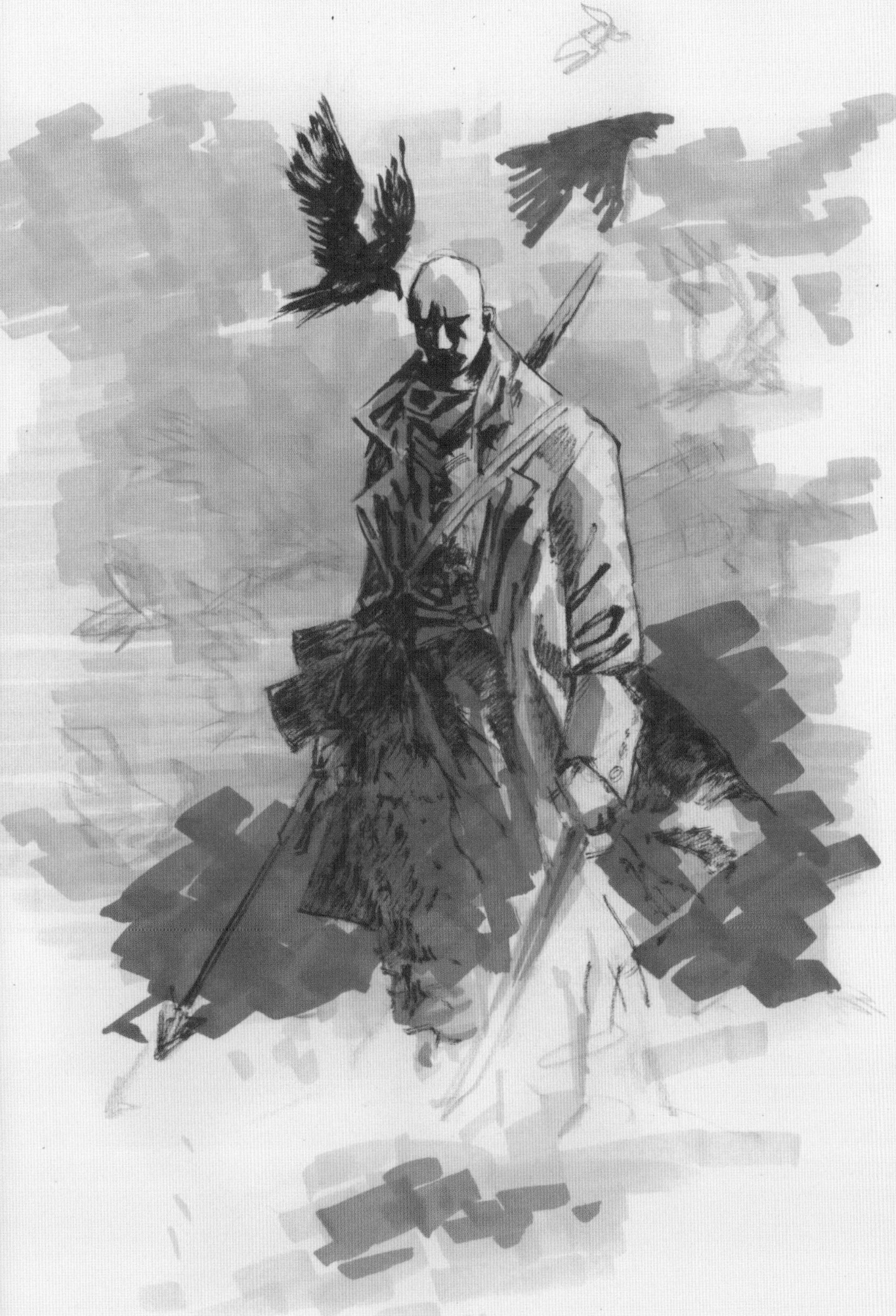

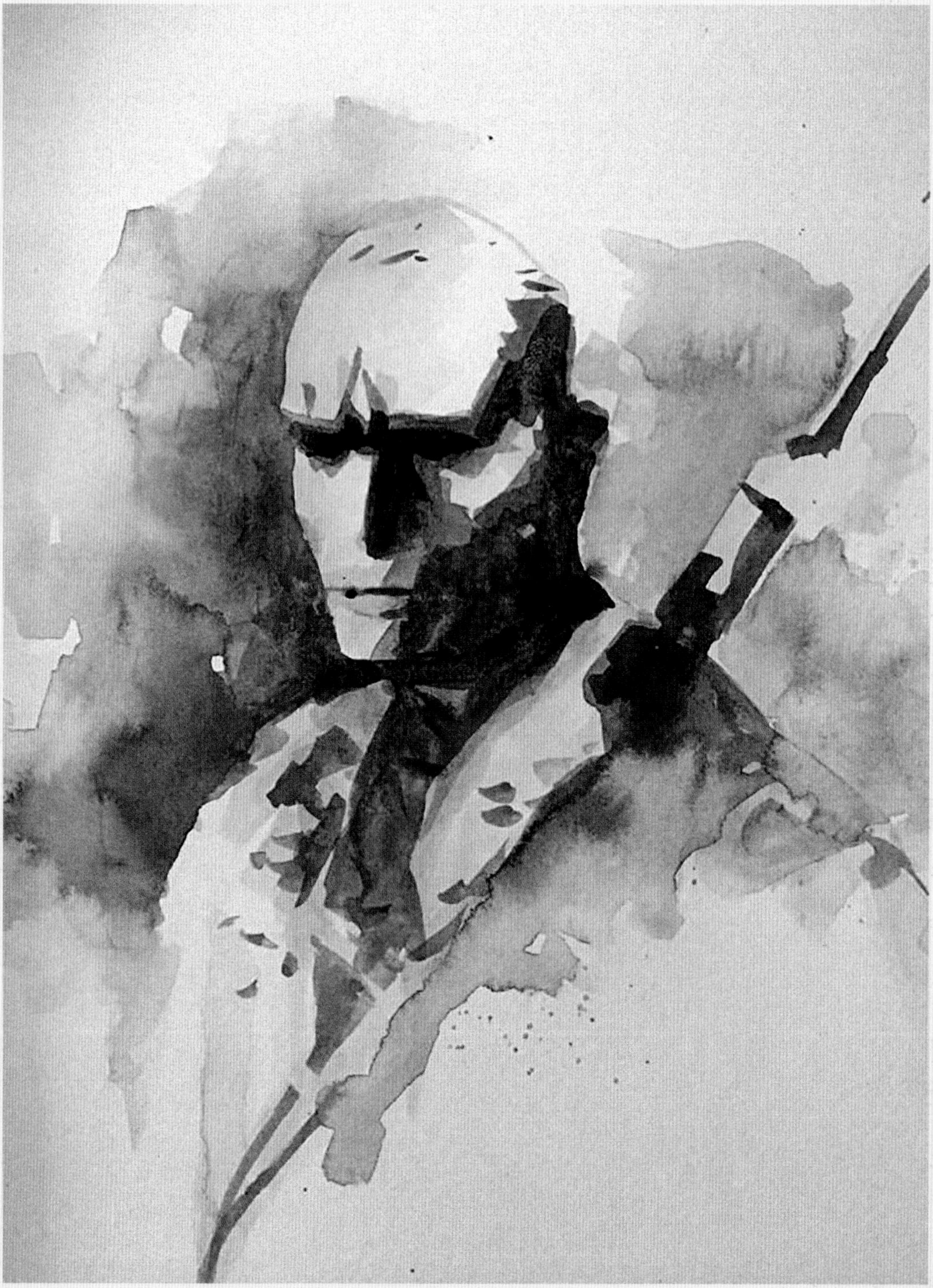

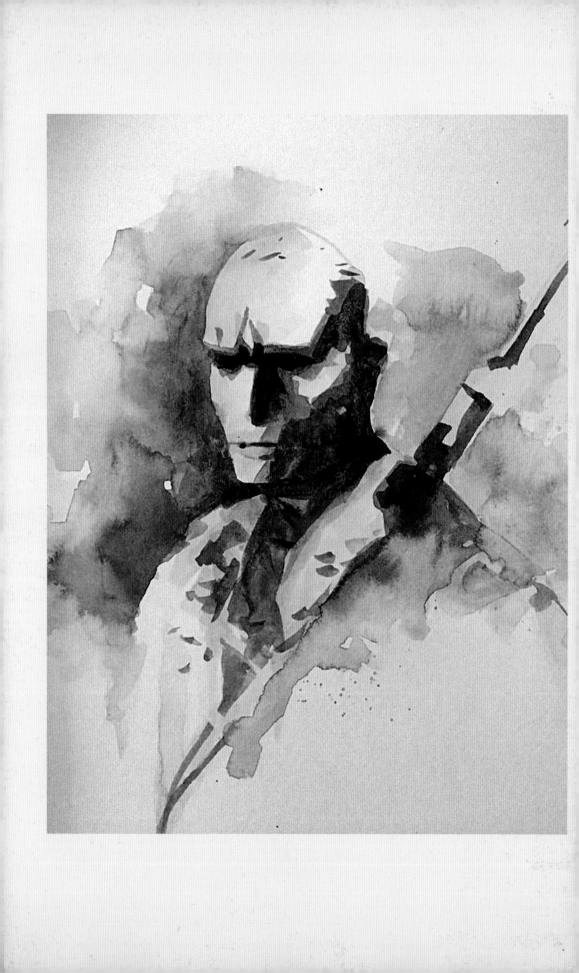

# *Also by* Mike Mignola

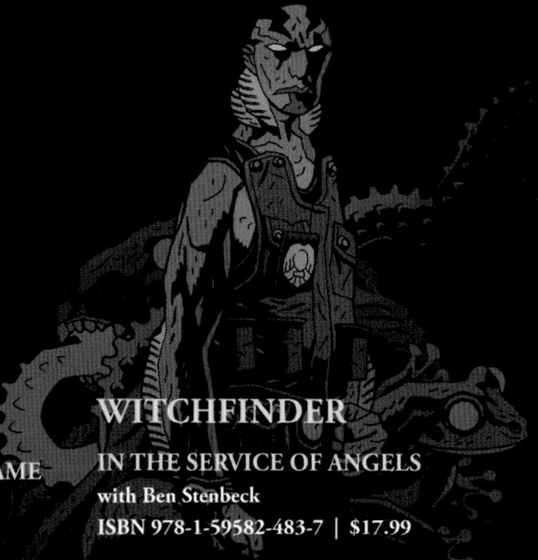

## .P.R.D.

LAGUE OF FROGS
olume 1
ith Chris Golden, Guy Davis, and others
C: ISBN 978-1-59582-609-1 | $34.99
PB: ISBN 978-1-59582-675-6 | $19.99

olume 2
ith John Arcudi, Davis, and others
C: ISBN 978-1-59582-672-5 | $34.99
PB: ISBN 978-1-59582-676-3 | $24.99

olume 3
ith Arcudi and Davis
BN 978-1-59582-860-6 | $34.99

olume 4
ith Arcudi and Davis
BN 978-1-59582-974-0 | $34.99

946
ith Joshua Dysart and Paul Azaceta
BN 978-1-59582-191-1 | $17.99

947
ith Dysart, Fábio Moon, and Gabriel Bá
BN 978-1-59582-478-3 | $17.99

948
ith Arcudi and Max Fiumara
BN 978-1-61655-183-4 | $17.99

EING HUMAN
ith Scott Allie, Arcudi, Davis, and others
BN 978-1-59582-756-2 | $17.99

AMPIRE
ith Moon and Bá
BN 978-1-61655-196-4 | $19.99

## .P.R.D. HELL ON EARTH

EW WORLD
ith Arcudi and Davis
BN 978-1-59582-707-4 | $19.99

ODS AND MONSTERS
ith Arcudi, Davis, and Tyler Crook
BN 978-1-59582-822-4 | $19.99

USSIA
ith Arcudi, Crook, and Duncan Fegredo
BN 978-1-59582-946-7 | $19.9

HE DEVIL'S ENGINE
ND THE LONG DEATH
ith Arcudi, Crook, and James Harren
BN 978-1-59582-981-8 | $19.99

HE PICKENS COUNTY
ORROR AND OTHERS
ith Allie, Jason Latour, Harren,
d Max Fiumara
BN 978-1-61655-140-7 | $19.99

THE RETURN OF THE MASTER
with Arcudi and Crook
ISBN 978-1-61655-193-3 | $19.99

A COLD DAY IN HELL
with Arcudi, Peter Snejbjerg, and
Laurence Campbell
ISBN 978-1-61655-199-5 | $19.99

THE REIGN OF THE BLACK FLAME
with Arcudi and Harren
ISBN 978-1-61655-471-2 | $19.99

THE DEVIL'S WINGS
with Arcudi, Campbell, Joe Querio, and Crook
ISBN 978-1-61655-617-4 | $19.99

LAKE OF FIRE
with Arcudi and Crook
ISBN 978-1-61655-402-6 | $19.99

## ABE SAPIEN

THE DROWNING
with Jason Shawn Alexander
ISBN 978-1-59582-185-0 | $17.99

THE DEVIL DOES NOT JEST AND
OTHER STORIES
with Arcudi, Harren, and others
ISBN 978-1-59582-925-2 | $17.99

DARK AND TERRIBLE
AND THE NEW RACE OF MAN
with Allie, Arcudi, Sebastián
Fiumara, and Max Fiumara
ISBN 978-1-61655-284-8 | $19.99

THE SHAPE OF THINGS TO COME
with Allie, S. Fiumara, and M. Fiumara
ISBN 978-1-61655-443-9 | $19.99

SACRED PLACES
with Allie, S. Fiumara, and M. Fiumara
ISBN 978-1-61655-515-3 | $19.99

## LOBSTER JOHNSON

THE IRON PROMETHEUS
with Jason Armstrong
ISBN 978-1-59307-975-8 | $17.99

THE BURNING HAND
with Arcudi and Tonci Zonjic
ISBN 978-1-61655-031-8 | $17.99

SATAN SMELLS A RAT
with Arcudi, Fiumara, Querio,
Wilfredo Torres, and Kevin Nowlan
ISBN 978-1-61655-203-9 | $18.99

GET THE LOBSTER
with Arcudi and Zonjic
ISBN 978-1-61655-505-4 | $19.99

## WITCHFINDER

IN THE SERVICE OF ANGELS
with Ben Stenbeck
ISBN 978-1-59582-483-7 | $17.99

LOST AND GONE FOREVER
with Arcudi and John Severin
ISBN 978-1-59582-794-4 | $17.99

THE MYSTERIES OF UNLAND
with Kim Newman, Maura McHugh,
and Crook
ISBN 978-1-61655-630-3 | $19.99

## THE AMAZING SCREW-ON HEAD AND OTHER CURIOUS OBJECTS

ISBN 978-1-59582-501-8 | $17.99

## BALTIMORE

THE PLAGUE SHIPS
with Golden and Stenbeck
ISBN 978-1-59582-677-0 | $24.99

THE CURSE BELLS
with Golden and Stenbeck
ISBN 978-1-59582-674-9 | $24.99

A PASSING STRANGER
AND OTHER STORIES
with Golden and Stenbeck
ISBN 978-1-61655-182-7 | $24.99

CHAPEL OF BONES
with Golden and Stenbeck
ISBN 978-1-61655-328-9 | $24.99

THE APOSTLE AND THE WITCH
OF HARJU
with Golden, Stenbeck, and Peter Bergting
ISBN 978-1-61655-618-1 | $24.99

## NOVELS

LOBSTER JOHNSON:
THE SATAN FACTORY
with Thomas E. Sniegoski
ISBN 978-1-59582-203-1 | $12.95

JOE GOLEM AND THE
DROWNING CITY
with Golden
ISBN 978-1-59582-971-9 | $99.99

AVAILABLE AT YOUR LOCAL COMICS SHOP OR BOOKSTORE! • To find a comics shop in your area, call 1-888-266-4226.
For more information or to order direct visit DarkHorse.com or call 1-800-862-0052 Mon.–Fri. 9 AM to 5 PM Pacific Time.
Prices and availability subject to change without notice.

DARK HORSE BOOKS
DarkHorse.com

# HELLBOY™

by MIKE MIGNOLA

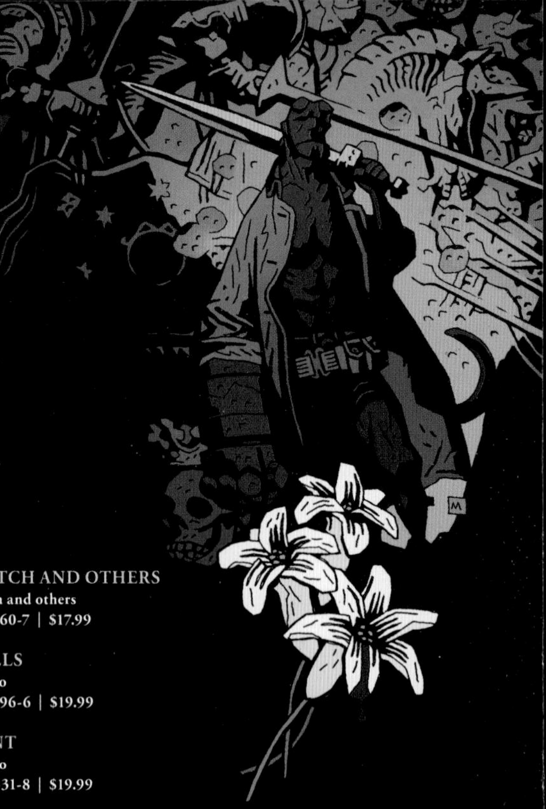

HELLBOY LIBRARY EDITION VOLUME 1:
Seed of Destruction and Wake the Devil
ISBN 978-1-59307-910-9 | $49.99

HELLBOY LIBRARY EDITION VOLUME 2:
The Chained Coffin and The Right Hand of Doom
ISBN 978-1-59307-989-5 | $49.99

HELLBOY LIBRARY EDITION VOLUME 3:
Conqueror Worm and Strange Places
ISBN 978-1-59582-352-6 | $49.99

HELLBOY LIBRARY EDITION VOLUME 4:
The Crooked Man and The Troll Witch
with Richard Corben and others
ISBN 978-1-59582-658-9 | $49.99

HELLBOY LIBRARY EDITION VOLUME 5:
Darkness Calls and the Wild Hunt
with Duncan Fegredo
ISBN 978-1-59582-886-6 | $49.99

HELLBOY LIBRARY EDITION VOLUME 6:
The Storm and the Fury and The Bride of Hell
with Duncan Fegredo, Richard Corben, Kevin Nowlan, and Scott Hampton
ISBN 978-1-61655-133-9 | $49.99

SEED OF DESTRUCTION
with John Byrne
ISBN 978-1-59307-094-6 | $17.99

WAKE THE DEVIL
ISBN 978-1-59307-095-3 | $17.99

THE CHAINED COFFIN AND OTHERS
ISBN 978-1-59307-091-5 | $17.99

THE RIGHT HAND OF DOOM
ISBN 978-1-59307-093-9 | $17.99

CONQUEROR WORM
ISBN 978-1-59307-092-2 | $17.99

STRANGE PLACES
ISBN 978-1-59307-475-3 | $17.99

THE TROLL WITCH AND OTHERS
with Richard Corben and others
ISBN 978-1-59307-860-7 | $17.99

DARKNESS CALLS
with Duncan Fegredo
ISBN 978-1-59307-896-6 | $19.99

THE WILD HUNT
with Duncan Fegredo
ISBN 978-1-59582-431-8 | $19.99

THE CROOKED MAN AND OTHERS
with Richard Corben
ISBN 978-1-59582-477-6 | $17.99

THE BRIDE OF HELL AND OTHERS
with Richard Corben, Kevin Nowlan, and Scott Hampton
ISBN 978-1-59582-740-1 | $19.99

THE STORM AND THE FURY
with Duncan Fegredo
ISBN 978-1-59582-827-9 | $19.99

HOUSE OF THE LIVING DEAD
with Richard Corben
ISBN 978-1-59582-757-9 | $14.99

THE MIDNIGHT CIRCUS
with Duncan Fegredo
ISBN 978-1-61655-238-1 | $14.99

HELLBOY IN HELL VOLUME 1: THE DESCENT
ISBN 978-1-61655-444-6 | $17.99

HELLBOY: THE FIRST 20 YEARS
ISBN 978-1-61655-353-1 | $19.99

THE ART OF HELLBOY
ISBN 978-1-59307-089-2 | $29.99

HELLBOY II: THE ART OF THE MOVIE
ISBN 978-1-59307-964-2 | $24.99

HELLBOY: THE COMPANION
ISBN 978-1-59307-655-9 | $14.99

HELLBOY: WEIRD TALES
ISBN 978-1-61655-510-8 | $24.99

HELLBOY: MASKS AND MONSTERS
with James Robinson and Scott Benefiel
ISBN 978-1-59582-567-4 | $17.99

## NOVELS

HELLBOY: EMERALD HELL
By Tom Piccirilli
ISBN 978-1-59582-141-6 | $12.99

HELLBOY: THE ALL-SEEING EYE
By Mark Morris
ISBN 978-1-59582-142-3 | $12.99

HELLBOY: THE FIRE WOLVES
By Tim Lebbon
ISBN 978-1-59582-204-8 | $12.99

HELLBOY: THE ICE WOLVES
By Mark Chadbourn
ISBN 978-1-59582-205-5 | $12.99

## SHORT STORIES

Illustrated by Mike Mignola

HELLBOY: ODD JOBS
By Poppy Z. Brite, Greg Rucka, and others
ISBN 978-1-56971-440-9 | $14.99

HELLBOY: ODDEST JOBS
By Joe R. Lansdale, China Miéville, and others
ISBN 978-1-59307-944-4 | $14.99

DARK HORSE BOOKS

AVAILABLE AT YOUR LOCAL COMICS SHOP OR BOOKSTORE! • To find a comics shop in your area, call 1-888-266-4226.
For more information or to order direct visit DarkHorse.com or call 1-800-862-0052 Mon.–Fri. 9 AM to 5 PM Pacific Time.
Prices and availability subject to change without notice.

DarkHorse.com